About the auth

Richard Ned Lebow is Professor of International Political Theory at King's College London and Bye-Fellow of Pembroke College, University of Cambridge. He is a Fellow of the British Academy, recipient of many honorary degrees, and author of more than forty scholarly books. Ned is an avid runner, tennis player, hiker, gardener, and lover of opera and chamber music. He and his wife Carol live in London; Cortona, Tuscany; and Etna, New Hampshire.

Cover photo credit: Mark Mniszko

OBSESSION
AN INSPECTOR KHAN MYSTERY

RICHARD NED LEBOW

OBSESSION
AN INSPECTOR KHAN MYSTERY

Vanguard Press

VANGUARD PAPERBACK

© Copyright 2022
Richard Ned Lebow

A CIP catalogue record for this title is
available from the British Library.

ISBN 978 1 80016 336 2

Vanguard Press is an imprint of
Pegasus Elliot MacKenzie Publishers Ltd.
www.pegasuspublishers.com

First Published in 2022

Vanguard Press
Sheraton House Castle Park
Cambridge England

Printed & Bound in Great Britain

Dedication

To my Cambridge colleagues and students

I: Friday Morning

They had been parked and idling for twenty minutes in a quiet residential street in a Toyota with an altered registration. The older man behind the wheel asked the younger one in the back if he had turned off his mobile and received a grunt in reply. The older man shook his head when his companion took out a cigarette package with the obvious intention of lighting up. He suspected the street might later be searched for discarded fags from which DNA might be recovered. He considered smoking a disgusting habit indulged in only by those lacking self-control.

Their target emerged from his neatly landscaped Victorian brick house. He held a rolled-up brolly in his right hand and a leather briefcase in his left. He tucked the briefcase under his arm, reached out to open the gate, passed through and swivelled gracefully to latch it from behind. He walked briskly down the street. The men in the car knew he was heading for the train station and London. They watched him turn into an adjacent street that led to a bike and pedestrian passageway running between two houses to another street that fed into a main road.

The driver noted the time when their target emerged and waited precisely eight minutes before pulling away slowly from the kerb. Having done several test runs, he knew that if he started now, he could overtake their target at the bottom of Bateman Street before it became one way in the opposite direction. Bateman Street was lined with terraced houses but also had a school. At this hour, numerous cars pulled up to drop off children, and this traffic would make their pickup less memorable. When they turned off Trumpington Street into Bateman Street, it was raining heavily, somewhat limiting their visibility. They nevertheless spotted their target ahead, with his now unfurled umbrella angled in front of him to deflect rain driven his way by the stiffening wind. The driver slowed down and came to a stop about five yards ahead of him, reached across and opened the window on the passenger side. As their target approached, he shouted out.

"Sid. Hop in. I'll give you a lift to the station."

Sid leaned over and craned his neck to see who was addressing him. "Oh, hello."

"Get inside before the passenger seat gets any wetter."

Sid hesitated for a moment but then opened the car door and eased himself inside whilst collapsing his umbrella. He pointed it downwards into the foot well and held it at arm's length to avoid coming into contact with its wet nylon.

"Thanks for the ride. It's a miserable morning."

The lad in the rear seat quickly and surreptitiously took out an EpiPen, held it against the back of Sid's neck, and pressed the plunger. Sid gasped and turned to face his antagonist but collapsed against the seat and window before having completed this movement.

"Well done," the driver said. He reached across to make sure that Sid did not fall forward. He searched for a pulse, and satisfied that it was very weak, engaged the gear and moved back into the traffic. He turned off Bateman Street and headed toward the centre of town. At the first red traffic signal, he leaned over to pick up the victim's briefcase and hand it to his accomplice in the back seat. He told him to find Sid's mobile and disable it by removing the battery.

They drove through Cambridge in the direction of Ely. After about fifteen minutes, they turned right into a narrow road that was soon flanked by two catchment basins. The driver slowed down and pulled over on a grass verge. There was a wooden dock just beyond that extended out about fifteen feet into one of the basins.

The driver got out of the car and went behind to open the boot.

"Help me with these weights," he said to his young partner, who had emerged from the back seat.

It took the two men several trips to carry eight ten-pound weights and four strands of rope to the dock.

"Why do we need all this junk?" the younger man asked.

"Remember what I told you. We're teaching Sid a lesson. When he wakes up, he'll be groggy and not fully in control of his movements. I want him frightened, even terrified. But I don't want him rolling off the dock and drowning himself. We're going to wrap him up — not too tightly — and secure his position with the weights. When he regains his strength, he'll have no trouble removing them."

"That's really clever."

"You don't know the half of it."

The young man bent down to pick up a rope, and following the movements of the older man, ran it through the holes in the middle of two of the weights. They did this for all four ropes and eight weights before returning to the car for their prey. The older man looked across the flat terrain, searching for movement before he opened the door, and they eased his body out of the front seat. They carried Sid to the dock and quickly secured, tightened and double-knotted the first two ropes around his torso and legs. They positioned the weights on either side of his body.

Following instructions, the young man bent down to do the same with the next rope and weights. As he inserted a rope through the hole of one of the weights, the older man, standing behind them, took a second EpiPen out of his pocket and placed it against his assistant's neck. He pressed the plunger, and the needle went into the young man's carotid artery. His surprised victim tried to shout, but only a gurgle escaped his mouth as he fell forward against the dock. The older man reached down with his gloved hands to empty the lad's pockets. He tossed the change in the water but pocketed his wallet, mobile, and keys. He bent down again to pull the rope out from underneath his body, strung it through two weights and then did the same with the remaining rope and weights. He arranged them perpendicular to the dock, rolled the comatose but still breathing young man over so he lay astride them. After putting the weights on top of both bodies, he tightened and secured the ropes around them. He rolled the young man over again until he was at the edge of the dock, squatted behind him, anchored himself with his hands behind him, and pushed with his feet until his former companion reached the edge and rolled off into the grey, still water. Body and weights made a splash and sank quickly. He did the same with Sid.

Our murderer stood up and peered down over the edge of the dock to satisfy himself that neither body was visible in the black still water. On a previous visit, he had used a drop line with a lead sinker to determine the depth of the water and discovered that it was a good six feet. The water was almost always murky because of its muddy bottom, which would also keep the bodies from being seen. With any luck, he thought, they will decompose, and weights and bones alike will sink into the mud. He allowed himself a smile. "One less nasty bastard and one less useless yobbo. I've done the world a double service."

He returned to his car and saw Sid's umbrella and briefcase in the footwell on the passenger's side. *"I'll have to get rid of these,"* he thought. On the outskirts of town, he stopped at a Tesco' to buy rubbish bags. He returned to his car and put his gloves back on. He found it difficult to open the bag — the sides were held together by static electricity — but he finally managed to do so and stuffed the briefcase inside. He drove into Cambridge and parked in an underground car park, dropped the rubbish bag in a waste bin and headed out of the cavernous building in the direction of a nearby café. He used the umbrella to keep himself dry whilst crossing the road and, once inside, put it in the stand to the right of the door. He ordered an espresso, sat down at a large leather chair that had just become vacant, and picked up the free local newspaper. He held it up in front of his face to make him less visible to other customers. The local rag contained little of interest, except the story about the arrest of a finance officer for embezzlement at one of the more distinguished colleges caught his attention. He sipped his coffee and noted with annoyance that it was bitter, and he was in yet another café that did not clean its machine as regularly as it should. Five minutes later he got up, walked to the door, took a different umbrella out of the bin, and crossed the street to the car park.

Now came the last and critical step. He had carefully backed his car into a parking bay in the far corner of the third level, out of sight of the lanes drivers used to negotiate their way in and out of the car park. He was fortunate, he thought, to have found such a space on a weekday morning. Perhaps the rain had deterred shoppers. He walked behind his car, opened the boot, and took out a rag and can of solvent. He sprayed the rag, looked around to make sure he was not being observed, and quickly dropped to his knees behind the boot of his car. He worked the rag over two of the letters and one of the numbers of its registration that he had previously altered with paint. It came off without much effort, and he wiped the metal clean and returned to the car. He put the rag and can in another rubbish bag, to be disposed of later. Having already paid for his parking at the kiosk, he negotiated the turns down to street level, inserted his ticket into the machine, waited for the gate to rise, and drove off.

II: Friday Afternoon

When Sid Mason failed to appear on time at a PhD viva at the London School of Economics, the chair of the committee became distraught. His student was not the best product of that august institution, and he had spent long hours helping him improve earlier drafts of his doctoral thesis. The final version was plebian but no longer structurally incoherent or so shoddily written. The student, sent to London as part of an exchange negotiated by the University of Beijing, was insecure and fidgety and the failure of his external examiner to appear ratcheted up the tension in the exam room. The committee chair thought even if Professor Mason did show up, there could still be trouble because he was not known for putting students at ease. In Cambridge's Leinster College, the students had given him the nickname "Sid Vicious," riffing on the professional name of the Sex Pistols bassist, and word of this had spread, as such things always do, throughout the profession.

The committee chair called Professor Mason's mobile several times to no effect. No one else could substitute on short notice because they had not read the thesis The now desperate chair called Leinster college. Sid was not in his office, and none of the porters had seen him that morning. They would not give out his home telephone number but took the chair's mobile and promised to call the professor's wife to see if she knew his whereabouts. Five minutes later, the committee chair received a call from Cynthia Mason, Professor Mason's wife. Her husband had left home that morning at ten minutes past nine, en route to London for the viva, and in plenty of time to walk to the station for the express train to King's Cross. She found it difficult to believe he was not in London. She wondered if the train had been delayed; it would not be the first time. But surely Sid would have called the chair of the committee to report the delay. If he and the train were sitting in a dead zone, he had been there for more than an hour.

Cynthia called the Cambridge station and learnt that the 09.50 had reached King's Cross two minutes ahead of schedule. After calling London to tell the chair that she knew nothing of her husband's whereabouts, she resumed work on the legal brief she was preparing but found it increasingly difficult to concentrate. She forced herself to have a cup of tea, but it did nothing to assuage her mounting anxiety. She excused herself from chambers and walked home hoping that perhaps Sid was ill, had returned to the house and was now fast asleep in their bed. There was no sign of him in the house. After trying his mobile several times and calling the LSE once more only to discover he still had not turned up for the viva, she called the porter's lodge and then one of his colleagues. She considered contacting the police, but he had not been missing for very long. She did not think they would do more than patiently record her concern and the little information she could provide.

Mid-afternoon, she gave up on trying to reach Sid and called one of her partners in chambers. He thought she should report her husband missing and insisted on driving her to the police station. If they both appeared, he explained, and one of them was a grey-haired male barrister, the police would be more likely to take her complaint seriously.

The duty sergeant was surprisingly solicitous. He ushered them into a quiet room, where a constable entered the information she provided, onto a standard missing person on-line form on the National Police Computer. He explained that they would make all the usual inquiries and contact the Met as well, as her husband had been on his way to London. The constable assured her that more than ninety per cent of people missing in Cambridgeshire were soon found, but if they failed to locate him within twenty-four hours, procedure required the handing over of the case to a nominated officer at the station who would organize future inquiries.

It took almost an hour to complete the form. The police wanted to know about relatives and friends her husband might have contacted, places he frequented, any medical conditions or anything else that might possibly explain his disappearance, and, of course, all the usual financial details. They would check to see if her husband had used any of his credit cards, withdrawn money from their bank, or contacted their financial adviser. The constable asked her to go home and return with some recent photographs, his toothbrush, or something else if he had taken it with him, from which they could extract his DNA. Cynthia directed them to his website for a recent photo and signed a consent form to let the police search her house, which they insisted was standard procedure and not something they were likely to do in any case. She signed another consent form to make a media appeal should it prove necessary. She returned home with her colleague, who offered to take the toothbrush back to the police so she could make more calls in the hope of locating Sid.

Cynthia was relieved to have gone to the police and was convinced they would make serious inquiries. She was also frightened. The police wanted his DNA, presumably to confirm that any body they found, was not her husband. She pushed the thought out of her mind and told herself that he was alive and well. There must be some innocent explanation for his disappearance, noting, however, that she now thought of him as a missing person. It was too soon to get alarmed — he had only been gone since that morning — and she refrained from calling their son or daughter, neither of whom lived in Cambridge. She did not feel like reading or watching the seven o'clock news on Channel Four. She often liked to relax by watching reruns of thrillers on ITV3, but that was out of the question tonight. She reflected, not for the first time, that Morse and Lewis solved murders in "the other place" and that an Oxford don's chance of being murdered, or of committing one, was totally off-scale. Cambridge, by contrast, was a peaceful university town.

By six p.m., Cynthia was convinced that something untoward had occurred. Minutes later, her landline rang, and she ran to pick up the receiver. Detective Sergeant Peter Leslie from the Cambridge police introduced himself.

"Has your husband returned or made contact with you?"

"No."

"Our inquiries have drawn a blank, I'm sorry to report. We double-checked with the professor at the London School of Economics, the rail company, and both stations. There were no medical emergencies or track jumpers, and both stations had staff look around and question the cleaners who went through the train on which he intended to travel after it arrived at King's Cross. The Met called the hospitals closest to King's Cross and the LSE. Neither hospital admitted or treated a Professor

Mason or has any unidentified patients who came through their A & E. We asked the college to have a peek in his set. There was no sign of him, nor in nearby loos, common rooms or the library."

Cynthia tried to process this information. She was reluctant to acknowledge its rather disturbing implications. After a long pause, she asked, "Where do you think he is?"

"We don't know. We were hoping you might. Can you think of anywhere he might have gone? Is there anyone he might have contacted?"

"I've racked my brains but come up with no answers. If he went to visit one of the children, he would certainly have told me. Or he would have called after he arrived. I've tried his office and mobile repeatedly, but they just ring. I've left messages, but he has not called."

"We'll keep checking, I assure you. It's early days, and something's bound to come up. We don't get many missing persons in Cambridge, and the few folk who seem to disappear, invariably turn up in short order."

"My husband did not just wander off, sergeant. Something has happened to him."

"That may be, Mrs Mason. If he's not back by tomorrow afternoon, his file will be turned over to an inspector."

"Is that going to make any difference?"

"Not really, I suppose. He'll follow the usual procedure in these cases, but if it comes to asking favours from other police forces, he's certain to get a more responsive hearing."

Following procedure, Detective Sergeant Leslie made a record of his conversation, noting that Professor Mason had still not shown up or contacted his wife. He agreed with her that he was unlikely to have run off or to have willingly missed his London viva. His disappearance was indeed a mystery.

III: Saturday Morning

Deputy Chief Inspector Rudra "Rudi" Khan nursed his tea and thought about the coming weekend. He was going up to London for a family do and would stay with his sister. He was smitten by his six-year-old niece and would go to Heffer's during his lunch hour to find a book she would enjoy having read to her. Now he turned his attention to a missing person's file. Not anything she would enjoy, nor he for that matter. Detective Sergeant Leslie had briefed him moments before about Professor Mason and his unsuccessful efforts to learn anything about his disappearance or whereabouts.

There was no body, but Inspector Khan thought it possible there had been a kidnapping. According to his wife, Professor Sidney Mason was addicted more than most people to his routine. He was always on time for classes and meetings. There was no indication that he was psychologically unstable or had run off with a lover. Mrs Mason had been adamant that he had not taken a suitcase with him, only a briefcase with his computer and a slim volume of poetry.

Inquiries at the university confirmed that the professor had not turned up that day, either in college or his department. Calls to the Mason's' bank and financial adviser revealed that no money had been withdrawn recently beyond the hundred pounds Mrs Mason acknowledged taking out of a hole-in-the-wall two days back. The Mason's' owned their home and had some investments, but not enough by any means to make either a target for ransom.

Reading through the file, Inspector Khan concluded that the constable and detective sergeant had done everything expected at the outset of a missing person inquiry and that the Met had been surprisingly cooperative. They would go through the motions and check again, but he was beginning to wonder if the professor would turn up. This afternoon he had a court appearance in connection with a robbery case, which left him free to devote the rest of the morning to Professor Mason. He collected DS Peter Leslie, and the two of them headed off on foot across Parker's Piece in the direction of Leinster College.

"What do you make of Mrs Mason, Peter?"

"She's distraught about her husband's disappearance. She called again this morning to see if we had discovered anything, just as I was about to ring her to see if he had returned home. She's close to sixty, I'd guess, wiry build, fit, carefully dressed, and very focused. She's a partner in a local law firm and was escorted to the station by a senior partner when she came to report her husband missing. Constable Huhn says she was careful in her choice of words, forthcoming in response to his questions, and struggling to control her emotions."

"You don't think she's covering anything up?"

"I'm inclined to take her at her word. I suspect they have a reasonably good marriage and that she is anxious to have him home."

"No chance he's run off with one of those leggy undergraduates?"

"Well, sir, we could check this out by hanging around at the college buttery. But no, I think it unlikely.

"And the children?"

"We didn't contact them at her request. She promised to call them this morning, and then we can follow up."

"OK, let's start in the buttery, then."

"Sir?"

"Had you for a moment, Peter. I called the master, and he'll make himself available for us."

Peter's mobile sounded. He pulled it out of his pocket, swiped his finger across the screen and held it up to his ear. "Leslie here."

Both men stopped walking as Peter spoke into his mobile.

"I see," Peter said. "Thanks so much."

He hung up and turned to Inspector Khan.

"The Met, sir. Mrs Mason told me that her husband walked everywhere he could and would almost certainly have hoofed it from King's Cross to the LSE."

"Even in the rain?"

"She was adamant. He's a fitness buff. If he got this far on his journey, she thought he might have stopped at the Café des Amis on Judd Street. He mentioned more than once that it had good coffee from a frequently cleaned machine, played classical music, and was an island of calm in the sea of London turbulence."

"Let me guess. He never made it to the café?"

"Spot on. The Met sent an officer around with a photo, and the barista recognized Professor Mason. Said he's something of a regular but insisted he did not make an appearance yesterday."

"Barista? You learnt a thing or two on that trip to Italy."

"I was really impressed at how they make coffee with elegant and economical motions and then create flowers or snowflakes with the milk foam they pour over your coffee. If you come back the next day, they remember what you ordered."

"There's at least one thing in common with our canteen. They always recognize you."

They walked alongside the stonewalls of Leinster College toward the front gate and porter's lodge. It was one of Cambridge's oldest colleges, and this section of its wall was all that remained of the original one. It was a composite of rough-hewn stones and mortar. The gate, by contrast, was fashioned of smooth, finished stone with an elaborately carved wooden arch. They passed underneath and entered the porter's lodge immediately to their right.

The on-duty porter was expecting them. He looked perfunctorily at their warrant cards and called the master's secretary to announce their arrival. She appeared quickly and led them across the main court through a narrow passageway that led to a smaller one.

"I'm always amazed at how perfect college lawns look," Peter said to no one in particular.

The master's secretary smiled. "The groundsmen have a ready answer. 'Seed, water and mow — for six hundred years'."

The visitors laughed.

The master's office was on the second floor of the "G" entryway. His secretary led the way up the narrow, steep, spiral, wooden stairs. Her sturdy, rubber-soled shoes made only the softest sound, and for a solidly built, middle-aged woman, she ascended the stairs with surprising rapidity. At the top of the second landing, she pushed open the door that led to the master's suite. They walked past her office, and the inspector noticed photographs of her family on the desk and a vase of tulips on a small end table.

The secretary rapped twice with her knuckles on the door to the master's office, and a pleasing baritone voice on the other side invited them in. The DCI and his colleague entered, and the secretary shut the door behind them. They introduced themselves to the master and shook hands.

"Please sit down," the master said, motioning with his left arm to a large sofa. He lowered himself into a beige upholstered chair that faced the sofa across a wooden butler's table that sat on what Inspector Khan recognized as a Bakhtiar tribal carpet. The master appeared sixtyish and gave the impression of being comfortable and confident in his surroundings. He sat back in his chair, waiting for the inspector to speak.

"Thank you for agreeing to see us at short notice."

The master moved his arms outwards and opened his palms. It's the least I can do in the circumstances. Do you have any news of Professor Mason?"

"I'm afraid not. He hasn't come home… at least he hadn't an hour ago when we last spoke to his wife."

"I imagine Cynthia is quite upset."

"Indeed," said Peter. "But it's still early days."

"I'm being impolite," the master said. "May I offer you coffee or tea?"

The officers declined. Inspector Khan asked the master if he had heard anything about Professor Mason. The master shook his head.

"I too made inquiries but turned up nothing. I've spoken to all the porters and Sid's colleagues in college and his department. Nobody has seen him or received an email from him since the night before last."

"Can you tell me about these emails?" Inspector Khan asked.

"Pretty routine. At about eight p.m. on Thursday, he exchanged messages with one of his graduate students about his data and how it was coded. Some minutes later, he emailed a colleague here about an upcoming meeting of the garden committee. Sid's been a member for years and takes great pride in our modest plantings. As far as I know, the last person to see him — other than his wife — was the on-duty porter when he left that afternoon. Sid gave him an envelope to put in the pigeonhole of a colleague."

Peter opened his mouth to speak, but the master pre-empted him. "I've already checked. The envelope contained a book with a Post-it Note expressing thanks for the loan. Nothing out of the ordinary. Nobody I've spoken to noticed any change in Sid's demeanour or anything that might give a clue about his disappearance. They are as baffled as I am."

"Is there anyone he is particularly close to in college with whom we might speak?" Inspector Khan asked.

"Nobody in particular. Sid is garrulous but quite private. His conversation is mostly about current events in the college, university, and the world. He has a fine sense of humour, but an acerbic one. He has been known to skewer colleagues, often in such a clever way that it is difficult for them to take public offence. He has been described as 'charmingly insulting'."

"Colleagues must resent him for acting this way?"

"Oh yes. A week ago, over port in parlour, he managed to anger two colleagues with the same barb. Young Prabhu, a promising neurologist, is married to a Jewish woman and recently converted to her faith. Sid told him he was living his life in reverse, as one is supposed to be born a Jew and then become a doctor. Suresh was at a loss for words. Professor Goldstein, sitting opposite, downed his glass and glared across the table at Sid."

"So," Peter said, "there are many in the college who dislike him?"

"He's on speaking terms with everyone, although a couple of colleagues do their best to avoid sitting near him at meals."

"Does anybody detest him enough to wish him harm?" asked the inspector.

"No. Not to my knowledge. There are those who regret he turned down a job offer from one of the Ivies a couple of years back, but nobody would wish him ill. This is a civilized place."

"What about this student he emailed? Might it be worthwhile to speak to him?"

"I believe they get on amicably."

"I'm hoping he might shed some light on Professor Mason's movements over the last few days."

"Yes, of course. Let me ask my secretary to contact him. If he's in college, you could meet with him in the inner parlour. It's usually free at this hour."

The master's secretary called back to report that she had set up a meeting. The master asked her to escort the detectives to the parlour.

"Is there anything else I can do for you?"

"You've been very helpful, thank you. You will, of course, call us if anything new comes up?"

"Certainly."

"I'll leave my card with your secretary."

The officers rose, shook hands again with the master, who opened his office door to usher them out.

They descended the same spiral staircase and crossed the court to another entryway. Once inside, the secretary held her ID card below the door handle and waited to turn the handle until she heard the soft click.

"Mr Krause should be along in a few minutes," she said. "Make yourselves comfortable. There's coffee, tea and biscuits if you like." Both men thanked her and waited until she had left and closed the door before speaking.

"What do you make of him?" Peter asked.

"Rather sure of himself. Not particularly upset by his colleague's disappearance. Treated it like any other problem. Open with us because he has nothing to hide. If he has any thoughts about what happened to Sid, he's keeping them to himself. He's convinced that nobody in the college is responsible. By being as helpful as he can, he hopes we will start looking elsewhere for our missing professor. Perhaps the college is in some way involved?"

"I'm not ready to give up on this place either."

Peter went to the sideboard to make tea, looked at his boss, received an affirmative nod, and took two cups from the cupboard. whilst waiting for the kettle to boil, he admired the oil paintings on the dark wood-panelled walls. There were several landscapes, presumably of East Anglia, as the terrain was flat. There were also several paintings of Cambridge and its colleges. A far cry, he thought, from police headquarters, where most walls were mere partitions. The only decoration was in situation rooms where pictures of dead people, suspects, timelines, and maps adorned whiteboards often precariously attached to partitions. He made the tea and carried the cups and saucers to the table along with two mini-packets of Dutch chocolate biscuits. He sat down opposite Inspector Khan and was struggling without success to open the packet when there was a knock at the door.

"Come in," the inspector said in a raised voice.

Carl Krause entered the room, black backpack draped over his left shoulder. He was solidly built with bushy black hair and an angular face. Clad in jeans, un-ironed shirt, and loose dark jersey, he was a postgraduate student from central casting.

"Mr. Krause, allow me to introduce myself. I am DCI Rudi Khan, and this is DS Peter Leslie."

Both men held up their warrant cards.

"May I have a look? I've never seen one of these."

Peter handed his over for inspection, and the student gave it a moment's scrutiny before returning it.

"Do take a seat," the inspector said in a tone that could be interpreted as friendly but firm." Peter used the moment to sip his tea and then felt a small surge of satisfaction as the package finally gave way, rewarding him with the sight of two dark biscuits studded with chocolate chips.

"Word has it that Professor Mason disappeared. Is that why you want to see me?"

"Correct," the inspector said. You exchanged emails with him the night before last, which makes you the last person aside from his wife known to have contact with him."

"He's still missing?"

"As far as we know."

"I hope he turns up soon. He's my dissertation supervisor."

"I'm told your emails were about one of your draft chapters?"

"That's right. He gave me some advice about how better to characterize my data set. He's a difficult but conscientious mentor."

"Difficult in what way?"

"Well, I've had no problems with him. I never contradict him, I'm always punctual, and I nod politely whenever he gets on one of his hobby horses."

"What would those be?"

24

"The importance of good data and quantitative research, the failure of Cambridge residents to sweep snow from the pavement in front of their houses, the inability to reach any real people when you telephone a bank or company to complain about their so-called service. There's a long list."

"I understand that there are some students who are less reticent about expressing their negative opinions of him?"

"Yes, that's right, but they don't end up working with the professor."

"He has a small number of students?"

"He had five, now three."

"What happened?"

"That's a tale and a matter of controversy in the college and POLIS — that's the Politics and International Studies Department."

"Yes?"

"The professor has his postgraduate students code his data. Depending on their language skills, they read Spanish, Italian, German, and Greek newspapers to find for stories about tax evasion and its prosecution. They scored these events with reference to several scales the professor has devised. It's painstaking and tedious work, but it provides the data he needs to write his articles."

"And the controversy?"

"Students don't get paid for coding the data. The professor insists it's part of their training and that he arranges good fellowships for them. Some students view it as slave labour. There's a rumour that every year some students fake the data to save time and, I suppose, get back at him."

"Is that easy to do?"

"Oh yes, especially in languages the professor does not read. He would have to go through the newspapers and do the coding himself to catch them. That seems to have happened this year. Supposedly, two students fudged the German data, and it's a language he knows well. He's charged them with an ethics violation and brought the matter to the attention of the college disciplinary committee. Word is that he's asked the committee to expel them. He's also complained to the department."

"This could be the end of their academic careers?"

"I'm afraid so."

"Do give us the names of these students. Is there anybody else he's antagonized?"

"There's another student, John Carnation. He was in Addenbrookes for a week or so under observation for some kind of heart problem. He's fine now, but the professor went to see him in the hospital to try to talk him out of writing his dissertation with a colleague he abhors. He's alleged to have threatened to make the student's life in the department very difficult. John was upset, and so was his mentor."

They learnt nothing else of interest in the interview, and the officers returned to the station still hopeful that Professor Mason would reappear.

IV: Saturday Afternoon

Back in his office, DCI Khan wrote up notes of his interview on his computer. He tried to catch up on other administrative tasks that consumed an increasing amount of his time. It was no longer "paper" work as it was almost all on-line. The ministry had paid God knows how much to software consultants to design a programme that, in theory, allowed police officers to submit all their reports on-line and to upload relevant files. This timesaving procedure was, of course, just the reverse. In the inspector's opinion, many of the functions were mislabelled or were enabled by icons that were incomprehensible or not in any obvious place on the screen. Some icons could only be accessed by turning on an editing function, and it was hidden in plain sight. Much like evidence, he told Peter. Perhaps the programme was designed by really clever people trying to make us better cops. He somehow doubted this most benign of interpretations.

His mind wandered, which it always did when he put more than five minutes into any tedious task. He remembered reading somewhere that Einstein attributed his success to his ability to concentrate for up to three seconds at a time. He wondered if this was a serious or puckish claim. His ex-wife had accused him of attention deficit disorder, especially when she was speaking to him. She insisted that he only paid attention to his police work. She should see him now, he thought, and Einstein too, for that matter.

He finished logging his hours but could not bring himself to face the next longer and more complicated form. He went down to the canteen in search of coffee. He intended to bring it back to his office as he was not in the mood for small talk with colleagues, but the duty sergeant motioned him to his table.

"Morning, Inspector Khan."

"Sergeant."

"I thought you might be interested in knowing that we have another missing person."

"Two in the same week? Most unusual."

"And neither of them runaway teenagers."

"Odder still. What's the story?"

"Young man, twenty-two, from Ely but lives here and works in a café. Didn't show up to work for several days and failed to contact his mother. She called his mobile repeatedly to no effect, and then the café. When they told her he had not come into work for the last three days, she began to worry. She called us this morning, and we had her come in and make the usual report. The lad has a bedsit here in town, and a constable has gone over to check it out."

"I don't imagine these cases are connected, but thanks for bringing me up to date. You'll let me know if and when he turns up?"

"Of course, Inspector."

Inspector Khan put the lid back on fast cooling coffee and scurried upstairs to his office. He had asked Peter to interview the several students and the professor that "Sid Vicious" — had offended. By the rulebook, this was premature because there was no evidence of foul play, and the professor could return home at any moment. He doubted this would happen and wanted to look into the professor's disappearance sooner rather than later. He knew from experience that the longer investigating a case is postponed, the more difficult it becomes to crack. He finished the form, and one that this time needed to be printed out. He sighed upon discovering that the sheet on which his signature was to be appended was on a separate page. Anybody could submit the form with a different signature page or a different form with his signature. His bank wouldn't do anything as silly as this, or at least he hoped not.

***

Peter had no difficulty finding the students in question, all of whom had heard about Professor Mason's disappearance. He interviewed separately the two students accused of fabricating data and got more or less the same story from each of them. Peter did not ask if the charge was true. He stressed that this was not his brief; he was only interested in finding the professor's whereabouts. The students were on edge, all the more so when he asked where they were on the morning Professor Mason left for London. The first student had an alibi that could easily be verified. The other said he slept late after partying the night before and did not show up for breakfast or even emerge from his room much before eleven a.m. As he had been alone, he acknowledged that nobody could verify his whereabouts. The students were not unhappy about the professor's disappearance, but neither gave Peter the impression that they would be likely to harm him physically. But you never know.

Professor Coates was in college to hold a tutorial and agreed to spend fifteen minutes with Peter before meeting his students. He was still agitated by what he described as Professor Mason's "unwarranted harassment" of his briefly hospitalized student. According to Coates, this was typical of Mason. He was the second person that day to take pleasure in confiding in Peter that the professor's nickname was "'Sid Vicious".' When asked his whereabouts on the morning Sid went missing, the professor said he had been working at home, alone after eight thirty, when his wife left for her office.

Peter made it to the courthouse in plenty of time to sit for an hour on a hard wooden bench waiting to be called to testify. The case was about a drug deal that went south, leading to a knife fight between a distributor and a dealer. Both had been arrested and taken to the hospital, where one of them, had nearly bled out. The police had tried, without success, to convince the distributor to do a deal and give them the next name in the chain up to the prime source of drugs. The distributor was clearly more afraid of him than of the police, who are severely constrained by law and regulations in their interrogation procedures. Peter and the inspector had a running joke about the utility of following the CIA in waterboarding offenders, which they both agreed would be unlikely to gain them much beyond the hostility of the victim. Thumbscrews would be better, the inspector insisted, and they argued from time to time about which of them would tighten the screws and which would pose the questions. Neither wanted the former task.

Connected to these conversations, Inspector Khan had asked Peter if he knew about the famous Milgram experiments conducted at Yale back in the 1960s. He told him how Milgram, a psychologist, had Yale undergraduates ask questions to someone strapped into a chair and wired up to a transformer. If the man in the chair gave the wrong answer, student participants were to shock him, and the experimenter increased the current each time they did. In fact, the transformer was a fake, and no current flowed through the wires, but the man in the chair — a research assistant — would pretend to react and begin screaming and convulsing when the current reached a certain level. Many of the students were undeterred by his apparent suffering and continued to apply shocks when he failed, purposely, of course, to answer their questions correctly. Milgram was appalled by this student insensitivity, and the inspector had wondered aloud if today's students would happily tighten their imaginary thumbscrews.

Peter was, at last, summoned into the courtroom, sworn in, and testified briefly about the circumstances of the arrest. The cross-examination, by a court-appointed barrister, was perfunctory and more respectful of him than Peter had expected. He surmised that the barrister must be basing his defence on something other than the police response. In less than ten minutes, he was released by the judge and headed back to the station.

In the interim, Inspector Khan had forced himself to fill out two more forms, one of which resisted for some time his efforts to submit it. He finally discovered a red asterisk three screens back opposite a question the programme did not think he had answered. He entered the same answer, only to find that he now had to answer all the following questions a second time because everything he had written had disappeared. He filled it out again, pressed submit, uttered an expletive, and breathed a sigh of relief when his submission was acknowledged. The process suggested to him that "submit" clearly had a double meaning.

Turning away from his monitor, he contemplated the coming weekend and his Sunday trip up to London. He enjoyed his extended family, especially his nieces and nephews, but not the inevitable and inappropriate questions from his mother and two aunts about his marital situation. And there was no way of indulging the former without putting up with the latter. It was almost lunchtime, and he calculated he could squeeze in a forty-five-minute workout at the gym and grab a sandwich on the way back.

Peter also bought a sandwich after leaving court. It was overcast and slightly blustery and one of those days when you feel foolish opening an umbrella but are likely to get wet if you don't. He had once heard an American refer to this kind of weather as "Englishing" and thought it an apt description. When he reached the police station, he engaged the duty sergeant in conversation, which he did regularly, as it was the best way of keeping informed. He learnt about the second missing person and his landlady's low opinion of the lad. She had not seen him for a couple of days and was willing to let the constable peek into his room.

"There was nobody there," the duty sergeant explained, "and the constable saw what looked like a package of cocaine on his desk. We're getting a search warrant. This sort of thing is becoming all too common."

"The drug scene seems to be getting worse," Peter agreed. "Unemployment is up among the young, but some professionals and businesspeople are making more money than ever before. I guess it creates incentives at the seller and buyer ends of the market."

The duty sergeant, a solidly built man with nearly thirty years' experience on the force, lifted his arm and raised a finger, gesturing for Peter to stand by as he answered the telephone. Peter heard a "hello" and several "yes, sirs" with short pauses between and then saw the handset returned to its cradle.

"We've got our warrant, and the drug squad will have a look. The usual, I would think. Someone believes he's found a low-risk way of supplementing his income. Maybe he's run into trouble with his dealer or a client and done a bunk."

"I wouldn't be surprised. I'm just back from testifying about a knife fight arising out of a drug sale. A young lad, a school leaver, kicked out of home after stealing from his parents and then striking his father when confronted with the theft. He was selling cocaine to a pharmacology student. You'd think they could make their own drugs."

Peter went upstairs, knocked on the inspector's door and walked in. He filled his boss in on his morning at the college, and they agreed that they now had several people with motives for a crime that may not have occurred. They knew that most adults who go missing are either elderly

31

people who get disoriented and are invariably found, sooner rather than later, or women escaping abusive partners. Every so often, a husband runs away, often to make a new life with someone. Their professor had all his marbles and was at the top of his game professionally. He had given no signs of psychological distress, and his offensive treatment of students was nothing new. It seemed unlikely that he would leave wife, college, and career in one fell swoop.

"But you never know," said the inspector. Supervising those students is a far sight more arduous than mentoring you. This last incident could have been the final straw and convinced our professor to throw it all in and start life anew as a blackjack dealer in Las Vegas."

"How did you settle on that profession?"

"It's what I've always wanted to do."

"Really, sir?"

"Got you again, Peter."

"Tedious job, but good tips, I expect. And you get exposed to all that second-hand smoke. Casinos are the last place where you can still light up."

"What made you think of it?"

"I suppose that it has the virtue of being far away from here and from research and teaching."

"Where do you think the professor's gone, Peter?"

"Run off with a long-legged student whose parents are fabulously rich and have promised to set him up in a yacht chartering business in St. Lucia."

"You wish. Maybe he needs an assistant?"

"Are you thinking of me or you, sir?"

"You, if you don't pass your Inspector's' Exam."

"It would be a nice consolation prize. And, sir, I would give you a good concession on a rental."

"I would need to find a companion with long legs first."

This oblique reference to their unsatisfactory love lives brought the conversation to an end. Peter stood uncomfortably, and Inspector Khan directed his attention to his computer screen. After a few moments of silence, he spoke to Peter in a lower tone of voice.

"I suppose you should send the professor's name out to the national list of hospitals and mortuaries to see if he's turned up. If not" — he looked at Peter and smiled — "I may have to check out St. Lucia."

Peter laughed. "I'll get to it right away, sir."

V: Sunday Morning

As always, Janice Clowes was the first in her household to rise. After making herself presentable, she shuffled into the kitchen, put fresh water in the kettle and placed it on the rear right hob of her cooker. She took butter, jam, and bread out of the larder to put on the table and reached into the cabinet for three teacups. Her husband Henry and teenage son John would soon be stirring and always started the day with toast and tea. A good morning greeting from both and a peck on the cheek from her husband would generally constitute the extent of their interaction. On occasion, she would get an appreciative grunt for refilling a teacup or toasting another slice of bread. Janice knew that both men loved her and would be more talkative later in the day.

As it was a weekend, neither father nor son was in his usual rush; they lingered at the table over a second cup of tea. Janice thought about the light household chores in store for her and "elevenses" at a café in Ely with friends. Henry and John had made plans to collect the small sailboat they had painstakingly built and sailed over the last two summers. They kept it moored in an inlet that ran near a friend's property. They could park their car at his house, walk along the road a bit and across a path that led to the boat. They could not keep it in the water during the winter and dragging it across the field to the road would be a daunting task and likely to damage the hull. Last winter, they had sailed it out of the inlet into a large bay, up another inlet, managed a short portage from the inlet to a catchment basin, and then across it to the dock by a road. John had stowed his bike on the boat, rode back to their friend's place and returned with the family car. It was not very far to pedal as it was much closer to a beeline than their circuitous water route. John felt considerable satisfaction at having worked this all out. He had used a local map, talked to another local sailing enthusiast, and reconnoitred the area on his bicycle to discover the dock. When he returned with the car, they loaded the boat onto the attached trailer for the short drive home. Wrapped in a tarpaulin, it spent the winter behind their house. They would do the same this year.

The men washed the breakfast dishes and prepared to leave the house. It promised to be a nice day, with a light breeze from the southwest, which would be perfect for much of their journey. In the canals, and against the breeze, they would have to pole. The bay aside, the channels were not wide enough to allow them tack or gybe.

***

Peter handed over his membership card to the woman at the reception desk of the Alex Stephan Tennis Centre. She logged him in and returned the card along with a neatly folded fluffy white towel. He double-checked that he had booked a court for nine a.m. and headed off to the locker room. His regular partner was an old school friend who worked in Cambridge for an accountancy firm. They were evenly matched in skill and inconsistency. Both played to win but took more pleasure from the exercise, camaraderie, the occasional well-placed shot, and well-executed returns. They complimented each other on good volleys and were generous in their line calls. Sometimes they went to the pub after showering, but his partner had a wife and young daughter and the usual family commitments, and this did not happen as often as Peter would have liked.

Suited up, Peter returned to the desk because he had forgotten to ask the number of the court on which he would be playing.

"Ah, Mr Leslie," said the woman behind the desk as he approached.

"Yes."

"Telephone message." She looked down at a slip of paper on which she had written something down. "It was your partner. Says his car won't start. Doubts the AA will arrive in time for him to make the game. Tenders apologies."

"Bloody hell."

"Frustrating, isn't it, when a partner cancels?"

"Tell me about it."

"Don't despair yet. I may have someone for you. We have a new member — she's in the locker room. I told her that the group of women

35

who regularly book three courts might be willing to slot her into one of their doubles' games. They're occasionally short a player, and if not, might let her rotate through, as they do when more than twelve women show up.

"A woman. Is she any good?"

"I don't have a clue. But she's a looker, and you do want to play?"

"I do. Tell me her name."

"I'll introduce you both."

Elaine Nichols came out of the women's locker room and was duly introduced to Peter. She held out her hand for him to shake, and Peter led her to court number four. She's definitely good-looking, he thought to himself. In her late 'twenties, he guessed, svelte, but with just enough roundness, front and back. She had a quick step, which boded well for her movement on the court. Peter soon discovered that he need not have worried on that score. Elaine was fast, more consistent in her play than he was, and obviously enjoying herself. Peter made a mental note to thank his regular partner for not showing up.

***

Henry undid the canvas that covered the sailboat cabin, and John came aboard carrying the bicycle, which he stowed just behind the mast. He had brought along several bungee cords for this purpose. They undid the first of the ropes tethering the boat to the shore before boarding and then untied the second. Using one of the poles they kept in the boat, Henry pushed them away gently from the grassy bank whilst John pulled on the halyard to raise the mainsail. He cleated it and took up the mainsheet. The wind, coming from behind, bit into the sail as John eased off the mainsheet. Henry, seated aft, used the rudder to position them down the channel and on a bearing likely to get the most wind. Something of a perfectionist, John tightened the Cunningham to put more tension in the sail. They moved silently down the inlet, admiring the oaks and shrubs that crowded the banks on both sides, broken only by the occasional lawn. The inlet made a gentle sweep to the right, which soon brought them perpendicular to the wind. John adjusted the sail and contemplated raising the jib when they reached the bay. It was not necessary, and it would add only marginally to their speed. But when running before the wind, it was wonderful to watch the mainsail flying to the starboard and the jib to the port.

Time stopped for both men. This is one of the joys of sailing in a world that otherwise compels people to compulsively check the time and measure their life in minutes. At sea, even in a protected bay, time slows down relative to the rest of the world and can even appear to stop. This state of bliss ended as they approached the canal, and John turned into the wind, let the jib luff before hauling it in, folding and stowing it in a bag stored in the hold. Henry steered back into the wind and entered the channel. They were now running abeam, and there was no need to pole. John pulled in the main halyard to accommodate and slowed the boat down. They wanted to move up the channel but not collide with the bank. The canal was narrow but ran perfectly straight. Keeping a steady course was not difficult.

Like many canals in the Broads, this one ran parallel to an artificially raised embankment. Grass covered both its sloping sides and a dirt path, ran alongside the top. There was a catchment basin, not visible from the boat, on the other side of the embankment. Most of these basins stored water to prevent flooding, and in some cases, were used for irrigation or raising fish.

Ten minutes later, they reached their first terminus, identifiable by a large pump rising above the embankment on the left. They moved the boat alongside, and John lowered and secured the mainsail. They reached the shore, climbed out of the boat, and slid it into the basin on the other side. Henry then hopped in, grabbed one of the poles and, holding on with both hands, used it to push the boat out into the water. As they approached the other side, John lowered the mainsail, and the boat glided five metres or so before coming to a stop.

John took out one of the poles and, standing up, pushed it down into the mud to propel the boat forward the last few feet whilst Henry sat and worked the rudder. They came alongside the dock, and John lowered his pole into the water, this time to sink it into the mud and steady the boat alongside the dock. The pole never reached the mud, six feet below, but was stopped by something solid at a depth of about four feet.

"I've hit something," John said.

***

Peter and Elaine finished their hour of tennis and moved quickly off the court to make way for an elderly male foursome waiting patiently outside the mesh gate for their game to finish. They walked toward the locker rooms, and Peter found himself facing an awkward moment when they reached the door to the women's changing room. He screwed up his courage and turned to face Elaine.

"I really enjoyed our game and would love to play again."

"I would like that too. Is next Saturday afternoon good for you?"

"Probably not, as that is when I meet my regular partner. I could do Sunday or some evening next week."

They agreed to play again the following Wednesday evening. Peter decided not to push his luck and ask Elaine for coffee. He said goodbye and took ten bouncy paces to the male changing room feeling very pleased with himself. He hoped nothing would interfere with his tennis date, but in his job, you never knew. Just once, he would like an urgent call from the station that drew him away from something unpleasant.

***

Inspector Khan was enjoying a quiet Saturday morning. He rose early, no longer able to sleep late on weekends. He made himself a boiled egg, toast and pot of tea and read what he had not finished of yesterday's *Guardian*. In the background, BR Bayern 4 Klassik was playing a Schubert piano and violin sonata to which he listened with one ear. Like many classical music lovers, he had become increasingly annoyed with BBC 3, which had dumbed down its music, played short selections and too many show tunes. A friend had put him on to Bavarian radio, which he much preferred. It played good music, from beginning to end, and had minimal chatter. Five minutes every hour was devoted to news in a language he did not understand. He ignored it, lowered the volume, and very occasionally listened in the hope of learning a little German. He had reasonable French and had spoken Urdu at home with his grandparents, but neither offered much help with this tongue.

On Saturday, the inspector had cleaned his flat and cooked for the week. His routine was to have meals and leftovers on hand for those days, most it usually turned out, when he returned home late from work. His plan for today was to do his laundry, shop at the Waitrose in Grantchester, and reward himself with a long bicycle ride in Thetford Forest. In the evening, he was looking forward to the football match between Arsenal and Juventus and the thriller he was halfway through reading. He kept his interest in murder mysteries to himself as his colleagues would find it laughable and his family and friends enigmatic. He had been drawn to the genre in his youth when he had devoured *Sherlock Holmes*. It had sparked his interest in becoming a detective. He loved puzzles and imagined the job of a detective as something akin to a medical specialist. Detectives and doctors solved mysteries by finding clues and using logic and professional experience to deduce the causes of crimes or diseases. As he abhorred the sight of blood, being a detective was by far the better choice and, he thought, more adventurous.

His parents desperately wanted him to become a doctor. They did more than hope; from about the age of ten, he could remember their encouragement, later, pressure, to become a doctor — "physician" was the term they used. Toward the end of his grammar school years, they finally accepted that this would not happen and held out a legal career as an acceptable substitute. The bar interested him even less, and he rebelled by sticking to his commitment to become a detective. He later wondered if he had joined the force because he wanted to or because his parents did not want him to. In university, he discovered that his interest in the police distinguished him from his classmates, who sought high-status careers or no careers at all in the case of two of his wealthy friends. It also lent a frisson of excitement to him in the eyes of some members of the opposite sex, especially, but by no means limited to, South Asian girls who were keen to rebel against parents pushing them to marry future doctors, lawyers, stockbrokers, and CEOs.

The job was nothing like what he had envisaged as a child, but it was interesting enough and put him in touch with very different classes — in uniform and in handcuffs. It gave him a better appreciation of British society and of himself. He quickly learnt to hide his education and cultural preferences from his colleagues but not with offenders from the least educated backgrounds. They seemed to respect learning, or at least respected him for making the effort to acquire it, and were, to his surprise, more forthcoming in interviews than they were with people they considered to be more like themselves.

Khan had advanced rapidly, given his intellect, commitment, and interpersonal skills. His big breakthrough came in a drug case when he was still a constable. His colleagues had pulled over a lorry driver for a traffic violation, and the driver's overreaction led them to wonder about his cargo. They got a warrant, opened the back doors, and discovered a load of drugs. Anxious to attend his daughter's school graduation and avoid the shame of prison, the driver did a deal, and the police got information about the next step in the chain of distribution in Cambridge. They also prised from the driver the name of his contact in London and passed it along to the Met's drug squad. Cambridgeshire police quickly picked up the local distributor, but he would not speak to them and soon had a competent solicitor representing him. A search of the warehouse he managed and of his home found no drugs or anything else incriminating. He had to be released. Without material evidence, the word of the lorry driver would not have been enough for a conviction.

Khan reasoned that the distributor had to have a stash of drugs somewhere as his business was not one of those modern enterprises that kept little to no inventory and brought in goods only in response to orders, or what they calculated to be the daily flow of business. Drug dealing in Cambridge was more hit and miss, even if demand was relatively steady. The problem was on the supply side. Drug shipments into the country were irregular and, occasionally, they were intercepted, or people were arrested for trying to distribute them. Local meth labs came and went; their presence was equally irregular. Shippers and dealers would occasionally lie low in response to successful busts, slowing or even stopping the supply from reaching the provinces. Internecine disputes that led to violence among suppliers had the same effect. Consumers, and even more so, addicts, demanded regular access to their drugs of preference, and local dealers wanted to keep them happy for economic and security reasons. It stood to reason, that distributors and dealers, sought to keep a ready stash on hand to protect themselves against the inevitable constrictions in their supply chain. So where were the drugs?

Khan did not believe they would be in the warehouse because too many people worked on the site, and someone was bound to discover them. They had to be in a secure location where the distributor could come and go unobtrusively to collect what he needed. He worked his way out on foot in concentric circles from the warehouse in search of some location where the dealer might keep his stash without attracting attention. On his second day of searching, he walked down a street of terraced houses with a construction site at the corner where the road joined a more heavily trafficked one. The construction site looked deserted, and residents he chatted to told him that work had stopped sometime in the previous year. There was a locked hut on the site, one of those rectangular prefabricated structures that fit neatly onto a lorry bed for transportation.

Khan shared his suspicions with a sergeant, who made the necessary inquiries. Construction had halted because of inadequate funding, and nobody worked at the site. Two residents nevertheless reported seeing someone entering or leaving the hut, although they did not think anything of it at the time and could not describe the man. With a warrant and lock cutter, Khan and his colleagues returned to the hut and found the drugs. The SOCOs were called in, dusted for fingerprints, and found several sets matching those of the distributor. He was convicted, as were two of his dealers. Khan was subsequently promoted and posted to CID.

***

Our murderer also looked forward to a quiet day. The only activity he planned was disposing of the remaining items that could identify his victims or connect him to them or the crime scene. He had pocketed their wallets, keys, and the two EpiPens used to immobilize them. He had read somewhere that a certain species of wasp immobilized grubs and other insects that it foraged for its offspring. Its sting did not kill but rendered its prey comatose. When the young wasps hatched, they would feed on these still living insects. Not a nice way to go, he thought. Sid and that lowlife he sniffed never suffered. They felt nothing more than a prick of

41

the EpiPen and drowned whilst unconscious. More ethical by far, he thought, than what American prisons did with those on death row.

He had resisted the temptation to get rid of their possessions at or near the dock. He brought them back to his lodgings and waited patiently, but not without some anxiety, for the weekend. To his surprise, he found this anxiety surprisingly pleasurable, not unlike sexual arousal. Using gloves, he now separated six keys from their two chains and emptied the contents of the wallet onto newspaper he had spread over a table. He looked down on a pile of dosh, totalling three hundred and twenty quid and an assortment of credit, debit and bus and train cards, photo ID's, family photos, business cards, and a few credit card receipts. Most of these items belonged to Sid, but the lion's share of the cash was Lowlife's. He had offered Yobbo five hundred pounds to help with the job, half in advance and the rest upon completion. He pocketed the two hundred and fifty that he had laid out and would arrange to give the rest to charity. He was not a thief. He had only taken the wallets to give the appearance of a robbery.

Everything else he cut up into little pieces that he stuffed into a small plastic bag along with the two keyrings. The yobbo's mobile was an older model iPhone, which he had probably bought used. He decided to hold on to it, which struck him as odd because he had no immediate plan for its use. He bagged it and stowed it inside a box of detergent under the sink. You never know when it could be useful.

He had put the EpiPens back in their plastic containers after using them. He now took them out, cut their cylinders in two with a sharp knife and rinsed them out thoroughly, and the knife as well. He put the cylinders back in the containers and into another small bag. This left the keys, which he pocketed. Satisfied with his labours, he took up his rubber gloves, dropped them into his own rubbish bag, and headed into town. En route, and well away from where he lived, he tossed the metal keys into a recycling bin. He moved on to a skip behind a shop and casually dropped his bags into it when nobody was in sight. He continued towards the centre of town feeling very smug. He regretted that the tingling feeling had passed.

***

Inspector Khan was enjoying his drive to Thetford Forest. It took him out of town in a northerly direction and past Royal Air Force Mildenhall. A bomber base during World War II, its primary purpose now was to support American refuelling aircraft and other far-flung operations. He had once interviewed an American major here in conjunction with a crime he was investigating in Cambridge. The captain had contacted him in response to a media request for assistance by anyone who might have witnessed an abduction. Unlike most callers who waste police time, the captain had useful information and was remarkably precise in providing it.

Khan had almost reached the forest when his mobile rang. He contemplated ignoring it and then checking to see what message, if any, the caller left. Responsibility got the better of him. He slid his finger across the screen to answer the call as he pulled off the road. It was the duty officer who reported that a body had been found in a catchment basin not far from the road to Ely. Whoever it was had not just fallen in. He was trussed up with ropes and weights. The coroner and SOCOs were on their way to the scene. Did he want him to call Peter?

So much for my bike ride, Inspector Khan thought. He put the phone in his pocket, turned the car around and headed back towards Cambridge. The desk sergeant had given him the precise location, but as the road was unmarked, they were posting a constable at the intersection.

**

The murder scene was much like any other. The first indication that something was amiss were the parked police cars with flashing blue lights, uniforms standing alongside to keep nosy parkers away, and a large area marked off with police tape. Other officers were walking around, eyes to the ground, looking for clues. Given the nature of the terrain, the tape stretched across the road on both sides of the dock. Inside the perimeter, several officers stood chatting with the coroner. Two men stood off to the side looking very uncomfortable. The SOCOs, in white suits and boots, were on the dock hovering over something. The inspector showed his warrant card to one of the uniforms, ducked under the tape and joined the circle of officers.

Inspector Khan declined a cigarette and stood quietly listening to the conversation. Latecomers should never make a nuisance of themselves by asking questions that have already been posed by those first on the scene. He would pick up enough information to get a general idea of what had happened. Only then would he make specific queries that his colleagues would be happy enough to answer if they could.

Henry and his son John, the two men standing silently inside the police tape, had discovered the bodies. They had sailed their boat across the basin to the dock, planning to transfer it to a trailer and take it home for the winter. John had used a pole to steady the boat against the dock and was surprised when it would not go into the mud on the bottom but hit something hard instead. He moved the pole around to figure out what it was and came up against something soft and something else hard that felt like wood or metal. His father said to forget it and help him get the boat on the dock, but John's curiosity was piqued, and he kept probing with his pole. They had a small grappling hook in the boat's hold, which they occasionally used to anchor or tie up when they wanted to swim. To his father's annoyance, John lowered it into the water and dragged it across the sunken object. It snagged on what turned out to be a rope, and with the reluctant help of his father, they hauled up a body. They had no choice but to call the police.

Father and son had made no effort to pull the body aboard the boat. They left the grappling hook attached to it and secured the other end to a cleat, with enough tension to keep the body from breaking free from the hook. The SOCOs were impressed because it allowed them to search a relatively untouched body and crime scene. They called in police divers, who, to everyone's surprise, found a second body not far from the first. When the inspector arrived, they were in the water helping the officers on land to bring both bodies up to the road via the embankment. They wanted to leave the dock free for the SOCOs. The inspector wondered if one of the bodies might be Sid. The second could conceivably be the missing young man, but he knew of no connection between the two men.

The SOCOs got both bodies up the embankment and then into body bags laid across stretchers on the tarmac. To do this, they had to cut the ropes and free the bodies from the weights. The divers were careful not to lose any of the weights and handed them one at a time and the ropes to officers ashore to deposit into evidence bags. Judging from the clothing, both bodies were men. One wore a suit, and the other was clad in jeans, trainers, and some kind of light jacket. They were covered with mud, and their faces were entirely obscured. The coroner bent down to peer at them and used a glove-encased hand to explore their jacket and trouser pockets only to discover they were empty. He used a cloth to wipe some of the mud off their faces, which he then illuminated with a small torch extracted from his kit. Finishing his initial examination, he stood up and walked over to DCI Khan.

The inspector was standing with Peter, who had just arrived, and another officer, who had been the first on the scene as he had been nearby when he heard the radio message that went out to patrol cars. The coroner was a spry man for his age but had a deeply lined face because he had so little body fat. He was due to retire in another two years, as was his wife from her civil service job. They were planning a move to southern California to be near their daughter and her family. The coroner had confessed some ambivalence about retirement to Inspector Khan. He enjoyed his job, although not its irregular hours, and whilst keen to spend time with his family, garden in a much nicer climate and hit the local golf courses year-round, he worried that it would be difficult to make a new life for themselves after living for so many years in Cambridge.

"Anything to report?" asked the inspector.

"Just the obvious for now," said the coroner. Two men, one is middle-aged and the other young, most likely in his 'twenties. They haven't been dead for long. I'd guess a week at most, but I'll know more when we clean them up and do the autopsies. No identification, or anything else for that matter, in their pockets. Unlikely that robbery was a motive as the older man is wearing what looks to me like a good watch. They both give evidence of drowning, and they were still alive when dumped in the basin."

"We've had two reports of missing persons this week," said the inspector. "Their gender and ages fit those of the bodies. We have a DNA sample from the first."

"And from the second too," Peter added. "I'll have a uniform bring them over to your lab."

"No need. We don't do our own testing; cheaper to send it out to a local lab. I'll have Jill come by to collect whatever you have. The usual toothbrushes?"

Peter nodded.

"She can bring them along with our swabs to the lab. Within twenty-four hours we'll know if they match."

The coroner asked if either man had any distinguishing marks, but Peter did not remember coming across any mention of them in the missing person forms.

There was nothing further to be gained from staying at the crime scene, and the detectives parted. They would read the SOCO and autopsy reports when they were ready, sometime tomorrow afternoon in all likelihood. The inspector headed home for dinner and a football match. At least that part of his day would come off as planned. Peter drove off and suddenly remembered that he had to take his washing out of the machine and hang it out to dry. By now, he thought, it will be all wrinkled.

VII: Monday Morning

Reporters are like fruit flies. You never see these flies in your kitchen until succulent, ripening fruit is left on a counter, and then they appear as if from nowhere. A ripe body attracts reporters just as quickly. They buzz around the police the way flies do with fruit, and it is no use waving them away as they come right back. They are more obtrusive even though there are fewer of them because they can pester you long distance by telephone and email. Unlike fruit flies, they have access to newspapers, news programmes, wire services and Internet blogs. This imparts a dramatic multiplier effect to their feeding frenzy.

On Monday morning, the *Cambridge News*, the London tabloids, and the BBC regional radio station carried the story of the bodies. All noted that the police had refused to comment beyond acknowledging that they had pulled two men from a catchment pond outside the city. The reporter from the *Cambridge News* closely monitored the local police scene and knew about the two missing person reports that had been filed. Inspector Khan was annoyed to read her speculation that they had now been found. She at least had the good sense not to mention any names. But the names quickly appeared on the Internet. Somebody had hacked into the police database, read the missing person reports, and posted them on-line along with additional information in the reports. The police were outraged and announced an investigation. Inspector Khan knew these revelations would complicate his investigation. He and Peter would have to proceed more cautiously in light of this unwanted publicity. He nevertheless derived some satisfaction from the security breach as the firm responsible for the software he so loathed would presumably catch hell.

***

Our murderer was more on edge than the inspector. He was shocked that the bodies had been found so quickly. He had been counting on them remaining undisturbed long enough to sink into the mud and decompose. He had thought there was a good chance they never would be discovered, making it very difficult to try anyone for murder. Now there was more risk. The police had found his victims and would search for some way of connecting them. He knew they would not succeed because, as far as he knew, there wasn't any connection. Their only link was through him, and he had been very careful to hire a helper he did not know. As he repeatedly reviewed the interactions between them, he was satisfied that he had left no trail the police were likely to pick up.

He did not think much of the police but told himself that it is always better to overestimate your adversary. Sid and Yobbo were lying at the bottom of a pond. He corrected himself. They were lying on slabs in the morgue because they had underestimated him. To be fair, neither had recognized him as a mortal enemy. He had an advantage in this regard; he knew the police were keen to arrest and put away the perpetrator of these murders. He had to make sure he did not come into their sights beyond his presence on their long list of people who knew Sid. He had been very careful in hiring Yobbo; he had worn a wig and false moustache and clothes that gave a false impression of his class and occupation. How he found and contacted Yobbo had also been very clever, he told himself. He had no alibi for the morning Sid disappeared, but who could say that he was not at home working. To discourage suspicion, he had turned off his mobile before he went out and used software that sent emails he left sitting in a queue on his laptop at arbitrary intervals. Any police check with British Telecom would show the record of this traffic and support his claim of having been home all morning.

He would go about his business as usual but give some thought to creating a false trail for the police. He recognized that things were not working out as expected, but this had been true of strategic plans since the days of Oedipus. The key to success was not to rely on your plan but to consider in advance what could go wrong with it and how you might respond. Whilst annoyed that the bodies had been found, the new situation would test his mettle. It was conceivable, he thought, that he might enjoy it more than the near-total security the absence of bodies would have conferred.

***

Henry and John, who had nothing to fear, were the people whose nerves were the most frayed. Their Saturday outing had ended terribly, and just at the moment when they felt a small sense of triumph for sailing their boat so efficiently through inlet, bay, canal, and basin. There was never any doubt about the need to call the police once they discovered a body, and the police came quickly enough. They were initially interested in the body, and it took some time for one of the detectives to direct his attention to them. He took their story and volunteered a constable to drive John back to his car. Henry rationed his cigarettes and was building up his courage to give up the habit, but he had consumed his entire day's allotment whilst waiting to be interviewed and then for John to return with his car. This would not have happened, he thought, if John had listened to him and not probed the bottom with his pole. But then it was good the poor blighters were discovered and would now have a Christian burial.

John was less conflicted regarding the day's events as a grand adventure. They had not interfered with his sailing, and he and his father were now headed home with the boat in the trailer. He had never seen a body before and had been thanked, as they both were, by the police for their discovery. He had enjoyed his ride in the police car and the expression on his father's friend's face when it pulled into his driveway. He had been working in the front yard and came running up thinking they had come to the wrong house. Tomorrow, he and his father would go into the police station to write out and sign a statement, and he was looking forward to it. His mates would hang on every word of his account of what had happened, and all the more so now that it was in the newspapers. Julia, too, he thought, might be impressed, and he had been looking for a while for a way to do that.

Janice began to worry when Henry and John had not returned home for lunch. But Henry had called her from the dock, reporting that they were held up and would explain when they got home. Once in the house, washed up and wolfing down their dinner, she knew they were safe. She listened with a degree of detachment to the curious and otherwise disturbing story they told.

"What made you poke around with your pole, John?"

"That's what young men do," said his father.

"Come now, Henry," said Janice.

There was a pause whilst John finished chewing his piece of stew. "Just curiosity really. The basin is a mudflat. If it had been a lake, I might have thought I hit a tree stump. I couldn't imagine what was lying on the bottom. I moved my pole around to see how big it was. I had no idea I was banging up against a body. But I thought it odd that my pole would prod something soft, then something hard and back again and decided to have a closer look. You know the rest."

"Could you sell your story to the *Sun*?"

"Not now, I suppose. I told much of it to the lady reporter from the *Cambridge News*. Anyway, it's not the kind of thing I would feel comfortable about making money from."

"Maybe," his father piped up, "you'll feel differently about that the next time you discover a body."

Silence ensued as father and son returned their attention to their dinner.

***

Elaine was on duty all day Saturday. As the newest and lowest ranking police constable in the British Transport Police, she had last choice in selecting her rotation. She really did not mind working one of the weekend days because she did not have much of a social life at present. She had broken off a relationship before her first posting and was new to Cambridge. It would take some time to meet people. She had made the right decision in joining the tennis club. The exercise was great and kept her from thinking about work or being lonely. She also met an attractive man who seemed interested in her. She had caught him checking her out. He played an acceptable game of tennis, and she was delighted when he asked her to play again on Wednesday. Somewhat shyly, he had shaken her hand before she disappeared into the locker room and had not asked her out. His restraint boded well, she thought.

The railway office station had the usual mix of responsibilities but few of its own detectives. It did the prosaic work of patrolling the neighbourhood around the station, liaising with local businesses, and, of course, safeguarding the station, trains, and passengers. Every so often it would assist in some operation where numbers mattered. Two weeks back, Elaine had participated in a roadblock. Stopping drivers to see if anyone of them resembled the suspect turned out to be a bore after a couple of hours on her feet in the rain. She preferred her more routine foot patrol as it gave her the chance to learn about her corner of town and provided an opportunity for casual and generally friendly interactions with people.

This morning she was on station duty. Nothing of any significance happened, but it was fun to watch the trains and passengers come and go. She played a little game with herself by trying to figure out which passengers were tourists and what percentage of the traffic they constituted. Her partner was content to stand around and check his watch frequently to see how close they were to a tea break. She had received instructions about what to do in all kinds of emergencies, including a terrorist attack. She thought that unlikely but had paid attention and memorized the procedures, the most important one being to call immediately for help. To date, her most important contribution to the peace and security of Cambridge had been assisting an old man who had dropped his eyeglasses on the platform. She then helped him to the exit and put his ticket through the reader, and the turnstile opened. She hoped something more exciting would come her way, but not too exciting.

VIII: Monday Morning

Inspector Khan and DS Leslie entered the Parkside Police Station with a sense of purpose. They both came in early, although they knew it would be many hours before they received the autopsy and DNA reports. It was another nice morning, and Peter had walked down Mill Road and made no attempt to board the bus that reached the stop as he approached. Inspector Khan came from the other direction, walking across Parker's Piece as he invariably did. At this hour, there were only a few students in sight, mostly heading into town along one of the several bike paths that ran through this greensward. He assumed that most were postgraduates, as undergraduates lived in college and tended to sleep late. There were the usual commuters, and as always, the runners and dog walkers, most of the latter with plastic bags in their hands.

Peter was already at work in the situation room setting up when his boss entered. He welcomed the break when the inspector invited him to the canteen for tea. It was crowded, but for the most part, colleagues took their hot drinks and anything they bought back to their offices at this hour. Nobody wanted to look like a slacker. The inspector and his DS could afford this luxury. The colleagues knew that they were in charge of a new murder investigation and had the commissioner and the media breathing down their necks. If they were sitting together nursing their tea, they had to be conferring on the case.

Everyone who expressed an opinion thought it likely that the recently discovered bodies were their missing persons. These kinds of coincidences happen rarely, and certainly not in Cambridge, where there had only been one murder in the last year. It was a sordid family affair with never any doubt about the perpetrator. Easier still for them, as the suspect had confessed when arrested. They agreed that Peter would call Professor Mason's wife, as he had made prior contact with her, whilst the inspector would phone the young missing man's mother. They would ask for more pictures of the missing men, and both of them would then meet up to interview the mother. They knew the missing men had mobile phones and had asked the wife and mother for the numbers. They were waiting for the phone logs and any information the phone companies could provide about the movements of the two men prior to and after their disappearance.

The SOCOs had found cocaine and ecstasy in the young man's rented room, not large amounts, but enough to suggest that he was dealing. They could not help but wonder if the murders were drug-related, but there was no evidence that the professor was either a user or pusher. From what they knew about him, it seemed unlikely.

The drive to Ely took them past the turn off for the catchment basin, and the inspector noted that he had driven by many times without ever taking any notice of it. Peter suggested that now he would never be able to go by again without registering the road and thinking of the double murder. Ely Cathedral sat atop one of the few rocky promontories in the region and was visible from some distance away. They did not drive into the historic centre as Mrs Peeker lived on the outskirts of the town in a badly designed and hastily erected post-war semi-detached home. She was house-proud. Her front garden, unlike that of several of her neighbours, was nicely tended and, Inspector Khan thought, artistically landscaped. It was a mix of shrubs and flowers, none of which he could name. They had called ahead and were invited inside after showing their warrant cards.

Mrs Peeker ushered them into her sitting room. The furniture was simple, and the sofa fabric had lost most of its colouring due to exposure to the sunlight that poured through the bay window on nice days. The tables and mantelpiece had framed pictures of her son and what the detectives assumed to be her late husband and parents. There were several potted plants beneath the bay window. She offered them tea and, as always, they declined politely.

The interview was delicate in the absence of any knowledge about the identity of the recovered bodies. They would not mention them and hoped that she would not either. Mrs Peeker had heard the news but refused to believe there was any connection between the dead men and her missing son. Her reaction could not be considered denial in the absence of any information about their identities. The three of them successfully skirted around the subject.

"Mrs Peeker," the inspector asked, "can you tell us one more time when you last saw your son?"

"It's been more than a week. Jaime came home on Sunday last week to have supper with me. He did his laundry, had a short nap in his room before we ate. He's a nice boy. He's hardworking and polite. And he never forgets my birthday."

"Did you speak to him at all during the week?"

"He usually calls about twice during the week to see how I am… and to check on his mail."

"Were you expecting him last Sunday?"

"I was. We have a regular arrangement. He usually shows up sometime in the late afternoon."

"How does he get here?"

"On his motorbike."

"You began to worry when he did not appear?"

"Yes, it's unlike him. If something had come up, he would have telephoned. When he wasn't here by six, I called his mobile and then the café. He didn't answer, and the people at the café had not seen him for a couple of days. I was concerned but did not call you for another two days because by then I was frantic."

"Can you give us the names of friends he might have contacted? And does he have a girlfriend?"

"He does have a few mates here in Ely, and I can give you their names. I don't know Johnny's surname, but one of the other boys will."

"Does he see them often?" Peter asked.

"I really don't know. He is somewhat mum about his personal life. I keep telling him that the café job won't lead anywhere and that he should plan some kind of career. He brushes me off and says he's not ready yet to make that kind of decision or commitment. He'll soon turn twenty-three, and he becomes irritated when I tell him time is moving on. I can tell. If he is standing, he shuffles his feet and looks down at them."

"What about a girlfriend?"

"No one in particular. For a couple of years, he was seeing a nice lass by the name of Sophie. They split up. I wouldn't be surprised if it was because he was doing nothing to advance himself. She went to a technical college and works for some company in Cambridge. I think she's now with someone else."

"You can give us her name too?"

"Yes, certainly. Are you sure you wouldn't like some tea?"

"That's very kind of you," said the inspector, "but we are in a hurry today. Before we go, could we trouble you for a few more pictures of your son? And would there be any chance of having a peek at Jaime's room?"

"Of course. But you won't find anything of interest. He keeps it neat, and I clean it regularly."

"If you wouldn't mind?"

"No, of course not."

Mrs Peeker led them up the narrow staircase and pointed to the bedroom on the left. The men entered and looked around. Without a warrant they could not open any drawers or search. Nothing in particular caught their eye. Like many young people, he had a poster of a rock musician hanging on the wall. There was no art and just one photograph of a young Jaime standing alongside his father, who had his arm around him. There was a nicely made model aeroplane on his dresser and no clothes or papers lying around. The only two books in the room were a biography of a famous footballer and a chemistry text. It struck the inspector as out of place and on the way out he asked Mrs Peeker about it. She had never seen him reading it and had no clue as to why it was there. They went downstairs, thanked her, and left the house.

On the ride back, the detectives shared their impressions. They were relieved that they did not have to say anything about the bodies but suspected that Jaime's was one of them and that they would soon be returning to bring the bad news to his mother. Jaime came across as another lad who had not yet found himself, although one without a police record or even any moving violations. They had checked him out earlier. Judging from his room and his mother's comment, he had a reasonable degree of self-esteem and social skills and gave no sign of depression.

"The only jarring thing," Peter observed, "is the chemistry text. What on earth is he doing with that?"

"I couldn't see if it was well-thumbed as it has a cloth cover. If the coroner comes through with a positive ID, we will get a search warrant and go through his room carefully. In the interim, what about checking on his motorbike? Get the registration and have the uniforms start looking for it."

Peter took out his mobile and relayed the inspector's request to the duty sergeant.

IX: Monday Afternoon

Twelve people gathered in the murder room, shuffling their chairs to get a better view of the paste and whiteboard on the inner wall. Nine were in uniform; the other three, detectives, wore suits. Four of the nine were holding mugs of tea or coffee, and two, paper cups with foam-topped coffees carried over from a nearby café. DS Leslie and a constable had attached to the whiteboard several photos of the victims obtained from their families and one of each body taken by police photographers at the crime scene. There were also photos of the weights and the rope used to truss them up. On another whiteboard, they had created a timeline. It began with the last known movements and communications of Sid and Jaime. Toward this end, Peter and several PCs had telephoned everyone they had connected to either man. They accessed the victims' telephone logs and had their IT person go through the computers in Sid's office and home. Within an hour of the bodies being found, constables had fanned out to locate and interview people who lived near the road that ran by the dock to see if anyone had seen anything or simply remembered a vehicle going by.

At the outset of his briefing, Inspector Khan, the senior investigating officer, told his colleagues that they were still waiting on the autopsy and DNA reports, both of which he expected shortly. The two weekend sailors had given their statements. Neither had any record and, as far as he could tell, were telling the truth. For the moment, he was not considering them persons of interest. A sweep of the crime scene had turned up no additional evidence. Nor had interviews of locals.

From his initial inspection of the bodies on the embankment, the coroner guessed that they had not been dead long. Not more than a week, he thought. One was middle-aged and the other young, in his 'twenties, the coroner was guessing. If so, they could be their two missing persons. All this suggested that Sid never made it to Cambridge train station last Monday morning.

"I am thinking abduction," the inspector announced. "Somewhere between his home and the station. If and when we get confirmation from the coroner or the DNA lab, we will have to interview and search along the route he would have taken."

Sid's movements prior to Monday morning suggested nothing out of the ordinary. During the week, he arrived at the college in time for lunch with colleagues then headed off to his office to work or meet with students. On Tuesday, he went from home to the department to teach his course. Porters or colleagues had clocked his arrival and departure on other days, including the Friday afternoon he had gone home early at three thirty. On Saturday, he had worked at home and made an outing with his wife to the Waitrose and garden centre in Grantchester. On Sunday evening, they went to a student performance of Medea. On Monday morning, Sid ate a light breakfast and left through the front door, never to be seen again.

Jaime was harder to track. His mother knew next to nothing about his movements. His landlady had a nine-to-five job and paid little attention to the comings and goings of her tenant. She had seen him go out and return on Sunday and leave early Monday morning, she assumed for work. Jaime's boss and workmates at the café were no more helpful. His last shift had been Friday afternoon and evening, and they had not seen him since. They described him as slightly withdrawn but polite to them and customers. He was a rapid worker and a good barista. The inspector looked across at Peter and raised an eyebrow as they heard this word used for his job description. Jaime invariably came to work on his motorbike and had done so on Friday. The police were searching for the bike but had not yet found it.

"The big mystery," the inspector told his colleagues, "beyond the identity of the perpetrator or perpetrators, is the connection between Sid and Jaime, if indeed these are their bodies. Any ideas?"

A constable tentatively raised his hand, and the inspector nodded in his direction.

"Maybe they met in the café? Has anyone checked if Sid frequented it?"

"Good idea. We will ask."

A burly detective sergeant's hand went up, and the inspector looked his way.

"Assuming no obvious social or professional connection between the men, there are two other possibilities to consider. Jaime is a pusher, and maybe Sid is a user. Older man, attractive lad, maybe they were lovers?"

"Certainly, worth looking into," the inspector replied. "The drug squad is trying to find out where Jaime sold his drugs and to whom. As for the romantic angle, we have no indication that either man is gay, but keep your ears open. We all know that most murders are motivated by money, love or hatred."

Another constable spoke up. "Hatred might be the operative motive in this case. Your three conversations in Leinster College indicate that the professor made enemies there. Two of them don't have verifiable alibis, and there are others you haven't interviewed. Any one of them might have done him in."

"Agreed," said the inspector. "We're going to pursue this line of inquiry. Get a more complete list of possible enemies and grill the lot of them. But what incentive would any of these people have had to kill Jaime? They probably didn't even know him. Somebody murdered these two men. There has to be some kind of connection between them."

"Not necessarily," the same constable replied. "Suppose two of the professor's enemies planned his murder in the café and became convinced that Jaime had overheard them. They would want him out of the way."

"That's a bit far-fetched," Peter suggested. "Why would you plan a murder in earshot of anyone?"

"Suppose they didn't plan it in the café," he shot back, "but were interrupted by Jaime whilst transporting the professor's body?"

"That makes more sense," Peter agreed. "It also puts a premium on finding his motorbike. Let's hold off on the speculation. It's premature. We need to get a positive ID on the bodies, locate Jaime's bike, and speak to his Ely friends and anybody in the university who had it in for Sid. With more information, we can narrow down the possibilities — I hope."

After assigning tasks and before dismissing his task force, the inspector reminded everyone of the information that had leaked. "I know it's not from any of you. Somebody hacked into the police computer system. Let's be careful and not communicate with each other by email in case that is insecure too. I'm going to keep our records off-line for the time being too. That's all for now."

The inspector and Peter walked back to his office after the meeting. They planned a return visit to the college and one to Sid's department. Peter telephoned ahead to arrange for interviews. There was a sharp double rap on the door, and a face peered around the half-open door.

"Come in, Detective Sergeant."

The sergeant opened and came through the door with a file folder in hand. "The preliminary autopsy report, sir."

"Thanks. We've been waiting for it."

Peter stood silently whilst the inspector read it through. He then held it out to Peter without saying a word. He read the two-page document quickly.

"What do you think?" the inspector asked.

"We've found our missing persons."

"It looks that way. Dead no more than a week, and the faces match the photographs. Presumably the DNA tests will be conclusive."

"Hardly surprising that the cause of death is drowning. But interesting that there was no sign of struggle. You would think they would have done their best to escape their bonds and get their heads out of water."

"And it wouldn't have taken a Houdini to do it," the inspector said. "They were loosely bound so might have been able to wiggle free, and the water is shallow enough that you could almost stand in it. Sid is on the short side, but Jaime might be tall enough to breathe standing on his tiptoes."

"Dr Argenella thinks they were drugged but hasn't found any evidence of it yet. It is suspicious, he said, that their arms were extended supinely at their sides and that there were no lacerations or abrasions on their jackets or hands. It suggests that they made no attempt to break free."

"Our killer or killers abduct and drug, or drug and abduct their victims, drive them to the dock, tie them to weights and drop them in the water."

"It certainly looks like it," Peter agreed.

"We're back to where we started — trying to find the connection between Sid and Jaime."

***

The two detectives walked to Leinster College. They cut across Parker's Piece walking by shops and several colleges. At this time of day, the vehicle and bicycle traffic were heavy, and the tourists were out in full force. They tended to congregate in King's Parade and in the outdoor market in the centre of town. Both men had learnt from experience to avoid some of the market food stalls whose proprietors falsely assured customers that what they were selling was fresh. They agreed there was a good vegetable stall but no fresh bread to be had.

"Do you think we should break the news to Mrs Mason?" Peter asked.

"No, not until we have the DNA report. We will then need to ask her to identify the body. Let's call Mrs Mason after our interviews and see if we can visit her after work. Best to tell her about the bad news at home rather than in her office. What do you think?"

"Sounds right, sir. And what about Mrs Peeker? We need to see her again too."

"Bearers of good news, we are not. It's the part of the job I hate the most. I could send you in my stead."

"Sir?"

"Pulling your leg is getting too easy these days, Peter. What if we split up these duties? I'll see Mrs Mason, and you go to Ely and Mrs Peeker?"

"That would be fine, sir."

"Make sure to take a family liaison officer with you. I don't know that we have two people trained for this. Maybe best to book the one we have, and I'll see if I can find a second one from somewhere."

Peter took out his phone, called the duty sergeant and passed along the request. The two men then split up. Inspector Khan walked through the portal of Leinster College, and DS Leslie headed down Silver Street and the bridge across the Cam. He cut through Coe Fen on the macadam

61

pedestrian and bike path and looked across the pond on his right to the Granta pub and back of Darwin College. It was a scenic spot, although occasionally marred by the debris of picnicking students and overflowing waste bins along the path. The pond and the grassy embankment behind Darwin College were a favoured hangout of water birds. Last spring, he had watched two geese looking after a dozen goslings. There were other geese in sight, busy feeding, and he wondered if they were the parents or if the geese had worked out some kind of childcare arrangement. He periodically walked across Coe Fen on his lunch hour and was impressed that by the end of the summer, there were still twelve goslings. No doubt, the now plump and sizeable goslings had profited from the offerings of passers-by. There was a certain irony, he thought, that the one place where natural selection decidedly did not work was on and about the lawns of Darwin College.

He crossed at the traffic lights at Queens Road, walked along the Backs admiring the outlines of Queens' and King's Colleges. He made a left onto West Street and soon entered the handsome new Alison Richard Building that housed POLIS. He was on time for his appointment with Professor George Chester, head of department, whose photo and bio he had googled beforehand. The professor was sixty-two, blue-eyed and silver-haired. He was an expert in bio-politics, a field new to Peter. He checked it out on Wikipedia. It was about how evolution was allegedly responsible for a range of human activities, including violence and war. Peter wondered how they could possibly establish the link but then dismissed his scepticism on the grounds that he was a mere layman.

The chair had an ante office with a secretary. He was handing her something to copy as Peter walked in and displayed his warrant card. Professor Chester ushered him into his spacious inner office. It had two large windows offering a view of other relatively new buildings on the Sidgwick Site. The back wall bookcases were full, and the spines of the books lining the shelves were neatly aligned. The chair's desk was devoid of the usual papers, envelopes, folders, pens, and coffee cups. His pens and pencils were stacked in a cup decorated by a college coat of arms, and there was only one file on the desk, to the left of a large computer monitor. There was a sideboard supporting a high-end coffee machine and related paraphernalia. Two plaques hung from the wall, awards for publications.

"I see you're struck by how ordered my office is. It makes some of my colleagues uncomfortable. I try to put them at ease by telling them that my desk may be neat but that my mind is every bit as cluttered as theirs." He chuckled.

Peter told him that Professor Mason was still missing and the police were treating his disappearance seriously. They thought it unlikely that he had run off and were considering the possibility of foul play.

"Foul play?" "I thought that kind of language went out with Agatha Christie?"

"How would you describe it, sir?"

"I don't know. What about criminal activity?"

"Okay, let's go with that. Can you think of anyone in the department or university who might be up to criminal activity when it comes to Professor Mason?"

"Not really, no. There are those who might wish him savaged by a reviewer, passed over for a grant, or made the target of the kind of derogatory but humorous remarks he routinely makes about others. But I wouldn't call that criminal. I don't think any of my colleagues would go further than calling him 'Sid Vicious'." And that only behind his back."

"Even Professor Lundgren after his visit to her student in the hospital?"

"You are well informed!"

"We try to be when it comes to foul play."

"You really think someone's done a dastardly deed?"

"You watch old film reruns too?"

"I thought you'd enjoy the turn of phrase."

"It's not really a laughing matter, sir."

"And why not? He's probably gone off to a conference on the continent and forgot to tell his wife."

"Is he absent-minded?"

"Not to my knowledge."

"Then he's hardly likely to have just flown the coop."

"I suppose not. But there has to be some innocent explanation."

"And why is that?"

"This is Cambridge, not the Other Place. Professors don't go around murdering other professors, even when they harass their students."

"I never said anything about murder."

"The newspapers and the news programmes have. There has been a lot of speculation since those bodies were found, and most of it connecting them to the two people who went missing last week. It's all rubbish. *In absentia lucusi*, these kinds of stories flourish. But maybe not, given that you are here asking questions about one of them."

"We don't have a positive ID on the bodies yet, but we are concerned about Professor Mason because there has been no trace of him for a week. Could we return to your colleagues and their relations with him?"

"If you insist."

"Tell me more about Professor Lundgren. Is the incident at Addenbrookes the only cause of bad blood between her and Professor Mason?"

"They have been on opposites sides of every department controversy. She has behaved professionally, as has our missing colleague. He has aimed several of his famous barbs her way, including one at a recent retirement dinner."

"What did he say?"

"I was sitting at the other end of the long table and did not hear it. Two colleagues told me later that he teased her about her cello playing. She's passionate about her music and plays in an amateur quartet. A few days before the dinner in question, her group gave a benefit concert for some charity that raises money for immigrant children. Sid is alleged to have said that her playing would have provoked the notice of Sir Thomas Beecham."

"Pardon my ignorance. Could you explain the reference?"

"Of course. During a rehearsal at which Beecham was conducting, he is alleged to have said to a female cellist whose playing he found unsatisfactory something along the lines of: 'You have between your legs the most sensitive instrument known to man, and all you can do is sit there and scratch it'.'"

"I see."

"I'm guessing that she was even more annoyed at the colleagues who laughed at what was obviously a sexist joke."

"Is sexism a problem in the college?"

"Discrimination against the fairer sex has a long history at Cambridge. Until quite recently, I am told, Peterhouse College may have had more Welsh-speaking fellows than women. Our department has a reputation for being hostile to women. As chair, I have made an effort to hire more of them. In the last two years, we hired two young female scholars who are helping to change the culture in the department."

"But it hasn't changed yet?"

"*Infinitus est numerus stultorum*. There is no end of fools. But there may be an end to our fools as they are close to retirement age."

"What about the hospital incident?"

"If true, it was over the top. Professor Lundgren filed a complaint. I interviewed her and the student in question. He acknowledges that Professor Mason came to see him in Addenbrookes but refuses to confirm or deny what she reports. In the circumstances, there was nothing I could do."

"Do you believe her story?"

"Professor Lundgren is not the kind of person to make up tales. She's the senior woman in the department, highly respected in the field, and has always behaved in the most professional way. I don't think anyone has ever heard her refer to Professor Mason as 'Sid Vicious'.' I suspect her student is intimidated and has probably been advised by his peers to keep his mouth shut on the grounds that speaking out can only hurt his career."

"Would Professor Lundgren look for a way of getting back at her tormentor? He's abused her student, made fun of her cello playing, and now appears to have finessed any disciplinary procedure against him. I'd be pretty miffed in the circumstances."

"I'm sure she was, but it wouldn't be the first time. She's had to deal with this kind of nonsense her entire career. Why would she do something stupid now when she's suppressed her hostility all these years?"

"Maybe because she's repressed her true feelings throughout her career. Could this be the straw that broke the camel's back?"

"She has always followed the rule of "*Cave quid dicis, quando, et cui* — Beware of what you say, when, and to whom. I don't see her changing now.""

"What about someone else in the department?"

"It's not all negative. Sid has friends, including a young Finnish protégé. But it's true, there are others who resent him. However, there's really nobody who would consider harming him other than verbally. That's what we professors excel at."

DS Leslie thanked him for his time. His next appointment was with Professor Lundgren, who asked to meet him away from the department. At her suggestion, they arranged to rendezvous at a very ordinary café in town not popular with her colleagues or students.

DS Leslie had googled her too and recognized her sitting in a leather chair in the back corner of the café. She was an authority on Japan and comparative politics more generally. Her most recent book was on feminism and why it had made such little headway in Japan, Korea, and China. Considering when she received her undergraduate degree, Peter calculated that she must be close to fifty. She was still attractive and had a shapely pair of legs. He introduced himself and presented his warrant card. She invited him to take a seat opposite her. There was nobody likely to overhear them as the café was all but deserted.

Peter explained why he wanted to see her and asked if she believed that Professor Mason had abused his student.

"Of course, he did. And it wasn't the first time."

"Oh?"

"There have been other incidents, but none as blatant. Sid has a reputation for abusing students and younger colleagues too. It's enough to make you sympathetic with the students he's brought before disciplinary committees in the department and his college."

"I've heard about that. Do you think he's justified?"

"I don't want to prejudge the matter, but I can readily understand why his students might want to get back at him. And what a perfect way to do it! Nobody would know but them. They could snicker among themselves at the claims he makes in articles based on this data. It would be very satisfying because Sid carries on endlessly about the sanctity of data and the superiority of quantitative research."

"And what about you? What would you do to get even with Professor Mason?"

"Me? That's an impertinent question, Detective Sergeant."

"At a dinner party, yes. But this is a criminal investigation, and like every other, it proceeds by asking unpleasant questions."

"Tell me then, the nature of the crime you're investigating?"

"The disappearance of your colleague."

"Is that a crime?"

"If he's been abducted, yes."

"Has he?"

"We don't know. It's early days yet."

"Then there's no crime to investigate."

"Don't forget the two bodies pulled out of the basin."

"Surely, they have nothing to do with me!"

"Then you should have no objection to answering my questions."

"Perhaps we could start by you answering one of mine?"

"If you like."

"Is one of those bodies Sid's?"

"We haven't identified them yet but haven't ruled out the possibility. Last week they were both here in Cambridge, and this week there's no trace of either of them."

"In Japanese, there's no word for last week or next week. They are described as the week below and the week above. If Sid has been pulled out of your pond, he's certainly had his week below."

"You don't seem very disturbed by the prospect?"

"He's a despicable man. Would I celebrate his death? No. Would I grieve for him? I would not. It would be a loss to the department. As we both do comparative politics, I would have to pick up the slack until we hired a replacement. As I'm desperately trying to finish a book, that's enough of a reason for me to want him alive, at least for the time being. Anyway, I abhor violence."

"Can you tell me where you were last Monday?"

"I was expecting that question. I was at home writing my book. I try very hard to work at home every morning and only play professor in the afternoons."

"Can you do that?"

67

"If you're insistent enough about it. I have a lecture course, tutorials, and meet the students I supervise on a regular basis. They, too, would rather meet in the afternoon. The problem is the odd committee that I'm stuck on, but I make it clear to colleagues I won't attend morning meetings."

"Can anyone verify that you were at home?"

"Not that I know of. I took out the recycling. I didn't see anyone, but a neighbour might have seen me out of a window. I made a phone call and received one, both on my mobile. I suppose you could check the time and location of the calls? I understand phone companies know which towers their signals come through."

"When did you leave home?"

"At 11.20. I know the time because it is a ten-minute walk into college, where I often have lunch."

"And which college is that?"

"Newnham."

"Did you lunch with colleagues?"

"Of course. I can give you the names of the people I sat next to, if you like, and those I had coffee with afterwards."

"If you wouldn't mind."

"One more question, if I may? Do you know anybody who might want to kill Professor Mason?"

"No, I do not. Only people who would be pleased to know that someone else had."

Peter took his leave and cut through King's College in the direction of King's Parade. The college often stationed a volunteer at the back gate to make certain that only members of the Cambridge community used this route, but no one was on duty today. He was to meet up with the inspector in the senior parlour of the college where his boss had dining privileges.

The inspector had given a guest lecture at this venerable institution whose front entrance was just off King's Parade. He was surprised by the size of the audience. But then, people are ghoulish and drawn to talks on the subject of murder. He had been invited to the High Table on more than one occasion since and asked by the students to give a second lecture. It had an even larger turnout as students told their friends it was certain to be good value.

The inspector enjoyed the experience, and the assistant commissioner, who got wind of it, encouraged him to establish a connection with the college. The department prided itself on community policing, and the Cambridge colleges were communities with whom they had relatively little contact. You can be our Inspector Morse, he said, only partly in jest. Inspector Khan had enjoyed the Colin Dexter books when he was younger and the *Morse* television series as well. He knew that Colin Dexter was Cambridge educated and had worked in Oxford, where he had a connection with Nuffield College. In the novels, Morse is an outsider but investigates murders in colleges or by their faculty. The current case aside, he was hoping to do the reverse: become a member of a college and investigate crimes outside of the university.

Inspector Khan met Peter at the entrance to the senior common room. They both opted for coffee, influenced, Peter allowed himself to recognize, by the impressively large, nicely burnished coffee machine with multiple option buttons. He pushed the one for a café macchiato and hoped that the machine's software was better than its police counterpart. The sound of grinding beans followed by the sight of dark liquid coming out of the twin spigots was immensely reassuring. He waited for the milk foam, put his cup in a saucer, picked up a small spoon and stood by as the inspector followed suit. They took their coffee into the parlour, and the inspector sat down in a high back chair. Peter eased himself into the companion chair and carefully placed his coffee on the small table between them. In front of them was a glorious Persian town carpet that covered much of the floor. It reminded the inspector of the theft from the college some years earlier of some precious antique carpets. The thieves pulled up in a white panel van and announced that they had come to collect four carpets from the master's lodge for cleaning and restoration. They were allowed in, collected these antique gems, one of them a rare tribal carpet, and drove off. The college, not the rugs, underwent the cleaning.

The room was modern and clearly a new annexe. The larger room in front was wood panelled, graced with another town carpet and had oil paintings hanging on its walls. Most were portraits of former masters.

What a difference from police headquarters and its canteen, the inspector thought. I should drop by more often. But then he realized it would only make him unhappier about his physical surroundings. He imagined a canteen in which the coffee cups were kept warm on a chafing tray and the walls graced by portraits of former commissioners. An oxymoron, to be sure, and whilst the chafing tray and espresso machine would be very welcome additions, he could do without the commissioners staring down at him during his few authorized minutes of relaxation. Like so much of life, the good and bad came bundled together.

"Did you learn anything interesting?" he asked Peter.

"Interesting, yes, relevant only maybe. Chair and professor alike can't imagine any of their colleagues committing murder. Character assassination is their preferred art, like our Professor Mason. The chair is pompous and has a need for order that borders on the clinical. He made an important point, however. Professor Lundgren has long been the butt of her colleague's barbs and has always turned the other cheek. This has garnered her some sympathy from her colleagues and presumably made it easier for her, the first senior woman in the department, to move up the pecking order. Now that she is a professional success, why would she put it all at risk by murdering her nemesis?"

"And Professor Lundgren?"

"She's got a tough shell. Not surprising in the circumstances. She wouldn't be unhappy if our professor turned up dead, but I don't think she's the type to commit murder. Too controlled and committed to getting her way by playing the system, or defying it, in ways that are acceptable. She says she was working at home the morning he disappeared and will have to fill in for him if he is not found soon. She is dreading the prospect."

"Is there a professor in the university who doesn't work at home on Monday morning?"

"You're thinking we've gone down the wrong career path, Peter?"

"It's worth considering."

"Maybe it's not so easy," said the inspector. "For a start, I'd have to learn a score of Latin phrases to drop at appropriate moments in conversation."

"That can't be too hard. Like Sacha Baron Cohen playing Borat, you could pretend to speak some obscure language and invent proverbs as you need them."

"I suppose so. You might come up with something like… I don't know, 'The dog barks, but the caravan passes'."

"When would I use such a phrase?"

"Anytime. That's the beauty of it. The more obscure and inappropriate it seems, the more impressive it is. Your audience is convinced that it must be profound or meaningful in some way they miss. Without knowing what the head of department said to you in Latin, I would bet even money he plays the same game. The number of people who study ancient languages today is marginal, so you don't need to resort to Kazakh or Urdu. Maybe better to avoid the latter."

"Do you understand it, sir?"

"Yes, but I don't speak it all that well. I was too busy assimilating as a kid. A South Asian professor spouting bits of Urdu wisdom won't win points in this competition. I'd have to do this in Sanskrit or ancient Greek to wow them."

"Do you know either of these languages?"

"Not a word."

"How did your visit to the college go?"

Inspector Khan recounted his morning, starting with his encounter with the master. "I wanted to acknowledge that I was on his pitch and keep him in the picture, at least in part, to maintain his cooperation. We had a short, inconsequential conversation and the master naturally wanted to know if one of the bodies they pulled from the basin was that of his colleague. I told him we didn't know at this point, and he didn't push me. He was remarkably restrained, as was everybody else to whom I spoke. Nobody but Mrs Mason seems upset by the professor's disappearance."

"He's not well-loved, is he?"

"Not in the least. I talked to the senior tutor, thinking that she is as likely as anyone to have her finger on the pulse of the college. An interesting woman, I'd say. An engineer, she's developing cheap and reliable technology for developing countries. I wish I had had more time to draw her out on her research and its applications. She avoids our

71

professor whenever possible, considers him a misogynist even though he supervises mostly women, she volunteered. He has verbal fun at the expense of his female colleagues but is always careful to avoid saying anything that is unambiguously outrageous. She called him 'a clever bugger' and can't imagine how his wife puts up with him."

"She's the only one who does, it seems."

"Yes, but then I can never understand anybody else's marriages and certainly couldn't figure out my own. They must have some kind of strong bond."

"What else did she say?"

"Only that it was inconceivable in her opinion that any of her colleagues would have done him physical harm. She knows the students he is trying to send down and admits they are terrified. She hinted that they are guilty as charged but believes the charges will be dropped if the professor is unable to testify against them. She wants him to reappear, she says, but also for the case to go away. The students have learnt a lesson. A disciplinary proceeding would not be in anyone's interest."

"The students have a good motive?"

"There's at least one other professor who also has a strong motive."

Peter's mobile rang, and he answered it and held it to his ear. The inspector could only make out the conversation on Peter's end, and that consisted of grunts and the occasional yes. Peter finished his call and pocketed his phone.

"The DNA results are in, and they confirm the bodies are who we think they are. No meaningful ambiguity, the lab said. Dr Argenella also called. He will make the bodies presentable for identification but wants to keep them for a few more days. Said he's happy to talk to us about the puzzle they pose."

"We need to inform the families."

"There's more, sir. The deputy commissioner is being barraged by the media and wants you to arrange a press conference."

"All that in one call? Are you sure they didn't pass along a message from my ex?"

"Nothing from her, at least nothing said to me. Do you think she's involved in the murders, sir?"

Inspector Khan studied his colleague's face and saw the expectant look he almost always had after making a joke.

"I do. I do indeed, Peter. She murdered them both, dumped them in the basin, arranged to have their bodies discovered, and is confident that we will never suspect her. It's her way of exercising power and taking me down a peg in the eyes of my superiors. I'm only sorry that you will have to pay the price too."

"It's fiendishly clever. What makes you think she's capable of it?"

"She's been trained by a master... her mother. Whenever she visited our flat, she would get up in the middle of the night, sneak into the kitchen and rearrange the contents of at least one of the refrigerator shelves. She knew that I was always first up in the morning and would set up for breakfast. I would open the fridge, and the change in air pressure would be enough to disturb what she had precariously unbalanced on the shelf. It would come flying out and land on my toes if I didn't jump out of the way in the nick of time. It's the domestic equivalent of the traps, guerrillas set in jungles for occupation forces."

"That's impressive."

"In fact, I wouldn't be surprised if my mother-in-law and ex-wife were in this together. It would help to have two people to overcome the two victims, transport them to the dock, and tip them over the edge. My ex-mother-in-law probably knows about some arcane drug, found only in the appropriately named Hindu Kush, that would immobilize them without leaving a trace. *Kush* in Old Persian means to kill. Maybe we should bring her in for questioning."

"I thought you didn't know any of these arcane languages?"

"I don't. I'm displaying crossword knowledge. What do you think? Do we bring in my mother-in-law, but maybe alert the press first?"

"We could hold them overnight in separate cells and interrogate them sequentially. You might just be willing to play the bad cop and use the thumbscrews or, at the very least, waterboard them."

"With pleasure, although it would only confirm my ex-mother-in-law's suspicions. She really believes that we beat and torture suspects. I could never persuade her otherwise. She once asked me if I had ever planted evidence on someone!"

"Have you, sir?"

"If this line of questioning continues, I could arrange for you to be busted for the drugs they conveniently find in your locker."

"A few months back, I read about a chief inspector in London who was arrested for drugs and drunk driving."

"I don't suspect you of the latter. You can relax on that score."

"I'm much relieved."

"What if you go see Mrs Peeker whilst I'll break the news to Mrs Mason? I'd love to see the coroner first, but I'm afraid of the media somehow getting their hands on this information and these women learning the bad news on the TV news. I'll go to the coroner, as you have the longer drive to Ely. I'll also arrange for my ex-mother-in-law to hold the press conference."

X: Late Monday Afternoon

Cynthia Mason was having a busy day in chambers. She saw two clients that morning, one of them new, the other a well-known pest, but a pest who never complained about how many hours she was billed. The new client was a partner in a start-up that had been bought out by a major corporation. The start-up's solicitor had done the numbers and calculated the amount due to each of the partners after costs were deducted. These costs looked inflated to the client, and she was suspicious of the solicitor, who was a close friend of one of the partners. She had gone to an accountant, but he could not give a definitive opinion without the relevant documents, which the solicitor was unwilling to share. It was the kind of challenge Cynthia loved.

The pest was another matter. She was involved in a messy divorce if that's not redundant. The firm had taken it on because they had previously handled her sizeable inheritance. There was ample dosh on both sides of the marriage, which, in theory, might make a settlement easier. Not in practice. Husband and wife fought over items of no value, including — Cynthia had difficulty in wrapping her mind around it — a recycling bin that was owned by the city. She and the husband's solicitor had tried, without success, to talk some sense into their respective clients. In another way, the conflict was rewarding because it kept her mind off her missing husband. When the pest finally left her chambers, Cynthia wondered how she would behave if she ever divorced Sid. She hoped she would be more reasonable but knew that Sid would not, although she doubted that he would make a claim on their recycling containers. They had two in any case, so it would be easy enough to take one each.

She ate a salad for lunch at her desk and then had a quick cup of tea with a partner. He inquired politely after her husband, and she told him that there was nothing new to report. He was sensitive enough not to try to reassure her by insisting that Sid would return. She now doubted that he would. His disappearance was totally out of character, and she had read about the two bodies pulled out of the water somewhere near Ely. She had called the police right after watching the story on the local news and had been put through to DS Leslie. He encouraged her not to jump to conclusions. The lab was doing DNA testing, and should one of the men turn out to be her husband, which he thought unlikely, she would be the first to know after the lab technicians and himself. One part of her hoped Sid would not return, but all of her hoped that it was not his body that had been found.

Late in the afternoon, she received a call from Inspector Khan. It came as a shock, although she immediately realized that it should not have. They had news for her that he wanted to report in person and volunteered to come to her office or home. Without thinking, she said her chambers and subsequently felt good about her decision. Unlike her house, it was her territory, and she felt more secure here. She assumed the news would be bad. If the police had something good to report, the inspector would not have hesitated to pass it along over the phone. She would do her best to busy herself in the couple of hours that remained before her appointment with the inspector.

***

The police did not have their own morgue; there was no need. They used the hospital facilities on the infrequent occasions they had a body to examine. Their forensic coroner worked for them only part time and was otherwise on staff at the hospital. He greeted Inspector Khan at the reception and ushered him through security and downstairs to the morgue. The inspector wondered why every hospital morgue he had ever visited was deep in the bowels of its building. He supposed it was to keep bodies away from patients and death away from their thoughts.

Inspector Khan did not like visiting the morgue. At his first encounter with a body undergoing dissection, he had suffered the most uncomfortable, actually painful, tingling in his bollocks. He had the strongest urge to rub them in an attempt to relieve the sensation but restrained himself for fear that others would stare at him and think he was getting off on the dissection. When he went for his next physical, he described this experience to his GP, whom he trusted. The doctor explained that his vagus nerve was responsible. When activated by the sight of blood, or any number of other things, it reduces the heart rate and blood pressure. This is why some people faint at the sight of a needle and many more in autopsies. It can also prompt people to vomit or, as in his case, to have unpleasant sensations in their testicles. It was perfectly normal and nothing to worry about.

Inspector Khan felt both relieved and annoyed at himself for his earlier concern. The experience had been made more troubling by his memories of Plato's *Republic*, which he had read in his first year at Cambridge. Socrates distinguishes *thumos*, usually translated as spirit, from appetite and shows how they can be in conflict. He described a character, Leontius, if he remembered rightly, who took pleasure in looking at dead bodies but felt great shame when he did. He suppressed his appetite to maintain his standing with his friends. The inspector had begun to think that he had some strange kink of his own.

Hospitals give the appearance of being clean, but he knew they were anything but. The police coroner must have read his thoughts because he told his visitor how carefully their bodies were preserved and how they hosed everything down after every dissection. The men entered the locker room, changed into scrubs, washed up and put on gloves and plastic hats. The inspector waited for the expected tingling but felt nothing, anxiety aside.

"These bodies present a challenge," the coroner explained. "They both drowned, which is evident from haemorrhages, pulmonary oedema, goose flesh, and the 'charlady' appearance of their hands and feet. Death occurs, at most, after four to five minutes in freshwater from cardiac arrest due to vagal inhibition."

Inspector Khan's testicles started tingling and itching, and he shifted around on his feet, hoping to ease what he was now feeling as pain.

"Are you all right?"

"I think so. My vagus nerve is stimulated."

The coroner made him sit down and sip a glass of water and asked him a couple of innocent questions having nothing to do with death or bodies. After a few minutes, the inspector felt better and insisted on giving it another try. They re-entered the room where the bodies were, and the coroner resumed his monologue.

"Nobody willingly drowns, not even people trying to commit suicide this way. Our bodies struggle to reach the surface and breathe, and there is no sign of struggle in either corpse. Their faces and hands have a relaxed appearance, and as I noted in my preliminary report, they give no evidence of trying to break loose from their bonds or propel themselves to the surface. There is no sign of prior struggle or physical harm, which is what you would expect in either circumstance. Nobody bashed them on the head, choked them with cord, or did anything else physical to render them unconscious or inactive."

"What do you think happened?"

"They were drugged. Some strong sedative knocked them out quickly and long enough for their bodies to be taken to the dock and tossed overboard."

"How are you holding up?"

"I'm fine now, thanks."

"Good. I looked for puncture marks and in places where the drug would most promptly enter the bloodstream and take effect. It took some time, but I found them. Both men were disabled by injections into the carotid artery in their neck. They must have collapsed very quickly afterwards. Both puncture marks suggest a standard bevel needle, possibly part of some auto-injector. Your murderer knew what he was doing. Hitting the carotid artery takes a little practice. However, both men were quite thin, and that makes the artery more visible. In overweight people it is usually out of sight."

"Why do you say that?"

"In the first instance, the location of the punctures. They are in the right place if the goal is to immobilize quickly. But to be fair, an amateur might figure this out on his own or do it after a few minutes of instruction."

"More telling is the choice of drug. I've run the usual tox screens to no effect. I've also tested for other common agents that might have done the trick. Whatever it was left no traces, and there are few agents of this kind. You certainly can't buy them over the counter. They are doubly hard to obtain because they have few legitimate purposes, and records are kept on those that are sold. The drugs would also be under lock and key, which presents another obstacle. I've written down their names for you."

"You are saying that we have a clever, probably well-educated killer, who somehow got his or her hands on some unusual and carefully controlled drug? That should make them easier to trace."

"Yes and no. Ask yourself why the killer would resort to a drug that would make him — or her — easier to trace."

"You have obviously given some thought to this question."

"My guess is that the killer did not expect the bodies to be discovered for years, if ever. They had weights attached to them and were dropped into a basin with a muddy bottom. Here too, intelligence shows. When drowned bodies begin to decompose, they produce a lot of gas, which forces them to the surface. Our killer used weights to keep them from rising and assumed, quite reasonably, that submerged they would decompose and their bones, and what was left of their clothing, would be gradually covered by mud. If the bones were ultimately discovered, nobody would know they had been injected with something. And if so, there would be no chance of identifying the agent."

"We got lucky, so to speak."

"Indeed. That's why we found the puncture marks but no trace of the disabling drug."

"Still, why would the killer take this risk? If I understand you, there was no perceived need for a special drug. A common one would have done just as well, provided it disabled its victims quickly."

"Yes and no. Any common muscle relaxer administered in a large enough dose would have killed the person injected by stopping their breathing. This drug acts very quickly, minimizing the resistance of those being sedated, but does not kill them. It slows but does not stop their lungs from functioning. This is useful and, I suppose, could be critical if the killer worried about being overpowered by his victims. Or perhaps, the killer had a reason to keep them alive for a while."

"Would it immobilize much more effectively than more readily available agents?"

"Yes, it would — if it's the one I have in mind."

"The real advantage would be for someone weak, possibly a woman, as you suggest?"

"There is another possibility to consider. Do you know why so many people are killed by guns in America?"

"There must be many reasons."

"Yes, but the big one is their availability. Angry people reach for what is in sight, and in America, it is often guns. It is conceivable that, for some reason, our killer has access to this drug. It might be a useful line of inquiry to pursue."

"That's very helpful. You think that some kind of auto-injector might have been used. Are they readily available, and is there a reason for our killer to use one?"

"Good questions. Auto-injectors are very common, but so are regular syringes. Someone inexperienced with giving injections might well prefer an auto-injector. It's easy to use, and you need no prior practice in sticking needles into people. But you would have to know how to remove its contents — usually, epinephrine — and substitute your poison, and I don't think that's easy."

***

John had written out his statement at police headquarters and arrived at the warehouse where he worked at about ten thirty, just as his mates were taking their tea break. They knew about his discovery of the body and were anxious to hear the details. John did not disappoint them as he enjoyed being the centre of their attention. He told the story in a straightforward manner, adding all kinds of details that set the scene but were not germane to his discovery. His mates wanted to hear more about his efforts to pull whatever it was up to the surface and why he had decided not to go further when he realized it was a corpse. None of them had ever seen a dead body, although one had seen his father taken away in a stretcher after his heart attack, from which he did not recover.

They also asked what happened when the cops arrived, and here too, John gave a description rich in detail. He and his father had been moved well away from the dock, and a detective sergeant asked them how they found the body and what they were doing there. Police divers had arrived and went into the water and found a second body. He couldn't see the bodies well as they were encased in mud. They were being washed down

80

with a hose when he and his father took their boat out of the water, and with the help of the police, loaded it onto the transporter.

The cops were very helpful. He was surprised. The PC who drove him to pick up the car seemed like a nice fellow. He told his mates the next time he needed some help that he was going to find another body. This got a hearty laugh.

"Have you heard," one of them asked, "about the disappearance of Jaime Peeker? The media were speculating that he and some Cambridge poofter might be the dead men."

A discussion ensued, and two of the lads owned up to knowing Jaime. Neither had seen him much since he had moved to Cambridge.

"The last time I saw him," Tashi volunteered, "was in his bedsit. He invited me to snort coke with him. I wondered if he was dealing."

"Coke?" two of the group said simultaneously.

"Yeah, coke. I've never tried it. Have any of you?"

There was silence and a shaking of heads.

"Did you do some of his coke, Tashi?" John asked.

"No. It's a rich man's habit and illegal. Better to stick with beer."

"Say, John, do you know which of the bodies you pulled up with your grappling hook? Was it Jaime?"

"That would be weird," he said. John's euphoria had disappeared by the time they all returned to work. Finding bodies was one thing, but altogether something else if they belonged to somebody you knew. Well, he didn't know Jaime well as he was a couple of years ahead of him in school. But it was still unsettling.

***

Peter was not all that far away from the warehouse. He was in the same chair he had occupied previously in Mrs Peeker's sitting room. There was no easy way to break the news, so he told her directly, and she immediately burst into tears. The woman constable he brought with him sought to comfort her, and it took some time for Mrs Peeker to stop wailing. The PC then went into the kitchen to make them all tea. Peter passed along the few details they had. He steeled himself to ask Mrs Peeker if she would come in sometime in the next day or two to identify

81

her son's body. She nodded. Peter asked if there was someone they could call to come over and keep her company. She suggested the neighbour next door, and the constable went across the lawn to fetch her. They left the two unhappy women and drove back to Cambridge, not exchanging any words for the first five minutes.

***

Inspector Khan arrived on time for his late-afternoon appointment with Mrs Mason. She was a solicitor and must have considerable life experience, he reasoned, and might be better prepared than most wives to take his news in her stride. He was right.

Mrs Mason had already guessed what was coming and had begun to process the information. She felt a great loss and a strange sense of liberation. Although she had a career, much of her life had revolved around Sid and his needs. His job, his research, his academic calendar, and his demands had always come first. She had made a life for herself in the interstices. She had lots of free time, but it was not always of her choosing. He dominated her in more subtle ways too, and she recognized some of them. During the last week, as she had begun to live her life without him, she had realized the many ways that she had been manipulated and been made to be dependent on him and she had become increasingly resentful.

The inspector could not know any of this. He was a detective and not a mind reader. He imagined that Mrs Mason was experiencing some of the same emotions that he had when his wife had left him. He was shocked by the loss but experienced some excitement at the prospect of his new independence. At first, he felt guilty about this pleasure but later had come to thoroughly enjoy it. Now he took his freedom for granted but was enough in touch with his needs to know that at some point, he would pair off again. Right now, he was like a rocket in free flight, at its apogee, before it gradually turned back towards the Earth and began its rapid descent.

He was ushered into Mrs Mason's office. She had put on fresh makeup, not that he noticed, and tried her best to put on a good face. The office was relatively neat but not compulsively so like that of the head of

POLIS. There was a nice, recently made, oriental carpet on top of the polished light wood floor. The walls were off-white, and what looked like a Malevich painting hung on one of them. On the other wall was a Chagall print. If the Malevich was real, it would be worth a fortune. He didn't think she and her husband had that kind of money. If he had come here for other reasons, he might have expressed interest in the painting.

Mrs Mason arose from behind her glass top desk to greet him. They exchanged the usual pleasantries, which both found even more ritualistic in the circumstances.

"There's no good way of expressing the news I have for you, Mrs Mason."

She looked him directly in the eye but said nothing.

"We believe one of the bodies we pulled out of the basin is your husband. The DNA matches, and there is a good likeness with the photograph you were kind enough to provide us with."

"I assumed as much. Was he murdered, as the newspaper reports? And if so, I'd like to know how."

"I'm afraid your surmise is correct. He was rendered unconscious with a drug injected into his neck and then dropped into the basin where he drowned. He would have felt no pain whatsoever, nor known what was happening to him."

"That at least is reassuring. What about the other man? Who is he?"

"His name is Jaime Peeker. He's twenty-three, single, from Ely but has a bedsit here in Cambridge. He worked part time at a local café."

"What was he doing alongside my husband?"

"We have no idea. We're very interested in discovering a connection between them."

"How could they be doing anything together? Did this Jaime have any university affiliation?"

"No, he never attended university."

"Then I'm at a loss."

"Could they have some interest in common? What hobbies did your husband have?"

"Hobbies? Work was his hobby, with a little gardening and a little me on the side."

"Could they have met at the café where Jaime worked?"

"I think it unlikely. Sid didn't hang out in cafés. That's why the London café's name stuck in my mind. It was so unusual. He hates the music they play in most places and doesn't like to be seen working in public or risk being interrupted when reading or writing. I've never known him to go to a café in Cambridge. He likes coffee and usually takes it after lunch in the senior common room of his college."

"Mrs Mason, I must ask you another question or two concerning the possible link between your husband and this man. I apologize in advance for asking, but it's part of my job to search for any possible link between these two bodies."

Cynthia noticed the shift in the inspector's language, with her husband now referred to as a body. *"I imagine that's what he is to him,"* she said to herself. *"He must have difficulty in visualizing Sid alive, just as I find it hard to think of him dead."*

"This Jaime lad sold drugs part time. It's likely that some of his customers were university people."

"At Leinster College?"

"We don't know yet."

"I hate to disappoint, Inspector, but my husband did not use drugs. He abhors them. He knows they are illegal and believes they are dangerous. I think, most troubling of all for him is that they encourage loss of control."

"Could he and the lad have had a sexual relationship?"

Mrs Mason laughed. "That's even more far-fetched. He was straight, I assure you."

"I see. Can you think of anything at all that might have connected him to Jaime? There has to be some connection, as they were murdered at the same time, presumably by the same person or persons."

"Was this Jaime fellow also injected with something?"

"Yes, he was."

"Isn't it possible that they were both murdered by the same person but for different reasons?"

"It is certainly possible, although that is not usually how murder works."

"What if they both had large gambling debts and a contract was put out on them? The connection would be to the bookie, not to each other."

"That's true. Did your husband gamble?"

"Absolutely not. I was merely offering it as an example."

"I appreciate your line of argument, and you are right in thinking that the connection need not be a personal one. Perhaps something will turn up, unconnected to drugs or sex. If you think of anything, let us know."

"Will I need to identify the body?"

"At a stretch, we could go with the DNA, but it would be extremely helpful if you would do so."

"Would tomorrow morning be all right? I have some free time in the late morning."

"That would be fine. I can pick you up any time you like."

XI: Tuesday Morning

The press conference was scheduled for nine a.m. Inspector Khan and DS Leslie arranged to meet in the inspector's office an hour before. Peter stopped at the café en route to the station to pick up an Americano with foam on top but no milk. He was tired of having to explain to so-called baristas what he meant by foam without milk. Nobody worked in one of these places long enough to get trained properly, and most came from somewhere in Eastern Europe and were still learning English. The odd native English speaker was no better. On one occasion, he tried to explain that what he wanted was like a macchiato but poured over an Americano instead. The young man behind the counter looked at him uncomprehendingly and finally said that a macchiato was an espresso. This morning he was lucky. The woman behind the counter recognized him and asked if he wanted the same as yesterday. He nodded his head but felt like giving her a hug. He wondered how good a barista Jaime was.

Peter climbed the stairs to the inspector's office, knocked and entered through the open door, said good morning to his boss, and lowered himself into the one chair opposite the desk. He pried the lid off of his coffee whilst the inspector took a sip of tea. He passed across a copy of John's statement about finding the first body and the coroner's final report. The latter had been hand-delivered thirty minutes before, another precaution against electronic snooping. He waited for Peter to finish reading both documents.

The inspector filled him in on his visit to the morgue and to Mrs Mason. They should follow up on the drug, see who had purchased it and from which suppliers. Peter could also ask around to see if any was missing from hospitals that kept it in stock. It was the first good lead they had. It was nevertheless a surprising development because somebody who had access to this drug would presumably also have access to much more commonly used and less traceable agents. Peter agreed that it seemed an unnecessary risk if the killer expected the bodies to decompose and never be found or discovered only when it would be impossible to find a trace of any drug.

"Maybe we are thinking too much," the inspector mused. "Perhaps the killer never considered these implications and used the drug because, for some reason, he found it easy to get his hands on it."

Peter agreed it was a possibility, but it was another reason to trace the source of the drug.

Peter told the inspector about his meeting with Mrs Peeker. Her reaction was more or less what you would expect. He didn't learn anything new. He got the names of some of Jaime's local friends and would interview them — this afternoon with any luck. He would also speak to the drug squad to see what their investigations had turned up. He was betting that the professor had not bought drugs from Jaime.

"His wife denies that he had ever been a user, and I tend to believe her. He was too smart to snort or shoot up in college, so it would have been at home, and she would have noticed. She also says that he had a fear of losing control which is one of several reasons why he shunned drugs. She dismissed any sexual connection with Jaime. Did you get any hints that Jaime tilted in that direction?"

"None. But I will have a chat with his former girlfriend and see what his mates have to say about his sex life."

"Mrs. Mason said something interesting that had also occurred to me. There could be an indirect rather than direct connection between her husband and Jaime. Suppose they never met, but both had dealings with a third party who wanted them out of the way for the same or even different reasons?"

"It's a bit of a stretch."

"No more so than finding the elusive and seemingly unlikely direct connection between them."

"I'll grant you that, sir."

"She's an unusual woman, our Mrs Mason. She's very bright, and her little grey cells, as a predecessor of ours would call them, were firing away unimpeded by her emotional distress. She'd figured out why I was coming to see her, was not shocked by what I said, answered my questions promptly but deliberately, and, most remarkably, was able to step back and reflect upon the situation. And another thing I noticed. She has some impressive art in her office, and I'd like to know how she affords it. I'll ask the finance people to get on to it."

The inspector's desk phone rang, and he picked it up immediately. It was the deputy commissioner who wanted to see him before the press briefing. He excused himself and said he would meet up with Peter before they confronted the press.

"We, sir?"

"Yes. I'll do the speaking, and you can stand there, look handsome and get us more viewers."

Deputy Commissioner Braham was neither old nor new school but something of a mix of the two. He knew all about traditional policing and had made a reputation for himself as a solid, if not particularly imaginative detective who had enough sources in the underworld and aboveground communities to keep him well informed. He had a deceptively cherubic face and a friendly smile, but people who judged his disposition on this basis made a big mistake. He would not hesitate to bite your head off if he thought you deserved it. Oddly, he was most benign when in a grumpy mood and, for this reason, Inspector Khan was happy to find him grousing about budget cuts that were being passed down the chain from London. The Tories had already reduced funding around the country for forensic officers and their labs, and this in an era when science was increasingly helpful, often necessary, in getting convictions. In the latest round of cuts, London and then the commissioner had given the deputy commissioner a certain leeway about what to axe. The end result would be both a less effective force and more hostility directed at him.

He reminded Inspector Khan that all press conferences present danger and opportunities.

"If we don't look like we are on top of things, our reputation will suffer. We also get a bad press if we are impolite and don't let reporters ask their silly questions. Answering them is another matter. That Johnson woman from the *Cambridge News* is particularly insistent, and I, for one, would like to know how she leant the names of the bodies before we had. Let her ask several questions, if she wants, but don't reveal anything you don't want to, especially to her."

"I assume you will confirm the names of the bodies? No reason not to tell the media at this point."

"Yes, sir. I also intend to let them know when they went missing. We have a reasonably precise time in the case of the professor. For Jaime, we only know the day. I'll appeal to anybody who saw either victim to contact us and hope someone does so beyond the usual creeps looking for attention. I've arranged for constables to interview anyone who calls or walks in. We've collected the data from the CCTV in the café where Jaime worked and will go through it to look for anything suspicious or any encounter with Professor Mason."

"Good. You seem to have it all in hand. Anything I can do to help?"

Inspector Khan brought the deputy commissioner up to date on their investigation, which, unfortunately, did not take long. He described the urgent need to check out the unusual drug the coroner found traces of in both bodies and to discover how the murderer got access to it. He wanted someone to look into the Masons' finances and the provenance of the art gracing the walls of Mrs Mason's office. The deputy commissioner agreed to both requests.

The press conference went better than expected. Inspector Khan confirmed the identities of the bodies, provided some background information about the victims and when they went missing and answered a string of questions. None were unexpected, stupid, or offensive. The reporters seemed satisfied by his explanation that the names had been withheld until their next of kin could be notified. Everyone wanted to know, or for him to speculate about, the connection between the bodies. He refused to do this but asked anyone who might have relevant information to come forward. He would be releasing photographs of both men and information about when and where they were last seen. He hoped the media would give them wide circulation. He said nothing about Jaime's involvement with drugs, and nobody asked about it, to his relief.

When everybody was getting ready to leave, he motioned to Rhianna Johnson of the *Cambridge News* to stay behind. He thanked her for holding back the names of the victims and asked if she had any idea how one of her colleagues had obtained them.

"Not from me," the tall, young woman said in no uncertain terms.

"I know that, and I owe you one for your restraint."

"Between us, I'm worried that someone has hacked into our system. I don't know enough about IT to even imagine how this might be done."

"Nor do I. Have you considered that it was one of your colleagues who leaked the information? The tabloids pay big money for news like this."

"I'd like to think that wouldn't happen."

"Don't be naïve. It's a common occurrence. Police salaries are low, and living costs are high. I don't know about Cambridgeshire, but it certainly happens elsewhere in the country, and definitely in the Met, where a couple of officers were recently tried and convicted of selling information."

"I'll look into it."

"Is there anything else you can tell me?"

"Not at the moment, but when I have something juicy for public consumption, I promise I'll come to you first."

***

Elaine had read about the murders in the local paper and heard about them on the local news, but they were of no immediate concern to her. The railway police were focused on other problems, and at the moment, drugs were high on the list. The Met had picked someone up at King's Cross bringing ecstasy into London on the express train from Cambridge. They suspected that it was being manufactured in Cambridge or its vicinity. The Cambridge drug squad had not noticed any increased use of the drug or change in its price. They assumed that if it were made in town or nearby, the producers had been smart enough not to sell it locally and draw attention to themselves. The carrot-and-stick strategy applied to their usual informants had produced no leads. The police thus concluded that the people involved were not connected in any way with the local drug trade.

Word had gone out to the police to keep their ears open, and the railway police, in particular, were keen to intercept another shipment of drugs. The mule the Met had picked up in King's Cross did not know the name of his supplier but helped a police artist construct an image of him.

He also reported that he had an odd gait, perhaps the result of some injury. Elaine and her colleagues were keeping their eyes open for him in the vicinity of the station because that is where the hand-off had occurred, in the large bicycle park to the right of the station. Elaine was dressed in civvies and given a bike. Repeatedly, she cycled around and then locked the bike up in a bike rack, walked off and returned for it ten minutes later. This way she could keep the area under direct surveillance for thirty minutes of every hour. A colleague did the same thing but on a differently timed cycle, making the surveillance constant. Backup could be summoned rapidly if the dealer was observed. The weather was accommodating, and Elaine was enjoying her assignment. It combined exercise with the prospect of excitement.

The suspected drug dealer was a no-show, but a bicycle thief was a good stand-in when it came to excitement. There had been a steady loss of bicycles at the park, and the police had not been able to do anything about it. So many people came and went, especially at rush hour, that any thief had an excellent cover. Elaine got lucky. On her fourth round of locking up her bike, she noticed someone reaching up two rows in front of her towards a high-end cycle on the second level of the rack. It was a young man who did not resemble the one for whom she was on the prowl. For some reason, boredom perhaps, she clocked his movements and noticed him take some object out of his back pocket and look around furtively to see if anyone was looking his way. He returned his attention to the bike, and Elaine could now see that he was holding a screwdriver-like device. He inserted it in the bike's lock, twisted it, and the lock sprang open. He looked around once more before removing the bike from the rack.

Elaine used her radio to summon help and moved to the end of her row to cut him off at the exit to the bike park. She and the thief reached the exit at the same time, and she ordered him to put the bike down and raise his hands. He pushed the bike at her to block her path and ran out of the bike park just as the two constables she had summoned arrived. One of them tackled him, and the other quickly handcuffed him. They hauled him to his feet and frogmarched him in the direction of the police station. The device he had used turned out to be a cleverly designed pick that was very effective in opening the most commonly used brand of bicycle locks.

The young man refused to answer any of their questions and demanded a solicitor. He obviously knew his rights, and a computer search revealed a string of prior minor offences. With a court-appointed solicitor present, he was offered a deal and agreed to give up the name of his fence. He was brought before the judge and released on bail, but not before Cambridge City Police arrested his accomplice at his place of work. This turned out to be a bicycle shop close to the centre of town. The owner stored stolen bikes out of sight in a back room until he had enough to fill a small truck. He sold them to a middleman who took them to Liverpool, where they were resold as used bikes. The Merseyside police, acting on the information provided by their Cambridge colleagues, arrested the dealer. Enough of his bikes were traced to their original owners, and he was easily convicted.

***

Cynthia Mason visited the college at the master's request. He wanted to organize a memorial ceremony for her late husband, but only if she thought it appropriate. Cynthia was receptive and spent the better part of an hour with the master planning the event. He suggested holding it in the old library, not the chapel, as Sid was avowedly secular. But if many people expressed an interest in attending, they would have to use the chapel.

The master had always considered Sid's radical secularism not only a matter of belief but, oddly enough, an expression of his strong desire to belong. He regarded this strategy as self-defeating because everybody knew Sid was Jewish and that this was a cultural heritage as much as a religious belief. His pro-Palestinian sentiments were part and parcel of the package and embarrassing. The problem, the master thought, was not only Sid's insecurity but the British culture that encouraged it. For centuries, the upper and educated classes had sent clear signals that Jews would never fully be accepted but that the elite and their Jewish acquaintances could both pretend they were, provided the latter conspired to hide their Jewishness. In Sid's case, the desire to belong was in tension with his acerbic wit, which alienated many of the people from whom he craved acceptance.

The master admired American Jews, who were frequent visitors to Cambridge, for being more at ease with their background. Some of them were practising and even those who were not were more open about their Jewishness and proud of it. He wished that British Jews would emulate them; they and British society alike could only benefit.

The master and Mrs Mason agreed on a relatively short ceremony of about thirty minutes. The master would offer an encomium to Sid and talk about his many contributions to the college. He would be followed by a few colleagues from the college and POLIS. Mrs Mason would have the last word, and everyone would then move to the master's lodge for refreshments. The master suggested, and Mrs Mason immediately concurred, that there should be some music. He thought it no problem to persuade two rather accomplished third-year students to play some Mozart or Bach on the piano and cello at the end of the ceremony. Mrs Mason said that her late husband would have been even happier with one of the Beethoven cello suites.

***

The inspector and Peter compared notes after the press conference. Background checks on the college's faculty had revealed nothing of particular interest. Only one professor had come to the attention of the police, but it was some years back and was the result of driving over the limit. The students were also clean. The two detectives agreed they did not have any real suspects.

The task force puzzled over the possible connection between Sid and Jaime. They remained hopeful that extensive media coverage would encourage someone with relevant information to come forward. They had no progress with the drug or with the EpiPens. The EpiPens used to kill the two men had not been left at the scene and would probably never be recovered. They could be purchased on-line with prescriptions and were stocked everywhere by chemists. Theft or purchase under a false name would not prove all that difficult. More problematic was substituting another drug for the one already in the EpiPen. They had contacted the leading manufacturer to find out how this might be done. The IT people drew a blank on Sid's computer. There was nothing out of the ordinary or suspicious about his emails. Almost all of them were professional in nature, plus the usual communications with friends and family and various bookings and appointments. Sid abhorred social media and had no accounts on Facebook, Twitter, Reddit, or LinkedIn.

"What do we do next, sir?" Peter asked.

"I wish I knew. I'm really feeling stymied. We're in the unhappy position of waiting for some responsible citizen to contact us with useful information."

"We could interview for a second time the staff and students who had it in for Professor Mason?"

"Let's do it. You never know when somebody will tell us something worthwhile. We also need to do more with Jaime."

"We could start with his college?"

"Jaime's college?"

"I got you that time, sir."

"Touché. To celebrate your victory, you can buy us both a drink after work."

"A drink? I thought you were a teetotaller?"

The inspector laughed. "Now, we're even."

"Did the drug squad turn up anything interesting?"

"Not yet. Following standard Vichy procedure, they brought in the usual suspects, but none had anything to report."

"Maybe they will discover there is gambling going on in Cambridge?"

The inspector considered the riff on *Casablanca* — a sign of their frustration. He remembered that he had forgotten to tell Peter of another line of inquiry that had led to a dead end. They checked up on the art in Mrs Mason's office, and indeed, a real Malevich hung on her wall. It belonged to the law firm. The partners had decided to invest some of their profits in art and some of their own money as well. They were hoping the market would continue to appreciate and that the partners could enjoy the art in the interim. Cynthia's Malevich was the most expensive piece they had purchased to date, and with the help of a loan.

"I meant to ask you, sir, how you knew it was a Malevich."

94

"There was an exhibition at the Tate Modern last year. It's a funny place. Cavernous but with relatively little display space. They have a representative collection of modern art, including one very controversial Rothko they received as a gift from the artist. The curator got lots of flak at the time as critics accused him of hanging it the wrong way."

"It wasn't obvious which way was up?"

"Not with Rothko. The curator waited without responding and let the furore build. He then revealed an exchange of letters with the artist in which he had asked how it should hang. Rothko told him any way he liked."

"Nice."

"I have no doubts about which way they will hang us if we don't solve this case."

"What about the CCTV?" Peter asked. "Did it turn up anything interesting?"

"Not really. The team retrieved the data from several cameras near the station and noted all the cars that drove by around the time of the kidnapping. Sid is likely to have walked up Bateman Street. They accordingly checked out the cameras by the school. There was lots of traffic, but no Sid. He was either picked up before he reached the school or perhaps took a different route."

"It's impressive technology," Peter said. "As you know, ever since CCTV's became capable of reading vehicle registration numbers, we can get details on the cars and their owners almost instantly from the licensing bureau's computer in Swansea. We've recorded and checked all the registration numbers of the cars passing by the school that morning within the relevant thirty-minute period. With two exceptions, everyone was local, and the Met and Thames Valley Police promised to check these two out. There was also a Toyota Auris with an unrecorded registration. This seemed odd, and we passed the numbers along to the traffic division. Their cars are equipped with ANPRs and will automatically scan registrations in search of this one. The CCTV tells nothing useful about the driver."

"OK then, let's go back to Leinster and lean a little harder on these people."

XII: Tuesday Afternoon

The interviews in the college consumed the rest of the day and did not tell them anything much they did not already know. Many staff and postgraduate students did little to hide their hostility towards Professor Mason, and few of them had ironclad alibis. Several of the professors noted his professional standing and how the college and POLIS benefitted from his presence. Two of the graduate students had been to the café where Jaime worked but did not know him. Nobody could suggest a plausible connection between the two victims. The hint of drugs or a sexual relationship encountered a range of responses from disbelief to guffaws. The only comment that caught their attention was from one of Sid's colleagues who reported that he seemed troubled in the week or two before his disappearance. He was edgier and withdrawn. When he asked if all was well, Sid said yes but unconvincingly.

The detectives walked back to the police station in silence. The inspector was struck by how students and staff had responded to him. They regarded him as an outsider who had entered their world without invitation. For the faculty, he and Peter were authority figures who threatened the autonomy of the college and the professoriate. They could and did demand appointments and asked them questions they would prefer not to answer. Accustomed to being beholden to nobody but themselves, the master and professors were uncomfortable with this sudden and unexpected reversal of the power balance. In the eyes of the postgraduate students, the faculty were yet another layer of authority with whom they had to deal... by flattery, finesse, and performance.

The inspector wondered if members of Leinster College would respond differently to him if they knew him better or had not met him in the context of a murder investigation. He told himself this was a delusion and that his identification with Cambridge was evidently stronger than its identification with him. Maybe he was just a policeman and should come to terms with it.

Peter had no similar concerns. He had committed himself to his career and did not feel that it closed off other avenues that might have drawn on and strengthened other selves. Each year on the job had provided more professional know-how and competence and was enabling his growth and sense of self-esteem. Peter wished he could say the same about his personal life. Perhaps, he thought, his upcoming tennis date might be a promising start.

***

John Clowes had his first normal day since the discovery of the bodies. His mates welcomed him at work, but his aura of celebrity had all but worn off. He took some ribbing at tea break; one of his co-workers, who had seen his brief interview on local television, wanted to know how many emails he had received from women hot for his body and whether he would send a few their way. Everybody laughed. John confessed that he had received a score of emails, but none of them romantic in nature. One was from a former first form teacher who told him how mature he looked. This revelation drew more laughter.

After break, John returned to the panel van, whose transmission he had neatly arrayed on the cement floor alongside. The owner reported that it shifted with difficulty, and John found a worn part that needed replacing. It had been on order and arrived with other morning deliveries. He was hoping to reassemble the transmission and take the vehicle for a road test. Most of the work the garage received was from used car and truck dealers who sent the vehicles they picked up, mostly at auctions, but occasionally from customers, for check-ups and, if necessary, repair before reselling them. It was a profitable business, and the garage had a good reputation. Its customers were another matter. Some were honest and committed to selling vehicles in good working condition. Others were content to hock wheels guaranteed to make it out of the shop and through the thirty-day warranty period, but nothing more. Some dealers insisted on the bare minimum of repairs, preferred used to new parts, and tried to cut corners with other costs. John disliked working for these customers but had little choice.

The husband and wife who owned the van were his kind of people. They were electricians who worked on construction and renovation sites. They had some eight electricians working for them and a small fleet of vans, which they regularly had serviced at the garage. They were high-end customers who wanted their vehicles looked after properly. If one broke down, they knew they would lose more money at the job site than at the garage.

John took a break to help a co-worker reattach an axle and all that went with it, a task much more easily accomplished by four hands. The van was supported by a hydraulic lift, and the two men were underneath talking about the order in which they would proceed. As they began the assembly, Tashi, his colleague, told him that he had heard from a mate that Jaime was dealing. This made two people now who told the story, so perhaps it was true, John thought. They agreed that it was a dumb thing to do and risky as well, John added, thinking about the body he had discovered. Tashi agreed and passed along the additional information that his mate had said that Jaime was anything but worried. He had met some man who hired him for some job and showed him the two hundred and fifty quid he had received as an advance.

"When was this?" John asked.

"I spoke to him a week ago Friday, before he disappeared."

"Of course, you spoke to him before he disappeared, you git."

"Well, you know what I mean."

"Did he say anything about what he was supposed to do for the money?"

"Nada. He shook his head when I asked. 'A man's gotta have some secrets,' he said. I got the impression he was showing off, but the money was sure real."

"He didn't describe the man or say anything about him?"

"No. Just that he had a real educated way of talking."

***

Mrs Mason had a troubled afternoon. She tried hard without much success to concentrate on her legal work. She forced herself to do it as the papers had to be filed by tomorrow afternoon. Her secretary would proof her text, and she would do a quick double-check on the case material her intern had looked up. She did not feel her normal self and thought it wise to ask one of the other partners to have a quick read through just to make sure there were no legal or other howlers. She felt reassured when he told her it was a good brief and should serve its purpose.

Both her children were shocked by the news, and her son promised to come up on Saturday. Her daughter managed to free herself and offered to come immediately, but Mrs Mason told her she needed another day or two by herself. The three of them arranged to spend the weekend together. She was pleased that her children were so responsive and felt very close to them. But it was her marriage, not theirs, and they could not help her remake herself as an independent person or deal with the growing hostility she now felt toward her deceased husband. She suspected that her daughter would relish a bit of dependence on her part, which was not about to happen. She felt a new sense of freedom, admittedly one that was struggling to express itself, like a chick pecking away at a shell from the inside desperate to break through.

Mrs Mason had already made several cracks in her shell, and they verged on the momentous in her mind. Sid had insisted that their bed covers be tucked in; it provided him with the sense of enclosure he needed to sleep. It made her feel trapped, and it had taken her a long time to feel comfortable sleeping this way. Yesterday, she had changed the linen, tucked in the bottom sheet but then substituted a duvet for a top sheet and blanket and left it loosely draped over the bed. Sid had had a close relationship with his mother, much too close in her opinion. The house was filled with her mementoes, many of them tasteless, and her mildly voiced objections had been studiously ignored. She had gathered them up, put them in two large cardboard boxes that she put in the back of a closet. She contemplated giving them to Oxfam but thought best to wait a bit before doing something irrevocable. Her third act of rebellion was taking down from the back of the top kitchen shelf the tea cosy she had knitted at age ten. Sid had banned it on the grounds that it clashed with their otherwise minimalist kitchen. Now it would keep the teapot warm and connect her to her pre-nuptial past.

Neighbours and friends had been, for the most part, solicitous. A few had come by with prepared meals, insisting that the last thing she needed to do at the moment was to shop and cook. She appreciated their kindness, and their meals as they were tasty, but continued to shop and enjoyed the ritualized encounters she had with shopkeepers. Two had discreetly expressed their condolences, which violated, but properly so, she thought, the norm of pleasant but impersonal chatter. A friend had warned her to steel herself against some of the outrageous things people were certain to say. Her spouse had died of a nasty cancer a few years back, and one of her neighbours had insisted on knowing all the details of his suffering. A colleague at work, clearly afraid of death, never mentioned her husband's illness, and then when he died, had the gall to say how happy she was that it was not her spouse.

Condolence notes poured into her office and piled up on her floor behind the front door letterbox. She collected them all but was not yet in the mood to open and read them. A few friends and relatives telephoned their sympathies, and these conversations she had to endure. Most callers were tactful; they voiced their horror at the murder, expressed sympathies for her, and offered to run errands or have her over for tea if she felt like a chat. Her children aside, nobody had forced themselves on her. The one exception was a colleague of Sid's who had called her twice to invite her out for a drink. She politely declined.

***

Jaime's motorbike was found parked in Silver Street. Constables had been given its registration and told to keep their eyes open. It was in full view for days and finally discovered by a constable looking for bikes that had parked in reserved spots. He phoned it in, and crime scene officers arrived within minutes. They inspected the perimeter and the bike and then had it removed to look at it more closely in their laboratory. Inspector Khan was notified and informed that there was nothing in particular to report beyond the discovery of the vehicle, a 1200 Suzuki Bandit. It had no luggage compartment, and its only accessory was a common brand of chain and lock.

Silver Street was well covered by CCTVs, and Peter asked the constables to access the data for the Monday morning that Sid disappeared. He thought seven to nine a.m. would be the timeframe to look at. On rainy or raw days, constables are not displeased at having to sit glued to a monitor for hours searching for something they may not find. It was a nice day in Cambridge, one of those warm spring mornings with the city splashed in sunlight. The two constables assigned to monitoring the CCTV footage were not looking forward to the task and were overjoyed to find their target only a few minutes into their session. Jaime drove down Silver Street and parked his bike at 07.05 a.m. on Monday morning. They couldn't identify him on the bike, but they clocked the bike and its parking place. They summoned Peter, who rushed over to have a look. They could make out the biker after he parked and removed his helmet, and sure enough, it was Jaime. He walked down Silver Street, cut into Laundress Lane, and disappeared. Peter asked the constables to check what coverage was available on Mill Lane, where he would presumably reappear, and in the more general vicinity. They should only have to look at the several minutes after 07.05 to find him. If they got lucky, they might be able to follow him to the murderer.

At five p.m., Peter checked in with the constables. They had Jaime on camera emerging from Laundress Lane and turning right on to Silver Street, where he crossed the bridge over the Cam and entered Coe Fen that extends along the river. They looked for him at all the exits where there were cameras but could not find him. There were gaps in the coverage, and he had perhaps intentionally chosen a route that allowed him to evade the cameras. They widened their search to include Queen's Road, Sidgwick Avenue, Barton Road, Fen Causeway, and Mill Lane, the last in case he had backtracked, but they could not spot him on any of these cameras. A very frustrated Peter thanked the constables and returned to his office to kill a little time before leaving for his much-anticipated tennis date.

XII: Tuesday Evening

Elaine was looking forward to tennis and seeing Peter and found herself thinking about the relative order of her anticipation. She confronted a strategic problem. She was in uniform and needed time to get back to the station and change before heading off to the tennis club. The last thing she wanted was for Peter to discover her occupation. Her friends on the force had told her, and experience had quickly confirmed, that being a cop was a passion killer. Men did not want relationships with women who carried guns and could, if necessary, have them supine and cuffed in short order. And the kind of men who warmed to such images she wanted nothing to do with. She was not prepared to lie to Peter about her profession but thought she could forestall any questions and keep it in the background until — if and when — their relationship developed. To make this easier, she would refrain from querying him about his line of work. On the basis of his seeming self-confidence, caution, and apparent interpersonal skills, she guessed he might be an executive in some company, with responsibility, perhaps, for sales or management.

Peter was unconcerned about Elaine's profession but did wonder if he had made a good impression on her. Was she attracted to him or simply looking for someone with whom to hit a tennis ball? He would focus on tennis, as here he felt on surer ground. Thinking about Elaine would interfere with his concentration and perhaps her assessment of him if he played less well. He left his office in plenty of time to walk to the tennis club via a shop where he could pick up a new can of balls at a discounted price.

***

The murderer was still feeling an unaccustomed mix of excitement and trepidation arising from the discovery of the bodies. It resembled an itch that would come and go in unpredictable ways and one he knew he should not scratch. He reviewed once again the steps he had taken to recruit his assistant, carry out the murders, dispose of the bodies, and then the evidence. All had gone according to plan except for the bodies, which had been discovered before they could decompose. He really had not counted on that. With bodies, the police could begin a murder investigation, which was worrying.

Our murderer reasoned the police would be looking for some relationship between the two victims and took pleasure in contemplating their inevitable failure to find one. There was nothing to connect Sid and Yobbo, except for their deaths, of course. It was your classic catch-22. To connect the dots between the victims, the police had to know the murderer but, to find him, they must first discover how the two men were related. He chuckled over this conundrum and how it would leave the police stymied. He wished he could be a fly on the wall of the chief investigating officer's office and enjoy their discomfort first-hand.

He knew that overconfidence led to hubris and invited punishment by the gods. He would not gloat. He reviewed his interactions with Yobbo and the precautions he had taken in this regard. He had initially intended to murder Sid by himself. It was simpler to do it alone and avoided all the risks of an accomplice who might not behave wisely afterwards, possibly even try to blackmail him. There was also the difficulty of finding an accomplice. He knew many people who disliked Sid, but nobody ready to do him in. If he approached a colleague, and they turned him down, he would have exposed himself and would have to exercise restraint ever after. The alternative was to do the job himself. This would be more difficult, as he would have to single-handedly subdue and kill Sid and dispose of his body.

Our murderer thought about the murder at length and how he could best pull it off. He concluded that it would be much easier with an accomplice and pondered ways of reducing the risks this entailed. The obvious solution, he realized, was to kill the accomplice as well. The elegance of this strategy greatly appealed to him, as did the double duplicity it entailed. First, he would find a pretext of getting Sid to go off with him, have the accomplice do the dirty deed, and then kill him afterwards. He would dispose of both bodies, if possible, somewhere they were unlikely to be discovered. It was like solving a chess problem with a set of moves that were original, artistic, and possibly profound. In this instance, he could not share the solution with others, but that was of little import. The satisfaction of finding it, implementing it, and getting rid of Sid was more than enough compensation.

How to recruit an accomplice? He needed someone willing to commit murder, do what he asked without questioning him, and could readily be disposed of afterwards. Such a person had to be unscrupulous, needy, or greedy — as he would be offered handsome compensation. He had to be naïve. He also had to be someone he had never met, and best yet, a person who had few connections elsewhere in Cambridge. This was a difficult bill of particulars to fill. A young, good-for-nothing, down-at-his-heels lad was the obvious choice. He would be easier to recruit and kill, and, our murderer thought, he would feel no remorse about doing him in. On his perambulations around Cambridge, he had noticed a young man selling drugs on the street and shadowed him. He discovered where he lived and worked, the hours he was on the street and at the café, and where he usually parked his bike. He seemed to have little in the way of a social life, which made him more attractive. He wondered if he used any of the drugs he sold. A high accomplice would be useless, but someone dependent on drugs would be more willing to accept money to assist in murder. He drove his motorbike well and gave no appearance of being high whilst dealing. Perhaps he would be all right.

The next step was the riskiest. He had to approach Yobbo and convince him to become his accomplice. Suitably disguised, he stationed himself near Yobbo's parked bike at an hour he was almost certain to appear after finishing work at the café. The effort at a rendezvous failed as the young man went off somewhere in town after work. Our murderer was nothing if not patient and tried a second time. Yobbo approached, helmet in hand. He crossed the street to confront him just as he reached the bike and leaned over to unlock and remove the chain running through the bike's wheel.

"We need to talk," he said in a quiet voice.

Yobbo stood up to stare at him with an obviously hostile look.

"I don't need to talk to you."

"I think you do. I have a proposition certain to interest you."

"A proposition?" Yobbo raised an eyebrow.

"That's right. It comes with a payment of five hundred pounds, two hundred and fifty of it upfront."

"And what do I have to do?"

"Help me."

"To do what?"

"To pay back somebody who's long had it coming."

"I'm not a thug; I don't beat people up."

"I have something gentler in mind."

"Yeah?"

"I'd rather not talk about it here. What if we go for a walk and continue our chat?"

"Sure, why not."

He led Jaime down the end of Silver Street, across the bridge and along the river path. It was largely deserted at this hour, although two people on bicycles passed them travelling in the opposite direction. Jaime wanted to know exactly what he would have to do. Before going into details, our would-be murderer reassured him that no real violence was involved in the sense that he would not have to hit, kick or strike anyone. He had something in mind that was painless but effective. Jaime — he made sure to address him by his first name — would only have to stick a needle into someone.

"I'm no doctor, you know."

"Indeed, I do. You're a barista and a small-time drug dealer."

"What makes you think I sell drugs?"

"I've seen you do it on Trumpington Street."

"Then you're mistaken, mister. And what did you say your name was?"

"I didn't. And I'm not mistaken. You're out there several times a week selling to a fairly steady clientele."

"You've been watching me?"

"That's right. I've even taken some photos of your deals. Be thankful it's me and not the police."

"Why should I be thankful?"

"Think about it. The police would haul you in and bring you before a judge. Your mother would be appalled and ashamed."

"My mother? Why are you dragging her into this?"

"How would your mother respond? If I know you are selling drugs, it must be obvious to the police. They haven't picked you up yet for reasons of their own. Perhaps they are waiting, hoping to discover your source. Whatever their reason, it's only a matter of time before they come and cuff you and take you away. I'm offering you a way to avoid this fate."

He could see that Jaime was mulling over what he had said and decided to press his advantage. He explained that this job could be followed by other ones, none as dramatic, but they would bring him a steady and safe income and for less work. Jaime went for the bait and began querying him in more detail about what he would have to do. He explained that Jaime would do deliveries and pickups on his motorbike, accompany him to meetings where he might need a backup, and even act as a go-between once he learnt the ropes. Jaime, of course, wanted to know the nature of his new employer's work, but he provided only the most elliptical explanation, suggesting that he would come to understand bit-by-bit as he slotted into the job. He could nevertheless guarantee payment of at least three hundred pounds a week for a start — all tax-free — and the sum would certainly go up if Jaime did good work.

Jaime expressed interest, and Sid explained that their first job was to teach a real bastard a lesson. They would pick him up in his car and, Jaime, sitting in the back, would stick a needle into his neck. They would use an EpiPen, and to do this, Jaime needed a little training. He had to identify the carotid artery and hold the EpiPen against it before hitting the plunger. Their victim was thin, his carotid readily visible. He need only reach around and press against it. He assured Jaime that the serum would do nothing more than put their victim to sleep. He would take over from there. They would drop him somewhere in the countryside, and he would have a real shock when he woke up.

Jaime's interest quickly switched back to the money, and his greed became apparent. Our murderer encouraged it and took out an envelope and handed it over to Jaime.

"What's this?" he asked.

"The advance I promised you."

"Jaime opened the envelope and had a quick peek inside. He looked around, saw nobody in sight, and tucked it into his pocket.

"There's more where this came from."

"How do you know I won't just walk off with this?"

"I'm not worried. You're a smart lad and won't look a gift horse in the mouth. In the unlikely opportunity that you do, I can always complain to the cops about the young lad who sells drugs openly on Trumpington Street."

"You would do that?"

"Would you walk away with my money?"

"Of course not."

"Then no worries about my dobbing you in."

The murderer told him he would be in touch shortly to tell him when and where they would meet up for their gig. For the moment, he suggested, he should go easy on selling drugs.

***

Inspector Khan headed home for a quiet evening of reading and watching a football game on TV. He warmed up the moussaka he had prepared on Saturday. He prepared a salad using a pre-packed base from Waitrose, into which he added some feta cheese, in keeping with the Greek theme of the dinner, plus pumpkin seeds and diced red pepper. He had his own dressing of oil and vinegar, with a little mustard and salt. He filled a glass with tap water as it was as good as almost any bottled water, free and without the carbon footprint of transport from God knows where. He poured a glass of wine from the bottle of Gigondas he had opened a couple of days back. It stayed fresh because he pumped out the air through a rubber stopper. He had Bayern 4 on in the background, and it was playing a Handel opera.

This daily routine allowed him to leave the office behind and enter into a different world. One of his mother's sisters had pointed out what she thought was the contrast between a day job that required him to rub noses with the worst kinds of people and evening and weekend escapes spent enjoying the higher accomplishments of the human race. He saw no contradiction, only relief from a job, one he thoroughly enjoyed five days a week, and especially when a murder investigation was in full swing. He had on more than one occasion conducted thought experiments of what it would be like to have a day job in the arts, say as a curator of oriental carpets at the British Museum or the business manager of a symphony orchestra. These jobs would be fun but would not provide the excitement of his current one or the opportunity to mix with such different kinds of people. He also thought that he would not take the same pleasure from culture if he had to earn a living from it. He had a school friend who became a cellist in a reasonably successful quartet who confided to him that, as a professional, he understood music much better but enjoyed it less.

His routine of leaving work at the office was not working this evening. The double murder investigation was not making any visible progress. They had no suspects and had found no way of connecting the victims. The media was asking why the police had not solved the case, although he was relieved that the local Cambridge paper was more sympathetic. His colleagues also expected results from their chief investigating officer, but he had heard of no griping on their part about how the investigation was being conducted. Peter was his eyes and ears on that score. The deputy commissioner had summoned him into his office that afternoon, and he had expected the worst when he held up a newspaper featuring a story about the murders. He asked in detail about how the investigation was proceeding and seemed satisfied with his answers. He told him not to worry about the press and just to get on with his job. His support could not last forever. He had to come up with some viable leads in the near future.

Inspector Khan had given considerable thought to the possibility that it might be a mistake to look for direct connections between the victims. Perhaps they had never met and were only connected through the murderer, who had it in for both of them for the same or different reasons. The more he thought about this, the more he thought Mrs Mason might be right. Professor Mason did not use drugs, was not gay, and did not frequent the café where Jaime worked. Nor did he drive a motorbike, which could have provided the opportunity for their paths to cross. They travelled in completely different circles and circles that did not seem to have any overlap. Professor Mason would have had to go out of his way to meet him, and the inspector could not figure out any reason why he would do that.

As for indirect connections, he also ran into a wall. Mrs Mason scoffed at the idea that her husband could have run up a gambling debt, and Jaime had no money to gamble. It was even more far-fetched to think they were having an affair with the same woman and were murdered by an irate husband. What kind of woman would be attracted to such different men, and neither Mrs Mason nor her husband's colleagues, thought it likely he was carrying on with someone. He could not come up with another plausible reason for why someone would have it in for both of them.

He tried to put himself in the mind of the murderer. Immediately, a puzzle arose. If he wanted to kill Sid and Jaime for whatever reason, it was safer for him to do this sequentially rather than simultaneously. Might he have killed them independently and then transported their bodies to the dock for disposal? The coroner thought this unlikely for several reasons. As far as he could determine, the two men were killed at the same time, or close enough to it, and they had both drowned. The murderer would have had to immobilize them sequentially and then transport them to the dock to drop them into the water. If he had used a car or some vehicle for transport, the first body would have been in the back or the boot whilst he went after his second victim.

He asked the coroner if the murderer could have kept one victim in a big freezer until he had immobilized the second, and the coroner explained that he would then have died of asphyxiation or freezing, not drowning. He killed the two men at roughly the same time. If the victims had been together — which Inspector Khan seriously doubted — he would have to overcome them both at the same time. If they were apart, he would have had to disable them within a few hours of each other. Doing this to a victim required just the right conditions; he had to be able to stick in a needle, load the body into his vehicle and drive off without being noticed by bystanders or CCTV. Getting two victims on the same day struck him as a far more difficult, if not impossible, task. But this is what he must have done, given the coroner's certainty about the method and timing of death.

A double murder might be feasible if two or more people worked together. Each could have taken care of one of the victims, or perhaps, together, they get them both. The problem here was motive. It was tough enough to come up with any reason why someone would want to kill Sid and Jaime. He could think of many reasons for doing away with Sid and many people who would be happy to have him dead. Presumably, Jaime had antagonized someone, perhaps multiple people, but it would be different people and for different reasons. How would two would-be murderers make contact, and what reason would they have for doing so?

Nursing his second glass of wine — his self-imposed limit — the proverbial light bulb turned on to illuminate another possibility. What if one of the victims was initially the murderer's accomplice, helping him immobilize the first victim and perhaps even carry him to the dock? The murderer could then have turned on him. This was an imaginative solution but not without problems of its own. Why would someone help a murderer kill someone he didn't know? If the helper was a close friend, why would you kill him too? If not, how would you recruit him? This query brought him back full circle to the problem of finding a connection between Sid and Jaime. And if you need help in killing one or two people, why not hire a professional killer, which Jaime was assuredly not. There were no obvious solutions, and he was going around in circles. Best, he thought, to do the dishes and watch football.

XIII: Wednesday Morning

Close to eleven a.m., Peter received a telephone call from John, who wanted to pass along some information. It was not an easy call for John to make. The previous evening, he had returned home from work and made the mistake of telling his parents what Tashi had said about Jaime. How he had become a small-time drug dealer and was expecting something big to happen soon. Henry and Janice insisted that he share this information with the police as it might help with their murder inquiry. John was reluctant to do this as his mate had spoken to him in confidence. If word got out that he was a snout, nobody would ever talk to him again. His parents were adamant, that he contact the police, and the impasse was only broken by his father's suggestion that John speak to Tashi and see if he would be willing to talk to the police. This way, John would do nothing behind his back, and the police would get the information second instead of third hand. Henry also pointed out that withholding evidence from the police in a criminal investigation is a criminal offence.

At work the next day, John approached Tashi and told him about his conversation with his parents. He apologized for speaking to them in the first place and confessed that he now felt squeezed. Tashi had no qualms about speaking to the police and saw no reason why he shouldn't share the limelight with John. John called the number on the card of the policeman who had driven him to pick up his boat and was immediately transferred to Peter. He agreed to meet one or both of the lads at work, or anywhere else they preferred. They both thought the garage would be best because everyone would see the attention they got, and the owner wouldn't dare dock them the time spent talking to the police.

Tashi had little to tell Peter beyond what he had told John. He had heard from another friend that Jaime was selling drugs, and Jaime had told him that he had received two hundred and fifty quid from an older fellow in return for some unspecified job. John had neither described nor identified the man but had flashed the money before him. Tashi assumed that their encounter was in Cambridge, but Jaime had not said so.

Peter drove back to Cambridge, wondering what all this had to do with the murder. Something perhaps, but without more information, it was hard to know. His life was full of ambiguities. His tennis date had gone well. Elaine seemed pleased to see him, and they had a good hour together. He won the first set and was even in the second when time ran out. They played hard but in a good-natured way. Afterwards, he asked Elaine out for dinner, and she accepted. They were scheduled to meet the following evening at a nice bistro Peter knew about.

Peter felt himself on the verge of a relationship, which was exciting, frustrating, and a bit frightening. Much of the excitement and frustration was in his loins. He had managed to suppress his sexual urges when no outlet was available, and now it was very much making its presence known. He was a bit frightened by the prospect of an emotional relationship. He very much wanted one, but his last relationship had not ended well. His former partner had been very unhappy about his unwillingness to make a commitment. He thought she should have given him more time and made a commitment less likely by pushing for it too hard and too soon.

After lunch, Peter and the inspector went over the several reports they received on the drug used to sedate both victims. Neither Addenbrookes nor the supplier acknowledged anything missing. The same was true of other hospitals in England. The manufacturer kept careful records, and the police had been unable to discover any loose ends. The coroner was convinced that he had identified the right agent. The police lab found nothing unusual about Jaime's motorbike, so another dead end. The only bright spot was the information that Peter had received from Tashi. Something had been afoot with Jaime; the cash was evidence that it had been more than talk. The inspector shared his earlier speculations with Peter, and the two of them wondered whether it had been the murderer who gave Jaime the money. Neither of them could figure out any way of following up on this tantalizing lead.

The two detectives attended the memorial service for Professor Mason. The Leinster College chapel was not as large as some and simpler than most in its design. It replaced an earlier chapel that had been taken down for some reason in the early nineteenth century. St. John's College had pioneered the neo-Gothic style at around this time in a new residential court and its famous replica of Venice's so-called Bridge of Sighs. Leinster employed the same architect for their chapel, and he had produced what was widely acknowledged as a masterpiece. On the wall outside was a plaque honouring graduates who had fallen in the Great War and another for those who had made the ultimate sacrifice in World War II and Korea. He noted a third plaque commemorating a small number of graduates who had died in subsequent conflicts, most recently in Afghanistan.

The chapel was about half full when they entered, and they took seats at the end of an aisle towards the back. The inspector recognized, and assumed Peter did too, several faculty and postgraduate students whom they had recently interviewed. Faculty had reserved seats at the front. How typical, he thought, for Cambridge colleges to maintain their hierarchy even when commemorating death, something that reduces everyone to ashes or dust. He whispered to Peter, "Are they long-legged enough for you?"

"Oh yes, sir," Peter replied whilst trying to repress what he thought in the circumstances would be an out-of-place smile.

The chapel filled up, and there was considerable chatter as most people were members of the college and knew one other. They quieted down when the master and dean entered, escorting Mrs Mason between them. They walked down the middle aisle and paused whilst she took a reserved seat in the front row. Several people in the aisle hugged her, and the inspector assumed they were family. Because the professor had been avowedly secular, the dean took a seat in the front row on the opposite side of the aisle, and the master took the two steps that led up to the chancel. The crowd went silent before the master spoke.

He delivered a short eulogy that focused on the better personal attributes of the deceased. They included his intelligence, wit, commitment to research with important normative implications, and willingness to spend long hours with students. Mention of his wit was greeted with some chuckles audible only to those in their vicinity. The master told everyone that Sid had all but finished the article he was working on, had submitted it to a journal and that colleagues would make

113

whatever revisions proved necessary. One of his former students, now a professor at Yale, had flown over for the ceremony and would be editing a Festschrift in Sid's honour. Several members of the college and POLIS, and one of his postgraduate students, spoke next and shared stories about Sid, all of which put him in a good light. Mrs Mason then rose and thanked the master and Sid's colleagues and students for their thoughtful remarks, which, she said, gave her great support and added to the good memories she would always have of her husband. She invited everyone to a reception in the senior parlour.

The master rose again to announce that they would close with Beethoven's second cello sonata played by two of their undergraduates. The piano and cello were already on the chancel and were moved forward as a solid-looking young man and a tall red-haired woman climbed the two steps and sat at their instruments. After the usual adjustments of chair and bench and last-minute tuning of the cello, they nodded at each other and began playing. Those assembled were treated to a more than passable rendition of the sonata. The cello sound was made richer still, the inspector thought, by the surprisingly good acoustics of the chapel.

When the music finished, the master applauded, signalling to others that it would not violate decorum to show their appreciation for the musicians. Everyone followed suit, and the musicians bowed in response. The master descended to the nave, waited to collect the dean, Mrs Mason, and members of her family before walking slowly down the aisle to the exit. The inspector and Peter waited for everyone else to leave and followed the crowd to the senior parlour. They eyed with interest the Masons' son and daughter. Murder is usually motivated by hatred, love, or money and, in most cases, committed by members of the victim's family. The inspector knew nothing about the Masons' family life, but from what he had learnt about the professor, he could readily imagine him having treated one or both his children in a way that they might wish for his demise.

The detectives were not above helping themselves to a glass of sparkling wine and hors d'oeuvres. They had agreed beforehand not to question anyone as it would be inappropriate to the occasion. Instead, they would pay their respects to the master and Mrs Mason and take their leave. Standing quietly in a corner, they were approached by two of Sid's colleagues whom they had interviewed. Neither could be counted as a friend of the deceased, and neither had a compelling alibi. They asked Inspector Khan if the police were making any progress with the investigation. Nothing worth reporting, he told them.

Outside the senior parlour and before leaving the college, the inspector and Peter turned their mobiles back on. They had messages asking them to return to headquarters for a ten thirty a.m. briefing by the deputy commissioner. It was already close to eleven, and this was out of the question. They nevertheless hurried back to the police station. They arrived after the briefing and went into the canteen looking for other detectives. They quickly learnt that the briefing had nothing to do with their investigation but with a warning they had received about an imminent terror attack. They went off to see the deputy commissioner to explain their absence. After exchanging the usual pleasantries, he looked across at both detectives and asked if they had heard the gist of what he had said.

"Only that someone phoned in a warning," said Inspector Khan.

"That's right," said the commissioner. "It's not much to go on, an anonymous tip-off of a likely terrorist attack in Cambridge. Not surprisingly, the caller wouldn't give his name and did not identify the target. I'm taking it seriously because we also received a warning from higher up to be on the lookout for some major act of violence."

"Two warnings? That sounds pretty serious to me," said Peter.

"Any information about the caller?" asked the inspector.

"The voice experts at the Met are working on it as we speak. They're hoping to tell us something about his background and education and are searching for any revealing background noise. I listened to the recording three times and got the sense that it is a London accent, and the speaker is holding something over the mouthpiece to muffle it. I don't think we're going to get much from the experts on this one."

"That's too bad," said the inspector. "How specific was the warning?"

"Very vague. We're told that an attack will take place in the next couple of days and nothing more. Then the phone goes dead."

"And the warning from higher up?" asked Peter.

"Not much there either, I'm afraid. The Home Office received warnings and passed them on to us. I've no idea if they are telephone tip-offs, gossip from snouts, or reports from agents who might have penetrated some terrorist network. London and local warnings together are cause for concern. I've contacted and warned leaders of the Jewish and Muslim communities, who are always a possible target, university security, and briefed your colleagues. There have been attacks on soldiers and police in London and elsewhere, and I don't want it happening here. I've ordered everyone to go in pairs and keep a low profile, but to keep their eyes open when off duty. I've stationed police along the routes to and from the station, and we're going to provide round-the-clock protection of the Beth Shalom Synagogue and the Jewish Student Centre, the two mosques and the Islamic Student Centre, and university labs — anathema to animal rights activists. Can you think of any other obvious targets?"

Peter shook his head.

The inspector filled the commissioner in on recent developments, the most promising being Jaime's drug dealing and encounter with some man who had given him two hundred and fifty pounds as down payment for some job he was to do for him. The deputy commissioner asked all the same questions that Peter had asked of Tashi and with the same result. There was no more information to pass along. Deputy Commissioner Braham wanted to know if Peter trusted his source, to which Peter replied affirmatively. He thought Tashi had nothing to gain by lying and believed that Jaime had waved a wad of banknotes before his nose.

"Where does that leave us?" the deputy commissioner asked.

"Up shit creek," Peter responded. "Nobody else phoned in with any useful information. The CCTV cameras show Jaime coming into town early on the day of the murder, but we lose sight of him somewhere in Coe Fen. The footage from his café is more disappointing. No evidence of Professor Mason ever entering the place and nothing else of a suspicious nature. Jaime goes about his work and has minimal interaction with co-workers and customers."

XV: Wednesday Evening

Terrified of being late, Peter reached the restaurant early. He was seated at the table he had requested in a side nook, thinking it would be more intimate. He tried to put the day behind him, but it was not helped by his habit of periodically checking for messages on his phone. There weren't any — to his relief. He looked at his calendar to remind him what he had on for tomorrow. The first event was Jaime's funeral, at ten a.m. It would be different in every way from Professor Mason's. Poor Jaime did not live long enough to have much of a life.

Elaine arrived right on time, handed her coat to the maître d', and was ushered to Peter's table. Peter rose to greet her, and the two shook hands. They exchanged the usual pleasantries, and Peter complimented her on her outfit, black leggings and top, the latter with some kind of silver-like thread. He asked her what she would like to drink, and they agreed on a bottle of sauvignon blanc after they decided they would both order the catch of the day.

This was the first opportunity they'd had to chat about anything other than tennis, and it seemed easier to Peter to start with that subject and then venture further afield. He told her how happy he was to have found a new tennis partner and asked how long she had been playing. It turned out they had both started in their school years and had played sporadically since.

Peter was keen to postpone the moment when he would have to tell her he was in the police. He accordingly avoided asking about her profession. Elaine did admit to working in Croydon before moving to Cambridge, in what she described "as basically a desk job." It took her to the city occasionally to collect documents, and she had once visited one of the top floors of HSBC. This led to a brief discussion of the latest banking scandal. Elaine passed along the latest banker joke she had heard, and they both lamented, tongue in cheek, not having the kind of assets that would make it worthwhile to have a foreign bank account.

Elaine's avocado salad arrived, as did Peter's tempura soft-shelled crab. There was a pause in the conversation as two hungry people tucked into their starters. They thought their respective dishes were very tasty, and Elaine reminisced about collecting crabs on the beach on holiday with friends a few years back. They boiled them up and ate them with lemon. There was nothing in the cupboard of the rented house from which she could make a sauce. Peter confessed that he did little cooking. He mostly bought prepared meals at the supermarket. Elaine told him that she generally prepared meals on the weekend to ensure she would have leftovers during the week.

"That's what my boss does," Peter exclaimed, careful not to refer to him as inspector. "He shops and cooks up a storm on Saturday or Sunday and eats better than I do."

"Maybe you should follow his example?"

"I'd first have to learn to cook. I can prepare a few simple dishes but nothing more. I confess that my mother cooked for me at home, and more recently, my partner."

Elaine thought it odd that he had brought up his former partner so early in their acquaintance, but perhaps he felt a need to talk about it. "How long were you together?" she asked.

Peter was equally unsure about why he had mentioned his ex but knew it was bound to come up sooner or later. Maybe it's better now, he thought. It will be out of the way. "Almost two years. It started well, but then she moved to Newcastle."

"Is that why you split up?"

"To be honest, the move was only the precipitant. She wanted more of a commitment than I was prepared to make. I'm not averse to commitment but felt it would be dishonest to her and to myself if I did so before I was fully comfortable about our relationship. There were some issues that needed working out. She also felt that a commuting relationship without a commitment was a recipe for disaster."

"Do you miss her?"

Peter was not sure how to respond to this question. Nor was he at all clear about what would constitute an honest reply. "Yes and no. We were close, and I have good memories, but it's no use to dwell on them since the relationship ended. In fact, she's found someone else in Newcastle."

"I see. So, it is a thing of the past."

"Yes, very much so. But it was good whilst it lasted, and good for me, as I learnt a lot about myself and relationships."

"You feel positive about them?"

"I do."

The conversation moved to less freighted topics, and the second glass of wine helped Peter and Elaine to relax. When the dinner ended, both were feeling good about the evening and each other. They agreed to get together again over the weekend. Elaine invited him to her place and promised to prepare a meal Peter would enjoy.

***

Our murderer was a busy fellow due to the demands of his job. They waxed and waned over the course of the year, and the last week had been particularly demanding. He wore his usual public face, and there was no difference in his demeanour. Nobody he encountered could possibly imagine that he had recently murdered two people. There was talk about the bodies the police pulled out of the basin, to which he listened with great interest. He was amused by the various theories he heard proposed and the links they established between the professor and Yobbo. This ran the gamut from gambling to drugs. Someone suggested that maybe they were lovers and killed by a jealous partner. The most imaginative and elaborate scenario involved MI5. Professor Mason had studied tax evasion, and the media gave this much play, although for no particular reason beyond fuelling speculation that he was killed as some kind of protest. The owner of the mini-market where our murderer regularly shopped had heard from another customer that the professor had a connection with the security service. Many people did in Cambridge, or so it was commonly believed.

"Wasn't the former master of Pembroke head of MI6?" the mini-market proprietor asked. "And weren't all those Soviet spies students or fellows at King's?"

"I've heard," said the murderer.

"If Professor Mason was working for MI5, maybe he was studying those animal rights protests on their behalf. Perhaps the young man they fished out of the pond with him was his informer. I reckon these animal rights groups are crazy enough to kill people to protect animals. If they found out he was reporting back to the professor, they wouldn't hesitate to kill them both. I hope the police are checking them out."

"It's a real possibility," the murderer agreed. He paid for his carrots, courgettes, baguette, and feta cheese and happily walked out into the sun-lit street.

***

Mrs Mason was home alone. Her children had resumed their lives, and her colleagues at work no longer treated her as if she were some kind of fragile doll. She welcomed both developments. It was psychologically easier for those around her to pretend that she was approaching her normal self again. She would not fool herself in this regard, nor did she want to. The shock of Sid's disappearance had worn off, but not the pain associated with his death. She could not return to her normal self because she did not yet know who that self was. It certainly wasn't the self she was before his disappearance, and her new self was very much a project in the early stages of construction. She found herself clinging to aspects of her former self as a shipwrecked person would to a life raft. Her morning routine — excluding preparation of Sid's breakfast — her job, mid-afternoon walks, pre-dinner drink, and the *Ten o'clock News* on the BBC before going to bed were more satisfying than in the past for this reason. They were also unsettling in the sense that they made her aware of just how much a creature of habit she had become.

Mrs Mason reflected on the problem of self-fashioning. The media, the cinema, and many psychologists emphasized the importance of discovering and nurturing your inner self. Nobody suggested this was an easy task, but it was always held out as a feasible one. She was discovering the extent to which she was a product of her roles and the routines they generated. One of those roles, that of wife, was now gone, and another, that of solicitor, had become more important. She had been cut adrift by the loss of Sid and wondered if she stopped being a lawyer whether there would be anything left of her. There was no inner self patiently waiting to be liberated and nurtured. This, she concluded, was another fiction of pop psychology and culture and one that had the potential to arouse considerable anxiety when such a creature eluded discovery. Perhaps we were nothing more than raw appetites and reflexive capabilities, both disciplined by our affiliations and roles. We were products of society, not the other way around. She was more unsettled by this recognition.

Mrs Mason knew something about the consuming nature of roles and the problem of letting go of them. She had experienced this with her children in her role of mother. It had been easier because that transition was normal and gradual. With Sid, she went from wife to widow when he walked out the door that morning, although full recognition of this truth only came with the discovery of his body. Sid was a difficult and demanding spouse, but he had been companionable and funny. They had a good rapport in bed, and she was beginning to miss their sex. Like so many desires, she recognized how this one was easily triggered by association. It was one of many reasons that made it difficult to enter their — her — bedroom in the evening. She wondered if she would ever have sex again. She found it hard to imagine outside of a relationship and found the idea of another relationship equally difficult to conjure up. Perhaps she would feel differently in time.

This train of thought led her to speculate about sexual partners and relationships. She ran through her male acquaintances at work, in Leinster College, and elsewhere. There were some very attractive young men, but none of them would have any interest in her. And to be truthful, she had no interest in them. The men her age or slightly older were almost all married, and they were out of the picture. The single men she knew her own age were gay or unappealing. One, a former colleague of Sid's, had been particularly attentive and had brushed up against her once, in a way she did not think was accidental. He had been among the many callers to express his sympathy and had invited her out for coffee. She had politely declined as she found him revolting. Slim pickings, she thought. Perhaps she would be better off in a relationship with a woman friend. She laughed.

XVI: Thursday

The investigation was in the doldrums. The police interviewed all of Jaime's friends and his former girlfriend but turned up nothing. Everyone thought Jaime was straight, only a few knew about his drugs, and most had not seen him much, if at all, since he had relocated to Cambridge. They re-interviewed his landlady but learnt nothing new from her... or his co-workers at the café. They rechecked the CCTV footage from the café just in case they had missed something the first time around. They showed Jaime's picture to the porters and other people at Leinster College, but nobody recognized him. They also reviewed the CCTV coverage of the porter's lodge on the day or two before Professor Mason's disappearance, but there was no sign of Jaime. Peter had attended his funeral, a sad affair as they always are when the deceased is a young person. Family, friends, and neighbours had turned up, and Peter had chatted to some of them. Nobody had any idea about why he was killed. They were baffled. Without any new information or line of inquiry, the inspector could see no purpose in making yet another visit to the college to talk to its master, fellows, and students.

Neither the inspector nor Peter was directly involved in the defensive preparations being put into place following the telephone warning of a terrorist attack. It had nothing to do with their investigation, and as yet, there was nothing to investigate. In most homicides, the killer is a family member, or somebody well known to the victim. Often, confession follows closely after murder or upon initial questioning by the police. Most murders are crimes of passion and unplanned. They are committed by people incapable of controlling their rage. For these reasons, they are rapidly solved even when perpetrators deny any wrongdoing. The police are not noted for their brilliance, but murderers are, on average, less intelligent and certainly less thoroughly organized. This, too, helps the clearance rate.

Inspector Khan and Peter agreed that their perpetrator or perpetrators were not lacking in grey cells. He or they had an elaborate plan, left no clues to their identity, had somehow got their hands on a controlled drug not reported missing from factory, distributor, or hospital, killed two people, not just one, and left the police guessing about their connection.

"This case," Peter suggested, "is more like one of those crime novels you love to read."

"In many respects," the inspector said. "There is a difference, though."

"What would that be?"

"In these novels, and even more in their TV versions, there are always multiple murders. Two at a minimum, and often three, with the murderer caught just on the verge of doing in victim four. I'm amazed that anybody is still alive in places like Cabot Cove, Oxford or Midsomer and its nearby villages. I'd certainly never go to a flower show or festival in Badger's Drift."

"We have two murders in this case," said Peter.

"Yes, but they took place at the same time, and it's been quiet since. We have a restrained killer, assuming it's one person. He kills his two people with little violence or fuss and almost succeeds in permanently disposing of their bodies. Nothing has happened since. It's absolutely minimalist. I wonder if his house or flat isn't similarly furnished. Perhaps we should search local residences and try to find him that way?"

"I'm sure the judge would give us a blanket warrant. Why don't you read some more murder mysteries? Maybe you can learn something useful from Morse or Barnaby?"

"More likely Miss Marple or Poirot. But no, I've stopped reading these things since we have our own real-life murder. But I'm hoping the murderer will live up to the standards of the genre and kill again, and this time in desperation and haste, leaving enough clues for us to find him."

"You don't really want that?"

"Not the murder, only the clues."

"I'll speak to his editor."

"You'll do what?"

"Got you!"

***

The deputy commissioner had pondered at length how he might respond most effectively to the warnings of a possible terrorist attack. He was as much interested in deterring it as stopping those who might carry it out. He accordingly insisted on a very visible police presence in places of possible interest to terrorists and more discreet coverage elsewhere. In distributing his forces, he had to take into account the wishes of the community. The local rabbi warned that armed police in front of the synagogue might frighten congregants as much as it would anyone with violent intentions. It would nevertheless be a wise precaution on Saturday morning when the community held its principal religious service. His Muslim counterpart thought nothing necessary at the moment but absolutely essential in the aftermath of any incident. Then the police should come out in force to protect not only the mosque but identifiably Muslim businesses like the halal butcher shop. Unlike the Cambridge Jewish and Muslim communities, the university had been the target of violent protests, but from animal rights activists. The new biology labs, well away from the central campus, had been constructed with security in mind. University authorities welcomed a visible police presence as they thought it would reassure their staff.

The railway police station was asked to provide backup, and Elaine was assigned to patrol duty at the Cambridge biological campus at the southwest end of Hills Road. The new Addenbrookes hospital was its core, and surrounding it or nearby, were the Rosie Maternity Hospital, the School of Clinical Medicine, the Wellcome Trust's stem cell institute, molecular biology laboratories, the cancer centre, brain imaging centre, the Institute for Public Health, and a number of laboratories sponsored by the government, the university or drug companies. Elaine was impressed by the size of the campus and pleased that her country was at the forefront of medical research. She could not understand why people would want to target facilities and researchers who were trying to save and extend human lives.

If the research here might prove exciting, her assignment was pure tedium. She was given a perimeter to patrol and told to look for anything out of the ordinary. Her beat took her through a large car park and around a complex of buildings that included the MRC Hospital, the MRI centre, the medical school, and the Hutchinson Cancer Centre. Staff and patients were constantly coming and going, just like at the station. From observation on train platforms, she thought she had honed her skills to detect anything out of the ordinary and hoped they would hold her in good stead here. She was one of several officers on patrol and assumed that her job was as much deterrence as it was detection. She was, of course, armed, but more importantly, had a telephone to summon assistance. The weather was good, people were friendly, and she slotted into her routine. She allowed herself to think about the rest of the menu for her forthcoming dinner with Peter.

**

Inspector Khan was working away at the usual forms when his telephone rang. It was the director of the police lab. The inspector was all ears and routinely reached for his pad and pen, even though his keyboard was in front of him on the desk. He moved it out of the way to make room for the pad.

The lab director explained that she was about to send a full report but wanted to give him a personal, heads up. They had been analysing the clothing of both victims and had come up with some fingerprints, and more importantly, a small bloodstain that did not belong to either of them. She explained that they could do nothing with the outer garments, as they were caked in mud and efforts to remove it had destroyed any prints that might have been present. Trussed up the way they were, their outerwear protected the clothing underneath, notably shirts and undergarments.

The inspector thanked her profusely and pondered the implications of what he had just heard. They would run the prints through the computer, of course. He suspected the lab already had and would have told him if there had been a hit. Most people unconnected with any crime are not in the database unless they have been civil servants or in the armed forces. He would take prints and blood samples from Mrs Mason and Jaime's mother to eliminate them. He would then face the unenviable task of asking the professor's colleagues and students to offer prints and epithelial cell swabs. He had no idea how many would agree, although the police would stress that their goal was to eliminate them as suspects.

Inspector Khan and his detectives were suddenly busy. As he had expected, there was no match for the prints in the database. The DNA extracted from the blood sample on Professor Mason's shirt was from a woman, and they immediately checked it against Mrs Mason, who went to the lab as soon as the inspector telephoned her. It was the usual wait until the next day for results, and they were negative. This was good news and perhaps their first real break in the case. Now they would ask female staff at the laundry that did Professor Mason's shirts for prints and cheek swabs and, if necessary, from female staff and postgraduate students at the college. If all these tests proved negative, they could expand their search to include women at Mrs Mason's law firm, Jaime's café and anywhere else that struck them as relevant.

When questioned about her husband's shirts, Mrs Mason confided that this was yet another way in which he had been demanding. He never wore shirts more than twice, and she took them to the cleaners once a week on her way to work. She remembered the shirt he wore on the day he disappeared. It was the second time he had used it. He always alternated shirts, and there was one hanging in his closet that he had worn the Friday before. The police collected it to send to the lab. The technicians found nothing of interest; the only fingerprints were those of the professor.

Most of the women at Leinster College agreed to be printed and swabbed. There were two exceptions. A postgraduate student insisted that this was sexist even after being told that the DNA they found on the professor's shirt came from a woman. A professor also declined on the grounds that her DNA and prints would go into a national database. Peter explained that standard procedure, dictated by law, was to destroy the files after they were no longer needed for the investigation or any criminal procedure that might result. She was unconvinced. He told her he could easily get a court order for the prints and DNA as this was a murder investigation but offered to wait to see if they got a hit from someone else.

XVI: Friday Morning

The lab reported that the bloodstain on the shirt was not from Mrs Mason, and constables descended on the dry-cleaning shop and Leinster College. The shop was owned by a Guyanese immigrant, now a British citizen, whose son and two nephews worked with him. The shirts were given plastic protective wrappings and kept hanging on a rack, and there was no way a customer could have bled onto a clean shirt. The constable, a thoughtful young man, asked if the shirt could have been exposed to blood before it was cleaned. Perhaps it was left in a pile on or near the counter? Absolutely not, the owner said. All shirts were immediately bagged, given a number, and then put into a bin well behind the counter.

***

The master let the police use the junior parlour to set up their equipment for fingerprinting and cheek swabbing. The work went quickly, and some forty women, faculty, postdocs, postgraduate students, and staff were processed. Professor Lundgren was overheard telling a colleague that Professor Mason would have been tickled pink by the queue of anxious women his death had caused. "This was something," she said, "that would never have happened when he was alive, unless, that is, he volunteered to put his head in the stocks at some fundraising event. Women would have queued for hours to buy water balloons to throw at him."

A postgraduate woman remarked to no one in particular that at least the police were not requiring a blood test. An older woman behind her suggested that that would be a prick for a prick. More laughter ensued.

It took a day and a half to process the prints and DNA. The lab found no match on the prints but did on the DNA. The blood came from Professor Lundgren, and the inspector quickly called her to make an appointment. He said nothing about the blood match over the phone, only that he had some additional questions that might help with their investigation. She agreed to meet them in her college set after her tutorial.

Professor Lundgren greeted Inspector Khan and DS Leslie when they arrived and asked how their investigation was going.

"Not all that well," Inspector Khan replied. "We are dealing with a clever murderer who has left few tracks."

"Did you get any results from the prints and swabs?"

"We did. The bloodstain turned out to be yours."

"Mine? That can't be. There must be some mistake."

"I'm afraid not. The lab did the test twice once they found a DNA match, and they are 98 per cent certain that it is yours."

"But how could it be my blood?"

"That's what I'm hoping to find out."

"I can't imagine. Let me get this straight. You found some of my blood on Professor Mason's shirt. I assume it was the shirt he was wearing when he was killed?"

"Yes, that's right."

"How large was the stain, and where was it?"

"It was a small spot, but I would rather not reveal where it was."

"Was there any other blood anywhere?"

"Not that we've found. It seems to have been a bloodless killing."

"The question is, what was my blood doing on his shirt, assuming your test is not a false positive?"

The inspector nodded his head.

"I haven't the faintest idea of how my blood could end up on his shirt. I don't remember cutting myself, and if I did, why would I bleed onto Sid's shirt? This is a real mystery. Does this mean I'm a suspect?"

"A suspect, no. But definitely a person of interest."

"I'm already a person of interest, I think."

"It's not really a laughing matter."

"That's a matter of opinion, Inspector. To think that I am a person of interest in the murder of Professor Mason strikes me as amusing because I know I had nothing whatsoever to do with this crime. And would you mind telling me just what a person of interest is?"

"It's a term with no legal standing but refers to someone who is cooperating with an investigation, may have information relevant to that investigation, or certain characteristics that merit further attention. In your case, it is the last category."

"I see. And what follows from it?"

"We would like to know more about your whereabouts on the day of the murder, for a start. We must also insist that you not leave town whilst the investigation is underway."

"That could take forever at the pace you are proceeding."

"We certainly hope not."

They went over in detail Professor Lundgren's movements the day her colleague disappeared. She had been working at home on a paper and had not left any email trail because, as she explained, she ignored her email when she wrote and let it sit in a queue until the afternoon. Nobody had observed her, nor had she made or received any telephone calls. She did not own a car, only a bicycle, and did not live close to her deceased colleague. Nobody could vouch for her presence until she came into college for lunch. That was enough time, the inspector informed her, to have waylaid and murdered Professor Mason.

"But there were two murders, I understand. Why would I kill someone I've never met? And even if I wanted to, how would I subdue two men? I certainly give you credit for not thinking of me as the weak sister type!"

"We recognize the difficulties you — or anyone else — would have in pulling this off," the inspector replied. "It can't have been easy for the murderer, even if he is built like a rugby player. Although I give you credit for being a very resourceful woman."

"I thank you for that. But let me assure you that this is not a problem to which I have devoted my little grey cells."

"That may well be, but you will remain a person of interest until you can come up with a compelling explanation for the bloodstain on the professor's shirt."

The two men took their leave of the only partly mollified professor and walked back to the station. It was raining, but they had the foresight to bring umbrellas. As it was not windy, they could easily talk despite the separation between them caused by their large, unfurled brollies.

"What do you think?" Peter asked.

"She does seem honestly perplexed. If not, she should be on stage rather than in the classroom."

"I don't think there's much difference between the two if you are a good teacher. But I agree. I think she's telling the truth. She's unlikely to be our murderer, but I can't come up with a scenario to explain her blood on his shirt."

***

Peter was hoping something would break in the case, but not today as he was to be Elaine's guest for dinner. He wanted to leave work early, pick up a nice bottle of wine on the way home, shower, and change into something informal. He tried to concentrate on his paperwork, which was difficult in the best of circumstances. He thought about going to the canteen for a cup of coffee but decided against it as he had already downed four cups today. He checked his watch for the third time in thirty minutes and had another two hours to kill, so to speak. Too bad he couldn't play the odd game of solitaire on his office computer to relax, but it did not come with any game apps, and he dared not download them. Instead, he plugged away at the form, accounting for his hours this week. Then he had an application to fill out. It would allow him with any luck to attend a training course on the latest advances in crime scene evidence collection and analysis. It promised to be useful and interesting, even if it was being held at the police conference centre in Slough. He remembered reading somewhere that its inhabitants, and with reason, he thought, thought it the most unattractive place name in the UK.

Form filling and daydreaming got him through the afternoon, and at five p.m. sharp, he was out the door and striding home with more than the usual bounce in his step. He stopped at the wine shop and picked up an already chilled bottle of Chablis. He thought about taking flowers but decided it would be overkill. He did not want to look too anxious, but anxious he was. Elaine was an attractive, intelligent, charming and, he thought, considerate woman. He wanted to make a good impression. He was also desperately horny.

***

Inspector Khan also put in some time on his computer and felt some satisfaction when he finished another mindless form. He rewarded himself by downloading a *Guardian* article on Siberian tigers. They were an endangered species but making something of a comeback because Putin was fond of them and had used his authority to put an end to poaching. The newspaper had a glorious head-on picture of the tiger, which he printed out in colour and put in an envelope with a note to post to his niece. Odd, he thought, how Putin was more interested in the rights of tigers than human beings. Just like animal activists here in Cambridge, who, he was certain, would take great umbrage at being compared to Russia's strongman.

XVI: Friday Afternoon

As senior crime scene officer, Inspector Khan had to stay in town and could not sneak down to London this weekend to see his family. And unlike Peter, he had not yet met another woman. He had only his cooking, bike ride, and football match in the offing. Even his bike ride would be constrained, as he would have to stay in the vicinity of Cambridge. He used a computer to chart a route that would allow a nice ride and end up by a pub set back from the Cam for his Saturday lunch. Peter was discreet about his social life, but Inspector Khan knew he had met someone and dragged the story out of him over coffee in the canteen. The tennis club made it possible for him to meet people, and the inspector wondered if he should do something similar. He did not play tennis, but he could join a biking group. The problem, he thought, would be having to pedal at their slower speed, and that would not be any fun.

He also rejected computer dating, knowing that it was ridiculously inefficient. On their websites, you had to fill out a form with pages of questions about yourself and your preferences. None of them were really relevant to whom you would find attractive, so the pairing done by whatever algorithm their computer programme used was meaningless. The only value of computer dating was putting people in touch with lots of other people. If you meet enough people, you might find one you like, and if you are really lucky, the feeling would be mutual.

Worse still was meeting women through your mother or aunts. He was convinced that the hit rate here was much lower but recognized that he did not have a sample large enough to justify his belief. And he was not about to collect one. At family parties, he had met two women obviously invited for the purpose of matchmaking. The first was lovely, and he had very much enjoyed talking to her. Off in a quiet corner — a rare find at one of his family gatherings — she confessed that she was gay, not yet out of the closet, and had not wanted to ruffle her aunt's feelings by turning her down. The two aunts were, of course, friends. The inspector admired her courage. He took her mobile number, and they would meet periodically in London for coffee or some cultural event. He and Aadila, which means honest in Urdu, kept their meetings secret. Both found her name amusing, given their little subterfuge.

Aadila was careful not to play matchmaker This still left him at the starting gate when it came to women with the potential of becoming partners. He kept hoping he would meet someone just by chance, but it had not happened. The last two attractive women he came face-to-face with were postgraduate students they had interviewed at Cambridge. He was certain that Peter noticed that one of them had long legs, although she was wearing jeans that kept them under wraps. If students were a no-no for professors, people encountered during a criminal investigation were even more so for detectives.

Inspector Khan had also thought about joining a book club, but they were relatively small, and there would be a couple of single women at most. Maybe when he had some leave time, he should go off to a singles Club Med or its equivalent. His musings were interrupted by the ringing of the telephone. It was Professor Lundgren, and her greeting was surprisingly friendly.

"Inspector," she said, "I'm delighted I caught you in your office."

"What can I do for you, professor?"

"It suddenly dawned on me how my blood got on the professor's shirt. It was such a small incident that I really had to dwell on the problem at some length to bring the encounter back to consciousness."

"Do tell me what happened."

"As I said, it was a really inconsequential matter. I nicked my finger on the door to the senior parlour. I keep meaning to turn in my old-fashioned metal key for a key card but somehow never get around to it. The keyhole is too close to the doorjamb, and I pinched my finger. The cut drew out a tiny bit of blood, which I licked off and promptly forgot about. I walked through the parlour to the main hall, where a buffet lunch is served. There are fresh rolls and a soup tureen on the counter before you get to the main courses. Sid was helping himself to soup, some creamy thing that did not appeal to me. But I wanted a bread roll, as the college does nice fresh ones covered in poppy seeds. I manoeuvred around Sid to grab one and, I think, touched his shoulder to balance myself as I reached out and across. It was a hot day, at least for Cambridge, and he was in a shirt, probably having left his jacket in his set. I touched him with the hand I had cut. It would have been on the back of the shirt, on the right arm, just below the shoulder. Is that by any chance where you found the stain?"

"Yes, it is. And it was only a trace amount. I was impressed that the lab managed to find it."

"Does that get me off the hook?"

"I think it does. It's a plausible story, and I deliberately refrained from telling you, where on the shirt, we found the blood."

"Well, sorry to disappoint, Inspector."

"It seems to be my fate today. Thanks so much for calling."

***

Elaine hoped for a quiet afternoon, and the gods smiled on her. She patrolled her perimeter endlessly and, for the first time, was pleased, not bored, by her seeming irrelevance. By now, she had developed some sense of the flow of people in and out of the hospital and nearby buildings. She recognized many of the faces, although not those of patients whose visits were less frequent. She processed what she observed in a way that she hoped would lead her to recognize something out of the ordinary but not otherwise obvious. Even if no alarm bells went off, it was still good training.

Early that afternoon, she watched a young man, pulling a small black suitcase, nervously approach the stem cell institute. It struck her as something worth investigating. Was he nervous because he was a patient or for some other reason, and what, she wondered, was in his suitcase? She followed him into the building, saw him check in at the reception, and take a seat in the waiting room. She approached the desk, showed her warrant card, and asked in a quiet voice about the man and his business. She was told that he was a salesman from a medical instruments firm and had an appointment with two of the researchers. It was a firm they dealt with on a regular basis, but the salesman was new. That probably explained his nervousness, Elaine thought. She thanked the receptionist, retreated from the building, and resumed her patrol.

She returned to the railway police station at the end of her stint, checked in her equipment, and changed into street clothes. She rehearsed the evening's meal in her mind and decided that she had purchased everything needed. She wanted the crab and sole to be as fresh as possible, so she had ordered them at the fish shop and would pick them up on her way home. She would steam the two small crabs and make a nice aioli to go with them. The sole she would do à la meunière, a simple preparation that brought out its taste, especially if you went easy with the butter. New potatoes and broccoli would be the perfect side dishes. The former was simple, like the fish, and the latter provided contrast as it was colourful and crunchy.

Elaine enjoyed cooking and was to some degree self-taught. Her mother had been committed to putting healthy food on the table but lacked all interest and imagination when it came to its preparation. Her energies went into keeping the family together, a challenging task given her ne'er-do-well husband who spent most of his time and money at the pub or in betting shops. She struggled to make ends meet and to provide Elaine and her younger sister with what they needed. The two grandmothers helped out when their mother took a second part-time job. Elaine had started cooking to do her share at home. She had read cookbooks in the library and had been befriended by one of the librarians, who encouraged her to start on simple and inexpensive dishes. The two became friends, and occasionally she was invited to the librarian's flat and given hands-on lessons in food preparation and cooking. Her younger sister was quite jealous but enjoyed the products of her labour.

Elaine showered and changed into a more alluring but not too revealing outfit. She wanted to look nice for Peter but not in too obvious a way. It occurred to her that she was deluding herself. She wanted him lusting after her but did not want to come on to him in a crude way. Her sister had given her a nice set of candlesticks for Christmas, and whilst the red and green candles that came with them were more Yuletide than romantic, they would do. She set the table and turned to the task of food preparation.

***

Peter had put work out of his mind, or so he thought. As he was getting dressed, and for no reason whatsoever, he thought about the car with the unknown registration that showed up on Bateman Street the morning of the professor's disappearance. All registrations were in the system, so there was something suspicious here. The most likely explanation was that a constable had read the number incorrectly. Tomorrow morning, he must remember to ask to have the plate read again from the CCTV recording. These images were never perfect, and perhaps there was a simple explanation. It was a loose end and worth following up on as they really had no other leads.

***

The coroner was also planning an evening out. He and his wife had a weekly bridge game with another couple, friends of many years standing. He knew that hardly anybody played bridge any more and that bridge parties were totally passé. It was yet another way in which he and Mary were social dinosaurs; their values and practices were on the decline, so much so, he suspected, that young people did not even understand them. In turn, neither the coroner nor his wife felt drawn to activities the young found so engaging. They were not on social media; Mary was computer illiterate. They owned neither jeans nor trainers, drank moderately, and had never tried drugs. It went without saying that neither of them was tattooed. They enjoyed ballroom dancing, golf, and long walks together. They would look even more out of place in California, he thought.

The coroner was a different person at work. He was au courant with the latest medical and scientific developments in his field. He attended grand rounds, continuing education programmes, and read widely. He was respected by his peers and was often consulted by coroners at other hospitals. He had developed a specialization in forensic science and had published a few papers on the subject. The previous autumn, he had been an invited speaker at an international conference in Honolulu. Mary had accompanied him for a holiday and stopover in California on their return, to visit their daughter and her family.

He could not make sense of the drug that had been used to sedate the two victims. It was not frequently used in hospitals, none was missing from Addenbrookes, and the police had told him that the manufacturer, supplier, and other hospitals could account for their entire stock. Could he have made a mistake? He thought it unlikely because he had found traces of the compound unique to this sedative. It was admittedly in a family of compounds, but his analysis was specific, and he had done it for both victims. He wondered how difficult it would be to synthesize, but this was a subject beyond his expertise. Perhaps he could seek out an organic chemist at the university and inquire?

He was also intrigued by the use of EpiPens and had been meaning to ask Inspector Khan if the police had made any headway on that front. Presumably, the extraction of the original drug from the EpiPens and the insertion of the drug used to anaesthetize the two men would require special equipment and skills. Was it possible that the killer had used something else, say a standard syringe with a needle that resembled those on EpiPens?

***

Professor Lundgren had an active social life, much of it with single women. One of her closest friends was a molecular biologist who worked in one of the buildings Elaine had been guarding for the last two days. They were meeting a third friend for dinner at her place. The professor was marking "fresher" essays in the two-term introduction to history in which she gave one lecture but held regular tutorials with the four first-year students in Leinster College who were studying her subject. Two of them were struggling, and two were performing well above average. She was pleased to mentor the latter and was doing what she could to help the former. The underachieving students had yet to learn how to read a text, formulate an argument, and express it succinctly and coherently in writing. She had her doubts that they would ever master these arts. Not for the first time, she wondered how such students were admitted to such an intensely competitive institution.

She was familiar with the law of large numbers, which presumably accounted for the variation in the quality of students she had seen over the years. She and her colleagues tried hard to recruit promising students from state schools but also not to discriminate against excellent ones

137

from public schools. It was a complex process, even an evolutionary one, an observation offered by one of her biology colleagues who studied birds. He did his research in Cambridge parks, where he observed interactions over the generations between magpies and other species. The magpies laid their eggs in the nests of other birds. Their eggs hatched first and pushed the other eggs out of the nest or monopolized the food, given their larger size. Some of the other species had adapted by laying eggs of a different colour so they could discriminate between their eggs and those of the interlopers or by producing eggs that hatched earlier. The magpies had evolved counterstrategies, among them copying the new colour of host bird eggs.

In Leinster and other colleges, faculty used interviews to try to identify the more promising students and distinguish them from those who merely performed well in examinations and essays. Public schools responded by conducting rehearsal interviews. Faculty tried to compensate by throwing questions at students that were unexpected, and the public schools then did the same in their rehearsals. Colleges attempted to set goals that would increase the percentage of state students admitted, and parents responded by sending their children to excellent state schools or to other state schools for their last two years and providing outside tutoring for them. It was not unlike the struggle between magpies and the birds in whose nests they laid their eggs.

Professor Lundgren routinely argued that interviews, introduced to help state school students, had the opposite effect. She supported more drastic measures along the lines of those adopted by King's College, whose percentage intake of state school students far exceeded other colleges. This worked in King's, she concluded, because it has been for a long time the most bolshie of colleges — and not surprisingly — among the least democratic and most authoritarian in its administration.

Leinster was more democratic, and she wanted to keep it that way. But she also wanted an admissions policy that would bring in more bright kids to Cambridge from minorities or underprivileged backgrounds and facilitate their entry into the British elite. The problem, as she saw it, was doing this cleverly and not relying on the hunches of faculty who interviewed applicants. They should copy American Ivy League institutions like Dartmouth that set up summer programmes for bright minority and otherwise disadvantaged young people and identified those who showed promise and performed well. Admissions officers then visited their families and urged them to apply, explaining that costs would all be covered, or a large part, by scholarships.

Professor Lundgren thought about admissions whilst walking back to college from the university library. She was doing research on the ways in which Japanese woodblock prints, especially those known as particularly *ukiyo-e* — pictures of the floating world — influenced Japanese social practices and expectations. It was a perfect subject as she loved Japanese art and the colour and minimalism of their prints. The Fitzwilliam Museum in Cambridge had a good collection, and the Victoria and Albert Museum in London a stupendous one. It provided an excuse to go to London frequently and offered her hours of pleasure when she examined their prints. She emailed the curator of Japanese art at the V & A beforehand, and the curator would assemble the prints that the professor wanted to examine. She would do so in a room set aside for scholars like the professor, but also for ordinary people who just wanted to enjoy the museum's collection as only a small number of prints could actually be displayed in the galleries at any given time.

The university library had good secondary sources on Japan and some useful primary sources as well. There was recent scholarship in Japanese on the sale and distribution of prints in the eighteenth and nineteenth centuries, and more interestingly, on the production and sale of copies. The copies were widespread and affordable to ordinary people. In her college set, she had framed originals of Eisen, Utamaro, and Kuniyoshi, supplemented by several Hiroshige in her departmental office. Like the V & A, albeit on a much smaller scale, she had more prints than she could or would want to hang on her walls; their colours faded if exposed to prolonged sunlight. She kept them wrapped in plastic envelopes and inside thick cardboard folders in a filing cabinet. Occasionally, she would go to the local frame shop and have them switch prints in frames to cycle through her collection.

Back in her set, she noted the prints on the wall and also the need to water her plants. Neither was her principal concern at the moment. She wanted to back up the notes she had taken on her small laptop on her desktop; she tried to keep copies of anything important in several places and to email files to herself. This way Google also had a copy. Unlike banking information, she was not worried about somebody hacking her account. There was nothing to be gained by doing so, except in the case of student records and those she was more careful about. Her desktop was wired into the university computing system, unlike her laptop, which connected via Wi-Fi. On this more secure computer, she conducted any correspondence she wanted to protect, although she was fully aware of the risk that anything sent over the web had the potential to become public. Still, it was less likely this way, and she took the extra precaution of using a different browser and email service.

She logged in and checked to see if there were any messages from Robert, her special friend in London. He was a handsome art restorer, two years younger, stuck in an unhappy marriage, but with considerable freedom, because his wife's principal office was in Brussels. She and Robert met up several times a month for meals and steamy sex. Sometimes they dispensed with the food. Robert was good in bed in the sense that he was keen to satisfy her, and she reciprocated. She also enjoyed their pillow talk and could not see herself having sex with someone with whom she did not have some kind of relationship. For various reasons, Robert did not want a divorce, and she was content to have him remain married. Their frequency of contact and degree of intimacy was just right for her.

There was indeed a message from Robert. Discreetly worded, to be sure, it described a seventeenth-century portrait of a reclining nude by a member of Velázquez's workshop, and how the texture of the skin was arousing, and even more so, the dimples above her buttocks, one of which was visible. Professor Lundgren had similar dimples, which Robert loved to admire and kiss. The email was intended to arouse her and succeeded admirably in its purpose. Robert was free the day after tomorrow and invited her to his studio to inspect the painting. She quickly confirmed their rendezvous, telling him what train she could make that afternoon. Feeling good about herself, she logged off, grabbed her handbag, and went to turn off the lights. She paused, noting that her large canvas holdall was not in its usual place. She looked around the room and in the set's closet and kitchen but could not find it. *That's odd*, she thought. *I'm pretty sure it was here yesterday*. She gave it no more thought, closed her door, double-checked that it was locked, and descended the stairs to the courtyard. She took the well-worn stone walk to the porter's lodge, the gate beyond it and the world outside.

XVII: Friday Night

Elaine felt a rush when her buzzer rang and ran to her apartment telephone. She heard Peter's voice on the other end and buzzed him into the building. Peter walked up the two flights of stairs and gave Elaine a peck on the cheek after entering. He handed her the bottle of Chablis and followed her into the kitchen. He commented on how light her flat was. She opened his bottle in preference to the pinot grigio she had in the fridge and poured them drinks.

Elaine had prepared some anchovy canapés, which Peter ate with gusto. Their conversation moved from the flat and its view to Elaine's adjustment to life in Cambridge, to tennis and a good time for them to play again. Peter asked if she had social contact with work colleagues but refrained from asking her directly what she did. She had been out for drinks with a couple of her co-workers, she volunteered, but hoped to develop a social life independent of her job. Peter said that this was also his preference. It gave him a life away from work and avoided the inevitable office gossip about any in-house relationship. Such chatter and often the ribbing that accompanied it made any romance more difficult to sustain, and there was nothing worse than a relationship that went sour, and the former couple had to confront each other on a daily basis at work. Elaine agreed and invited him to the dinner table.

The conversation returned to food as Peter was effusive in his praise of the crab and accompanying sauce and the Japanese seaweed on which she had placed the crab. He didn't know where you could buy this in Cambridge, and she told him about her secret source. She was a regular at a Japanese restaurant not far from the station and had become friendly enough with the owner to get some from him. Peter complimented her on her initiative and asked if she would take him to the restaurant sometime as he was not really familiar with Japanese cuisine. She agreed. What they did not talk about were their respective jobs. This was now their fourth encounter and second evening together. Each sensed that for some reason, the other did not want to broach the subject, and they both began to treat it as taboo. They were relieved but also ever more curious why the other kept the subject off the table.

After dinner, Peter helped to clear the table and do the dishes. He declined yet another glass of wine, but Elaine convinced him that there was not enough to save in the bottle. They should divide it between them. Feeling euphoric, quite the reverse, they returned to the sitting room and took seats on the sofa.

"Would you like some music?" Elaine asked.

"Oh, I'm quite content to talk, but please put some on if you like."

Elaine did this not because she wanted to hear music, but it required her to get up to put the sound system on and gave her the opportunity, when she returned to the sofa, to position herself closer to Peter. Peter could smell her perfume, which had been very discreetly applied.

"That's a nice fragrance."

"I'm glad you like it."

"What is it?"

"I'm embarrassed to tell you."

"Why is that?"

"It has a very suggestive name."

There was a pause before Peter could formulate an appropriate reply. "Then it's well named considering the effect it's having on me. Sorry, I meant… that you are having on me."

"How sweet of you. It's mutual, you know."

Peter took this as a green light and put his arm around her; Elaine cuddled him in response. Peter gently turned her body with his left arm, so they faced each other and moved his lips close to hers. She opened her lips, and they began to kiss, gingerly at first, then more passionately. Peter began stroking her back, and she did the same to him. They paused for a moment, but not for long, as Elaine pulled him close to her again. Peter began to stroke Elaine's leg, and she let out a slight moan. Peter had earlier shed his jumper, and she began to undo the buttons of his shirt.

"Let's go into the bedroom," she said.

Peter rose and followed Elaine into her boudoir. He thrilled at the sight of Elaine disrobing hastily but gracefully. He shed his clothes, but unlike women, men can rarely just kick off their shoes. It was a more laborious process. Their foreplay became more serious once they were undressed. They had both put the quotidian world behind them when Peter's telephone rang. He had two, both of which were in his trouser pockets, and this ring was from his police phone. The last thing he wanted to do was answer it, so he decided to just let it ring. Like Peter, Elaine was momentarily distracted but pleased that her partner had not let the outside world interrupt their intimacy.

Peter's phone was set to ring twelve times before switching to message mode. On the tenth ring, Elaine's phone went off from somewhere in the closet, summoning her in no uncertain terms with Darth Vader's theme. Peter looked at her quizzically. She disentangled herself from him and went to the closet to retrieve a solid-looking mobile. Peter got up and fished his phone from his trousers and dialled in his code to retrieve his messages. Both were silent as they held their phones to their ears. Peter caught Elaine's attention, and she signalled her discontent at the situation by raising her eyebrows. Peter grimaced in return. Elaine went to grab pen and paper and wrote down an address. Peter just listened intently to his message.

Their call and message completed, two embarrassed naked people with their electronic devices in hand stood staring at each other. Peter saved the situation with a quip that Elaine would long remember.

"I don't think I've read about this form of *coitus interruptus* in *The Joy of Sex.*"

Elaine laughed. In keeping with his efforts to make light of the situation, she asked how he had arranged for their phones to ring almost simultaneously.

"I have a confession to make. I'm a detective, and that was the duty sergeant summoning me to a crime scene."

"You're a cop!"

"Yes. I've been trying to keep it out of the picture as long as possible. It's usually a passion killer… although not like two ringing phones, one of them with the Empire striking back on the other end."

"I wish it were sometimes." She hesitated for a moment to build up her courage. "It's another cop shop."

Peter was speechless, and a long pause ensued as they stared at each other.

"You're a cop too?" he blurted out.

"Yes, I'm posted at the railway station. You must be at Parkside, which is why we've never met."

"And you've been called for the same reason?"

"I expect so. A bomb at Leinster College."

"Yes. Well, we'd better get dressed and back to, I hesitate to say it, real life."

Peter reached for his clothes and Elaine for her knickers and bra. As Peter got dressed, Elaine reopened the clothes closet and took out her uniform. After dressing, she reached back in for her boots, cap, and other paraphernalia, including her whistle and service pistol. Looking at her fully outfitted, Peter smiled. Elaine blushed and thought how odd her reaction was, as she had not done that when they were in their birthday suits.

Elaine had a motorbike and offered Peter a lift to Leinster College. She had been instructed to report back to the railway station. Peter hugged her from the back of the saddle and lamented that this was as intimate as the evening would get. She dropped him off a hundred yards or so from the college. This way they would not be seen together, and for the same reason, they avoided embracing before she did a neat turn with the bike and headed back down Trumpington Street in the opposite direction.

***

Armed and helmeted police blocked the college gate, and another officer stood in front of the metal gate off to the right that cyclists used. Peter assumed that other entrances would be similarly closed. He showed his warrant card and passed through the archway into the main courtyard. The usual officials were on hand, although he saw no evidence of the coroner or his assistant, which he considered a positive sign. Students were milling about questioning one another and the police, if they could, about what was going on. A constable who recognized him came by to report that the action was in a stairwell accessed through the inner

145

courtyard where he would find Inspector Khan. Peter thanked him and eased his way through the mob of students, totally uninterested in checking out any long-legged women. What a nice evening it had been, he thought, and what a rotten ending. Better, he supposed, than losing his erection at a critical moment, but that had never happened.

Once in the inner courtyard, he could see tape and police protecting the relevant entryway. The buildings surrounding the lawn were Gothic revival in style and apparently not the only thing that was faux in the college. Behind the Gothic façade, he knew from previous visits, were ordinary and not very comfortable structures that incorporated none of their elegance. He suspected this was true of many members of the college as well once they took off their robes, medals, and scarves. Were they attracted to the place for this reason or came to resemble it in the course of their time here? The professor's murder and this event made it evident that the college and the image it projected of itself were two different things.

Peter could see Inspector Khan talking to the bomb expert at the other end of the court. He made his way to them along the stone path that formed a perimeter around the largely grass court. He knew that only fellows were allowed to walk on the lawn of the inner courtyard, a rule students and the police, were obeying. He thought the respect the police were showing was inappropriate to the situation, but he was still careful to walk the two sides of the square to reach the inspector.

Peter knew the bomb expert and exchanged greetings with both men. The inspector apologized for dragging him away from what he hoped had been a pleasant evening.

"You don't know the half of it, sir," Peter said.

"The inspector decided against pursuing this line of inquiry any further and briefed his colleague on what had happened.

"There was a bomb in the office of Professor Nejami. Fortunately, it didn't explode, and nobody was hurt."

"It's a very ordinary device," the bomb expert said. "It's constructed from simple materials, and the design is right off the Internet. I had no problem disabling it by cutting the wires between the timer and fuse and the fuse and the charge. As soon as the SOCOs finish, I'll do a more thorough analysis."

"Was it a large device?" Peter asked.

"Large enough to do considerable damage," the bomb expert replied. "It would have destroyed the office and badly damaged the rest of the building, I'm guessing. But we will know more when we have analysed the explosive."

The bomb expert was named Joseph. He was a small man who somehow gave the impression of being much larger. Perhaps it was his deep voice and commanding presence, although he was eminently polite and even deferential. This was another seeming contradiction, Peter realized. He attacked bombs the way Inspector Morse did crossword puzzles. They were problems to be solved, and the joy was more in the process than the product. Unlike Morse, for whom puzzles were a commitment with which work often interfered, the puzzle, in this case, was the work. This made Joseph a happy man and an even more contented one today because he had an intact bomb with which to work, not just the scattered fragments he was accustomed to piecing together.

Peter asked what he could do.

"Nothing really," the inspector answered.

Peter began to bristle but then noticed the smile on the inspector's face and forced himself to suppress any residual rage.

"The bomb was in a canvas bag," the inspector explained. "The SOCOs will give it a fine going over. I imagine that we will get more useful information from a bomb that hasn't exploded. Is that right, Joseph?"

"Absolutely, Inspector. Once we fully understand its design, we will be in a better position to track down its components and perhaps find its builder. The only thing we won't know for sure is how much damage it would have done. Just the opposite of a bomb that goes off."

"I'll take this situation any time," said the inspector. "No dead students or staff and all the other horrors that accompany bombs."

The men stopped talking when they saw one of the SOCOs coming out of the stairwell carrying the bomb in a large plastic bag. He handed it to a colleague to transport to the police laboratory and approached Inspector Charles Davidson, who was in charge of the investigation. The inspector had just emerged from the entrance that led up to the master's suite. The two men conferred, and neither Peter nor Inspector Khan could overhear their conversation. The SOCO returned to the stairwell where the bomb had been found, and Inspector Davidson turned to walk in their direction.

Inspector Davidson said the master was baffled by the bomb and the warning that led to its discovery.

"What warning?" Inspector Khan, Peter, and Joseph asked almost in unison.

"At 8.30 p.m. sharp, the master's phone rang. The master is careful about giving out his number. He assumed it was someone he knew reasonably well. A muffled male voice told him there was a bomb in the "N" stairway set to go off in an hour. The master shouted something like 'what,' and the voice on the other end shouted 'Allah Akbar' and the line went dead. And no, his calls are not recorded, but I've already ordered the phone logs to see where it came from. We will almost certainly find it is from a throwaway mobile. The master called the porters, asking them to evacuate the college immediately. It seems they have an emergency plan that they have rehearsed, and porters, staff and students responded with remarkable efficiency. He then dialled 999, and we and the fire department were immediately notified."

"It was a bit of a crush when we arrived," Inspector Davidson continued. "There were students milling about on the streets outside the college. We pushed past them, as did the SOCOs, and Joseph arrived shortly afterwards. The chief porter insisted on escorting us despite the danger. He used his master key to open all the doors in the "N" stairway, beginning with the set of Professor Nejami. The bag was in the middle of the carpet on Professor Nejami's floor, and the top of the bomb was visible. It didn't take long for Joseph to determine it was a dud, and just to be sure, he cut the wires as a backup precaution. We searched carefully for another device, on the off chance that this was a decoy to lure us into the stairway to get blown up by a second, hidden bomb. There's absolutely nothing there and no basement to worry about. I gave the all clear, and I imagine the students began to file back in around the time the two of you arrived."

"Why did the porter start with Professor Nejami's set?" asked Inspector Khan.

"Because he had received prior threats, including a death threat yesterday."

Peter kept shifting his weight from one foot to another.

"Ignore him," Inspector Khan said to Inspector Davidson. "He was probably out on the town and enjoying himself."

"Did we drag you out of someone's arms?" Inspector Davidson said jovially.

Peter refused to be drawn and said nothing.

"Must have from the look of it," Inspector Davidson said.

"What do we know about Professor Nejami?" Inspector Khan asked.

"Just enough to guess why he may have been targeted," said Inspector Davidson. He studies ethnic and religious identities and their implications for politics. According to the master, he's just completed a study of British Muslims based on an on-line survey and follow-up interviews. Some of the results have been reported in newspapers, and *Channel 4 News* interviewed him several weeks' back. He's a controversial figure in the British Muslim community because he is secular and opposed to the wearing of headscarves in schools or the workplace."

"A man after my own heart," Inspector Khan told himself.

"The master was much relieved," Inspector Davidson continued. "He didn't want to think about the possibility of two of his professors murdered in the same term, and possibly a student or two as collateral damage."

There was another pause as the three men reflected on this last statement.

"I doubt there is any connection between our murders and your bomb incident," Inspector Khan said.

"I'm sure you're right, but I'll keep you abreast of everything," Inspector Davidson promised.

The group broke up, and Peter and the inspector left the college in the direction of the Parkside Police Station. They were ambushed outside the entrance arch by Rhianna Johnson of the *Cambridge News*.

'Good evening, inspectors," she said.

They greeted her and kept walking. She followed and shouted, "You're not going to escape so easily."

Neither man responded.

"Inspector Khan, I have some important information for you."

Against his better judgment, the inspector stopped and turned around. Peter followed suit.

"I've learnt something about the hacking of the police computer network."

"'This is a serious matter," the inspector replied. "Perhaps it would be best to discuss it at the station."

"Happy to oblige, Inspector. But you realize my information does not come free."

"Look, Ms Johnson, if you have information about a crime, you're required by law to pass it on to the police."

"Don't be such a stick-in-the-mud, Inspector. You're not going to run me in. If you did, I'd deny I know anything. But perhaps you know something about what's just happened at the college, and we can inform each other?"

"I can't trade information."

"All right, I understand that. But certainly, you can provide an anxious public with information they crave, and that might reassure them. Isn't that one of the responsibilities of the police force? Just as responsible citizens should provide useful information to the police."

"Tell me what I should know."

"Could we do this in a pub, Inspector? We could all use a drink."

After a short discussion, they retired to an agreed-upon watering hole where Rhianna took their orders. The inspector objected that even if the cost of the drinks was trivial, it could be construed as a bribe if she picked up the tab. Rhianna and the inspector dutifully went to the bar together and returned with three pints of bitter. Rhianna's information was useful but not pertinent to their investigation. A reporter from a national daily had boasted about one of his colleagues hacking the police computer system. She considered this a violation of press ethics and something that would come back to bite them all on the behind. The inspector agreed to pass along the reporter's name to the deputy commissioner, who he thought, would be most grateful if the information helped to plug the leak. He gave Rhianna an edited summary of the evening's events — just enough information to provide the morning edition of her paper with a scoop.

Before parting, Rhianna asked if, like Louis in *Casablanca*, the police were rounding up the usual suspects.

"I wish we had some to round up," the inspector replied.

XVIII: Saturday

Both detectives came into the station early to discuss recent developments. They agreed the bomb was probably unrelated to Professor Mason's murder. But could it be mere coincidence that Leinster College was central to both events? Inspector Khan thought it useful to return to the college for another round of interviews. Perhaps they could establish some connection between the two professors. In the interim, he would pass along Ms Johnson's tip to Deputy Commissioner Braham, and Peter would try to find out as much as he could about Professor Nejami. If the bomb had been planted by Islamic extremists and motivated by hatred for a secular professor of Middle East origins, it had nothing to do with their investigation. They would nevertheless look for any possible connection between Islamic extremists, anti-Islamic groups, and their murder victims.

Peter returned to his office, where his first thought was not about Professor Nejami but Elaine. He called her mobile, whose number he now had, and imagined the sound of its Darth Vader ring. It reminded him of one of his teachers who enjoyed telling her students at the beginning of the term that she had such a reputation for low marks that her former students nicknamed her "Darth Grader."

Elaine responded on the fourth ring. She was just leaving her station and, suspecting it was Peter calling, had waited to answer until she was outside. She was fine and pleased to hear that he was also well. They had a good-natured chat about the previous evening, and Peter's comment that his dash to the college proved anticlimactic provoked a laugh on the other end of the line. Elaine's post-bedroom evening was even less exciting. She had been sent back to patrol her hospital beat for a few hours just in case it too was a target. She was exhausted, having only a few hours' sleep before having to report back to work this morning so suggested that they get together the evening after. Peter asked her if she knew the old joke about the fellow who was afraid of flying for fear a bomb would go off on the plane. She had not. He explained that the man's friend suggested he carry a bomb with him as the chance of there being two bombs on a plane was infinitesimal. He was considering phoning in a bomb threat from her flat when he arrived on the assumption that two bomb threats in one evening in Cambridge were that much less likely.

Inspectors Khan and Davidson agreed to go to Leinster College together. Davidson was in charge of the bomb investigation, but Khan knew the college and its master and had spoken at some length to a number of fellows and students. Peter called the master to schedule an appointment and asked him to arrange meetings with colleagues he thought most knowledgeable about Professor Nejami and his research. He checked the professor out on the Internet and discovered that he had authored two controversial books, one of them on suicide bombers. He had written numerous academic articles, the occasional piece for the *Guardian*, and had his own blog. He was the son of a Lebanese doctor and educated in France. He was an outspoken enemy of extremism and very much in favour of assimilation.

Professor Nejami opposed headscarves and argued that Muslims who immigrated to the UK had to accept the country's values. He nevertheless acknowledged that those values were one-sided, as allegedly secular national holidays and school curricula were very Christian. Muslims should nevertheless recognize that in Britain, religious beliefs are a private affair and that it is deeply offensive for any group — Muslim, Christian, or Jewish — to attempt to impose their values and practices on others, including members of their own faiths. The professor was well known to the Cambridge community, had something of a national profile, and periodically received abusive mail and even a few death threats. He had reported these threats to the police, but they proved impossible to trace. On two occasions, the Cambridge police had provided a constable to accompany him to public talks where they feared disruption or possibly an attack against his person. The first talk encountered no opposition, and whilst protestors showed up at the second, they held their placards aloft and otherwise behaved decorously.

The most recent death threat was the most explicit and arrived the day before the attempted bombing. In letters that had been cut out and pasted onto an ordinary sheet of printer paper, it warned that Professor Nejami was courting death and would be blown into smithereens by a bomb that with any luck would take out some atheist students along with him. He immediately contacted the local police. They did not miss the irony of the possibility of the professor being turned into an unwilling suicide bomber. He was about to leave for a conference in Lund, Sweden, and the police urged him to stay away for a few more days. He refused to do this on the grounds that he had responsibilities to his students and did not give in to threats.

The master knew the police would ask for the files from any CCTV coverage on the day of the bomb and perhaps a few days prior. He had the porters download and copy them and then hand-deliver the CDs to the police station. He asked two porters to review the coverage because they knew all the students, fellows and staff and could identify faces new to the college. The back gate was left open on weekdays, and many members of the Cambridge community used it as a shortcut. Inevitably, there would be people the porters did not know. Again, on his own authority, the master sent an email to everyone in the college asking them to contact one of the porters if they had seen anyone or anything suspicious. The porters were instructed to forward to the police the name of anyone who came forward.

The SOCOs had readily determined that the lock on the door to Professor Nejami's set had not been picked, so it must have been opened with a key. The professor, contacted in Sweden, insisted that he had left the door locked, and the master checked and assured the police that no staff had entered the room between the professor's departure and the discovery of the bomb. Someone had a key, which heightened the possibility of an inside job. A member of staff would be less likely to attract notice entering and leaving the college and the "N" stairwell.

The master was keen to convince the police that nobody in the college was responsible for the bomb. When the two detectives came to see him that morning, he told them that there had been a public lecture in the college that ended only a few hours before the bomb was found. It would have provided a good cover for anyone wanting to plant a bomb in the college. He suggested they concentrate on the CCTV coverage before, during and after the talk. The lecturer was a visiting fellow from

154

"the other place", and the subject was the sexual practices of Oxford students between the two world wars. As expected, there was a sizeable turnout, almost all students.

The interviews with two members of faculty and two postgraduate students took up much of the day and did not produce much of interest to either investigation. Fellows and students described Professor Nejami as a good colleague or diligent mentor. He had no known enemies in college or even people with whom he had clashed. He was considered polite, tactful, and full of bonhomie. He was invariably among the last to leave the fruit and port gatherings after High Table. He was something of a heartthrob but very careful to maintain absolutely proper relations with students. He had a partner in London and frequently went there to spend time with her. He had brought her to the occasional High Table and feast in college, where she had made a favourable impression for both her looks and personality.

Towards the end of their last interview, Inspector Davidson received a call and excused himself from the room. After finishing with the student, his last planned interview, Inspector Khan went outside in search of his colleague. He found him standing on the forbidden grass of the inner court. Inspector Davidson gestured for Inspector Khan to join him.

"It was the police lab," he said in a low voice to the now adjacent Inspector Khan. "They traced the phone used to warn about the bomb in the 'N' stairwell. You'll never guess to whom it belongs."

"Gary Glitter?"

"Guess again."

"My mother-in-law?"

"The young man whose body was found alongside the professor."

"I'll be damned!"

"It looks like our two investigations are connected."

"Joined at the hip, I'd say."

"It does put everything in a new light."

Inspector Davidson wanted to know what his colleague could tell him about Jaime, who now seemed connected in some way to two professors at Leinster College. Or at least, his phone was, Inspector Khan observed. He told his colleague how they had struggled without success to link Jaime to the professor and suspected they would fare no better with Professor Nejami.

"Let's keep in mind," he said, "that it's Jaime's telephone, not Jaime, implicated in the warning. Jaime's dead, and somebody else used his mobile. The worst-case scenario is that Jaime had it with him when he was killed, that his murderer tossed it someplace, and that our bomber, or someone connected to him, found it and decided that it was the perfect instrument to use because it could not be traced to them."

"And the best-case scenario?"

"That the murderer kept the phone, made the warning and placed the bomb."

"Wouldn't that be splendid! It would give us more to go on and turn two investigations into one. And as I have seniority, it would make me the senior investigating officer in two murders and an attempted bombing."

"That could lead to a third murder," said Inspector Khan.

Inspector Davidson laughed. "I have enough on my plate as it is."

Their conversation was halted by the appearance of a student who had emerged from one of the entryways and was striding along the stone path in their direction. He stopped at the part of the path closest to them and shouted out, "You can't stand on the lawn. Only fellows have that right."

The two inspectors looked at each other and across to him.

Inspector Davidson shouted back at the student. "You can't put bombs in fellows' rooms either. Now bugger off."

The student was not quite sure what to do and stood looking at the two men before shaking his head and walking away in the direction of the main court.

"Where do we go from here, Rudi?" Inspector Davidson asked.

"A good question. I haven't heard anything about the professor's mobile, so let me ask Peter to check up on that. I assume the letter sent to the police is being examined for prints, but I suspect whoever sent it was careful enough not to leave any."

"I'm sure you're right, but I sent it over for analysis after we made a copy. I did the same with the recording of the phone warning. It's a male voice, but that could be half of Britain. The interesting question for me is why the warnings? Why not let the bomb go off?"

"And why place it in Professor Nejami's set on a day when he was leaving town?" Inspector Khan said. "The note warned that the professor would be made an unwitting suicide bomber. That doesn't tally with what we found. The bomb might have killed some students, if they were in the stairwell, but not Nejami. And if somebody else sent the warning, which strikes me as unlikely, why go to the effort of spelling out a scenario which is not going to happen?"

"I suppose the most logical explanation is that the bomber posted the letter and made the call because he wanted the bomb to be found and defused. But why do this? It's a mystery within a mystery."

"Something else troubles me, Charlie. Why use Jaime's phone unless you just happened to come upon it by accident? It automatically links the murders and the bombing, and you would not want to do that if you were the murderer."

The inspectors agreed that they had many more questions than answers and were not sure which of the former were worth pursuing. They would wait and see what the bomb expert and police lab came up with and have a long talk with Professor Nejami when he returned from Sweden.

***

Our murderer had a singularly satisfying day. He started it with a full English breakfast minus the baked beans. He enjoyed his coffee from what he judged was a recently cleaned machine and took his time with the morning newspapers. The front-page story in the *Cambridge News* carried the by-line of Rhianna Johnson and was about the bomb discovered and defused the night before at Leinster College. There was a dramatic colour picture of the college with police and fire engines parked, students milling about and two well-armed policemen standing at alert with helmets, bulletproof vests, and assault weapons. The reporter's "well-informed sources" said the bomb would have destroyed a wing of the inner court and could have killed a lot of people. He chuckled when he thought about the confusion that must have reigned at the college last night and even more, he imagined, at the police station this morning. Dickens' *Bleak House* came to mind, where the fog, rolling up the Thames, was thickest of all in the judge's chambers. Not much had changed, he thought. Just a shift in venue.

He gave the police credit for intelligence and good investigative procedures, but he was leading them on a wild goose chase. The bomb was not designed to go off, only to put the police on the wrong track. This ploy had been facilitated by two clever moves on his part. The first was saving Yobbo's phone, which he had used to warn the college of the bomb. He had since destroyed the mobile and tossed its parts into the Cam. The second was an initiative he had taken some two years back. He had been a lunch guest of a colleague in Leinster College, and following custom, they had taken the next free seats at one of the tables. By chance, he found Professor Nejami on his right, and they had an interesting conversation.

After lunch, his host invited them to join him for coffee in the inner parlour. They talked about Muslim students at Cambridge and how some of them were caught between two worlds. His host was called away by another colleague who needed to consult with him urgently on some college matter. He and the professor finished their coffee and conversation. Nejami had placed his keys and book on the small round wooden table around which they had been sitting and excused himself to go to the loo. Most people take their coffee or tea in the senior parlour, and he had the room to himself.

Having damaged a tendon in his hand due to a fall, the NHS had given him a putty-like blob to squeeze and strengthen surrounding muscles. He took it out of his pocket and used it to make impressions of the two college keys on Professor Nejami's chain. He later used the impression to make a cast and then copies of the keys. At the time, he wanted access to Sid's office and considered this opportunity a godsend. One of those keys, he hoped, would get him into the college at night through either the back entryway or the gate used by cyclists. He would then pick the lock to Sid's set. This had been one of his hobbies as a youngster, and his skills, although dormant for many years, were still active.

There was no longer any reason to break into Sid's office because he had, so to speak, broken Sid instead. He would throw another spanner in the works by creating a diversion. As he had a key to Professor Nejami's office, it was the obvious place to put a bomb. It was also a serendipitous choice, given the subject of the professor's research. The police would run themselves ragged looking for some Muslim "lone wolf" or terrorist cell responsible for the bomb and reframe the murders as connected somehow to headscarves, assimilation, or suicide bombers. He imagined himself as an imam or bearded fundamentalist and smiled at the thought. His ploy would spread police resources thin, taking people and time away from their primary investigation. This could only work to his advantage.

He knew his diversion would be more convincing if the bomb had gone off. He had decided against this because it might kill or maim some innocent person, and in all likelihood, a student. He knew that Professor Nejami would be away, which is why he chose to put it in his set that day. He would not be around if and when it went off, and he had made sure that it would not. His fuse looked like the real thing but was filled with an inert substance. He had been keen to do away with Sid and was untroubled by killing the good-for-nothing yobbo, but he was not a mass murderer or terrorist. Such people were sick and should be hanged; he deeply regretted the end of the death penalty. Violence ought to be surgical and remove tumours from the social body whilst doing its best to avoid damaging healthy tissue. Sid had been a tumour, and Yobbo would sooner or later turn into one. He had done society a favour by removing them. Cambridge was a healthier place.

***

Mrs Mason was making strides in her adjustment. Business, family, and friends had been helpful but not as important as self-reflection. With Sid gone, she could think more clearly and objectively, or so she told herself, about her marriage and life. She had always resented what she saw as her domestic subservience and had tried to make up for it in her professional life. She was very committed to it and fiercely independent in her practice, so much so that it occasionally became a source of friction with colleagues. She realized that she was overcompensating and hoped that now she had a private life of her own, she could ease off at the office. She was all the more committed to this resolution in light of how supportive everyone at work had been, including people she had occasionally rubbed-up the wrong way.

She came to work this Saturday morning with two potted orchids in hand, presents for the receptionist and her secretary. She wrote a warm note of thanks on the accompanying gift cards and left the orchids on their respective desks. The florist had told her, and she would pass along the tip, that it helped to let water sit for a week before adding it to the plant. This way, many of the minerals sank to the bottom of the glass. The purer the water, the healthier the plant. There was an analogy here to her work. She viewed cases as puzzles and was always tempted to jump right in and start gathering the information she needed to write a brief or begin negotiations with the other side. Experience had taught her that her initial framing of a case could be inappropriate and that revising and starting anew was hard to do once she had organized it in a particular way. She had learnt to have a careful read through any materials, and to get, or ask for, any additional documents or court opinions that she might need. But she refused to begin work on the case unless it was absolutely urgent. The delay gave her the opportunity to consider different ways of approaching the case, strategically and legally, although the two were certainly related. Even when she selected a strategy, the others she had rejected stayed in the back of her mind, discouraging her from overcommitting herself, making her more open to the possibility that a particular strategy might not succeed, and remaining available as alternatives should she need one.

Her caseload had been moderate, and work was going well. The pest had not been around of late, and she had quickly resolved the case brought to her by a client who thought he was receiving less of a company's worth than he was due. The solicitor for the start-up had initially cold-shouldered her but changed his tune when she served papers on him. He made a new offer to her client, but she had subpoenaed the relevant documents and insisted on reading them carefully before responding. They made it evident that the initial offer was quite unfair, and that the solicitor had not honoured his fiduciary responsibility. He was in an awkward position, and she needed to do little more than resort to veiled threats to negotiate a significantly better deal for her client.

Mrs Mason had periodically contacted the police to see if they were making progress with their investigation. They were invariably polite but not at all encouraging. They could find no connection between her husband and Jaime and hastened to assure her that they had given up on the possibility that her husband bought drugs from or was having a sexual relationship with the young man. Inspector Khan, who struck her as an intelligent fellow, had told that he was exploring the possibility that the two victims were related only through a third party. He quizzed her at length about Sid's interest and activities in search of hints about the nature of this indirect connection.

***

Inspector Davidson was at his desk earlier than usual. The café where he bought his morning coffee was still closed, and he was annoyed, not for the first time, at how late Cambridge cafés opened. He supposed it was due to the difficulty of getting staff to appear early in the day. He made himself a cup of tea in his office and would hoof it over to the café later for a decent macchiato. The walk and the coffee could only help his thinking.

The two inspectors had a good professional and personal relationship. They were representatives of so-called minority groups and the first two detectives from their respective backgrounds on the Cambridge police force. Their relations with their colleagues were complex. Nobody accused them of unfairly receiving preference in promotion, but both were sensitive to the charge. They had discussed the problem once they felt comfortable with each other. Inspector Davidson, the senior of the two, had broached the issue over a drink at the end of a workday. He assured his younger colleague that nobody had ever said anything to him, but he could imagine what some of them might be thinking. All the more so since his prior posting had been elsewhere. Inspector Khan had the advantage of working his way up from constable in the same station and was a known quantity.

Davidson explained that he felt compelled to have a higher closure rate than everyone else, which was hard at first because he lacked the necessary contacts in the community. He earned the respect of his colleagues, which was manifest in diverse ways. This included racial ribbing, which began in a gentle way after about six months or so on the job. In the pub or at social events, but never at work, his colleagues would sometimes refer to him as a Rastafarian, and once he was asked if he would put a voodoo curse on a local councillor who was causing them trouble. He smiled and asked if anyone had some long pins, a comment that provoked good-natured laughs.

At first, he had taken umbrage at being called a Rastafarian, but as he thought about it, it was no different than being called a Paddy or a Taffy. A sergeant of Irish extraction was routinely called Paddy to his face and took it good-naturedly. He decided to do the same. A couple of months later, he was asked a serious question about his background and identity. It was apparent from his facial features and skin colour that one of his parents was Caucasian and the other of African origin. A fellow detective wanted to know with which, if either, he identified and the extent to which Whites and Blacks accepted or rejected him because of his mixed parentage. He explained that Whites invariably regarded him as Black. So-called Blacks, more of whom were of mixed parentage, were more accepting. They were also more sympathetic, he thought, because any identifiably Black features led Whites to consider them Black. And no, he had no identity problem or conflict. He was an "Afro-Saxon," simple as that. His self-description provoked a confused silence and then good-natured laughter. It quickly made the rounds; Inspector Khan had not been on the job for two weeks before hearing it from someone.

In Cambridge, one saw relatively few Black faces in and around the university in comparison to South Asian ones. Inspector Khan had been one of these faces as a student and was now rising up the professional ladder, albeit not in the kind of prestigious profession his parents had hoped for. He had benefitted from a middle-class upbringing and a good school that prepared him well for Cambridge. Inspector Davidson, by contrast, had gone to a state school in London and then to Royal Holloway in Surrey, to which he had commuted from home. He had taken a degree in information security, one of the university's more distinguished programmes. From there, he went into the Metropolitan Police Force. He paired off with a woman who worked for Cambridge University Press, and after a year of unpleasant commuting, he sought a transfer to Cambridgeshire Police. It took another year for a position to open up.

In spite of their different backgrounds, the two inspectors got on well from the start. Inspector Davidson went out of his way to show his younger colleague the ropes and had him over for dinner on two occasions. Inspector Khan appreciated this courtesy and reciprocated by cooking an Italian meal for him and his partner. Asked if he ever prepared Indian food, he said no, as he ate it, every time he visited his family. It was also highly labour intensive, far more so than the risotto he had just made, which was the outer limit of his patience with food preparation.

The bomb expert telephoned Inspector Davidson a few minutes after ten a.m. He was about to send over his report but wanted to discuss his findings and their implications. The device could never have exploded, he said, because the fuse would not have worked. A bomb, or any explosive device, has several components. There is a charge to be detonated, a fuse that triggers the charge, and in bombs of this kind, a timer to set off an electrical current to trigger the fuse. All must function for the device to explode.

"The fuse was a dud. In a design of this type, the timer is connected to batteries that convey a charge to the fuse. But this fuse was filled with an inert substance, and the electrical charge would have had no effect. By itself, it could not have triggered the main charge."

"Why use such a fuse?" Inspector Davidson wanted to know.

"There are two possibilities," the bomb expert explained. "This bomb is what I call a standard Internet device. There are any number of websites with diagrams, pictures, and instructions on how to make them. The timer and wires you can buy anywhere because they are ordinary items with multiple legitimate purposes. The fuse and explosive you have to assemble yourself. I understand, however, that ready-made fuses are available for sale illegally. Perhaps our bomber bought one thinking it would function."

"Is there no way of testing it beforehand?"

"Testing involves using it, and you can only do that once. A cautious bomber could buy, say, three fuses of the same kind from the same supplier and set off two with an electrical charge from the same timer. If they worked, he could be reasonably certain the third would as well."

"Do we know this fuse was purchased?"

"No, we don't. The bomber may have put it together himself. Fuse parts are readily available."

"Then there are the warnings," said Inspector Davidson. "If you want the bomb to go off, you don't put a warning in the mail and phone another one in. If there's overkill in this project, it is in the warnings, and we can reasonably infer that the bomber wanted to make sure that his device was discovered before it detonated. But I have a question for you."

"Fire away… if that's not an inappropriate expression."

"What time was the bomb set to explode? Can you tell that from the timer?"

"You're right on the money. That's where I was going next. The timer was set hours after the warning, another precaution to make certain that the bomb did not detonate when the police and SOCOs were on the scene."

"How considerate."

"So even a working fuse would not have made a difference as I would have cut the wires from timer to fuse well in advance of the timer going off and the batteries sending their charge. We might even consider the possibility that the bomber deliberately used a faulty fuse."

"You think that a possibility?"

"Why not? He gave two advance warnings. Perhaps the faulty fuse was a fail-safe device to make sure there would be no detonation even if the warnings were ignored."

"Then why put a bomb in the professor's office?"

"That, Detective, is your problem."

XVIII: Saturday Evening

Constable Ryan was a patient man and known to be good with computers. He had designed a couple of apps he was now trying to market. For both these reasons, Inspector Khan gave him the task of identifying the Toyota Auris with the registration that did not show up on the national database. Several of the constable's colleagues looked at the CCTV again and agreed that he had read the registration correctly. One possibility the inspector and constable considered was that the driver had altered the numbers. With one letter changed, there were twenty-five possibilities, and with one number changed, there were nine possibilities. Changing one letter and one number created two hundred and twenty-five possible combinations. Two letters and one number raised it to five thousand six hundred and twenty-five. Doing it the stubby pencil way would require him to write out all these combinations and search for them one at a time. He wasn't sure if madness or retirement would come first. Instead, he wrote a simple programme to do the work for him; it would generate all the combinations arising from possible changes and search the national database for each of them.

The challenge was to collect the results in an efficient way. Normally, they appeared on the computer screen, and those initiating searches were expected to write them down or copy and paste them into a file. To do this manually for even two thousand and twenty-five searches would take a long time. With any luck, there would not be much information to capture because they were limiting the search to one make of car. But he would still have to monitor two thousand and twenty-five searches for car types. He wrote his programme to scan the results for any Toyota Auris that appeared on the screen, to temporarily halt the search at that finding, and to make a sound to get his attention. He thought of using the "Silly Farts" sound clip for this purpose, as it seemed so à propos, but it would not go down well in an open office where he had his cubicle. Instead, he chose "Crickets Chirping at Night". It took him only a few hours to write and test the programme and less than an hour to debug it. As the final test, he typed "Toyota Auris" and broke into a big smile when the crickets started chirping. He immediately lowered the volume when another constable in the next cubicle suggested in an irritated voice that he call the exterminator.

The next problem was conceptual: should he change the first letter and one or more numbers, and if so, which of them to change? In theory, the owner could alter all the letters and numbers, although this would be a challenge. He would also be at risk driving a car with a registration that looked like it had been tampered with. Changes in four letters and four numbers resulted in over two billion possibilities. If a search took five seconds on average, a comprehensive search would take 3,559,570 hours or a little more than four hundred and six years. By then they would all be dead, and of equal importance, his programme, and the language in which it was written would be history, and in all likelihood, so would automobiles. Perhaps the owner of the car knew something about probability and reasoned that he would be safe from detection.

The constable needed to shorten the search process, and this was not a software problem. He put himself in the owner's shoes and asked what he would do if he were to change his own registration. It had two numbers and five letters. Some letters and numbers would be harder to change than others. The letters "A" and "X," for example, are not easily transformed but could be pasted over, he supposed. The letter "E" is easily made into an "F", "P" into a "B", "B" into "I", "G" into "O", and "V" into "W". With numbers, "1" could be made "4", "6" transformed into "8" and possibly, "9" into "8", although that would be more difficult. By reading the two letters and four numbers that showed up on the CCTV, he could work backwards and construct a smaller number of possibilities by changing only the letters and numbers that were easiest to transform with a few strokes of brush or pen.

He pursued this strategy, and to be more confident about it, asked two colleagues to do the same. They all agreed that the letter "F" on the CCTV picture of the registration could have been an "E" and on the two numbers that were easiest to change. This gave them two thousand and twenty-five possibilities, a manageable number to search. The other constables were now as interested as he was to see if they got any hits.

They discovered that one thousand and ninety-six of the two thousand and twenty-five possibilities had been assigned to motor vehicles, and of those, twenty-nine were Toyota Aurises. This was not surprising as it was a popular model. One of the vehicles was reported as stolen in Bradford, where its owner lived. They flagged it right away and sought an update. It was still missing, and they asked the deputy commissioner to make its whereabouts a national police priority.

It was five p.m., but the constable and his associates were charged up and keen to continue with their search. One of them confessed with a grin that he would have to miss dinner with his in-laws. They directed their attention to the remaining vehicles. The CCTV was in black-and-white, and they could not eliminate cars on the basis of colour. Year of make was of little use because recent models looked very similar, and the CCTV footage they had did not provide full side views of cars. They decided to concentrate on owners and their addresses. Here too, there were choices to make. Owners were not necessarily drivers; they could not automatically rule out an Auris owned by a seventy-year-old pensioner. Such an unlikely suspect for a double murder could have loaned his car to his grandson. It made sense to concentrate, at least at the outset, on vehicles registered in Cambridgeshire and its environs, and there were seven. They divided up the task of running owner names through the police computer to see if any of them had a record.

***

Elaine and Peter had an early evening booking at the tennis club. Each would have preferred another form of exercise, but they were loath to lose their time slot, which could easily happen if they cancelled. They met at the edge of the court, and this time embraced. They waited behind the wire cage for the foursome in front of them to finish, collect their balls, sleeve their racquets, put towels and balls in holdalls, and exit the court. Elaine and Peter entered in turn, warmed up and played an hour of hard tennis. Peter did not know which he was enjoying more: the game or the prospect of what was likely to follow.

They showered, changed, and met up at the front desk. They travelled separately to Elaine's flat as she had come on her motorbike

167

and he in his car. Inside the flat, the door carefully locked, and their weapons and mobiles even more carefully set aside, Elaine opened her bottle of pinot grigio. She filled their glasses and motioned to Peter to follow her to the sofa in the sitting room. They exchanged stories about what happened after being dragged out of Elaine's bed by their telephone summons. Peter recounted how he had arrived at Leinster College only after the bomb expert had severed the wires to the fuse and given the all clear. He and Inspector Khan were largely superfluous to the crime scene, and like everyone else, had to wait for the SOCOs to finish their work. There was really nobody they wanted to interview again at the college about Sid's murder, and certainly not at night and in the immediate aftermath of a bomb scare. Inspector Davidson was in charge of the investigation They largely stood around and, when they finally left, were waylaid by a local reporter. Elaine's return to work had been equally inconsequential. She was given her hospital beat as a precautionary measure and spent a quiet and uneventful night.

"What do you propose we should do?" Elaine asked.

"The choice is yours," Peter replied.

"We could start where we left off."

Peter took Elaine into his arms.

***

The coroner had nagging thoughts that perhaps he had been too quick off the mark with his report. He needed to consult a chemist. He might know if the active ingredient in the drug that had been used to immobilize the murder victims could be produced in a laboratory and how easy it would be to do. He remembered meeting a university chemist at a bridge party a year or two back and had been racking his brain for his name. His wife did not remember him at all, and he was not sure he had provided her with much in the way of a useful description.

At lunch the next day, his wife had a pleasant surprise for him. She had called a couple of her card-playing friends, and one of them remembered the evening and the man in question. He was Ian Bricknell, a Cambridge chemist, and a very good bridge player. Her friend recalled a rather ordinary hand he had played in a daring and successful manner that evening. The coroner would normally have been interested in the details but was anxious for his wife to finish her description and pass along the contact details. Her friend had Professor Bricknell's home and office phone numbers.

The coroner was not going to disturb him at home, so called his office and left a message. It was returned later in the day when he was working in the garden and did not hear the landline ring. Their telephone tag continued into the next morning when the two men finally connected. The coroner explained that he was involved in a criminal investigation and might benefit from a chat with a distinguished chemist. He regretted that he had no funds to offer a consulting fee but promised that he would not take much of the professor's time. The professor said he would be happy to help the coroner and the police. He surmised that it was a matter best not discussed on the telephone and invited the coroner to come to his office in the chemistry department in Lensfield Road. They agreed to meet at six p.m. that evening.

Chemistry departments are busy places. More than in many university buildings, undergraduate and postgraduate students and postdoctoral fellows are everywhere in evidence. There were proportionately fewer women, and jeans and T-shirts for both sexes were the norm. The coroner was suited, which was his normal outfit, and was pleased to be greeted by a similarly attired professor. Professor Bricknell's office was large, with many books and manuals on shelves and tables and two posters on the walls on either side of a large recently cleaned window. One was a periodic table of the elements in an attractive range of pastel colours on a black background. The other of a chubby student in a lab coat asking an invisible interlocutor: "Have you heard any good sodium jokes." His response, printed below, was "Na."

The coroner asked the professor if he knew about two bodies discovered northeast of town.

"Of course. It headed the local news until that bomb was discovered at Leinster College. Has something else happened?"

No, the coroner reassured him. He explained that he had done the post-mortem on the bodies and discovered that they had drowned, but before that had been immobilized by a drug used only occasionally in medical procedures.

169

"Addenbrookes and other hospitals can account for their small stocks. The same is true of the suppliers and manufacturer. We cannot figure out where the killer or killers got their hands on the drug."

"I see the problem," said the professor, "but what does this have to do with me?"

"There's more. The anaesthesia in question relies on a natural substance that is extracted from a tropical plant at a particular time in its cycle. It is then refined. The molecule that is the active ingredient is found in tandem with a closely related one that is even more toxic. Unless the two are effectively separated, the drug cannot be used safely."

"How interesting."

"I've been wondering if the molecule might be synthesized. Could someone with access to a university laboratory produce it, or perhaps even do this at home if they had the relevant technical knowledge?"

"That would depend on the molecule, how much of it you need and in what degree of purity."

The coroner had previously asked the police to ask the drug manufacturer for information on the chemical makeup and took copies of their letter and accompanying appendices out of his briefcase to show Professor Bricknell. The professor read the letter and studied the formulae and diagrams of the molecule in the appendices.

"This is a tricky business. How much chemistry do you know?"

"I did organic and inorganic in university and a couple of courses specific to my profession."

"What I am about to tell you is a first approximation, of course. I'll do some reading and perhaps consult a colleague or two. I could get back to you with a written report. Before I go on, it would be helpful to know how soon you need this."

"Let's start with your off-the-cuff thoughts. If you rule out the prospect of an amateur replicating the drug, I probably won't need a follow-on report. I'll advise the police to go back and look again at the chain of supply from manufacturer to hospitals."

"Well, the short answer is no, an amateur would not be able to synthesize the drug. The molecule in question appears to be highly unstable and needs to be bound to another one to keep it from breaking down. Once bound, it is inert and of no medical use. It has to be released

170

from its bond by a catalyst, and that must happen immediately before use. I don't know how a highly trained amateur, or even a chemistry professor like me, would be able to do this on his own. It requires — I'm fairly certain about this — some very specialized and expensive equipment and a lot of knowledge about the compound. If I were to look anywhere, it would be for some rogue technician who pilfered some of the refined drug and diluted the container from which it came to cover up his tracks. But I'll make some inquiries anyway if you like."

"This is enormously helpful. You put my mind to rest about my earlier report. I'll tell the police to redouble their efforts."

The two men shook hands, and the coroner took his leave.

***

Inspector Khan was keen to get away from Cambridge. But Peter had made it unambiguously clear that he had plans tonight and wanted no interruption this time. Inspector Khan accordingly had a chat with Inspector Davidson, who promised, if necessary, to cover for him. He took a crowded rush-hour train to London but had reached the Cambridge station early enough to walk towards the south end of the platform and secure a seat in the lead car of the train. When it reached King's Cross, he would be out of the station in no time.

He looked forward to the forty-five-minute journey and planned to catch up on two days of the *Guardian*. It was not to be. Across from him sat a rotund, thirtyish man in a Chelsea shirt with a tablet on the table that separated their seats. As they pulled out of the station, the sound of the train was insufficient to block the cheering and commentary coming from the programme on his machine. The inspector looked around and noticed that he was not the only one displeased by the noise. The two people sharing the table on the other side of the aisle were obviously uncomfortable but had not said anything. How English, he thought. They would suffer all the way to King's Cross rather than risk an incident. The yobbo responsible for the disturbance was undoubtedly counting on their stiff upper lips. Still hopeful that one of the other passengers would speak up, the inspector tried to concentrate on an article about reduced speed limits in certain London boroughs, but without much success. Exasperation prodded him into action.

He leaned across to address the man making the disturbance, asking him politely to use his headphones instead of the speaker. The man ignored him. The inspector tried again with no effect. He asked a third time and pointed out that the noise was probably bothering at least half the passengers in this section of the car. Nobody else spoke up, and the man looked up and told him to bugger off. Inspector Khan was now angry. He paused to calm himself before confronting his antagonist. "I'm going to ask you once more," he said, "to use your headphones and lower the volume. If you don't do as I ask, I'm summoning the conductor."

"Fuck off," the man said.

"Turn it off, and I'll leave you alone."

"And if not?" came the belligerent answer.

The encounter had now escalated uncomfortably. Reluctantly, Inspector Khan reached into his jacket and took out his warrant card and shoved it under the man's nose.

"Turn the machine off, or I'll turn you off," he said in a firm and loud voice.

The man glowered at him but swiped the tablet, the screen went dark, and the sound ceased. The inspector stared back at him for a moment, put his warrant card away, and picked up his newspaper to resume reading. The woman next to him immediately thanked him, and the man opposite nodded his approval. Standing by the door at the end of the journey, two other people thanked him for his intervention. *A bloody bunch of cowards*, he said to himself before pressing the exit button when the little ring of lights around it came on. The door slid open, and he made a dash for the Tube.

The underground line ride was crowded and uncomfortable but blessedly silent. He exited at Belsize Park, suffered through the lift queue, as one of the two lifts was being serviced, and emerged from the station in the warm London evening. His aunt lived a short walk away in a large second floor flat. She was in good enough shape to climb the stairs, even with her shopping, and she must have done a lot of that given the spread that awaited him. She had invited his mother and his sister and her family. Her flat was opulent, with thick beige carpets everywhere and a few antique prayer rugs to break the monotony and add colour. He particularly liked the one under the glass coffee table, whose design and odd imperfection revealed imagination and impatience. Girls made such rugs for their trousseaus, and this one he would have liked to have met.

His interest in tribal carpets derived from exposure to his aunt's collection. She would go to auctions and bid and, on several occasions, had invited him to join her at Bonhams or the Victoria and Albert Museum to admire their collections. Her taste above floor level differed from his, and more so at every additional increment of altitude. Her coffee and side tables were mahogany and tasteful, although more elaborate than he liked. They supported a few attractive objects, including a Ming vase turned into a lamp sometime early in the last century and a small and very elegant Benin bronze antelope. The animal was poised as if ready to jump and had incised circles on its body that also invoked the expectation of imminent movement.

These stunning pieces shared the available table and shelf space with a host of other items of less artistic merit, including many family photographs in gold and bronze frames. The few works of interesting art were almost lost in the crowd. To admire them required a major mental effort to block these other objects out. Hanging on the wall were several prints, but also several tempera paintings of the Dorset coast, where his aunt went for holidays. The paintings were of uneven quality. His aunt might have purchased them more as mementoes than as works of art. On the ceiling was an ornate and, he thought, garish, rock crystal chandelier. Somehow, almost everything seemed to fit together, and he had pondered more than once why this was so. After much thought, he came to the conclusion that his aunt's character and force of will imposed unity, or more accurately, collaborative coexistence, on the diverse things she had collected.

Making sense of her furnishings helped him make sense of her life and, to some extent, that of his parents and his own. Inspector Khan's aunt and mother were born in England a few years after their Siraiki parents had emigrated from the Sind. Their father was a classic rags-to-riches story. His first job in Birmingham was for a Hindu neighbour who had recently opened an auto parts shop. He worked there for two years under the benign eye and guidance of the owner. He noticed that certain parts were relatively simple and cheap to produce but had astounding markups because they came from the car manufacturers. With the money he had saved and some co-investment from his Hindu neighbour, he bought on hire purchase the few machine tools and other equipment he needed to produce these parts himself. Beforehand, he had tried to interest existing car parts shops in stocking his products. His former employer aside, they had no interest because their profit margin would be smaller. He used the front room of the space he leased to set up a small shop to market what he fashioned. It was a near thing at first until word got round to car owners that he sold cheap, reliable parts. Soon, dealers were sending employees to buy them in bulk and then billing their customers at higher prices for official parts. After a few years, he was able to expand his product line and open a second store in another part of town. Ten years later, he had multiple stores and many more products. Twenty years into the business, he sold his first franchise.

He was an observant Muslim, but he saw that as no barrier to assimilation nor to friendship with South Asian immigrants of other faiths. He quickly learnt English and was deeply thankful to the United Kingdom for providing economic opportunities to him and a good and secure environment for his children. He raised his two daughters as English Muslims and was pleased that they spoke native and educated English. They excelled in school and went to university, one to Manchester and the other to University College London. Khan's mother, the younger of the two, stayed in Manchester, read maths in university, one of the few women of her generation to do so. She became a teacher in a grammar school and married a pharmacist from a family with a similar background. To her father's delight, she named her son "Rudra," a Hindu name, to honour his father's by now closest friend and business partner, the man who had first employed him.

His aunt worked in the British Museum after graduation, initially as an assistant in the business office but later as an assistant to a curator. He specialized in Persian carpets, and she was delighted to learn from him and handle these beautiful objects. She married an English South African, a pairing that initially provoked a family crisis. She wanted a secular wedding, his family a Church of England ceremony, and her parents a Muslim one. Her father was nothing if not practical and, over

174

the course of several conversations, came to realize that his daughter had different views and plans for her life. He respected her for it, although was saddened to see her assimilate to the point where there was little of her heritage left. He and his wife became reconciled to a secular wedding as it had the advantage of forestalling a Protestant one.

This generation's view of integration was not the same as their parents. Their parents mistook the ideal of British meritocracy for the practice and were highly motivated to sustain this illusion because they had left their family and homeland in the hope that they and their children would have better chances in life. Their children had fewer illusions about their acceptance in Britain but ironically were successful beyond their parents' expectations because of their greater mastery of British customs and life.

The older generation sustained their culture in a way their children would not. They tried to be as British as they could at work but sloughed off office or shop floor clothes when they came home. They sat on the floor, ate with their fingers, sang tunes from the old country, and socialized with others like themselves.

His aunt had neither entirely abandoned her parents' culture nor accepted English culture uncritically. She rejoiced in an increasingly multi-cultural Britain because it opened the space for her to mix and match from diverse traditions. This was evident in her personality, dress, cooking, and above all, in her art. She created pastiches of seemingly unrelated things that somehow came together, in her hands at least, to form new wholes. His parents did something similar, but on a muted scale, more privately and less adventurously. His aunt had accordingly been his role model since early adolescence and inspired his first efforts at self-fashioning.

His sister experienced a more troubled adolescence and initially recoiled from the choices she faced. Refuge is a common teenage strategy. Not infrequently in girls, especially those who mature physically before they are ready to cope with the consequences, and wear clothes designed to hide their curves and make them less attractive. Inspector Khan thought his younger sister had done the Muslim version of this by adopting a hijab. In her case, the headscarf was intended to forestall cultural choices. For almost a year, she took refuge in a more traditional version of Islam, much to the horror of her parents, brother, and many of her school friends. She emerged from her headscarf a more confident person and more at home in her two cultures. Unlike her brother and aunt, she sought no synthesis but rather appeared to live contentedly with her dual identifications.

The crisis came when anti-Muslim and anti-immigration sentiment heated up in the UK. She responded by becoming less secular and more religious, but also by demonstrating her Englishness to all those around her. In the interim, she had married a gentle and successful physician, also of Pakistani background, but a Punjabi. He worked at UCL hospital and specialized in geriatric medicine. Punjabis traditionally looked down on Sindhis, and it took some fast-talking before his parents agreed to the marriage. Relations between the families were correct but cool until the young couple produced a child. They then warmed up quickly.

Their six-year-old daughter Elizabeth was the apple of the inspector's eye. He sat next to her at dinner and spent a half-hour afterwards reading together the new Dr Seuss book he had brought her. His sister and her husband were delighted with the attention he showed her, as was Elizabeth.

***

For the first time in weeks, our murderer was unhappy. The elation promoted by his crime, the ensuing investigation, and his faux bomb in Leinster College had disappeared. This kind of high is intense but short-lived, and efforts to extend it are bound to fail. Repetition of the behaviour that brought it about is the only effective strategy. Just like sex, he thought.

For our murderer, the two forms of elation became reinforcing. He experienced a figurative tingling in his head and one of a more literal kind in his groin. This arousal was a response to what he had accomplished but also to what he envisaged. His future actions were focused on Mrs Mason, for whom he increasingly carried a torch. He did not know how this had happened and why he had become so smitten by her, more accurately, consumed. She was attractive, but not noticeably so. She had thick brown hair, with a nice sheen to it, and a long angular face whose most prominent feature was a pair of attentive dark eyes. She had a longish neck that nicely complemented her face, and she moved in an elegant and cat-like way. She was not particularly curvaceous, and he had always been drawn to full-figured women, whose fleshy protuberances he loved to stroke and fondle. There was little on offer here, and his fantasies about her focused more on her submission and the mutual pleasures this would provide.

In the course of time, this fantasy had become a fixation. He thought about Mrs Mason many times during the day, took the occasional furtive photograph of her, and had even purchased a good camera and telephoto lens for the purpose. He had a bulletin board in his bedroom where he tacked up these photos and a story that had appeared in the local paper about her a little over a year back. He made attempts, not always successful, to get himself invited to events she was likely to attend. He was careful never to stalk her, or at least not to do what he considered stalking. He did not follow or telephone her, at least not until Sid was out of the way. And he did this only once, after what he thought was a decent interval, to invite her for a drink. She turned him down and did not hide her irritation at his phone call. He chalked this off to her roiled emotional state and decided to be patient before approaching her again.

Her rejection nevertheless ate away at him. He had taken an enormous risk in murdering her husband. He had done her a huge favour. Even casual encounters with Sid indicated what a bastard he was, and he had interacted with him on many occasions over the years. Sid had dominated his wife in an offensive and public way. It was not at all, he told himself, the kind of domination he had in mind. She would fulfil herself, not become imprisoned, by giving in to him. This and less exciting forms of liberation were now available to her since Sid had been removed from her life. He hoped she would come to realize this and be thankful for it. Ultimately, he would make it known that he had been responsible for her liberation. But that would have to wait until well after they had paired off. That recognition, he expected, would make her even more beholden to him.

He was feeling down because of the telephone call, which he played over and over again in his mind. He had no control over Mrs Mason's emotions, so he would have to wait until things took their natural course and she became interested once again in men. This might take some time, and there was nothing he could do to hasten the process. He did not like this at all because it brought home his powerlessness, something he had always tried to avoid. It put him in a position where any effort to influence events had the potential to make him more powerless. He had enough insight to know that he was responsible for the dilemma he now faced.

XIX: Monday Morning

Inspector Khan walked to work at his usual time feeling very much refreshed by his Saturday evening in London and uninterrupted bike ride in Thetford Forest on Sunday. He had not thought much about the double murder over the weekend. He knew that time away from the office was good for his emotional wellbeing and his job. He might return to the case with a new perspective, which in this instance was desperately needed. He had a couple of ideas whilst walking to work and was anxious to share them with Peter. The two men would have preferred to do this in the local café, but Inspector Khan thought it wise to put in face time as he had left early on Friday. Peter was in a particularly good mood; Inspector Khan had not seen him like this for some time. He could only conclude that his Friday engagement had been the start of a very satisfying couple of days.

Peter had also put the case aside for the weekend, along with his and Elaine's weapons and mobile phones. The phones had remained blessedly silent, and they were not disturbed until the Monday morning light came through the windows to awaken them. In the heat of the moment, Elaine had forgotten about the need to draw the curtains the night before. They had a relaxed breakfast of toast, jam, and tea, and Peter then showered, dressed, and sauntered into the office. Elaine had a free morning.

The two detectives talked their way through the case from the beginning. They started with Sid's disappearance.

"Scotty didn't just beam him aboard," Peter said.

"And even if he did," the inspector responded, "somebody must have given him the order to do so."

"Just where was he abducted?" Peter asked. "It wasn't in the station, as somebody would have seen a ruckus. It wasn't on the train or in King's Cross for the same reason. It might have been in London, and if so, it had to be between the station and the café where he never showed up. That rules out the LSE, although one of the professors I interviewed at

Leinster, told me that this institution hijacked several faculty from Cambridge, in recent years. The logical place is somewhere between his home and the Cambridge station."

"Agreed," said the inspector. "Although nothing shows up on CCTV on his expected route to the station, and he never appears at the station."

"There are gaps along the route, and the murderer could have figured out where they are so he could snatch Sid out of their sight."

"An abduction is not an easy thing to pull off," the inspector said. "In old gangster films you see people hustled into cars and forced to sit silently between two thugs, but that's the cinema. Even in these films, it takes several people to pull off an abduction: a driver and a couple of heavies. If we follow this line of argument, we are talking about a murder conspiracy involving two, possibly three people — and a double abduction."

"I see the problem. Something of this nature would not have gone unnoticed, especially during rush hour when lots of people are on the streets. Although, it was raining, and people had umbrellas up limiting their visibility."

"Even so, an abduction would almost certainly have attracted someone's attention unless they pulled it off with absolute precision."

"I'll throw another spanner in the works," Peter said. "Sid was hardly an easy-going type. He was prickly, aggressive, and suspicious, certainly not the kind of person to climb meekly into the back of a car when ordered to do so."

"That sounds right to me. For all these reasons, I don't think he was abducted. It's much more likely that he entered a car willingly. It's a nasty day, you're on your way to the station, a car pulls over, the window comes down, and somebody shouts, 'Morning, Sid. Want a lift?'" Sid looks across, recognizes the driver, and unless he's an exercise fanatic, opens the door and hops in."

"And then what?" asked Peter.

"Here's where it gets more speculative. Somehow, the murderer needs to disable Sid to drive him out of town, carry him unresisting to the dock, and tip him into the basin. How do you do that, without Sid resisting, and whilst you are behind the wheel of a car?"

"Beats me," said Peter.

"Me too," said the inspector. "It would be difficult to pull a syringe out of your raincoat or even lift it from the dashboard, wave it at Sid and somehow jab him in just the right place where the sedative would have an almost instant effect."

"And if he did," said Peter, "what's to keep Sid from keeling over? Somebody driving through Cambridge with a passenger's head against the dashboard might be noticed."

"Especially if the body shifted during a turn and came to rest against the steering wheel."

"Indeed," said the inspector. "That's why he needed an accomplice. What if Jaime was in the back seat and jabbed Sid in the neck the moment he sat down? He could also have reached around and steadied him as they drove."

"He would also be useful in carrying him to the dock," Peter added. "A deadweight body is heavy and would be hard for one person to remove from the car and drag any distance. As I recall, there was no sign of drag marks between the road and the dock."

"That's correct," said the inspector. "There had to be at least two people."

"The same with Jaime then," Peter reasoned. "He was young, fit, and presumably harder to abduct and subdue. But do they make two runs: Sid first and then Jaime? It would have been that much more difficult to abduct a second person with the first one sedated and visible in the front seat."

"There's another problem to consider," the inspector said. "And that's the link between Sid and Jaime, and between them and the murderer. We've got nowhere on this puzzle, and not for lack of trying."

"What do you think happened?"

"The most elegant explanation," the inspector suggested, "is to make Jaime the accomplice. Then there's only one abduction, and the murderer has help in the car and at the dock."

"But Jaime was also murdered," said Peter.

"Here's the ingenious part," the inspector said. "Jaime was hired by the murderer to help him out. They get to the dock, haul Sid from the car, and truss him up with rope and weights. At that point, the murderer pulls a second syringe out of his pocket and jabs it into the back of the unsuspecting Jaime. He doesn't have to drive or carry him anywhere. All he has to do is weigh him down, tie him up and tip both bodies into the basin. What could be easier and more elegant!"

"And more heartless," Peter added. "The killer recruits Jaime, who is keen to make a quick bundle, and probably with some cock-and-bull story. Jaime does not seem the type of lad to become a hired gun. But who knows what the killer told him? Maybe Jamie never knew he was going to be an accomplice in a murder. We're undoubtedly up against a man with absolutely no scruples and with the intellectual ability to conjure up and execute a complicated scheme."

"All the more so," the inspector said, "when you factor in his ability somehow to get hold of the sedative and load it successfully in the syringes. But any of the alternative scenarios are far less credible."

The two men speculated about how the murderer recruited Jaime. Where had they met, and what inducement had he been offered? Did he know that he was taking part in a murder, or was he naïve enough to be hoodwinked?

Their discussion was interrupted by a telephone call from the coroner. He reported on his conversation with the chemist. He explained how he had begun to wonder if the drug used to immobilize the two victims might be synthesized. A chemist at the university ruled it out on the grounds that it was a difficult compound to extract or reproduce and needed to be combined with another substance for use. He urged the inspector to redouble his efforts to discover how some of the drug had been diverted from the factory, supplier, or hospital. He passed along the chemist's speculation that it was probably an inside job and not noticed by anyone because the batch, or batches, from which it had been extracted had been diluted with a neutral agent.

The telephone call was followed by a knock on the door from the constable who had been working on the car registration problem. The inspector invited him to take a seat, and he and Peter listened to his detailed narrative of his efforts to discover the owner of the car. One good prospect, he thought, was a Toyota Auris stolen in Bradford and still missing. Their creative manipulation of registration numbers had turned up nine possibilities in Cambridgeshire. They had run the owners' names through the computer, but none had a record or seemed suspicious in any way. Nor were they associated with Leinster College, or at least with the list the master had provided them. The constable handed over a memory stick to the inspector with the list of names and whatever other information Internet searches had turned up about them.

The inspector thanked the constable, and he and Peter resumed their conversation once he had left.

"Where does this leave us?" the inspector asked Peter.

"I suppose we should revisit the drug question. Maybe someone with the right qualifications could speak to the drug company and probe the possibility of something along the lines of what the chemist suggested."

"Yes, we can do that. I'll ask the deputy commissioner to look into it. It will have to be a detective on whose turf the drug lab or labs — I don't know how many they are — are located. The labs are almost certain to deny that it can happen or happen on their premises. But it's worth a try. Another visit from a detective may just prick someone's conscience or encourage some administrator to look more closely at their procedures for safeguarding this and other drugs."

"The car angle doesn't sound very promising," Peter said.

"I agree. But after all the creative work this constable did, we're duty-bound to follow it up. Can you ask a couple of members of the task force to check out these cars and their owners?"

"Will do, sir. I'm not optimistic. We'll find the owners without difficulty, but I'm not persuaded the car is related to our case. Our clever constable has manipulated letters and numbers to get a match, but by his own admission, he may not have changed the right ones. He said something about there being some millions of possibilities."

"I agree," said the inspector. "But it's all we have to go on, and we have to give it our best shot."

"We could try yet again to find some connection between Sid and Jaime. Working on your assumption that Sid hired him, how did he find him, and where did they meet? Certainly, Sid would not have taken him to the college or home, and we know that he never showed up at Jaime's café."

"I've considered this problem. The murderer needed an assistant and best to find some young man up to the job physically, but not all that swift. Not that Jaime lacked any marbles, but he was inexperienced, greedy, and easily misled. We know he sold drugs, which offered evidence to any passer-by that he was on the far side of the law and likely to break the law in other ways if the money was right. We also know that he had a wad of cash and was expecting more from some sugar daddy."

"Let's go back to our murderer and how he found Jaime," Inspector Khan said. "He's unlikely to be an addict as his planning and cover-up have been clever and consistent. But he might well have seen Jaime on the street selling drugs, checked up on him, and then made contact on the street telling him he had a proposition that would bring him bigger rewards than drug dealing."

"He should show up on CCTV then," Peter said.

"Jaime thought about that too and chose a place in a black zone for his drug deals. Maybe he's visible arriving and leaving, and the murderer too if we knew who to look for, but we don't."

"It's too bad we lost him in Coe Fen."

"More evidence," said the inspector, "of his practical intelligence. He took a route he knew would lead him off camera. Presumably he and the murderer would have met someplace where they would not be recorded and where nobody was likely to recognize them. I take back what I said earlier about Jamie's intelligence."

"Any thoughts about where they might meet?"

"Last week I bought some jeans. I used the changing room in the back of the store to try them on. It would be a perfect place to confer unobserved with someone. The other person, assuming it was someone of the same gender, would only have to come into the store, grab some jeans and change in the adjacent stall. We could talk quietly through the walls or even in the foyer if no other customers were around. Then we come out separately, pay for or hand back our jeans, and go off in separate directions."

"You don't think we're going to find any evidence of their meeting?"

"I doubt it. If we knew what the murderer looked like, we could circulate his picture, and something might come up."

"We don't and looking at hours of CCTV coverage won't yield anything even if the murderer walks by five times."

"You're right, sir," said Peter. "If only we had some description of him from one of Jaime's friends. Jaime was indiscreet in bragging about his newfound source of wealth but careful to protect the man's identity."

"There's a briefing coming up on the bomb in Leinster College," said the inspector. "Shall we mosey over and have a listen?"

"By all means. Have they something new to report?"

"I think not. It'll cheer us up to hear another investigation foundering."

***

Inspector Davidson had made little progress on the bomb through no fault of his own. He had interviewed Professor Nejami upon his return and found him a thoughtful, soft-spoken, and attractive fellow. The professor could provide a long list of groups that might want to harm him, and, as the police knew, he had received prior threats. He was shocked by the bomb but pleased to know it had been meant to scare, not kill. He inferred that it was a message to him to keep a lower public profile.

Inspector Davidson voiced his suspicion to the gathered group of police that the bomb might not have been directed against Professor Nejami. They had received a telephone warning from Jamie Peeker's phone, the young man killed together with Professor Mason. The two cases seemed to be connected in some way — or somebody wants them to think they are. He quizzed Professor Nejami at length about his relationship to Professor Mason and discovered, to his surprise, that the dead professor had always treated him with courtesy and respect. He could never figure out why he had a bye on being the target of his colleague's vicious barbs. He never complained, just considered himself lucky. He had no light to shed on the Mason murder case.

There was no new information on the bomb. The bomb expert reported that it was an easily assembled device made from readily available components. No special knowledge was needed.

"Ages four and up, and some assembly required," quipped one of the detectives in the audience.

"Yes," Inspector Davidson said, "but in this kit, the batteries are included. We've interviewed extensively in the college and looked at all the CCTV footage, not only that evening but back to the time when Professor Nejami left his office to catch a flight to the continent. There are lots of people coming through the college, especially during daytime hours because the back gate is open, and a walk through the gardens and courts offers a pleasant shortcut into town. There are only three CCTVs on site: at the two gates and in the underground car park. Faculty and students are adamant about their privacy and voted against installing the surveillance equipment found at many other institutions. Ironically, Professors Mason and Nejami were among the most outspoken opponents of the cameras. The master convinced the fellows to permit the three they have on the grounds of necessary security. Until now, it was a workable compromise."

Inspector Davidson looked briefly at his notes before continuing. "We've had no better luck with the two warnings. The written one sent to the college was composed of letters cut from an opinion piece Professor Nejami wrote for the *Daily Telegraph*."

"How do we know that?" one of the detectives asked.

"The title of the article was in a larger font and in bold typeface. We treated these letters as a rebus and played with them until the title emerged. It was an article about British Muslims, and we did a Google search, and voilà, Professor Nejami was identified as the author."

"Very impressive," said a detective.

"Maybe, but also frustrating. There were no fingerprints, the glue was a common brand, and the paper a standard kind used for photocopying. And the envelope told us nothing."

"Finally, there's the telephone call," Inspector Davidson said. "Our experts say it is a man trying to sound like a woman by speaking in a falsetto voice. The mouthpiece of the phone was covered to muffle his voice, and as you know, it was made on the pay-as-you-go mobile that belonged to the young man dragged out of the basin with Professor Mason. The voice experts say it is an educated person trying hard, but not succeeding, in sounding like a less educated Geordie."

"A Geordie?" said another detective.

"Sorry to disappoint," said Inspector Davidson, provoking laughter. "According to our expert, it was a parody of a Geordie voice."

"What's the difference?" someone else said, provoking laughter.

"Here's the question," Inspector Davidson said. "Why place a bomb designed not to explode in Professor Nejami's office and send two warnings to alert the police and the college? Whoever did this, accepts risks for little gain. And the telephone message links the bomb to the murders, making us that much more intent on finding the perpetrator of the bomb hoax. If we could fathom the bomb maker's motives, we might have a chance of finding him."

"Have you ruled out hatred of Professor Nejami by Muslim extremists?" a member of the task force asked.

"No, I haven't. But it's not at the top of my list. Why would they send a bomb that didn't explode and multiple warnings about it? More to the point, why would they use Jaime's telephone? And where would they get it from if they had not been somehow involved in these two murders? There's nothing linking Professor Mason or Jamie to Islam."

Inspector Davidson looked across to Inspector Khan and asked him if he could shed any light on this mystery.

"None whatsoever," he replied. "We've examined this question in reverse. We've asked ourselves what the bombing might have to do with our murders, and we've drawn a blank. If the same culprit is responsible for the murders and the bomb, he would presumably want to keep us from reaching this conclusion. He would have every incentive not to use Jamie's mobile. We therefore considered the possibility that there is no connection, and the bomber just found the phone somewhere and chose to use it because it could not be connected to him. This seems unlikely as none of Jaime's other personal effects, like keys or wallet, have turned up, nor have Professor Mason's. Their killer or killers were careful to dispose of them and presumably would have done so with Jaime's mobile as well."

"How do you explain it then?" asked a uniformed policeman.

"We considered a third possibility, a bit far-fetched but logical. The perpetrator deliberately used the phone to make us think the murders and the bomb are connected. He would only want to do this if the two events are unconnected, and he somehow believes he will benefit from making us think otherwise."

"Why would he do that?" the same policeman asked.

"That's what Peter and I have been asking ourselves. One possibility is to direct our attention to Islamic extremists and away from, let's say, members of Leinster College or anyone we've identified as having a personal grudge against Professor Mason. That would be a clever move. But it would backfire if we figured it out. We would become even more intent on looking closer to home for the killer and someone from within the college who would have no problem going into Professor Nejami's entryway without arousing suspicion. A member of college would also find it easier to get access to a key that opened his set. We are redoubling our efforts to check out the alibis of fellows and staff, and the master as well. If we are right, Davidson and I are looking for the same perpetrator."

This last comment created a buzz in the audience. Until now, most of the detectives working on the bombing assumed that Muslim extremists were responsible, although they recognized the many anomalies of the case. The ensuing discussion made it evident that Inspector Khan's logic was accepted, and Inspector Davidson suggested that they work together. They would continue the formal structure of two investigations and would not rule out the possibility that the bomb was somehow connected to Professor Nejami's political views but would coordinate their efforts even more closely in the future.

XX: Monday Afternoon

Inspector Khan and Peter decided to have yet another chat with the master, the students involved in the coding scandal, and then with Mrs Mason. They would push the master harder than they had in the past. Both agreed that he was hiding something and trying hard to put relations among the fellows in the best light. As for Mrs Mason, she'd had ample time for reflection since the murder and their last interview and might remember something that might point the finger at one of her husband's colleagues. In the interim, detectives and constables would interview the local owners of any Toyota Auris that fit the description of the one caught by CCTV in Bateman Street. They would reconvene as a group later that afternoon.

The interview with the master was frustrating. Peter came away even more convinced that he was a master at obfuscation. The master was perfectly charming, offered them tea and coffee, and regaled them with amusing tales about the college and its fellows. When confronted with the argument that the bomb was almost certainly an inside job, he was just as adamant as before that none of the fellows could possibly be responsible. He thought it equally unlikely that a student had done it but confessed that he did not know them nearly as well as he did the fellows. He insisted that they had the highest admission standards and rarely encountered behavioural problems among the students. The inspector was unconvinced that the student body was problem-free and did not see intelligence as a deterrent to crime. He was tempted to say so to the master but restrained himself.

The meeting with Mrs Mason, once again at her office, was more pleasant but no more productive. They asked many of the same questions they had before and received the same answers. She still couldn't think of anyone who would want to kill her husband as opposed to seeing him taken down a peg or two. He had antagonized many of his colleagues, but none to the degree, she insisted, that they would commit violence against him. Even she — she smiled as she spoke — had never considered the option.

Inspector Khan asked Mrs Mason in an elliptical way how she was coping. He meant his question to be interpreted as an expression of sympathy, not prying, and it was received as intended. She thanked him for his concern, said she was doing as well as one could in the circumstances and was very thankful for the support of her children, colleagues, and friends. The occasional person — not the police, of course — she hastened to say, asked inappropriate questions about her husband's demise, or made equally uncalled for suggestions about how she should now lead her life as a widow. But no, she assured the inspector and Peter, nothing had happened to arouse her suspicions with regard to the murder.

They returned to the college to have one more go with the students against whom Professor Mason had brought disciplinary proceedings. In the interim, other members of the investigating team had followed up on their alibis and questioned other students about them. Most of the students claimed to be studying in their rooms, and one had a neighbour who had heard him pottering about through the thin wall that separated their flats. They all had alibis for the evening the bomb was discovered, but then it could have been placed at any time after Professor Nejami left the college. The students were ill at ease when interviewed but impressed the detectives as honestly shocked by the murder and bomb threat. One of the students Professor Mason had brought before the disciplinary committee lamented that his death had given publicity to the data scandal and did more damage to his career. The inspector acknowledged the possible truth of his remark but noted to Peter afterwards that it would not be the first time that people did something that had the opposite effect of what they intended.

**

The investigating team reconvened at five p.m. in the same room they always used. As smoking had long since been banned in public buildings, it did not reek of stale tobacco as it would have in the old days. Rather, it had the aroma of stale coffee. The cleaning service went through it early every morning but, by midday, the usual collection of food wrappers and other detritus was evident. There were whiteboards covered with photos, names, charts, scribbled text and connecting arrows, and they could be read as a sign of progress or the opposite. The mood was glum, as it had been for a whilst now because the investigation appeared to have reached a dead end. There had never been any real leads, and none of the less obvious lines of inquiry had produced anything worth pursuing, let alone promising a breakthrough.

The inspector gave a short summary of the morning's interviews. As there were no questions, he turned the floor over to DI Crawley, who had coordinated the interviews of Auris owners. He was ruddy-faced and overweight and a few years from retirement. He had a reputation as a competent detective who tended to do things by the book because he was thought to lack the imagination to do otherwise. He briefly explained how they had gone in teams of two to interview the six owners living in Cambridge and its surroundings.

"People are not usually at home on weekdays," DI Crawley explained, "so we telephoned or emailed them to make appointments at home or at work. We wanted to see the cars as well as photograph the plates and take swabs of the registration that the lab might check for paint or paint remover. We've done this with only two cars but hope to do a third this evening when the owner returns from work. She uses public transportation and leaves her car at home in a lockup. Two of the other three owners we reached we have provisionally ruled out. One of the cars was in the shop getting serviced on the day the professor disappeared, and the garage owner confirmed this for us. The other owner was on holiday in France and offered to show us his tickets and the photographs he took in the Dordogne. We're checking it out, of course, but expect to confirm his alibi. The sixth owner has not returned our telephone calls. You will be interested to learn that she works at a Cambridge college."

"Not Leinster by any chance?" Peter asked.

"I'm afraid not. But it's a nearby college if that's any consolation."

"Not really," Peter said. "Have you checked her out?"

"Nothing more at this point than running her name through the computer, and she's clean."

"What about the other three?" Peter asked.

"We can probably rule out the two whose cars we examined. They allowed us to photograph them and take a swipe of their registrations. The lab is processing the swipes, but I would be very surprised to find anything. Frankly, I think the exercise is something of a wild goose chase. As I understand it, these registrations were generated by a computer programme that selected on the basis of the fewest changes of numbers of letters. What if the owner of the car that drove down Bateman Street changed one more or less number or letter or changed a more difficult number or letter? He wouldn't be on our list. And we have nothing to link this car with a possible abduction in the vicinity."

"All true," Peter said. "But we have nothing else to go on. It makes sense to pursue this line of inquiry even if it may appear a bit far-fetched. Tell us about the person you are seeing this evening?"

"He's a Cambridge professor." Inspector Crawley looked down at his notes. "He's in the chemistry department. He was helpful enough on the telephone and agreed to shift another appointment to accommodate us at five thirty this evening."

"A chemistry professor?" asked Inspector Khan.

"Yes, that's right."

"Out of curiosity, what's his name?" asked Inspector Khan.

Inspector Crawley looked down at his notes again. "Bricknell, Ian Bricknell."

"That name rings a bell," Inspector Khan said. "What do you know about him?"

"Nothing really," said Inspector Crawley. "He came to Cambridge as a postdoc in 1983 and has been here ever since. No record, no traffic violations, divorced, no children. We could undoubtedly find out more in short order if he turns out to be a person of interest."

"If I recall correctly, this is the professor the coroner sought out for a second opinion on the anaesthetic. It could be a coincidence, but as we all know, a key rule of policing is to be suspicious of any and all coincidences. That said, there's nothing to set off alarm bells here. The professor's name came up the first time because we went to him for assistance."

"If you like," Inspector Crawley said, "we can dig around."

"I don't think it's necessary, not yet anyway," Inspector Khan said. "Treat him as you have the others. What about the woman who didn't return your calls? She seems more promising."

"I've sent Constable O'Grady to her office, and they said she called in sick this morning. It's suspicious. She's not at work and not at home. I'm going to stop by her house after work. If I don't find her, I'll see if her car is in the street. She lives in Great Wilbraham, and it would be easier to find a space there."

"You'll call if you have anything to report?"

"Absolutely," replied Inspector Crawley.

The meeting broke up, and everyone went off to perform their respective tasks with no particular enthusiasm.

***

Peter was one of the few people to leave the meeting in a good mood. He was heading off to see Elaine. She had proposed a quiet evening at home, a suggestion he found very appealing. He stopped off at the wine shop and asked the owner's advice for a red wine that would go well with the lamb shanks Elaine had promised to prepare. He suggested a pinot noir and pointed him towards one he thought excellent value.

"Have a new friend, I see."

"How did you know?" Peter replied.

"This is the third time this week you've bought a bottle of wine, and each time you put more effort into selecting it. I hope she has been appreciative."

"Oh, she has," Peter said and blushed. "And she's a fine cook."

"Have a lovely evening," the wine merchant said after Peter had paid and turned towards the door.

Peter told Elaine about his wine shop encounter and brought a smile to her face. She confessed that one of her colleagues had picked up a change in her demeanour and asked if she had met someone.

"It's hard to keep a new relationship a secret." So far I think I've succeeded at work, but the DI did make a remark in passing."

"It wouldn't be a problem if we weren't both cops."

"Thank God we work at different stations."

This last comment led to an exchange of professional gossip. Peter explained that both their investigations were stalled and how they were now busy wasting their time — but not his time, at least — tracking down the owner of the mystery Toyota that had shown up on Bateman Street the morning the professor went missing.

"Couldn't it be a real lead?"

"I doubt it. The registration seems reasonably clear on the CCTV, but there are so many ways of altering the numbers and letters that there's little reason to think our computer programme has identified the real registration."

"What's new with you?"

"Not much. A woman collapsed at the station, and we had to call an ambulance. There's still a drug watch, but we haven't caught any of the mules. It's all the more difficult to do this in Cambridge, where half the passengers are students. I'm convinced they use well-dressed professionals. They are the greediest class of people as they crave possessions that they can't afford. Some of them undoubtedly reason — and rightly so, I'm afraid — that the chance of getting caught is minimal. They also have a ready defence, just in case. They will claim that someone slipped the drug package into their briefcase when they weren't looking and that an accomplice of that person must be waiting to steal it once they arrive at King's Cross."

"Who would believe them?"

"Oh, there's always some judge willing to convince himself — and they are always men — that an educated, well-spoken, white professional from a good family must be telling the truth. And if not, he'll give him a year in prison, or perhaps only two years of community service — unlike the five or six years some other offender would get for the same crime. Our best chance is finding them with the drugs taped to their body. That's hard to explain away."

"Have you ever caught someone like that?"

"Not me, and not our station, I believe. But I've heard of it happening elsewhere."

"Do you have a profile you use to identify possible drug mules?"

"Yes, although I don't find it helpful, and neither do my colleagues. I use my intuition and look out for people who appear uncomfortable. Of course, at the beginning or end of the term, that's most of the young people on the train. Tourists also look nervous as they worry about being on the right track for the right train. They seem unlikely possibilities as it is so much easier to recruit locals, but it would be a great cover."

"Even better would be someone in a constable's uniform."

"Don't even joke about it. My colleague today zeroed in on some football fans. He's one himself and knew there were no games on in London. He wondered where they were going. Two of them were also carrying large duffel bags. He called it in, and the Met drug squad was waiting for the train. The dogs sniffed the men and the bag, and they were clean."

"Do you ever stop and search people?"

"Only if they are handsome and give some indication of being well-hung."

Peter laughed.

"Don't you have to have one of your male colleagues do a strip search?"

"Yes, if the man to be searched requests it — but they never do when it's me about to feel them up."

"I can believe it. When you finish your drink, would you show me your technique?"

"Delighted to."

XXI: Monday Evening

Inspector Davidson wondered if you could trace the computers of people who accessed bomb-making sites the way you could those who click on paedophile webpages. The department's IT person explained that the police routinely monitor these sites as well, and he could easily submit a request to see who had accessed them recently in Cambridge. A few names came up, which was more than Inspector Davidson expected, and they were all Cambridge students. Two of them were in the same college, which allowed him to interview them together.

Inspector Davidson had met with them that morning over coffee in their college's buttery. They were impressed that the police saw fit to question them but dismissed the inspector's concerns.

"We're students, not terrorists," the taller of the two young men said.

"Isn't it possible to be both?" Inspector Davidson asked.

"In theory, yes," the shorter student with tousled blond hair replied. "But we're just students, and I can easily put your concerns to rest."

"How would you do that?" the inspector asked.

The student took his laptop out of his backpack, opened the lid, waited for the screen to light up, and passed it across to the inspector to look at the page that had come up on the screen.

"This is the syllabus for a course in radicalization given in POLIS. We're writing a joint paper on websites that encourage radicalization and violent acts. We have searched a range of sites, including bomb-making ones. We're interested in finding out the extent to which they were neutral about who used them or if they were set up specifically for radicalized students." He reached into his backpack a second time and removed a copy of their paper and handed it over to the inspector.

"You're welcome to it. Perhaps you or one of your colleagues will find it interesting."

"I'll certainly have a look and get back to you if I have any further questions. My guess is they will be about the subject, not about the two of you."

The students smiled.

"One more question before I go. There's a third student at St. John's who has also visited these sites."

"That would be Sonia Beddow. She's on the same course, and we arranged a division of labour. We're mostly focused on the network of radicalization sites and where they funnel people who access them. She's looking at possible targets these other sites might encourage people to attack. I'm sure she would be happy to speak to you."

Inspector Davidson asked them to email him a copy of the syllabus and to make sure it had the name of the instructor on it.

***

Inspector Crawley had a slower than usual drive to Great Wilbraham. It was rush hour, and a bus had broken down on the main road and at a point where it was impossible for the driver to pull over. There was only one lane passable. Police were on the scene and alternating the use of the good lane by traffic in both directions. The queue coming out of Cambridge was long, and it took him a good twenty minutes to get past the bus. He arrived in Great Wilbraham later than he intended and in a bad mood as his stomach was now incessant in its demands for nourishment.

He found Ranelagh Lane without difficulty. It was a quintessential middle-class street with brick terraced houses on both sides nicely set back. There was little variation in the architecture but somewhat more so in the landscaping. Only one house had a noticeably overgrown lawn. He drove down the lane slowly, looking for a Toyota Auris. He found a metallic maroon one directly in front of number thirty-one, the house of Mrs Buttle, the owner. He parked, grabbed the camera on the passenger seat and walked over to the vehicle. There was nothing remarkable about it. He limited himself to snapping a few pictures before returning the camera to the car. He did not want to do a swipe of the registration without first asking for permission. He had a court order in his pocket should she refuse. The judge had issued six warrants for car swipes and also for removal of the cars by SOCOs, if necessary.

Mrs Buttle opened the door within ten seconds of his ringing the buzzer. He presented his warrant card, and she invited him inside and introduced him to her husband. They were in the midst of a takeaway Indian meal. He could smell the spices from the sitting room, and the open doorway to the kitchen revealed three standard metallic containers on the counter. He apologized for interrupting their meal and explained his mission giving the cover story he had carefully prepared. The police were interested in a suspect in a major robbery who may have altered his car registration to facilitate the getaway. The new number coincided with theirs, unfortunately, and he wanted to look at the car to rule it out. Mrs Buttle was a little slow in taking this in, but not her husband, who encouraged her to assist the police in any way she could. Mrs Buttle, in whose name the car was registered, signed a consent form. Mr Buttle asked if he could come out and watch, and Inspector Crawley readily agreed.

Before going outside, he asked Mrs Buttle where she was earlier in the day as he had tried reaching her at home and at work. She told him that she had phoned in ill because of a severe toothache and had spent much of the day waiting at the clinic to see a dentist.

"The National Health Service is getting worse. Fortunately, it was not life-threatening but bloody uncomfortable, and I had to sit on a hard plastic bench for nearly three hours. And that after standing for twenty minutes until a chair became free. I didn't get home until the early afternoon and fell asleep not long after taking the sedative they gave me. I was not up to preparing dinner and asked my husband to stop at the local Indian restaurant for a takeaway on his way home."

Inspector Crawley expressed his sympathies and asked about her usual route to work. She explained in more detail than was necessary, but he did learn that she went nowhere near Bateman Street. This made sense given her entry point into Cambridge and the location of the college at which she worked. She had a parking space inside the college, which greatly facilitated her commute.

Followed by Mr Buttle, the inspector went out to the street and his car, where he removed the kit the lab had given him, for taking several swipes from the registration. The constable had previously briefed all the officers about which letters and numbers were easiest to change and hence the ones to swipe. He returned the swipe cloths to their envelopes, made notes on the outside with a marker pen, thanked Mr Buttle for his wife's cooperation, and drove off. He seriously doubted that the swipes would reveal anything. Now, he thought, time for a beer and meal.

***

Constable Krauss pressed Professor Bricknell's doorbell at precisely five thirty p.m. The drive from the police station to the neighbourhood of Newnham was not very far, but anything could happen at rush hour. He arrived five minutes before his scheduled appointment and, as it was a nice day, permitted himself a walk down the road to where it ended. Beyond was a turnstile and a path that skirted the River Cam and playing fields of the various colleges as it made its way to Grantchester.

He showed his warrant card. The professor, expecting a policeman and seeing one in uniform, hardly glanced at it, and invited him inside.

"How can I help you?" he asked.

The constable told the professor the cover story that they all had rehearsed and that a detective had given earlier to the professor when he telephoned to make an appointment. The constable later reported that the professor gave every appearance of being relaxed and went with him to his lockup and backed his car out so he could take a photo and swipes of its registration. The car was spanking clean and must have been through a car wash recently. The entire encounter took no more than three minutes, and the professor wished the constable and his colleagues' luck in finding the robber.

***

Rhianna Johnson was as unhappy as the police were about their progress with the murders. This gave her little to report and certainly not the scoop that Inspector Khan had raised as a possibility for her cooperation. She had been flirting with a constable who was about her age in the hope he would provide some useful information. They had met for a drink after work, and she had done nothing to discourage the young man's obvious sexual interest in her. He was not on either investigating team, but constables shared information among themselves more freely than detectives did, and he had a general idea of what was going on. He told her about their efforts to trace a possibly false registration on a Toyota Auris. She immediately grasped the connection between the car and the possible abduction and subtly probed for more information. The constable let slip that one of his colleagues was visiting one of the five or six cars identified as those that might have changed their registrations.

Rhianna decided to follow this colleague to see where he went. This was easy because it never occurred to the constable that he might be tailed. He took the most direct route to Newnham and parked in front of the house he intended to visit. Rhianna stopped well short of the house, which, fortunately, was on a long street. She left her car, walked in the direction of the house, and watched as the constable disappeared inside. She turned around at the end of the street and slowly retraced her steps. She saw the constable and a middle-aged man emerge from the house and walk together around the side of the house to a lockup. She stopped, took her mobile out of her pocket and pretended to answer a call. She jabbered away whilst keeping a close eye on the scene. She saw a Toyota Auris back out of the lockup and saw the constable take several pictures of it and then a couple of swipes of its registration. She continued down the street to her car and sat there waiting for the constable to drive past her, which he did shortly.

Rhianna contemplated trying to interview the car's owner but decided that she probably knew more than he did about what was going on. There was also a downside of doing this because the police would be furious with her if they found out. They would want to know how she found out about their search of Toyotas and would not be convinced by some story that she was following a constable at random to see where he was going. Best that she file away the information, for the time being. You never knew when it would come in handy.

***

Inspector Khan was still mulling over the coincidence. These things happen, he told himself, particularly in a relatively small place like Cambridge. The coroner needed a chemist, and the university department was the obvious place to turn. Professor Bricknell was an obvious candidate because the coroner had met him at a bridge evening. The professor had been adamant that the anaesthetic could not be produced easily outside a laboratory dedicated to this purpose. He was insistent that it would have to be stolen somewhere in the course of its production, distribution, or storage by hospitals. Inspector Khan reasoned that if a registrar told him he had an incurable illness, he would be deeply depressed and would immediately seek a second opinion. He had an incurable case of murder, so why not seek a second opinion in this instance as well. He had nothing better to do as there were still no promising leads.

When seeking a second medical opinion, one must be discreet. You do not want to antagonize your physician, which you will almost certainly do if he or she finds out about your second consultation. The inspector thought he could call the chair of the Cambridge chemistry department and ask him to keep his consultation a secret from his colleague, but this was risky. The two men might be close friends. As with a medical consultation, you need to go to a different practice, and better still, to one on the other side of town. He Googled Anglia Ruskin University and discovered to his delight that it not only had a chemistry department but a programme in analytical chemistry that specialized in pathology and drug analysis. It was located off East Road in Cambridge, an easy drive from the station. He called ahead and made an appointment with the programme director for nine o'clock the next morning.

XXII: Tuesday Morning

The inspector announced himself at the visitor's' desk at Anglia Ruskin University and was told someone would shortly appear to escort him to his appointment. The new building was modern, attractive, and light, and a very different setting from most of the Cambridge colleges.

The director of the analytical chemistry programme soon appeared and ushered him upstairs to his office, which had a courtyard view and was separated from the busy hallway by a large outer office occupied by his secretary and assistant. Once in the office, he passed over his warrant card for inspection. It was immediately handed back, and he was offered a seat. Inspector Khan was intrigued by the degree of attention people paid to his warrant card. Those expecting him generally nodded their heads or otherwise indicated they recognized the formality of presenting identification but had no need to inspect it. He reasoned that many thought it would be impolite to do so. Others were unintimidated and stared closely at it the way immigration officials in police states shift their glance back and forth between the photo on a passport and the face of its holder.

"What can I do for you, Inspector?" the programme director asked.

"First, let me thank you for graciously agreeing to see me at short notice. I am very appreciative."

"I'm happy to help and pleased that you have come to me. Usually when some authority wants scientific advice they go to Cambridge. It's as if we don't exist, yet we are a leader in the field of analytical and forensic chemistry."

"I recognize that, and it is one of the reasons I come to see you. There's a second reason that will become apparent in a moment."

"I'm all ears, Inspector."

"I'm investigating a double murder. You may have read about it in the papers."

"The two bodies found in the pond just outside of town?"

"Yes, that's right. I'm going to tell you something about them, and I would appreciate it if you would treat this information as highly confidential."

"You have my word."

"Thank you. We have not told the media, but we know that the two men were disabled with an anaesthetic not often used in hospitals. It almost instantly sedated them and made it easy for the murderer to transport them to this catchment basin and then roll them over the edge of a dock into the water."

"What an unpleasant way to die!"

"It was barbaric but painless. They were unconscious the entire time and did not know they were drowning. At first, we thought the anaesthetic had been stolen from a local hospital. But Addenbrookes, other hospitals that stock it, and both the manufacturer and distributor insist that none of it is missing. They all claim to keep careful logs, and I suppose we should believe them."

"We do the same here in the department, not that we handle anaesthetics. But we have drugs and chemicals that could do great damage if they fell into the wrong hands. They are carefully controlled, and all the more so as this is a university where people largely come and go as they please."

"That must present problems," the inspector said.

"It does. We log everything in that is either a controlled substance or dangerous and keep it under lock and key. People requesting any of these substances need a good reason, have to sign for it, and someone else must countersign. We're also careful about the amounts we let people use. We pretty much know the quantities needed for various teaching and research purposes."

"It's good that you are so careful. You will better understand our dilemma then. If none of this drug is unaccounted for, how did the murderer get his hands on some?"

"I see the problem."

"Our coroner has lost much sleep over the question. He wondered how easy it might be to synthesize the anaesthetic and how much knowledge and equipment you would need to do so. This was outside his area of expertise, and he sought out a chemist for advice. This chemist is on the faculty at Cambridge, but that's not why he sought him out. He and his wife play bridge, as does the chemist. He had met him socially and thought it would make it easier to approach him."

"I'm sure it did."

"He agreed to see him, and the coroner asked his questions."

"And what did the chemist say?"

"He was insistent that the anaesthetic would be all but impossible to produce outside of a lab dedicated to the purpose."

"I see. Why come to me?"

"I think it worthwhile to get a second opinion."

"You don't trust this other chemist for some reason?"

"He is highly regarded in his field, and I have no reason to doubt what he said."

"But you still want a second opinion?"

"Yes, I do. It's a murder investigation. We have precious few leads, and before we invest enormous resources in tracing the drug from production to hospital pantry, we need to make sure this is the only route by which it could be obtained. All the more so because all the inquiries would have to be carried out by other police forces and as favours to us."

"I understand. Why don't we begin by you telling me the name of the chemist and the drug."

"And will you assure me that this information will remain confidential?"

There was a gentle rap on the door followed by a woman's head peering around the now partially opened door to announce that the public affairs director of a pharmaceutical company was on the line.

"Tell him I'm dealing with a troubled student on the verge of a breakdown and that I'll call him back." He looked across and smiled at the inspector.

"Do I look that troubled?"

"Not yet."

The inspector smiled and waited a moment or two after the door had closed to continue with his presentation.

The professor in question is Ian Bricknell. Do you know him?"

"Not well, but our paths have crossed at professional meetings and occasionally at seminars in Cambridge. His area of specialization is different from mine. He has an excellent reputation as a scholar and teacher. And what about the drug?"

"It has a long, multi-syllabic name that's not so easy to remember. I've taken the precaution of writing it down to make certain I get it right." He took a piece of paper out of his jacket pocket, unfolded it, and handed it over to the programme director. "Professor Bricknell says it comes from a South American plant, and the active ingredient is a molecule that is bound together with another one even more powerful, and thus poisonous to people. The less deadly molecule must be separated, which is a difficult process. To have its desired effect, it requires a catalyst that must be introduced moments before the anaesthetic is injected."

"That's what Professor Bricknell said?" the programme director said in a questioning tone of voice.

"Yes, the coroner made notes on his conversation and passed them along to me."

"Did he tell this to the coroner off the top of his head?"

"No. The professor told the coroner he would have to do a little research and would get back to him, which he did the next day."

"And you're absolutely certain about what he said?"

"Yes. Our coroner is an experienced and cautious man. He wrote everything down almost verbatim and handed his notes over to us. Is there a problem?"

"It makes no sense to me. I've heard of this drug, and yes, I believe it comes from a South American plant. But the rest of what he says is news to me. It is presumably urgent that you get accurate information?"

"Correct."

"Bear with me then. Let me return that telephone call. It's important to keep sponsors happy, and the sooner I get back to him, the more important he will feel. I will cancel my next appointment, do a little quick research, and offer you a more confident opinion. Would that be all right?"

"More than all right. I am very grateful."

"In that case, why not get a coffee or some air as it's a nice day and come back in say thirty minutes. I work best when I am undisturbed."

"No problem. I'll find my own way out and come back at ten a.m. Would that be about right?"

"That would be just fine. Thanks for being so understanding."

Inspector Khan took the stairs down to the ground floor, decided against a coffee but in favour of a walk. The neighbourhood was mixed business and light industry with a new condo across the road. The sun was shining, and there was no wind. He walked away from the university and the main road in search of some quiet. He noted the time on his watch.

The inspector was puzzled by how his interlocutor had responded to what Professor Bricknell had told the coroner. He knew that academics frequently disagree among themselves. Controversies drove knowledge in most disciplines. No doubt this was true of chemistry too. But what he was asking about, or so he thought, was a relatively straightforward matter of fact. Either the drug could be synthesized or not, and if so, with relative ease or varying degrees of difficulty. He put the question out of his mind as best he could because he would hear soon enough from an authority.

Inspector Khan made certain that he did not appear at the office until 10.05 just in case his host needed more research time. He was immediately ushered into the programme head's inner office and offered the same seat, this time by an excited man. He waited for his host to speak.

"I was puzzled by what Professor Bricknell told you and did some quick research. I checked out the drug and its active ingredient and looked at a paper about it I found on-line. Our programme has a relationship with the company that produces it, and I called them and spoke to the chemist I occasionally liaise with. He confirmed my suspicions."

Inspector Khan was now leaning forward to catch every word. He had his notebook in hand, ready to write down what he heard to be able to give as near as possible a verbatim report.

"The drug does in fact come from a South American plant, and a serum is extracted on site, quickly chilled, but not frozen, and sent to processing plants in several parts of the world. There's only one in Europe, and it's here in Britain. This probably rules out the possibility of, say, stealing it in France or Germany and then bringing it unnoticed through customs." The programme head paused to allow the inspector time to finish writing his notes.

"The story about the other molecule from which it needs to be separated is nonsense. The serum needs to be refined and combined with a stabilizing solution. No catalyst is required before use, but the drug has a short shelf-life."

The inspector made more notes and asked a question or two just to make sure he understood correctly.

"I cannot imagine why Professor Bricknell told that coroner what you say he did. He's a fine chemist, and even if he knew nothing about this drug, a little on-line reading would tell him what he needed to know. And I assure you, the truth of the matter is nothing like what he is said to have told your coroner."

"And what about synthesizing it?"

"It's not easy, but not impossible. A knowledgeable chemist, or even an experienced lab technician, could do it with access to the right equipment."

"What do we mean by the right equipment? Could it be done in a spare room or basement by an enthusiast?"

"Definitely not. You need some highly specialized equipment, notably a centrifuge."

"Let me ask a more direct question," said the inspector. "Professor Mason, one of the victims, was not widely loved in his college or the university at large. Suppose a student or colleague who studied or taught chemistry wanted to do him in, or help someone do this, would they be able to synthesize the anaesthetic in one of the university labs?"

"In theory, yes. Whatever they came up with would not come close to the quality of what the drug company produces. But this is unimportant because the killer would not be concerned about impurities that could complicate or retard post-operative recovery."

"You're reasonably confident about what you are telling me?"

"Absolutely certain. It was confirmed by the chemist at the drug company to whom I spoke."

"There's no way to reconcile your judgment with that of Professor Bricknell. Could there be a reasonable difference of opinion?"

"No, I'm afraid not. What he is said to have told you is simply wrong."

Inspector Khan finished making his notes and offered profuse thanks to his host, who insisted on escorting him downstairs and out to the car park. On the drive back to the police station, he mulled over what he had learnt. Somebody was not telling the truth. There were three possibilities: Professor Bricknell fobbed the coroner off with a lot of nonsense; the coroner, deliberately or inadvertently, misheard what he had been told; or the programme head was not telling the truth because he wanted to tarnish Professor Bricknell's reputation. He trusted the coroner and doubted that the head of the programme would be so unimaginative as to tell an easily discredited porker. And then there was the nagging matter of coincidence. Professor Bricknell's car was one of those identified in the search for the mystery vehicle on Bateman Street the morning Professor Mason disappeared. If anybody lied, it was likely to be Professor Bricknell.

Inspector Khan was excited. This could be the first breakthrough of the case. Professor Bricknell's misleading information and his car were enough to classify him as a person of interest. He was now keen to learn if the lab had found anything on the swipes taken from the professor's car. He wanted to speak to the detective or constable who had interviewed him to see how he had acted during their visit. The inspector parked at the police station and rushed in to tell Peter his news.

***

Peter spent his morning speaking to colleagues who had interviewed the car owners. Inspector Crawley and his colleagues had nothing of interest to report. Nobody they visited appeared suspicious or unhelpful, but there was still one car and owner outstanding. Inspector Crawley was confident that both the people he interviewed could be ruled out. Constable Krauss made no secret of his belief that it had all been a waste of time. He described Professor Bricknell as a distinguished-looking man who had been helpful in every respect. The professor had told the constable that he had read nothing about the bank robbery in the local paper, which he thought odd. The constable had no ready explanation for this omission, and the professor had not pushed him any further. The constable thought he had seen through their cover story but decided, for whatever reason, to play along with it.

Rhianna Johnson then called to ask if he had anything of interest he could share with her, and he said no.

"I've played straight with you two," she said, "and you're shutting me out of the investigation."

"It's a police matter," Peter replied, "and we do not confide in anyone not on the force." He stopped himself from adding, "Especially the press."

"I've done you favours by keeping interesting information under wraps."

"Oh? What information haven't you published?"

"That you're going around swiping car registrations and taking pictures of these cars."

"And how do you know about this?"

"That's none of your business. You don't share your sources with me, and I respect that."

"I'm frankly baffled about how you found out about this."

"Good. It's time you and the inspector develop some respect for my sleuthing skills. I also know the cover story you're giving to people about why you want to look at their cars. Permit me to suggest that a bank robbery that's never been reported is likely to arouse more suspicion than not."

"It doesn't matter. People agreed to let us swipe their registrations. And what if they recognize it as a cover story? It hides our real intentions."

"I don't suppose you will tell me what those are?"

"What do you think?"

"I think not. But if I did, I might be able to help. And I would certainly refrain from publishing the story about the registrations. That might be useful to you."

"Look, Ms Johnson. I'm not about to trade information for silence."

"Oh, do call me Rhianna. And I'll call you Peter. Do you think we could make that kind of deal?"

"No offence, but you're beginning to try my patience. It would be helpful if you held off for a day or two on publishing this story. If so, I can't promise, but I think there is a good chance the inspector would be willing to tell you what it's all about."

"All right, I will exercise restraint at the expense of a scoop."

"It's not much of a scoop. I can't imagine your paper will put it on the first page."

"Maybe not, but the Cambridge police will not look good if they are exposed for telling tall tales to people to persuade them to let them examine their cars."

"You do have a point there. But surely you can understand that we may have a very good reason to keep our real motive quiet for the time being?"

"Yes, I do, and so did Professor Bricknell."

"Professor Bricknell?"

"Yes, one of your constables took photos and swipes of his car."

"Did he call you to report it?"

"No, he did not. I called him to ask why the police paid him a visit."

"How did you know about that?"

"Sources, remember. We don't share them. He actually denied everything until I told him that I had a photo of him watching a constable rubbing cloths over his number plate."

"I see. What did he say then?"

"I could come by, and we could talk about it."

"I don't know about that. Let me get back to you later in the day."

"Fine, but remember I have to make a decision whether or not to print. If I do go ahead, I have a deadline to meet."

The lab reports arrived whilst Peter was on the phone. He watched the three pages coming through the printer one page at a time and was anxious to get Rhianna off the line so he could read them. They were disappointing. No sign of paint or paint remover on any of the registration plates, followed by the usual disclaimers and boilerplate language about false negatives and positives. Inspector Khan would not be pleased.

At that moment, the inspector stuck his head through Peter's half-open door and was invited inside.

"We may have our first break," he announced.

"Do tell," said Peter.

XXIII: Tuesday Afternoon

Inspector Khan told Peter about his encounter with the programme director at Anglia Ruskin and how Professor Bricknell was now in his sights.

"I know the coroner well and feel certain he was telling the truth. But let's give him a ring and double-check that he got it right."

"I'll call him now, sir."

The coroner was examining a corpse, and an assistant took a message. Peter stressed that it was important for him to call back as soon as possible.

Peter agreed with the inspector that something odd was going on. The two men talked about what motive Professor Bricknell might have for lying to the coroner. Throwing them off the track was the obvious explanation, and if true, they agreed, it suggested that he had some role in the murder. Perhaps he had manufactured the anaesthetic in his lab.

"Maybe he's the killer," said Peter.

"We can't jump to conclusions," said the inspector. "But we certainly can't rule it out."

"It doesn't help," Peter said, "that they found nothing on his car."

"Do we have the lab report?"

Peter handed it over to him and waited whilst the inspector read it through carefully.

"All that effort for nothing," he finally said.

"It looks that way, but it still might be worth pursuing. If we could find evidence that Professor Bricknell had fiddled with his number plate, we would have two counts against him. Any chance we could have his car impounded?"

"On what grounds? There's nothing in the lab report to suggest a further look, and we have no evidence connecting him with the abduction. All he's done is tell a porker, and that will never convince a judge."

"Let's phone the lab. Maybe they have some thoughts they did not risk putting in writing."

"Worth a try."

Peter picked up his telephone. He knew the deputy head of the police lab well, and they exchanged the usual pleasantries before getting down to business. The inspector could hear only one end of the conversation. It went on long enough for him to infer that something was up, an impression heightened by the nature of the questions Peter posed.

"It's ambiguous, sir," Peter said when he finally put down his phone. Jonathan says that there was no trace of anything anywhere with the exception — you will like this — of Professor Bricknell's registration plate."

"They found something on the swipes?"

"Not exactly. There is a hint of what could be solvent, but not enough to warrant a confident positive identification. Jonathan says the photographs show a recently cleaned car. If Bricknell changed the registration and then used solvent to wipe off the paint, he then used something else to remove any sign of solvent. The registration is cleaner than the car, which suggests it was repeatedly scrubbed. There was no dirt or residues in the usual places."

"Well, he is a chemist," said the inspector. "He would know exactly what to do. Maybe he used some kind of paint that does not need a solvent to remove it or had some other chemical that removes all traces of solvent. Either way, it's suspicious."

"What should we do?"

"The first thing is to summon the constable who took the swipes. Let's get his first-hand impression of the professor."

"There's somebody else we need to talk to in this connection," said Peter.

"Who is it?"

"You won't like this. It's Rhianna Johnson."

"What's she done now?"

"Somehow, I don't know how, she found out that we were taking swipes of registrations and — forgive me — giving out an inane cover story about a bank robbery. She also discovered that Professor Bricknell

213

was one of the car owners we targeted. She telephoned and interviewed him after the constable had left."

"Damn. Do we know what he told her — or what she told him?"

"No, we don't. She told me that she would hold back on publishing for the time being if we made it worthwhile for her. I told her we don't do deals but indicated that you might be interested in speaking to her."

"Passing the buck, eh?"

"It's a freighted issue. I didn't want to commit us to anything until we knew what had transpired between her and the professor. It seemed a good way to stall and keep her story out of the paper for the time being."

"You did well, Peter, as usual."

"Thank you, sir. Shall I call and summon her?"

"Yes, but let's speak to the constable first. In the interim, I'll ask the deputy commissioner if he thinks we have enough to get a warrant to search the professor's home, office, and lab. Let's assign someone to keep a discreet eye on the professor on the off chance that he tries to leave town."

***

The constable hurried along the corridor to Peter's office. He was not quite a two-year veteran and still intimidated by the prospect of being grilled by two detectives. He assured himself that he had done what was asked of him and had nothing to hide. At the inspector's request, he recounted his encounter with the professor from the beginning.

"No," he explained, "I did not initiate the contact. Inspector Crawley or one of the detectives called him and made an appointment for five thirty p.m. And no, I don't know when the professor was called. Sometime in the morning, I think. Surely, the call would have been logged."

"He had all day to prepare for your visit," Peter said. "How did he come across?"

"He opened the door very quickly after I rang, only glanced at my warrant card when I displayed it and invited me inside."

"What does his house look like?"

"Nicely furnished. What is the word? Uncluttered. There were a few decorations on the mantelpiece but no photographs or anything else. There were some framed prints on the walls. I was only in the hallway, but I could peer into the sitting room."

"You are observant," Peter said. "What happened next?"

"We went outside and walked around the house to his lockup. I waited at a distance as he opened it and backed out his car. I eyeballed the inside, which was spanking clean and contained nothing out of the ordinary that I could see. Whilst still in the house, I told him what I intended to do with his car and repeated the story I was instructed to use as our justification. I think he had already been told this tale by whoever called him. He smiled as if to signal that he saw through this ruse, but he did not challenge it or raise any objection when I took a couple of photos of his car and three swipes of his registration."

"How did the registration look?"

"Very clean, otherwise very ordinary."

"Did he say anything to you worth passing on?"

"Not really. The conversation was limited to the car. I thanked him afterwards, and he wished us good luck — with a smile again — in catching the bank robbers."

"One final question." "Was there anyone else around or watching you do the swipes?"

"Come to think of it, yes. There was a woman walking by on the street. When I finished the swipes, she was standing on the pavement talking on her mobile."

"What did she look like?"

The constable offered a description whilst Peter googled Rhianna Johnson and asked the constable to come behind his desk to have a look at his computer screen.

"Yes, that's her," he said.

"Son-of-a-bitch," Peter exclaimed. "How did she do it? You didn't tell her anything?"

"Absolutely not," the constable said as he shook his head.

"She must have a source somewhere in this building," Peter said.

"And we are going to find out who it is," Inspector Khan added.

***

Rhianna Johnson arrived on time for her appointment. Inspector Khan took no chances with her, even at the risk of offending her. He had a female constable look through her purse and pat her down to make sure she had no recording device. She was miffed but went along with it as she knew it was the only way she could see the inspector. The constable took her mobile and promised to return it at the end of the interview. She was ushered upstairs, this time to Inspector Khan's office. She was greeted politely but coldly by him and Peter.

The inspector invited her to take a seat and wasted no time in asking what Professor Bricknell had said to her in their telephone call.

"I've already told that to your colleague here."

"I'd like to hear it directly from you."

Rhianna recounted her conversation and made sure she relayed the professor's amusement at the not very well considered cover story the constable had used to explain why he wanted to inspect his car. Inspector Khan did not rise to the bait but asked her how she happened to call Professor Bricknell. She was reluctant to divulge her sources.

"Ms Johnson," said the inspector, "we have every right to inquire about your source if it is inside the Cambridgeshire Police."

"Let me set your fears to rest then, Inspector. None of your colleagues is my snout. And I didn't hack your computer system. Nothing exciting has happened in Cambridge, and I had some free time. I followed a couple of your colleagues around town. I tailed Inspector Crawley to Great Wilbraham and watched as he took a photo and swiped the registration of a car. Today I followed Constable Krauss, who did the same with Professor Bricknell's car."

"Do you realize, Ms Johnson, that following — no, let me say, spying on — the police in the course of their duties constitutes an offence?"

"Are you interested in my information, Inspector, or do you intend to harass me?"

"I'm interested in what you learnt, but I am frankly appalled by your efforts to play detective. They could seriously interfere with our own."

"Could Professor Bricknell be a person of interest to you?"

"I don't think you have done any damage by speaking to him but imagine the consequences of speaking to someone who was of interest to us and tipping him off."

"There is a simple way to avoid that, Inspector. Take me into your confidence."

"I really think you misapprehend your role here. You are a reporter, not a detective, and have no right to be briefed as if you were one of us."

"We are on the same side, Inspector. You should recognize that I'm an asset to you. People in Cambridge read what I write, and my paper is a vehicle for you to reach them when you need help from the public. I'm a responsible person so, within reason, I also refrain from publishing what you think could be damaging. You should share more information so I can make better informed and more responsible judgments."

"If I share with you," the inspector said, "I have to share with other journalists as well, and not all of them are, shall we say, so responsible."

"You don't have to take everyone into your confidence. I'm the leading crime reporter in Cambridge, indeed the only one aside from a BBC stringer. This is a good reason to make an exception."

"I'll tell you what, Ms Johnson. To date, there is little to share on either the murders or the bombing. I can assure you we are leaving no stone unturned, but we have no information that is newsworthy. When we do, you will be the first journalist we will call. Perhaps until then you could call a halt to your private investigation."

The conversation went on for another five minutes as each side sought to avoid making an explicit concession but communicating the promise of restraint on the one hand in return for the promise of information on the other. When Ms Johnson finally left, the inspector felt drained. Peter too, who had the additional strain of having remained silent for the entire interview. The two men decided to go out for a coffee, but not before the inspector made a visit to the deputy commissioner in search of warrants.

***

Deputy Commissioner Braham was more respected than feared by those who worked for him. He was solicitous of his staff and ready to praise people who performed well. He was supportive of women on the force and had tried to manage recent cuts in a way that did as little real damage as possible. He adhered closely to the rules in the belief that it gave him more leeway in other respects. Inspector Khan understood and generally approved of his strategy but recognized that it would work to his disadvantage this morning. He would be asking for search warrants on the flimsiest of evidence, and the deputy commissioner would not want the humiliation of asking a magistrate for them only to be turned down.

The deputy commissioner's office was larger and better furnished than those of his colleagues. He had a penchant for plants, especially bromeliads, some of which produced colourful flowers that varied considerably in their size. He had figured out a new way of using fertilizer by flushing out its otherwise retarding salts. Inspector Khan was always careful to begin any encounter in his office by admiring whatever plant was in flower and wondered if others did this too. The office was devoid of the usual plaques and awards that hang on the walls or litter the tables of high-ranking police officers. The desk supported only a telephone console, a large computer screen, and a couple of photographs of his wife, children, and their partners. His youngest son was gay, and one of the pictures on his desk was of him hugging his partner. Everyone had seen the picture and presumably got the message.

If the deputy commissioner had a fault, it was his temper. It was fierce, but never to the inspector's knowledge, provoked by anything trivial. It was most often directed against Westminster civil servants who thought they knew better how a police force should be run and the level at which it should be financed; the media, whose search for sensational stories led to distortions, public fears, and political pressures; and the occasional detective or constable who did something stupid. The last officer to run afoul of him was a constable who hung up his suit jacket in an overheated café only to have some thief make off with it with his warrant card inside. So far nothing had happened, but the deputy commissioner was rightly worried that the thief, or someone to whom he or she sold the warrant card, might use it to pose as a police officer causing real damage to the force once the media got word of what had happened.

Today the deputy commissioner was in his usual grumpy mood but not in any way angry. Inspector Khan brought him up to date on the combined investigations and the possibility that they had some kind of breakthrough. The deputy commissioner was intrigued by the method the constable had come up with to locate the enigmatic auto. He agreed that it was unlikely to be a coincidence that it belonged to a chemist who had lied about the difficulty of synthesizing the drug used to anaesthetize the two murder victims.

Inspector Khan made his case for warrants to search Professor Bricknell's home, office, and laboratory. Deputy Commissioner Braham remained silent until he finished his pitch.

"Bricknell is certainly a person of interest and clever of you to get a second opinion on his report to the coroner. What do you make of it?"

"We had no other leads. I had time on my hands."

"Well done, I must say."

"Thank you, sir."

"The higher-ups keep asking when we will solve the double murder case, and I fob them off with assurances that we are working on it but, until now, we've really had nothing to show for our efforts. Do you think Professor Bricknell is our culprit?"

"I can't say for sure, but why would he try to throw us off the track unless he is involved in some way. At the very least, he may have produced the drug in his lab, and that would make him an accomplice."

"I presume he would synthesize the drug if he was the killer, owed the killer a big favour, or got paid a lot of money for his efforts. Any sense of which?"

"None. To date, we've found nothing to link him to either Professor Mason or Jaime. The two professors' paths had crossed, but that's probably true of almost all Cambridge faculty. He doesn't belong to a college, which is not atypical among scientists. We had a quiet talk with the steward at Leinster College, who checked his records and discovered that Professor Bricknell has been to lunch and dinner on multiple occasions. He has a friend, another chemist, who is a member of the college."

"Is there any indication of tension between him and Professor Mason?"

"None whatsoever."

"And no hint of a motive?"

"Afraid not."

"If it's money, maybe we could convince him to reveal the name of the killer."

"I don't know that he has much to gain by doing so. He'll still go to prison, lose his professorship, and his standing in the field."

"Yes, but we might persuade the prosecutor to give him two years instead of ten. That's a big difference."

"Unless he believes that he can avoid prison altogether if he stiffs us. After all, we have no real evidence against him. We can't prove that he altered his registration or produced the drug, and he's smart enough to suspect this if we offer him a good deal."

"True. How would you like to proceed?"

"I want his home, office, and lab searched in the hope that the SOCOs come up with something definitive."

"This is where I was afraid you were going. It's not the easiest case to make to a magistrate. It will look like a fishing expedition, and if we find nothing and the professor goes to the media afterwards, we are going to look terrible. I'll catch hell from the commissioner, and you'll get the same from me. Do you think it's worth the risk — assuming we can find a compliant magistrate?"

"I do, sir. It's our only promising line of inquiry. If we hit pay dirt, we might solve the case. And consider the alternative. What if we do nothing and discover later that our professor was responsible for multiple murders. We will be accused of a cover-up, unfairly in this case, to be sure. But we will look no better than Rotherham, where our colleagues appear to have turned a blind eye to underage girls being exploited as sex slaves. It will be the end of both of us."

"You do have a point. I'll see what I can do."

***

Deputy Commissioner Braham consulted with the chief prosecutor, and he knew which magistrate to approach. Fortunately, he was on rota and issued the warrant after asking only perfunctory questions. The SOCOs were alerted and, together with detectives with warrants in hand, descended on Professor Bricknell's home, office, and laboratory. The professor was not at any of these venues. One of the SOCOs, a qualified locksmith, took what he needed from his toolkit, and, within minutes, the police were inside his house. They found nothing of immediate interest. The house was clean and well cared for, but it still took them several hours to go through its contents and to collect samples of various kinds for testing. They did the same in his lockup. Needless to say, neighbours appeared on the street, and Inspector Davidson, who was overseeing the operation, questioned them at length. The professor did not socialize with any of them but was polite when he encountered them on the street. His wife had been more sociable, but they had been separated or divorced for at least five years. Nobody reported visitors to the house beyond the usual delivery and repair people. Two neighbours reported seeing the constable who took the car swipes.

Peter oversaw the visit to the professor's office, where they presented their search warrant to the department secretary. She immediately called the chair on his mobile, and he came rushing over from his laboratory. Nothing like this had happened before in his experience. He asked the police to be as discreet as possible to staunch the rumours that were certain to spread among the students. Peter explained that they would do what they could, but SOCOs in white suits were hard to hide. If it were Easter, perhaps they could wear rabbit ears. The chair was not amused and decided the best thing to do was to hide in his office with the door closed.

The SOCOs needed less time in an office than a house. It was a crowded scene, and Peter waited for them to finish before going through the desk drawers and file cabinets. One of the drawers was locked, and the secretary did not have the key. A SOCO pried it open with a crowbar. Inside they found the key to the filing cabinet. Peter took some files with him, and the SOCOs took the professor's computer back to their lab. Peter signed a receipt, which he left with the secretary. The chair never emerged from his office, although colleagues and some students watched from down the corridor, and soon a small crowd had gathered. They quickly made way for the police when they exited. Peter found a file that had clippings from the Cambridge News and other papers about the twin murders and the bomb found in Leinster College.

The lab operation was a more dramatic affair. It was a large facility, with multiple rooms, shared by many people and one of several, run by the chemistry department. Inspector Khan made sure that his colleague had a copy of the warrant to present to the chair of the department along with the one to search Professor Bricknell's office. Upon his arrival at the lab, he had the SOCOs, and other staff wait outside whilst he entered to present the warrant to the director of the lab if he could find him. He had deliberately not called ahead to avoid alerting anyone to what was about to happen.

He found the lab director in his office conferring with his assistant, a tall woman with bright red hair. Neither was wearing a lab coat, violating his stereotype of what people in this setting should look like. They were both in jeans and cotton shirts, as was just about everyone else he had encountered on his walk up to the second floor. They were speechless when he presented them with the warrant and explained his purpose and told them that a half dozen crime scene officers were about to scour the building for clues in a murder investigation. They stared at each other, presumably waiting for one of them to react.

At last, the director said, "You're really going to go through the entire building looking for what you call clues?"

"That's right. Although your cooperation could help us limit our search to the areas where Professor Bricknell works or could have synthesized a particular drug we are interested in."

"And just how would your crime scene officers know what a clue was even if it stared them in the face?" the deputy director asked. "And are you prepared to pay for any damage you do here? Your herd of rhinos is the last thing we need in this lab. We have delicate experiments underway, and any damage could set us back. Worse still, you could cause a serious accident."

"We're not the fools you take us for," said the inspector. "Our SOCOs are professionals, and for this operation, we have put together a task force with appropriate expertise drawn from police forces in the region. They are being assisted and supervised by a professor of forensic chemistry."

"And who might that be?" the director asked.

"Professor Carr. He's head of the programme of analytical chemistry at Anglia Ruskin."

"Yes, we know where he works."

"You know him then?"

"Yes, we do. Surely, you can't expect us to agree to let a professor from another institution search our lab?"

"You don't have any choice in the matter," the inspector said in a firm voice. "Perhaps you would prefer my herd of rhinos to stampede through your lab without the guidance and oversight of a chemistry professor?"

Neither director nor deputy director had an appropriate comeback, as indicated by their ensuing silence.

"Now, let me ask you both a few questions," said the inspector. "For a start, what can you tell me about Professor Bricknell?"

"Professor Bricknell?" said the director. "Why are you interested in him?"

"If you'll forgive me, I ask the questions. However, I will share our concerns with you in the hope that you can help. Do you understand?"

They nodded their heads in unison.

The inspector began by apologizing for the inconvenience he was causing them and insisted they were only searching the lab in conjunction with a murder case. The director and deputy director were incredulous when he explained that it was the double murder. He gave an abbreviated version of the automobile registration tracing and how it put Professor Bricknell on their radar. He went into more detail about the story the professor had told the coroner, reasoning that he had two top-of-the-line chemists before him.

The inspector confided that Professor Mason and the young man found alongside him had been anaesthetized before being tipped off the dock and drowned. The police had identified the drug in question beyond any reasonable doubt. He handed over several sheets the manufacturer had provided them with its chemical composition and general details of its collection and refinement. The police had done their best to ascertain that neither the drug company, distributor or hospitals had lost or mislaid any of their drugs, making its availability to the murderer all the more enigmatic. The coroner wondered if it could be synthesized in a lab and had sought out Professor Bricknell for an opinion. He told the coroner it was all but impossible and insisted the police redouble their efforts to find some leak from the drug company.

The inspector explained that, on a hunch, he had sought a second opinion from the chair of the analytical chemistry programme at Anglia Ruskin. He had thought it best to go elsewhere to avoid throwing any unnecessary suspicion on Professor Bricknell. He also discovered that Anglia Ruskin had a prominent forensic chemistry programme. It seemed a natural place to make his inquiry. Professor Carr said the drug was not easily synthesized, but this could certainly be done in a university lab by an experienced chemist. It appears that Professor Bricknell lied to the coroner, perhaps to throw him off the track.

His two interlocutors were visibly agitated but said nothing and directed their attention to the materials he had given them to read. The inspector stood by quietly until they were finished. After a couple of minutes, the director turned to his colleague to ask for her thoughts.

"It could be done. We have the necessary centrifuges and other equipment. But there's no way we could produce anything that would meet pharmaceutical standards."

"Unnecessary," the inspector replied. "Our murderer would not have worried about any collateral damage or even the accidental death of his victims from an overdose. All the better, perhaps."

The director grimaced. "I must agree with my colleague," he said. "We could duplicate the drug or something like it."

The two chemists began to talk in scientific language the inspector did not understand. He interrupted to ask if they wanted to send someone to escort his team to where they could do their work and perhaps identify equipment that might have been used. They went to look for a colleague to do this and one who knew where Professor Bricknell's workbench was. The inspector then went downstairs to let in the SOCOs.

Inspector Khan returned to the director's office, where the director and his deputy were still engaged in their conversation. They stopped talking when he entered.

"Inspector," the director said, "we are both of one mind here. Something like the drug could be produced here. With your permission, we will consult with a couple of colleagues just to make certain and, if you like, send you a written report."

"That would be very helpful, thank you. Would Professor Bricknell have the expertise to synthesize the compound?"

"Yes," the director said. "But so would any professor in the department. Do you have evidence connecting the professor with the compound in question?"

"None. I'm hoping to find it here, in his office, or perhaps in his home."

"You're searching all three?"

"As we speak."

"I see," said the director. "You are really treating him as a suspect."

If that was intended as a question, the inspector let it pass. He asked several additional questions about Professor Bricknell. The chemists volunteered that he was a bit of a loner but highly professional, a good mentor of students, and had never been a cause of any concern.

"Did he know Professor Mason?" the inspector asked.

Neither of them had any idea, but the deputy director suggested that as they were both on the university faculty, it was likely that their paths would have crossed. The inspector showed pictures of Professor Mason and Jaime, but they did not recognize either man.

The telephone rang and was answered by the deputy director. The inspector heard her instruct the caller to come right over. She replaced the phone and told the inspector that a copy of the centrifuge log would shortly be in his hands.

"This log would list everyone who has used the device for the last six months you assured me earlier?"

"That's right," the deputy said. "There are two centrifuges. They are locked when not in use, and only the director and chief lab technician have keys."

"Then there is no way that Professor Bricknell or someone else could access the centrifuges without your knowledge?"

"That's right. You not only have to sign the log before using the machines but must also submit a prior request that one of us has to approve. The professor occasionally uses a centrifuge in conjunction with his research, and we will have a full record of the dates and purposes."

There was a light rap on the door, and the director looked up to see a technician wearing a lab coat, much to the inspector's satisfaction. He handed over a thick folder to the director and disappeared.

"This is the logbook, actually a copy," he said as he handed it over to the inspector. "If you like, we will go through the original and look for anything that might be suspicious."

"I would appreciate that," said the inspector. He tucked the folder under his arm and took his leave.

XXIV: Late Tuesday Afternoon

On the drive back to the station, the inspector's mobile rang. It was the duty sergeant telling him that the master of Leinster College had phoned and asked for him. He would like you to call him back as soon as convenient. He gave me his mobile and said to call at any hour.

Inspector Khan pulled over to the kerb, called the duty sergeant back to get the master's number and punched it into his phone. The master picked up on the second ring and thanked the inspector for returning his call.

"There's something you ought to know," he said. "Liam Stanley, one of our students, has disappeared."

"Disappeared?"

"Yes. Nobody has seen him in college for three days now. We've interviewed his friends and the other students in his tutorials. One of them saw Liam leaving with a suitcase." "

"Would this be a normal time for a student to leave the college? I know classes are over."

"That's right, but exams are coming up, and so is the May Ball."

"Ah yes, the May Ball. The end of the year event that always comes in June."

"Very Cambridge, isn't it?"

"Most students are still in college?"

"They are. And we insist that students sign out in the porter's lodge if they are going to be away overnight. We try not to act in loco parentis, but we are responsible for these young men and women and try, within reason, to keep an eye on them."

"I understand. He didn't sign out. I assume this would not be the first time a student failed to sign out?"

"It happens occasionally."

"There must be something else of interest here for you to call me."

"Liam is one of the students Professor Mason was bringing before the disciplinary panel. I didn't say anything about this before, but he apparently told several students that he would find a way of getting even with him."

"Why didn't you tell me this at the time?"

"It was only gossip, and the college needs to protect its students."

"Even if they may have murdered someone or two people, for that matter? I don't suppose you know of any connection between Liam and Jaime?"

"Jaime?"

"The young man whose body was found alongside that of Professor Mason."

"None that I know of."

"Have you contacted Liam's family or anyone else he might have gone to visit? Does he have a girlfriend at another college or somewhere else?"

"We checked and have drawn a blank."

"What about his room? Have you searched it?"

"No. We did not want to contaminate any evidence, if there is any. We opened the door to see if he was there and closed and locked it when he was not. I've posted a porter at the door to make sure nobody else gains entry."

"Other than calling me, that's the first sensible thing you've done in this matter. I'll send a detective over later. Everyone is tied up at the moment. In the interim, could you send me a picture of Liam and any other information you have about him?"

Inspector Khan called Peter, who had just finished overseeing the search of Professor Bricknell's house. They agreed to meet back at the station and to ask the duty sergeant to see if Inspector Davidson was free to join them.

***

Peter had come into work early, and he was hoping to leave early. He was meeting Elaine at her place, which had now become a routine. He spent more nights there than he did at his flat and missed her on those nights he slept at home. At first, he left some toiletries in her bathroom, then some clothes. He wondered where this was heading. Would he move in? Did he want to make this commitment? He recognized how easy it would be to let things move along in small steps until they were, in effect, living together. Deciding against the relationship at this point would be difficult and painful. Saying no now would be easier, but he had no incentive to do this. He was enjoying Elaine's company in and out of bed. He had not eaten so well, or so healthily, in a long time. They had much in common, beginning with tennis and their jobs, as they had discovered in awkward but amusing circumstances. For the time being, his loins were in agreement with his mind, and he felt elated at the prospect of seeing Elaine in another few hours. He would have to call her to tell her he would be delayed.

The search of Professor Bricknell's office had gone quickly as it was only one room. The SOCOs had done their usual searching, dusting, and photographing, and he had also had a look around. They did not expect to find a written confession in his desk, but here and at his home, they were anxious to uncover anything that might link him to the crime or suggest a motive. There was a consensus among the detectives that he was probably involved with the synthesis of the drug used to sedate the victims. Nobody had come up with a plausible motive for his doing this, let alone murdering two people, one of whom he had probably never met.

The only interesting thing Peter found in the office was a folder in a file cabinet with a set of clippings about the murder and the bombing. In itself, this proved nothing, but it did reveal something other than a passing interest in these events. It was more circumstantial evidence that heightened their suspicions of the professor but offered no evidence of his involvement.

The three detectives convened in Inspector Khan's office. The constable who had allowed himself to be followed by Rhianna popped his head in the door and offered to go to the café and buy them all coffee. He took their orders and refused any money. Inspector Davidson suggested he was feeling guilty, as he should, about giving away their interest in Professor Bricknell to a pesky journalist.

The lab reports would dribble in over the course of the next few days. The SOCOs had collected so much material for analysis that they were compelled to distribute much of it to other police labs in the region. Deputy Commissioner Braham had coordinated this effort and the borrowing of additional SOCOs. These requests came with a price: other police forces would now be monitoring and judging their progress. Up to this point, the deputy commissioner had given a free hand to Inspectors Khan and Davidson and defended their efforts in the occasional telephone call from higher authorities. Those calls would come more frequently and further search warrants or extra forces, to say nothing of the additional expenses, were out of the question in the absence of some noticeable progress in the investigation.

There was no way to hide the SOCO searches from the local press. The story had gone national given the interest in the double murders and the bomb that did not go off in Leinster College. Deputy Commissioner Braham was now personally under scrutiny in the media and would be branded incompetent or an abuser of police authority — most likely both — if the searches failed to come up with anything. He was beginning to have second thoughts about asking for the warrants. To reassure himself that something positive was happening and to be in a better position to respond to intrusive inquiries from above, he asked to meet with Detectives Khan and Davidson.

Each of the detectives brought the other up to date on his investigation. Inspector Davidson reported that the professor's house was clean, as far as they could tell. He found nothing to connect him with either victim or the bomb, but they would have to await the lab reports to know anything with certainty. Neighbours and local shopkeepers had nothing of interest to say. The professor was interested in photography and had set up a small room as a lab. They had confiscated a large number of photographs and negatives and books of mounted photos from his home office. He and a constable would go through them later today. The SOCOs had taken a digital camera with them. They suspected that he had a second, fancier one, a Nikon, with interchangeable lenses because they found an additional Nikkor lens.

Peter described the search of the professor's office and his discussions with the professor's colleagues. They considered him somewhat odd and unsociable, but — Peter read from his notes here — "a consummate professional and dedicated mentor of his students."

Nobody could imagine him synthesizing a drug used to kill people or fathom a reason why he would do so. And nobody had seen him do anything suspicious.

Inspector Khan recounted his experience at the laboratory. By far the most interesting part, he thought, was dealing with the director and deputy director. They were initially hostile but quickly decided that it was in their best interest to cooperate. They confirmed, at least provisionally, the opinion of the Anglia Ruskin chemist that the drug, or something like it, could be synthesized in their lab. They promised to consult with colleagues and submit a written report. They suggested it would be much easier to design a similar molecule that would have roughly the same effect and would lead the coroner to conclude it was the drug used by hospitals.

Inspector Khan pointed to the folder on his desk, the copy of the logbook he had been given. "The professor had used the centrifuges on multiple occasions, but seemingly for legitimate purposes relevant to his research. The director was going to eyeball the logbook and talk to the technician in charge of the machines to see if he could have used a centrifuge for some other purpose."

"I also asked them about bomb-making," Inspector Khan said. "This would require some machine tools and other equipment, some of it not in their lab but available elsewhere in the university. Here too, they promised to ask around but were dubious. Someone would have seen him with this equipment and wondered what was going on."

"What if he went into the lab at night?" Inspector Davidson asked.

"They're checking on that."

"Is it possible he assembled a bomb at home or in his lockup?" Inspector Davidson asked.

"The SOCOs went through the garage," Peter said. "There was nothing in sight to attract their attention."

"Did any of you encounter Professor Bricknell?" Peter asked. "He was not at his office, and his colleagues had not seen him all day."

He had not been at home or in his lab. Inspector Khan called the head of the chemistry department, whose mobile number he now had, to ask if he had seen him, which he had not. He promised to call around and get back to the inspector.

"Maybe he's done a runner?" said Inspector Davidson.

"I almost hope he has," said Inspector Khan. "It would be an admission of guilt. But it would leave us with two suspects who have hightailed it."

"Two?" said Peter and Inspector Davidson in tandem.

"Yes, two. There's another suspect in this case."

Inspector Khan described his telephone call with the master and the disappearance of Liam Stanley from Leinster College. Liam had told other students he was going to get even with Professor Mason and his sudden disappearance made him a person of interest. The inspector had filled out the missing person form and wanted Peter to go to Leinster to interview some of the students. The master would provide a list of relevant names, but Inspector Khan thought it best to start with the other students implicated with Liam in the data fudging incident. He had asked the master to make sure they were all available after six p.m.

Peter nodded his head and tried to hide his disappointment. He would almost certainly be late for his rendezvous with Elaine and doubted he would learn anything of interest at the college. There was nothing he could do about it. He asked if he could head over to Leinster now as there was probably little more they could do until the lab reports began to come in. Inspector Khan agreed.

"If you get over there now," he said, "you might make your appointment on time."

"What appointment?"

"Lay you five-to-one odds it's either tennis with your new woman or another well-known indoor sport."

"How did you twig this?"

"The bounce in your step and freshly ironed shirts. And I've caught you twice today looking at your watch. I'm a detective, after all."

"You won't hold this against me?"

"Hold it against you? I'm envious. Get yourself over to Leinster College so you can have a free evening."

After Peter left, the two inspectors continued their conversation. Could it be another coincidence, they wondered, that these two men had disappeared at the same time? Were they in some way connected? Liam did not study chemistry, and Professor Bricknell was not affiliated with

Leinster College. Professor Bricknell had photography as a hobby, and perhaps Liam did too. Inspector Khan called Peter on his mobile to have him add this to his list of questions to students.

"Could they have gone off together?" Inspector Davidson asked.

"Too good to hope for," Inspector Khan said. "It would give us a young man with a motive for murder and an accomplice, presumably in it for the money."

"But it would still not solve the problem of Jaime. Why kill him? And what connection did he have with the professor or this student?"

"Hang on a minute," said Inspector Khan, reaching again for his phone. He called Peter a second time.

"Another question for your students, and perhaps for the master. Did Liam come from a wealthy background or have money for some other reason?"

"Any more questions, sir?"

"Only the personal one that I'm not going to ask."

XXV: Tuesday Evening

Peter arrived at Leinster College as the sun dipped behind the chapel of the college across the street. He was escorted to the same common room he and the inspector had used for interviews on their prior visits. He spoke to two of the students who had heard Liam voice his threat and to another two students the master had identified as his mates. The students had not volunteered this information to the master but had made the mistake of telling friends, and word had spread through the college. The master had summoned them to his study and told them it was in their interest, and that of the college, to speak to the police. They got the message and reluctantly agreed to meet with Peter. They had little to add to what the inspector had heard already from the master. On two occasions, both in pubs, Liam had carried on at length about what a turd Professor Mason was and how he exploited his students to code data for his research. He wished him an unhappy end. One of the students insisted that he never heard him actually threaten to do physical harm to the professor, let alone kill him. The other reported that Liam had said something along the lines of wanting to put arsenic in the professor's much-loved Torrone, a nougat-based Italian sweet, and watch him writhe in agony.

Liam's friends thought it inconceivable that he would have done anything of the kind. He had it in for the professor, to be sure, and was deeply concerned about his future; an academic career was out of the question if the committee upheld the charge that he had fudged data. They thought Liam was sounding off, in part because he could think of no course of action likely to improve his situation. To their knowledge, he had no stash of dosh. He came from a middle-class background, was the first member of his family to attend university, let alone do postgraduate work. Like other PhD students, he struggled to make ends meet because their fellowships never covered all their expenses. They had no idea where he had gone; he had not confided in them before he took off.

Peter had a careful look around his room and found nothing to arouse his interest beyond a newspaper story about the discovery of the professor's body that Liam had cut out and tacked on to his bulletin board. As Peter expected, Liam had taken his laptop with him; there was a rectangular space on an utterly cluttered desk indicating where it had sat.

Satisfied that he had done a thorough, if disappointing, job of quizzing the students and searching Liam's room, he set off with time to spare to meet up with Elaine.

***

Our murderer had been lying low for some time. He was enjoying the national press coverage and endless speculation in the media. Most titillating of all were the blogs and other on-line posts, many of which smelled a conspiracy. Professor Mason studied protest, and some of the conspiracy theorists suggested that MI 5, or even the CIA, had done him in. Others saw the hand of Muslim extremists behind this and other evil deeds. They had planted the bomb at Leinster College and murdered the professor because of what he had found out about them. Some of the bloggers who pointed the finger at the intelligence agencies surmised that they had planted a bomb at Leinster College to make it look like the work of Muslims. Another blogger insisted that UKIP had done it in the hope of mobilizing political support. The only consensus seemed to be that the police were incompetent, although a few bloggers suggested that their failure to catch the culprits was deliberate because they were being restrained by MI5 or covering up for it.

The murderer thought the police were doing a credible job in the circumstances. He knew they had more or less rejected the idea that the anaesthetic he used to immobilize Sid Vicious, and Yobbo was stolen from the manufacturer, distributor, or end-user hospital. The police were looking elsewhere, and earlier today, the local radio station had informed him, a squad of SOCOs in white suits bumbled their way through a

235

Cambridge chemistry lab. They wouldn't find anything, he told himself with some satisfaction. I'm still a step or two ahead.

He had covered his tracks carefully. The police had nevertheless picked up on the altered car registration. This was really quite impressive. He understood that CCTVs could read registrations and assumed there were likely to be a number of them caught on camera between Sid's home and the station, and perhaps one or two where they had abducted Sid. He had changed two letters and a number on the plate of his borrowed car. He hoped that it would slip by CCTV coverage, and if not, send the police after some innocent car owner, who would swear he was nowhere near Bateman Street that morning. He had calculated the number of permutations generated by a change in two letters and one number and concluded that it was large enough to keep several police forces engaged for decades. He could not figure out how the police had worked backwards from the altered plate to a small range of possible ones. There should have been millions of possibilities for them to eliminate. By his reckoning, they should be searching the national database for months, if not years. Maybe they had picked people at random to question and swipe their registration in the hope of forcing the murderer's hand? It would not work.

He faced a different problem. His two operations had required strategic insight and street smarts, and few people, he told himself, possessed both qualities. In another life, he might have been a general. But his choice of profession was preferable. Generals take orders from politicians, who are rather unimaginative, ego-driven people more interested in power and the obedience of their subordinates than they are in positive policy outcomes. He was outcome-focused and eschewed publicity. Better to have the satisfaction of having done something good for society — and there was no question that removing these two men was a social benefit — than the plaudits of the crowd. The only admiration he sought was from Mrs Mason, and that was eluding him.

This problem he could not solve by strategic planning or street smarts. He had removed the principal obstacle to his goal: Sid Mason. Making Cynthia fall in love with him was a different kind of challenge. He had fallen into the common trap of focusing on the first step of a plan that required multiple steps to reach the pot of gold. He felt like the bank

236

robber who meticulously planned how to enter the vault and grab the jewels inside but had not given much thought to how he could sell them without getting caught. Sometimes the unforeseen can be beneficial, as with the murder of Yobbo. He had hired him because he needed help with the murder and had killed him because he was a witness to it. He later realized that the police must be tearing their hair out, trying to find a connection between Sid and Yobbo.

You are being too hard on yourself, he thought. For the bank robber, breaking into the vault was only a means to an end. For him, the double murder was an end in its own right. He had rid the world of an intellectually arrogant shit and a social parasite and had enjoyed what he did. This had only dawned on him afterwards. He was surprised by the thrill of the deed and the subsequent satisfaction of avoiding discovery by the police. He put the bomb in Leinster College as a diversion to misdirect the police and make them think there was some kind of connection between the murders and Islamic extremists. He now believed he was motivated as much by the excitement of a second operation as by its putative benefits. He knew he would enjoy a third operation of some kind but also recognized the added risk each time he did something like this. Not that he was a serial killer, but he knew from reading about them that they were not usually caught until they had killed multiple people. Knowledge of their modus operandi or a mistake ultimately made it possible for the authorities to track them down.

The police were more capable than he thought, but they would never have anything more than circumstantial evidence linking him to either crime. All the physical evidence he had disposed of effectively, and there were no witnesses. Had there been, they would have been on to him by now. It would be his word against theirs, and no prosecutor would consider pressing charges for fear of being made a fool of in the courtroom. If he did nothing, he would be safe. But doing nothing would not get him any closer to Mrs Mason. He had tried the normal social route of asking her out for a drink but had been turned down. Something else was required, but anything he could think of that had any prospect of success could backfire and expose him to the authorities. He was at a loss to know what to do but felt increasingly compelled to do something.

Inspector Khan went home late to a satisfying meal of leftovers preceded and accompanied by a glass of Albarino, a white wine from Galicia. He had opened the bottle on Sunday night to accompany the octopus and potato he had cooked, another Galician speciality. Neither then, nor now, was he in a particularly Spanish mood, but he had found some exotic and interesting looking Spanish potatoes at his local greengrocer and thought octopus would be an appropriate accompaniment. On Sunday night he made a concession to the Spanish-themed cuisine by listening to Verdi's *Don Carlos* whilst he ate. Based on a play by Schiller, it offered a chilling account of a regime where all human feeling was overridden by political calculations, to the disadvantage of everyone. It was a depressing libretto, but beautiful music and singing, and hearing it always left him in an elevated state. Try as he might, he could never fathom why listening to or watching depressing operas put him in such a buoyant mood.

***

Elaine was also having some second thoughts, but not enough of them to hold her back from a relationship that was moving down the runway like a jetliner whose pilots were anxious to take off for fear of losing their slot. She enjoyed spending time with Peter and experienced a tingle at the prospect of seeing him again. For a man, she thought, he's sensitive, treats her as an equal, has a good sense of humour, and is dynamite in bed. She thought she enjoyed the sex largely because of how these other qualities affected his lovemaking. It was much easier to cook for two, and especially for someone who was so full of praise for her efforts. They enjoyed a number of activities together, including tennis. There really was no downside, she thought, except for the uncomfortable coincidence of their shared profession. At least they did not work at the same cop shop, only in the same town, and so far, had been able to keep their relationship a secret. How long this would last, and what the consequences of exposure would be, she could only guess at.

Her only real concern was her social isolation in her new job and town. Peter solved this problem, and she had to be honest with herself here. She recognized that loneliness made any relationship more attractive and wanted to be certain that it was not in any way driving her interest in Peter. He was on his way over, and she pushed these thoughts out of her mind. She quickly changed out of her uniform, showered, and put on jeans and a shirt. She had a wicked thought. Why not, she told herself, and promptly undressed. After her outer garments, she shed her bra, knickers, and socks. She strode into the kitchen and wrapped herself in her cooking apron, deftly tying it behind her. She looked at herself in the bathroom mirror. Mighty sexy, she thought, and the outfit would leave no doubt about her willingness to cater to Peter's appetites and her own.

***

Mrs Mason was also in her kitchen but primly dressed. She had always enjoyed cooking and found doing it for one more challenging. It was also more interesting as her husband had fairly limited food tastes and some quite rigid requirements about what got served and when. She felt liberated when she cooked but lonely when she ate. At work she never felt this way because her chambers and the courtroom were spaces she had never shared with Sid. Her colleagues, still solicitous, were no longer treating her with kid gloves. She encouraged this return to normalcy by not talking about her situation or asking for any kind of special privilege.

Only one person had suggested that she think about her social life, and she had responded with a long hard stare. The topic had not been raised again. Her daughter had implied something along these lines, but far more discreetly, when she asked her if she was getting out of the house. Mrs Mason had been taking her usual walks, going to local cultural events, and was looking into the possibility of a tour of the Silk Road. A colleague from another law firm was thinking of going and asked if she was interested in joining her. It would be good to have someone along she knew, and it would be cheaper if they shared a room. She had always wanted to see more of the world and was attracted by the exotic character of the itinerary. Her friend said it was a good tour company and glowingly described a previous voyage she had made with them. Travel would have the additional advantage of getting her out of Cambridge and away from anybody who knew about her tragedy.

Mrs Mason had made herself a boeuf bourguignon. She had prepared and cooked it the evening before and let it stew whilst she was at work. She heated it up and let it simmer some more when she came home. She prepared a salad to go with it and had fun adding fennel, peppers, pumpkin seeds, and finishing it with an oil and mustard dressing. She treated herself by opening a bottle of Domaine de Vieux Télégraphe, a present a couple of years back from a couple who knew how much she liked Châteauneuf-du-Pape. They had invited her for dinner recently, and she had cautiously accepted. It had been her first night out, and she had thoroughly enjoyed herself. They had the good sense to not invite any male to make a fourth and not to ask her how she was coping or what she was feeling. It was the closest thing to a normal night out that she had had since the murder, and she was deeply grateful to them.

XXVI: Wednesday Morning

The following morning everyone was at work on the early side. There was an air of excitement as they waited for the lab reports. The detectives knew they would not filter in until late morning, so there had been no real reason to rush to work. But they all had, and their excitement fed on one another as they speculated about what the technicians might find. They nursed their cups of tea and coffee and expressed hope that the SOCOs would come up with evidence of bomb-making in the professor's lab or something equally incriminating in his home or office. Peter thought they might get lucky with the camera and books of pictures. Maybe there would be a shot of Jaime.

"And what kind of connection could they possibly have?" asked Inspector Davidson.

"What if he convinced Jaime that he could make more money selling boutique drugs and that he would synthesize them in return for his assistance in killing Professor Mason? Then he killed Jaime to avoid having to produce the drugs."

"That's a stretch," said Inspector Khan. "And what was his motive for killing Professor Mason?"

"I haven't gotten that far."

"Neither have we," said Inspector Khan. "Perhaps we need to look more closely into the relationship between the two men. Would you give Mrs Mason a ring and ask her if she knows Professor Bricknell and, more to the point, if her husband might have known him? Could you also send constables over to the professor's lab and office with a photo of Professor Mason and see if anybody recognizes him? I'll call Jaime's mother and ask her if he had any interest in photography."

The first report arrived, and the three detectives gathered around the machine, waiting for the pages to print out. There were only two, and they were from the lab that tested the swipes taken in the professor's home, garage, and office for evidence of explosives. The swipes were negative. A second report arrived moments later. It reported that the swipes sent to another police lab also came back negative.

"That's a downer," Peter said.

"Let's not jump to conclusions yet," said Inspector Khan.

His remark was greeted by silence and desultory conversation ensued as they waited for more news. Inspector Khan asked Peter if he had a good time last night, to which he received a simple "yes" in reply. The inspector recognized the construction of a new no-go area, as it had been customary until now to chat about their off-duty activities. Inspector Davidson directed their attention to the bomb and whether it was possible to assemble one without leaving any traces. Peter suggested that you could buy a ready-made bomb to put in your briefcase or assemble it in some other location.

"Let's look at his briefcase, backpack, or whatever he uses to carry things to and from work," said Inspector Khan.

"We have to find him first," said Peter. "He hasn't turned up at the lab, office, or home. I asked the lab director and the head of the department to call me if he had, and we have his house under surveillance. I'll call the lab and office to double-check."

Peter continued speaking as he punched in the first number in his mobile. "He could have some workshop somewhere else, perhaps at a holiday cabin?"

"It's the drug we should be focusing on," said Inspector Khan. "That's what we suspect him of producing. I think we're getting ahead of ourselves talking about the Leinster bomb."

"True," said Inspector Davidson. "But the conversation was triggered by the lab reports. It's hard to know how we would know he had produced the drug unless someone observed him doing it."

"There are also the centrifuges," said Inspector Khan. "The head and deputy head of the department seemed to think that they would be essential in producing the drug or any substitute. We need to see what they make of their logbook. I've had a look, and it tells me nothing beyond fairly regular use by the professor."

Peter had slipped out of the office when the first number he called started to ring. He now returned and announced that Professor Bricknell had not appeared at either office or lab. "It looks like he's done a bunk."

"Do we know if his car's in the lockup?" Inspector Davidson asked.

"I'll ask a constable to have a look," said Inspector Khan. "If he's not on our radar by five p.m., we will upgrade him to the category of suspect."

The printer hummed again as Inspector Khan's office phone rang. The inspector picked up the handset. Unlike most people, he did not grunt, mutter, or say words like "yes", "right", or "perfect" to communicate to the person on the other end of the line that he was still there and paying attention. He finally said, "Thanks, that's very helpful. I'll be here."

"That was the lab director," he informed his colleagues. "He and his deputy have put their heads together on the anaesthetic substitute and are convinced it could be produced without much effort in their lab, provided there was no concern about its purity. They also went through the logbook with the technician in charge of the centrifuges. They're on their way here now. What about the lab?"

"Nothing to report as yet, but they are continuing their tests," Inspector Davidson said.

***

The lab director and his deputy had done something of an about-face in their attitude toward the police. They had been put off by a detective marching into their office with no prior notification to present them with a warrant to search anything and everything in their lab. They also felt protective toward Professor Bricknell. He was a responsible colleague. They had never received a complaint about him, and unlike some of the staff, he was scrupulous in cleaning up after himself, following regulations, signing in and out, and leaving under lock and key that which needed to be secured. They were aware of the historic "town-gown" tensions in Cambridge, largely quiescent at the moment but easily aroused by SOCOs turning a university lab upside down.

The SOCOs turned out to be careful, asked intelligent questions, tried to cause minimal disruption, and did not flaunt their authority. Researchers in the lab were nevertheless stunned by the intrusion, and one refused to budge from his bench and became quite emotional in his

243

protests. The head of the SOCO team refused to be drawn, asked his colleagues to give the researcher a wide berth, and had a quiet talk with the deputy director. She resolved the matter by explaining to the researcher that the SOCOs were only doing their job, and she would stand by to make sure they did not interfere with an experiment of his then underway.

After everyone had left, the lab director and assistant had a quiet chat in the director's office and wondered if there could be any substance to the police suspicions about Professor Bricknell. They quickly came to the conclusion that the best way to satisfy the police as to his innocence was to cooperate fully with them. Toward this end, they went through the centrifuge logbook with the responsible lab technician. They reasoned that on the off chance that Professor Bricknell had done something wrong, they did not want to be accused of a cover-up. The deputy director noted that politicians and bank executives frequently got into more trouble for their efforts to cover up misdeeds than they did for committing them.

The logbook showed that Professor Bricknell had used the centrifuge several times, and each time appeared to have a legitimate purpose for doing so. The lab technician said he had observed him on two of the three occasions and had left for lunch on the third. The professor knew how to use the machine, and he found no reason to miss his lunch hour. Professor Bricknell had told him to go enjoy himself and that he would stay by the centrifuge and clean up afterwards. When pushed, he admitted that the professor could have used the centrifuge for some purpose other than what he had requested it for. He could, in theory, have checked up on him by analysing the residue in the cylinders he had used. But there was no reason for him to do this, and they were cleaned as a matter of course.

At the Parkside Police Station, the director presented Inspector Khan with a written report describing the feasibility of producing a variant of the drug that would quickly and effectively immobilize someone. He explained that the drug company prepared their product from naturally collected serum for reasons of cost and simplicity. They had no evidence that Professor Bricknell had used the centrifuges to make the substitute drug but no evidence that he had not. It would have been possible for him to use a centrifuge for this purpose whilst the technician was on his lunch break.

The director was pleased with his findings. They had done everything possible to help the authorities but had not done anything to incriminate their colleague. Inspector Khan and his colleagues were frustrated, an emotion they did not hide. They grilled the director about the prospect of doing something else to find evidence that the professor had produced the drug. The director could not think of anything they had not already done.

The telephone rang not long after the chemists had departed. Inspector Khan picked it up on the first ring.

"That was the chief lab technician," he told the inspectors after finishing his conversation. "I asked him to call on the off chance that Professor Bricknell made an appearance, and he's just walked into the lab."

***

Professor Bricknell was greeted by technicians, students, and staff who knew him. Word quickly spread that he was back, and it didn't take long for a colleague without much in the way of interpersonal skills to tell him all about how the police had been over the lab with a fine-tooth comb and were especially interested in his workbench and the centrifuges. The professor expressed total bafflement and asked what the police were looking for. Nobody had any idea. He had a look at his workbench to make sure it was in order and went about his business, although not for long. Inspector Khan and Peter entered the lab and headed his way.

"Professor Bricknell?" Inspector Khan asked as he flashed his warrant card before him.

"Yes?"

"I think you had better come with us, sir."

"Why would I do that?"

"We have some questions for you."

"Can't we do that here?"

"Unfortunately, not. You will have to accompany us to the police station."

"The police station! First you photograph and swipe my car, then you search my lab, and for all I know, my home. This is harassment, and I'm going to complain to your superior officer and to the media."

A small crowd had gathered, and it was apparent where their sympathies lay.

"Why don't you leave our professor alone?" said a bearded postdoc.

There were murmurs of approval from those around him.

In a voice loud enough for everyone to hear, Peter said, "This is a murder investigation. We have some questions for the professor. If he answers them to our satisfaction, he can return to his lab."

The word "murder" brought silence.

"Are you ready to go, sir?" Peter asked.

"Let's get this charade over with." Turning to the postdoc who had spoken out, he told him to call Rhianna Johnson at the *Cambridge News* and alert her to what was happening.

***

At the police station, they put the professor in an interview room and waited to question him until his solicitor arrived. He first called his lawyer, a divorce lawyer, who had made it clear on the telephone that he was not qualified to represent his client in this kind of matter. There was someone from his firm — a Michael DuBois — who specialized in criminal law, and he would see if he was free. He called back to report that he was with another client and could not get to the station for at least an hour. Professor Bricknell spurned the offer of coffee or tea but asked for his laptop. Inspector Khan refused. He had taken the professor's briefcase and car keys from him at the lab. He arranged for a constable to pick up the car and drive it to their lab for inspection. He handed the computer over to their IT expert.

"Am I supposed to sit here and twiddle my thumbs?" the professor said to the constable who escorted him to the consultation room. He received no reply.

Neither detective felt sorry for the professor. "Let him stew for a while," Inspector Khan said to Peter when they learnt that Bricknell's solicitor would be delayed. "He'll be even more anxious to leave and possibly more compliant."

"Just what are you going to ask him, sir?"

"His whereabouts for the last day-and-a-half for a start. I want to know what he's been up to. He obviously twigged that we were on to him and took off. But he's come back, and he must be fairly confident that we have nothing on him."

"Unless the miracle workers in the lab come up with something."

"I'll call over. We really can't hold him beyond twenty-four hours on what we have."

The phone rang, and it was Rhianna Johnson. Inspector Khan confirmed that they were questioning the professor or would do so when his solicitor arrived. "No," he told her. "I have nothing to say at this time." He broke off the call.

"We don't need her breathing down our neck," Peter said.

"If we don't get something on the professor, we will be in a worse position. The deputy commissioner will be all over us. Let's find out what's on the professor's computer before we interrogate him."

Inspector Khan called the IT expert, who had just finished a preliminary analysis and promised to come right up.

Susan Trivers was a geek, but did not look like one. After a pint in the pub one night, Peter had confided to his boss that he loved to watch her walk. She had feline elegance and grace. Inspector Khan agreed and noted that this was high praise coming from Peter as she did not have long legs. Sergeant Trivers announced herself and was invited in and offered a chair.

"You won't like this," she said. "The laptop you took from him is a brand-new machine on to which he has uploaded files and programs. He did this yesterday afternoon. I can do more searching if you like, but I've scanned the files and found nothing about the drug or chemical that interests you, nor about bomb-making or the Jaime lad. My guess is there was something on an old computer he did not want anyone to see. He accordingly bought a new one and uploaded only what he thought was innocent enough. I've checked with Apple, and he bought this machine yesterday morning from their shop in Covent Garden."

"I wonder what he did with the other one?" Peter said.

"Destroyed it, I'd wager," said Susan.

"What about his email?" asked Inspector Khan.

"I just started going through it when you called, but I don't expect to find anything. I imagine he's smart enough to know that nothing you upload can be kept private. Downloads are more difficult to track but not impossible. If his old machine was a university computer, we could get its serial number and other identifiers. We could then check to see if he accessed any bomb-making sites. If you could get your chemist friend to give relevant URLs, we can also see if he searched on-line for ways of synthesizing the anaesthetic."

"Thanks. That would be helpful. I'll get you the relevant web addresses."

***

The three detectives conferred before interrogating the professor. In the interim, Mr Dubois had arrived, and they gave him fifteen minutes to introduce himself to his client and, they assumed, instruct him to look his way for an affirmative nod before answering any question. They could fit four people comfortably in the interview room, and Inspector Davidson volunteered to let his colleagues confront Professor Bricknell. He would continue his efforts to track down the professor's former wife and call the missing student's parents to ask if they had heard from him. They agreed that Mrs Bricknell might tell them something useful about her ex.

The interview room was spartan. The off-white walls were bare, there were no windows, and the floor was badly scuffed grey linoleum. The only furnishings were a sturdy metal table with a Formica top, flanked on each of its longer sides by two wooden chairs. There was no ventilation, and the temperature was rising from the body heat of Professor Bricknell and his lawyer. The two detectives entered the room, Peter with a laptop they would use to record the conversation. Inspector Khan introduced himself and Peter to the professor's solicitor. Peter recognized him from a previous case, and the two men nodded at each other.

Inspector Khan addressed the laptop, noting the time and who was present. He turned to the professor and asked him if he knew why he was here.

"Because you bloody well insisted that I accompany you here." He sat with his hands clasped in front of him.

Inspector Khan continued. "You know that we are investigating the murder of two men, both disabled with a drug administered to them intravenously. The coroner sought your advice about the feasibility of synthesizing the drug in a lab, and you told him it would be exceedingly difficult to do. This turned out to be a cock-and-bull story. We sought the opinion of an outside chemist and spoke to the head and deputy head of your department. They all agree that the drug could be synthesized, but it would be easier still to produce something like it that would have the same effect. The substitute would respond to the same tests and appear to the coroner like the actual drug used in hospitals. Why did you lie to the coroner? Why did you insist that the drug must have come from the producer, supplier, or hospital?"

"I did not lie to the coroner. I offered him my considered professional opinion. The drug is hard to synthesize, and it would not be easy to remove all the impurities necessary to make a hospital-grade product."

"But it would be good enough to immobilize someone if you were not concerned about side effects?"

"Almost certainly, but that's not what the coroner asked."

"You are a good enough chemist to know that the drug or a substitute could be made in your laboratory. Do you still maintain this is not the case?"

"The substitute did not occur to me, perhaps because I was asked about the drug itself. I recognize now that it is a possibility."

"And what about the centrifuges? Did you use them to make a substitute?"

"Of course not. Every time any of us uses one of the big centrifuges, we must fill out a request, be assigned a time, and be supervised by a technician. How could I make this chemical I knew nothing about without being observed?"

"Because you encouraged the technician to take his lunch break, leaving you alone with the centrifuges."

At this point, Mr Dubois broke in to assert that this was all speculation. Did they have any evidence that the professor had synthesized the drug? Inspector Khan had to admit they did not.

"On what basis then are you holding my client?"

"I'll come to that, but first," Inspector Khan said to Professor Bricknell, "I want to know what you were doing in London yesterday."

Professor Bricknell looked across to his solicitor for guidance. Mr Dubois nodded at him.

"I went to a museum and a musical. I have stubs from both if you are interested."

"You bought a new computer too," Inspector Khan said.

"Yes, that's right. I have that receipt as well."

"What did you do with your old machine?"

"Its hard drive crashed, and I disposed of it."

"You didn't try to have it repaired?"

"No, it was beyond repair."

"How did you dispose of it?"

"I tossed it in a bin outside of King's Cross."

"That's not a very convincing story."

"Then why don't you invent one you like better."

"How did you upload your files to the new machine without the old one?"

"I store everything important on the Cloud, and it was easy. I imagine this investigation is there as well."

Mr Dubois reached across and put his hand on Professor Bricknell's arm to signal restraint.

Inspector Khan showed no outward sign of irritation but understood the interview was not going anywhere. "He's free to go," Inspector Khan said to the lawyer. "But he's to remain in Cambridge until further notice."

"Can they restrain me like this?" the professor asked his lawyer.

"Yes, they can. So please don't leave town."

***

250

Inspector Davidson made little headway on the missing student, Liam. He had not returned home nor contacted his parents. A call to Leinster College indicated that he had not shown up there either. He had taken his computer with him, and it was his personal machine, not a college or university one, so difficult to trace. The inspector had put in a request to Apple to see if he had bought a machine from them and was waiting for a reply.

The three inspectors met up to exchange information.

"That professor is a smarmy bastard," said Peter. "He's guilty as hell and sits there and mocks us. He knows we know he produced the drug but can't prove it. I'm wondering if it was the right thing to bring him in. He'll be even cockier now."

"Maybe not," said Inspector Khan. "It's a thoroughly unpleasant experience to sit isolated in that room as the temperature goes up. He was outwardly calm, but I bet he was squirming as much inwardly as we were. He knows he's an accessory to murder and that we have him in our sights."

"And then there's the bomb," said Inspector Davidson. "That's still a mystery, although there is nothing to connect the professor with it."

"Agreed," said Inspector Khan. "And let's not forget the missing student. The simplest explanation is that Liam paid the professor to synthesize the drug, and the two of them carried out the murders and put the bomb in Professor Nejami's set to throw us off the track. But there are too many holes here. Liam has no resources that we know of. There's no evidence that he knew Professor Bricknell. He has a good motive to kill Professor Mason, but not Jaime, whom, as far as we know, he never knew. Either we've not been good at finding these connections, or they don't exist. If the latter, we're on the wrong track."

Inspector Davidson revisited the possibility that Professor Bricknell had done it all by himself. "He made the drug, hired Jaime to help him administer it, killed him because he was a witness, and lied to the coroner to direct suspicion away from his lab. We're missing a motive, I confess."

"And the bomb?" asked Inspector Khan.

"Either he made it, or the murders and bomb are unconnected. I'd like to believe he was responsible, but we found no evidence of bomb-making, nor have we even thought about how he would have gained entry to Professor Nejami's set."

"There's a third possibility," said Peter. "On the blogosphere, there are a lot of people who have directed their intelligence to this problem. Perhaps we could learn something from them."

Inspectors Khan and Davidson remained silent, and the latter's eyebrows were now furrowed.

Peter continued. "Maybe the case is so difficult because we are looking too closely at the facts. If, on the other hand, we consider the premise that MI5 is behind both murders, then things neatly fall into place."

"You can't be serious!" said Inspector Khan.

"Gotcha," said Peter, with a big smile formed on his face.

"You two play this game often?" asked Inspector Davidson.

"And he usually wins," said Peter.

"The truth of the matter is that we are all losing," said Inspector Khan.

XXVII: Wednesday Afternoon

Professor Bricknell returned to his lab and was immediately surrounded by colleagues and students curious about what had happened. He gave them a version of the story that put him in the best possible light and the police in the worst. The detectives had confiscated his briefcase and computer, which they refused to return. They made him sit and wait in an airless room for over an hour just to torment him. Their questions were ill-considered and little more than a fishing expedition. Their tone and language were insulting, but fortunately, his solicitor made them release him. "It was truly appalling," he said to the now large gathering. "The police in this town need to be reined in."

His diatribe fell on receptive ears. The lab director, standing off to one side, took it all in and was sympathetic. She nevertheless wondered how accurate an account the professor was giving. He did not take liberties with the facts in his work. Today he was playing up to the crowd and revealing a side of himself she had never seen. Professor Bricknell was clearly enjoying himself. She watched as the professor returned to his bench after the hubbub had died away. He moved several items around, stood staring at a beaker for some time before picking it up to examine it. He left the lab abruptly.

***

Rhianna Johnson recorded Professor Bricknell's description of what he called his "imprisonment" to make sure she represented him accurately. She would contact Inspector Khan to see if he would offer a comment. She had learnt from long experience never to accept as accurate first-hand accounts from people with axes to grind. And Professor Bricknell had a very large and sharp axe. She called Inspector Khan but reached his message service. She asked that he give her a ring. She then called Peter, who was in his office.

"I've just interviewed Professor Bricknell," she said. "He's furious with you lot and passed along all the lurid details of his interrogation to his colleagues, and to me, of course."

"What did he tell you?" Peter asked.

Rhianna relayed the gist of what he said.

"That's nonsense," Peter said. "He sat in the interview room because he had to wait for his solicitor to arrive. His lawyer did urge restraint, but on his client, not on us. We did not harass him but asked straightforward questions, for most of which he had no answers."

"Can I quote you on this?"

"I need to be careful here. We never publicize what transpires in police interviews. One of the reasons, ironic in this instance, is to protect those whom we interview."

"I understand. What if I say something along the lines of the police deny any wrongdoing? They insist they had ample reason to categorize Professor Bricknell as a suspect and treated him with every courtesy. Any delay was the result of his need to find a solicitor."

"That would be very helpful, but would you mind referring to him as 'a person of interest' and not a suspect? And could you send the text over so I can pass it by my boss?"

"Of course… and remember, the ledger has just become more imbalanced in my direction."

***

The deputy commissioner was perfectly composed when Inspector Khan entered his office. This was a bad sign, the inspector thought. I'm in for a rough time.

He was right.

The conversation began pleasantly enough. The deputy commissioner asked after his health and about his niece before getting down to business. "Where do we stand?" he finally asked. "Are there developments I don't know about?"

"I'm afraid not, sir."

"That's what I feared. It's been some time since the bodies were discovered, and we've made no visible progress."

"Not for lack of trying, sir."

"I grant you that. But the media and the powers that be are interested in results, and we have nothing to show them."

"Are you being hassled, sir."

"You bet I am, from the commissioner, but by no means ending there. The higher-ups want a written report on the murder investigation. And you can rest assured someone will try to outguess us and say we would have had results if we had proceeded differently."

"Do you believe that sir?"

"Of course not. Some cases are just tough to crack. I'm sure the grand panjandrums know that too, but it doesn't stop them breathing down our necks and trying to second guess us."

"Is there anything you can do about it, sir?"

"Would you please stop this 'Sir' business. Once at the outset of a conversation is enough."

"Yes... certainly."

"It's what *you're* going to do about it. Prepare a detailed account of what your team has done, how thorough you have been, and what avenues you have and have not explored, and why. Get it to me by close of business tomorrow. I'll get back to you if I have any questions and otherwise edit and submit it under my name. Maybe that will buy us a little time."

"Any restrictions on length?"

"No, be as thorough as possible. Better to bury them in detail than not."

"Any other instructions?"

"No. But you will need to justify this interview with the professor. I gather you got nowhere with him?"

"Yes and no. We couldn't pry anything out of him, but we got an account of his movements over the last two days. Thanks anyway for getting us the search warrants."

"They are another source of grief," said the deputy commissioner. "You found no smoking gun, and so far, to our knowledge, nothing that promises a breakthrough in this case. Unless you do, it's going to be much harder for the judge to issue me warrants in the future, and the media is certain to carry on about police heavy-handedness. And I will catch the flak, not you."

"I understand. I haven't given up hope that the labs will turn up something; they're still doing their work."

"You'd better have more than that the next time I see you."

***

Back in his office, Peter came by and briefed him about his conversation with Rhianna.

"She's being remarkably responsible," the inspector said after hearing Peter's account of their telephone conversation. "And did she email her text?"

"She did, sir."

"Look, Peter, why don't we drop the 'Sir'? We're friends and colleagues, and we both know I'm the boss. There's no need to confirm this in every conversation."

"I'm happy to oblige," Peter said as he handed over a one-page printout from Rhianna Johnson.

Inspector Khan read it quickly and handed it back. "You're right. I wonder what got into her? She's passing up the possibility of a juicy exposé in favour of the truth. Police abuse would make a far better story than suspect interviewed without obvious result."

"She did make it clear that she expects something in return."

"Maybe we have something to give her?"

"We do?"

"I'm tempted to say 'gotcha,' because we don't. But I have an idea. Perhaps we can flesh it out together."

***

Our murderer nursed a cup of coffee in his kitchen and pondered his dilemma. He had only bought time. It was abundantly clear that the police did not have a clue about either the murder or the bombing. Whatever hard work and cleverness had led to their registration breakthrough was not evident in their subsequent inquiries. The

Cambridge News story about their harassment of Professor Bricknell was bound to arouse public concern and pressures from above on the police to tread carefully. He would be the direct beneficiary of their restraint. He could go about his business secure in his relative invulnerability.

He asked himself if he had made any mistakes and done anything that might trip him up. The big surprise had been the discovery of the bodies, but that was not the result of any error on his part. Those damned sailors had found them, a one-in-a-million chance. Their discovery set off a murder investigation, initially down the wrong pathways. The police looked for a leak in the drug supply from manufacturer to hospital, and more amusingly, for a connection between Sid and Yobbo. He had not thought beforehand of the ways in which his choice of drug and accomplice would confuse the police but subsequently took great pleasure in their unexpected but beneficial consequences. He convinced himself that they had not been entirely unintended. He was a really clever fellow whose planning must subconsciously have considered these possibilities. His crime was even more perfect as a result. The only loose end was Professor Bricknell, from whom he borrowed the car. He would have to remain alert here.

And what to do about Mrs Mason? Any overt attempt to court her was likely to be rebuffed, given how she cold-shouldered his invitation to buy her a drink. Should he continue to bide his time or risk exposure? The former strategy was certainly the safer of the two but got him no closer to her. She might even find someone else in the interim, putting him back at square one. Restraint was as big a gamble as intervention. Even his brilliance in planning and execution had its limits.

He reached a decision, at least for now. He would continue to plan "Operation Bondage" as if he were committed to carrying it through but defer its implementation for the time being. Executing this plan was a real challenge, and that required a false trail, leading the police to point the finger at someone else.

***

Elaine was having another boring day at work. She was on duty at the railway station, and nothing much ever happened. She believed that she had further honed her sense of how people behaved at railway stations and directed her attention to people who violated her expectations. She approached a woman who turned out to have a medical problem and a man with a child who, she thought, should have been at school. He turned out to be a foreign national separated from his British wife, who was in the process of abducting their daughter to his home country. Her superiors were delighted, as it was one more success that helped to justify their presence in an environment of severe cuts in funding.

Watching trains and passengers come and go made her anxious to get on a railway carriage herself. She recognized that she had already done so in a metaphorical sense. She and Peter were on an express train to Commitment that she had unwittingly boarded, and, she suspected, so had he. It made only one stop en route, at the twin cities of Doubtful and Frightened. She would soon have to decide whether to get off or continue on her journey. She needed to discuss this with Peter but worried that bringing it up would encourage him to leave the train. And unlike some of the trains that left Cambridge, there was no conductor who would come through the carriage, ask for their tickets, and eyeball his and read its destination.

The railway police had been warned once again about a possible drug shipment, and she remained alert. Since the economy had gone south, the number of needy people had risen dramatically. Some of them were not averse to becoming mules. So far, they had not caught anyone despite repeated so-called tip-offs. They never came up with a description of the mule, only with a never-changing profile that was all but useless. In a police state, they could stop people at random and search them. But this was Britain, where probable cause was necessary, and she was pleased about the law. Some of her colleagues would otherwise abuse their authority, and the police would be regarded as a public nuisance, if not a direct threat. This would make their job less appealing and more difficult and lead to more abuse. A vicious cycle was the term that came to her mind, and she wondered where she had picked it up.

For ordinary people, she did her best to exude a friendly air. They felt more relaxed and were more likely to ask for assistance. To expose a mule, she thought, it helped to look fierce enough to unsettle them. She could not do both simultaneously and sometimes flipped a coin in her mind to determine her demeanour. She was generally pleased when the friendly side of her imaginary coin won the toss, as it had this afternoon. It paid an almost immediate dividend. Within the first half-hour of her shift, an anxious woman approached her as she walked through the station. She was to have met her mother on the 15.05 train from King's Cross. As far as she could tell, it had arrived on time, but her mother was not on it. She had stood outside the turnstiles waiting for her to appear. Perhaps her mother was on the platform looking for her there? She gave Elaine a description, and off she went to track one to have a look around. The platform was almost deserted as the train had returned to London with almost all of the people waiting on the platform. She easily identified the missing mother and escorted her to her daughter. The mother looked disturbingly like Miss Marple, and Elaine began to wonder if she had walked onto a TV set. Mother and daughter thanked her profusely.

She resumed her lookout for this mythical drug mule, focusing her attention on the platform where the local to Liverpool Street was due to depart. She had read in the *Guardian* about some woman who had recently been caught with drugs in her bra. She did not share this information with her male colleagues. They were already fixated on knockers and would now have a justification for their sometimes-obvious ogling. As a well-endowed woman, she had become used to this kind of attention but found it irksome when a man to whom she was talking clearly did not register what she said because his attention was engaged elsewhere. Her police uniform did not advertise her curves, and she was thankful for it.

Nobody looked nervous, but perhaps the mule was experienced enough to feel immune to scrutiny. Her uncle was a pilot and told her that most accidents caused by pilot error happened when pilots began to feel comfortable in the cockpit and had not yet been frightened by some unexpected event or near-accident. She hoped her mule was in the vulnerable category and would make some mistake or do something to attract her attention. People boarded the train, it left on time, and Elaine, disappointed but not surprised, returned to the police station.

XXVIII: Wednesday Afternoon II

Liam Stanley had heard informally from Professor Lundgren that the charges Professor Mason had brought against him, and two other students would be dropped. The professor had died before he had submitted the dossier documenting his allegation, and he was no longer available for questioning. Instead, the three students would be asked to make an appearance before the disciplinary committee, where an academic version of the riot act would be read to them. They would be let off with a stern warning, and their academic careers could proceed as planned. The department had arranged for a noted authority in their field from King's College London to serve as their informal supervisor and external examiner. The students were overjoyed but wondered how their new supervisor would treat them. They decided to meet with him as soon as possible in the hope of getting off on the right foot.

After lunch, Liam travelled to London to meet up with the two other students. They gathered in front of Somerset House and made their way through to the new supervisor's office on the seventh floor of the Strand Building. It was not large but had an impressive view of the Thames. They could see west as far as the London Eye and the Houses of Parliament and east to Tower Bridge and beyond to the Gherkin, Shard, and the newest skyscrapers under construction. Liam and his colleagues were impressed by the vista but also by the professor, who made no mention of the scandal. They commiserated together over Professor Mason's death, and he quizzed them about their research. Normally, an external examiner is not involved with the students prior to the completion of their theses, but in this case, an exception had been made. After the meeting, the students walked through the courtyard of Somerset House to the Courtauld Gallery. Admission was free with their Cambridge IDs. Liam had convinced the other students to join him to see the museum's stunning collection of Impressionists. They lingered in front of a portrait of a reclining nude by Modigliani, which they agreed was wonderfully erotic.

Afterwards, they gathered in the basement café for coffee and cake and discussed their encounter with their new supervisor. They were surprised that he had not asked them about the charges Professor Mason had brought against them. One of Liam's companions suggested that perhaps the department had said nothing about them. They agreed that this would be typical of the department, always trying to put the best face on everything to maintain, if not improve, its middle of the pack standing in the field of politics. They further agreed that it was in their interest to keep mum as well and behave as professionally as they could with their new adviser. Their degree and job prospects would depend on it.

***

Inspector Khan was hard at work on his report for the deputy commissioner. He was known to have a knack for writing such things, which actually made it more difficult for him because recipients had high expectations. He wanted to produce a document that would convince readers of the thorough and professional nature of their investigation and would also justify the search warrants and continuing interest in Professor Bricknell. His narrative began with the discovery of the bodies but was not chronological. Rather, it was organized around the relevant subjects of their investigation: means of death and the source of the anaesthetic; who had motives to murder the professor or Jaime; what connection, if any, was there between the two dead men, and the possible relationship between the bombing and the murders. There was a final section on Professor Bricknell.

Inspector Khan passed his draft by Peter and Inspector Davidson and incorporated their suggestions before hand-delivering it to the deputy commissioner. He knew that, at most, the report would buy them some additional time, so the pressure was really on them to solve the case. His colleagues were fully aware of the situation when the three of them met to decide what to do next. Inspector Davidson confessed that he had made no progress in tracking down Liam Stanley. He argued, and no one disagreed, that he had a motive for murdering his professor, but there was no evidence implicating him. He was only a person of interest because he had done a bunk.

Professor Bricknell was another matter. But here too there was consensus that the evidence against him was entirely circumstantial, as Inspector Khan had acknowledged in his report. They considered the counterfactual of whether they would be so interested in him if they had other leads. Peter insisted they would be because he had lied to the coroner. At the very least, Peter said, he was guilty of manufacturing the anaesthetic. They had no motive to connect him to the murders, and he had no real link to Professor Mason.

Inspector Khan told his colleagues that he had a plan for smoking him out. They listened with interest as he described it and went on to consider its pros and cons. It involved a third person, everyone's favourite journalist, and they batted about the wisdom of involving her. As no one had a better idea, and Rhianna would almost certainly be willing — downright enthusiastic, Inspector Khan thought — they decided to go ahead.

"Don't you think we should clear it with the deputy commissioner?" said Inspector Davidson.

"Definitely not," said Inspector Khan. "He's already having second thoughts about persuading a soft judge to issue the warrants. He would hardly be receptive to our scheme."

"I suppose you're right."

"Best just to go ahead with it as planned."

***

Inspector Khan gave Rhianna Johnson a call and asked her to meet him in a nearby café. She accepted immediately but needed an extra thirty minutes because she was filing a story and had to double-check a fact or two.

Inspector Khan arrived a few minutes early, largely because he was bored. There was no queue. He bought himself a cappuccino and grabbed one of two adjacent leather sofas that had just become free. He put his suit jacket on the other chair to save it for Rhianna. She sailed through the door at almost exactly the appointed hour, wearing her usual summer outfit of jeans and T-shirt. He could not help but notice her breasts as the shirt was at least a size too small. It had "Cap d'Antibes" written across it, and he could readily imagine her there lying on the beach without the shirt. The musings reminded him how sexually frustrated he was and how envious he was of Peter for having found a partner.

He averted his eyes from her shirt, hoping that she had not caught him clocking her. He doubted she would mind and wondered if she deliberately wore this size shirt to draw attention to herself and soften up — maybe not the right turn of phrase — men from whom she wanted something. He did not doubt that it gave her a useful edge as a reporter.

He took her drink order and got on the end of the queue that had now formed. Funny, he thought, how queues came in waves and for no particular reason he could fathom. He was sure some mathematician could prove that random entry into cafés was more likely to result in bunches than evenly spaced arrivals. One might make real money by figuring out the patterns and the occasional gaps that appeared in queues. You could design an app for people to time their entry into cafés, or better yet, into railway ticket offices and security checkpoints at airports. But if enough people planned their entry into these places, their arrival would no longer be random, and that would defeat the algorithm, rendering his envisaged app useless. It would only work if used by relatively few people, and that would not make him any money unless, of course, he charged a king's ransom.

His musings kept his mind off the queue, and he was now the next customer. He remembered — he had nearly forgotten — that Rhianna had asked for green tea. The heavily tattooed and multi-nose ringed server fetched a china pot, filled it with steaming hot water and placed it on a tray along with a cup, saucer, spoon, and teabag. He paid with cash, pocketed his change, and carried the tray to the table. He was pleased to discover his coffee was still warm; Rhianna had covered the cup with the saucer. He watched her put the teabag into the pot and sit back, waiting for it to brew.

"Would you like some sugar?" the inspector said. "I forgot to ask."

"No thanks. I'm not the sugary type in case you hadn't noticed."

The inspector sipped his coffee, waiting for the right moment to explain what he wanted from her.

"Any break in the case?" she asked.

"I wish. Frankly, we don't seem to be getting anywhere even though we now have a suspect."

Rhianna leaned forward and poured herself a cup of tea, satisfied that it had steeped long enough. "That would be Professor Bricknell?"

"Yes. What's your impression of him?"

"He was very polite and very anxious to please, indicating, I think, just how much he wanted to use me as a conduit to embarrass you."

"And why would he want to do that?"

"Come on, Inspector. Embarrassing the police is like cheating Her Majesty's Revenue and Customs or, better yet, British Gas. It's a real high and, unlike other underhanded acts, one you can share with friends and bring smiles to their faces."

"Do you really believe that?"

"About the tax authority and British Gas, absolutely. But not about the police. I was teasing you. I think he hopes that it will constrain you. I googled him, and he's a distinguished chemist. He's obviously an intelligent man and has reasoned this through carefully. Public sympathy and support from his colleagues is likely to bring pressure on you from above. Your bosses will insist the case is solved ASAP but will not want you to do anything that will backfire in the PR department. You will be constrained."

Rhianna paused to sip her tea.

"Taking this a step further, perhaps he feels vulnerable and imagines something you could do, but now are less likely to, that would expose him or at least increase his vulnerability."

"And what do you think that would be?"

"I don't have a clue. I'm hoping you might."

"I wish I did. Off the record, let me share a confidence with you. For the time being, you'll have to keep mum about it."

"Of course."

Inspector Khan filled her in about the use of a tightly controlled drug to anaesthetize the two murder victims, how they initially searched without success for a leak from the producer, distributor, or hospitals, the coroner's speculation that the drug might be synthesized, Professor Bricknell's insistence that it could not, and subsequent evidence that it could. Professor Bricknell had lied to them, but a search of his home, lab, and office had not found anything incriminating. Professor Bricknell's car had also connected him to the case, Inspector Khan explained.

Rhianna listened carefully. "You've put a lot of work into this," she finally said.

"We all did."

"What made you second guess Professor Bricknell on the drug?"

"It was just a hunch as I had no reason to doubt him at the time. I think I was so desperate for some kind of breakthrough and had time on my hands and decided to seek a second opinion."

"Do you believe in intuition?"

"Not really. I suspect it is the result of unconscious rational inference and that it is as often wrong as it is right. We just remember those occasions where our intuition was correct."

"I had an intuition about you from the outset. Do you remember our first encounter at the press briefing you attended following the breakup of a drug ring some five years back?"

Inspector Khan remembered the press conference well and how he and his "intuition" were singled out for praise by the deputy commissioner. But he didn't remember meeting Rhianna at the briefing. But then she was probably dressed less provocatively, and he was a married man at the time and much less aroused by other women. But what could he say? "Of course, I do."

"It was obvious that you were a cut above your colleagues, socially as well as intellectually. I saw the wedding ring on your hand and thought, now there's a lucky woman."

Inspector Khan wondered where she was going with this and was anxious to return to the matter at hand. By now he had finished his coffee but felt the need to fiddle with something, as he almost always did when feeling uncomfortable. He took out his ever-present pad and a pen.

"Surely, Inspector, you're not going to take notes on my first impression of you as a sexy and attractive man?"

Inspector Khan smiled and put his pad down. "No, certainly not. Tell me about your encounter with Professor Bricknell? Did he come across as sexy?"

Rhianna laughed. "Just the opposite, I think. For a start, he didn't stare at my boobs the way you do. I got the impression that I turned him off."

"Do you think he's gay?"

"No, definitely straight. He likes women all right, but not those he thinks might be available."

"How did you ever form that impression?"

"I'm tempted to say intuition. I don't want to appear conceited, but believe me, a lot of men have looked my way in the two decades since my adolescence. After a while you learn to read them like a book. Take you, for example. You enjoy looking at my breasts but are trying your best not to show it. You also feel a little bit silly about your prurient interest. Am I right?"

Inspector Khan did not quite blush but looked away from her before he agreed with her observation.

"Nothing to be ashamed of, Inspector. And don't you think we could move to a first-name basis now that we are discussing my mammary glands?"

"Let me ask a question, as we seem to be getting personal?"

"Please."

"Your tight shirt accentuates your natural endowment. Did you wear it to arouse me and reap the psychological rewards?"

"I'm not always this calculating, Rudi. I'm more a spontaneous kind of girl. You just haven't seen this side of me yet. I'll own up to dressing in a calculated way today, but here I'm afraid I'm going to disappoint you. I didn't have you in mind. My first appointment was with a young man who works for a local company about which I'm gathering evidence in the hope of writing an exposé of their violation of environmental regulations. I'll tell you about it on another occasion. On the basis of an earlier encounter, I thought I could get a lot more information from him this way."

"Did it work?"

"Oh yes, better than I had hoped. Now I have to deflect his attentions."

Inspector Khan laughed. "A double-barrelled weapon, so to speak."

266

"Yes, and I do apologize. I didn't have time to change before coming here. I would have worn a more professional top. But my shirt does seem to have had an unexpected benefit."

"And what is that?"

"It's broken the ice between us. We're relating like normal people. You know, if we spent more time together, you would feel more comfortable with me."

"I'm sure I would, but let's get back to the matter at hand if that's all right."

Rhianna agreed.

Inspector Khan felt relieved, as he very much wanted to keep this relationship a professional one.

"As I told you, all of our evidence is circumstantial. We're doing more tests, and the SOCOs are using some new technology to see if they can locate any hair or other organic matter in the professor's car that would connect him to either victim. But I suspect he's vacuumed and scrubbed the inside clean. And here's where you come in."

Inspector Khan outlined his plan of action, and Rhianna listened with interest. She agreed to go along with it and promised to report back to him as soon as she had done what he asked.

***

Liam and his friends returned to Cambridge, and he to Leinster College. The porter on duty confided that everyone had been worrying about him and that he was sure the master wanted to speak with him. Liam agreed to meet with him, but after he had taken his bag up to his room and cleaned up.

As expected, the master dressed him down for not having signed out and provided the porter's lodge with a destination where he could be reached. And why didn't he answer his mobile? They had tried to call him several times, as had the police.

"The police?" he asked.

"Yes, the police," the master replied. "There's an ongoing murder investigation, and you're a person of interest to them."

"But they've interviewed me twice."

"And then you disappeared and renewed their interest. I hope you have a good explanation for your absence?"

"I don't know if it's good or not, but I have an explanation."

"Yes?"

"I needed to get away for a few days. First there was the charge of fudging the professor's data, then his murder, and finally, the bomb in Professor Nejami's set. The police grilled me at length because they thought I had a motive for killing the professor, which, of course, I did. But I assure you, the thought never crossed my mind. I've benefitted from his death, but I'm sorry that he's dead. I feel sorry for Mrs Mason. I've met her on a couple of occasions, and she's a very nice woman."

"So where were you?"

"My parents have a little hideaway in Dorset, and I went there. I needed to get away and reflect on all that has occurred and about my future. It was very relaxing, and I'm sorry if I caused you or the college any trouble. I then went up to London to meet up with other students of Professor Mason and see our new supervisor."

"How did that go?"

"Very well. We're grateful to you for not telling him anything about the cloud over our heads here."

"It served no interest, and there is no longer a cloud. You may have heard that the committee decided to let the matter drop as Professor Mason is no longer around to pursue it. Get on with your work and your life and benefit from this experience."

"I will do that. Thank you again, Master."

"And for god's sake, call that police inspector and let him know you are back."

The master wrote down Inspector Khan's name and number and handed it to Liam, who pocketed it and took his leave.

XXVIII: Late Wednesday Afternoon

Mrs Mason was in her office dreading her afternoon appointment with the pest. She had not been in for a while, and Mrs Mason could not guess why she was coming today unless it was the fact that she had left her alone for at least ten days. She had the legal variant of hypochondria, and it would be nice to invent a term for it. They were very similar. Hypochondriacs are not deterred by unpleasant and costly medical procedures, and the pest was not kept away by steep legal fees. Mrs Mason felt uncomfortable about their meetings because it was unethical to bill clients for legal advice they did not need. She had tried unsuccessfully to discourage her from coming on several occasions, to no effect. So be it, if the pest found her time with her a form of entertainment worth paying for, she would do her best to accommodate.

In the interim, she had an interesting libel case. Here, her gripe was with the law, not with her client. British libel law was notoriously one-sided, making it far too easy for people to sue successfully for defamation of character. This encouraged people and institutions with deep pockets to threaten authors and publishers with legal action if they printed something offensive to them. The law had a chilling effect, even when what would be printed was factual and defensible. Certain people and institutions develop reputations for suing publishers and effectively deflect unpleasant but truthful things that would otherwise be written about them.

On this occasion, her client was a young Cambridge historian who had authored a book about the National Health Service. He had criticized their willingness to pay for forms of alternative medicine, noting that there was no scientific evidence that they had any beneficial effect. He described how the supporters of this alternative medicine had used political influence to intimidate the NHS. His publisher insisted he would have to resolve any possible libel threats at his expense before they published his book. Like most academics, he had little money and could not afford the kind of legal aid he required. A colleague in Leinster College sent him Mrs Mason's way, thinking she could give him good advice and would go easy in her billing. Mrs Mason was sympathetic to his plight and was considering taking him on as a pro bono client. The pest's money could be redirected to support something worthwhile. She would have to clear this with her partners, but they devoted a percentage of their hours every month to pro bono work, and she thought this case should appeal to them.

She had decided to do the Silk Road tour with her friend and was looking forward to a preparatory shopping trip after work. She had received a list of things she should take from the tour company and thought most of them sensible. She had not bought new clothes for a while and certainly not of the kind she would need for this adventure. Once she finished with the pest, she expected to be in a good mood.

***

Our murderer felt compelled to act when he learnt that Mrs Mason was soon to leave the country for a holiday. He chose the code name "Operation Liberation" and fantasized what it would be like to tie Mrs Mason up in soft cords that immobilized but did not hurt her and how he would gradually transform her into his sex slave. He believed that this side of her, repressed until now, was waiting to emerge. She would be surprised and initially uncomfortable with herself when it did but ultimately beholden to him for making it possible. This bonding would not happen instantly, and that posed practical problems. At the outset, she would resist. Bondage was not only a means of ultimate liberation but also a necessity in these circumstances. It was fortunate that he had a secluded safe house where she could be kept away from prying eyes. The hideaway had also come in handy for readying the syringe and fashioning the bomb.

Mrs Mason would be missed at her office, and at some point, a nosy neighbour would almost certainly worry about her. Best to abduct her on a Friday afternoon. Unless she had weekend plans he did not know about, this would give him a two-day grace period before she was missed. He had considered tapping her home and office phones but decided it was too risky to do the former. Instead, he tapped her home phone and hacked her personal email account, which provided all the information he needed.

On one of the occasions, he followed her, he saw her check to make sure the spare key to her house was still in its hiding place. Knowing to some degree her schedule, he realized that she was walking to work. He waited until she was out of sight, took the key, and entered her house. He had a good look around but concentrated on the bedroom she used as a home office. Her computer sat on a desk, and he searched its two drawers. There under a plastic divider for pens and the like, he found a Post-it Note with several codes, which he copied onto a pad. One of them looked like a bank code, and the others were clearly passwords for computer accounts. He had no difficulty in figuring out which code was her user ID, and which was her email password. Satisfied with his efforts, he put everything back in place and exited from her house when he thought the street was clear. He ignored her bank account but read her email on a daily basis. He did this in the middle of the night when she was almost certain to be asleep.

This coming weekend was looking good because, to the best of his knowledge, Mrs Mason had no appointments. He was relieved to see there was no other man in her life, not that he expected to find one so soon after Sid's death. He pegged her as the monogamous type and quite proper, despite what he believed to be her deeply passionate nature. Her husband, he was convinced, had not had a clue about how to reach and arouse it, but he did.

The abduction would be easy even without the help of Yobbo. He had another syringe, which he had filled with what he calculated as just enough of the drug to keep her anaesthetized for several hours. He hoped that there would be no side effects. He would monitor her pulse and deposit her at an A & E if any problems arose. Being a careful planner, he noted on his map where the hospitals were between her home in Newnham and his hideaway in the Norfolk Broads. He had spent many hours getting the place ready to accommodate her. He had purchased appropriate restraining equipment and anything else he thought they might need. This included some excellent bottles of Burgundy and prepared foods to accompany it. He would also pick fresh flowers before he kidnapped her.

***

Rhianna was delighted that Rudi had taken her into his confidence, and he really had. She had expected some information but not a full account of where the police stood and their frustration at having only circumstantial evidence against their primary suspect. She had now become part of their investigation, so could not publish anything they had told her beyond what they agreed was in the public interest. But she would be the first to know the facts when the story finally broke and get a real scoop. Better yet, she would be part of the story. She was no longer in the back of the stalls but right on stage, which was exciting. She would show Rudi and the other members of the cast just how well she could play her part.

She called Professor Bricknell and left a message for him. Looks count on stage, and she carefully considered her wardrobe. Anything provocative was out of the question. She would dress conservatively but still make herself look attractive. Charms that were not displayed, but only hinted at, might appeal more to the professor.

***

Elaine was still on the lookout for her mule but was increasingly despairing of success. Lots of people looked nervous at the station for many perfectly innocent reasons. She thought the most likely mules would be students and the unemployed, many of whom were in need of funds, or well-off businesspeople, some of whom were greedy. But there were so many student and business travellers, and perhaps the mule was a perfectly respectable looking middle-aged woman desperate for money to pay for old-age care for one of her ageing parents. She gave up on profiles and decided to rely on instinct.

For no reason she could put her finger on, her attention was drawn to several workmen, one of whom was carrying a holdall that seemed packed with something light judging from how he carried it. She went over and chatted with them and told them that she was in training and told today to act as if there had been a bomb alert. She asked if he would mind if she looked inside the bag. The three men smiled, and the one with the bag took it off his shoulder and unzipped it for her. Inside was a doll nicely wrapped in plastic with a pink ribbon tying it at the top. He smiled and explained it was a present for his daughter. She wished him well and walked down the platform to the sound of laughter behind her. So much for intuition, she thought.

***

Back in the police station, the three detectives were crowded into Inspector Khan's office reviewing the lab report on Professor Bricknell's car. It was inconclusive. They had found hairs, but none with DNA that matched Jaime or Sid. They presumably belonged to the professor, but they did not have a DNA sample from him. There was no sign of blood. The car had been scrubbed clean as if its owner knew that it would get a going over.

Liam Stanley had called Inspector Davidson at the urging of the master. After speaking to him, the inspector had called his friends and the professor at King's College London, all of whom confirmed his story. His disappearance, whilst irresponsible, was explicable. Inspector Davidson removed him from his mind as a suspect.

Inspector Khan spoke to Professor Bricknell's former wife, who still lived in Cambridge and worked as a payroll officer at one of the colleges. It had taken some effort to find her because she had gone back to using her maiden name. She agreed to meet with the inspector and did not seem surprised that he was interested in talking to her. She preferred to do it on neutral ground and requested that he not be in uniform. He readily agreed, explaining that his normal attire was a business suit. They met at a café in town whose seats were not jammed too closely together so they could have a modicum of privacy.

Inspector Khan had no difficulty whatsoever in recognizing Mrs Bricknell — now Pauline Sousa — when she walked into the café. She was conservatively dressed, had her hair in a bun, wore what looked like designer glasses, and had a trim but undistinguished figure. He rose to

273

greet her, offered to buy her a coffee, and invited her to take a seat. There was no queue, and he thought again about the app that might make his fortune. He ordered and paid for two cappuccinos and returned with them on a tray to their table. Mrs Sousa thanked him and asked how she could help.

"If I may be frank, we're interested in your ex-husband."

"I'm glad somebody is. I'm certainly not."

Inspector Khan explained their recent history with Professor Bricknell and their inability to come up with any definitive evidence to connect him with the synthesis of the anaesthetic or the murders.

"He lied to you too. I'm not surprised. That's how he is; self-centred and ready in equal measure to delude himself and others. It was a real problem for our relationship, and it looks like he's done the same with you."

"You could put it that way," the inspector said as he reached for his coffee cup.

"I could see him making the drug if he was strongly motivated to do so."

"Would enough money do the trick?"

"I wouldn't think so. He lives well, but within his income, or at least he used to. I doubt that's changed. He would have to want something very expensive to be unable to afford it, and that would be out of character."

"Can you think of any other reason why he might put his career on the line by making this drug?"

Mrs Sousa sipped her cappuccino, looked across at the inspector and said, "Perhaps the challenge of it? It's why he became a chemist, and most things he likes in life, crossword puzzles, for example, he views as challenges. He builds self-esteem by overcoming them. Well, I take that back. He's really a man of low self-esteem, and he engages in puzzle solving to convince himself that he is someone of value. One of the difficulties between us was that he expected me to pander to his endless need for recognition as a clever fellow. Enough is enough, you would think. But not in his case."

"He might be manipulated by someone who posed it as a challenge and might even have suggested that he doubted the professor's ability to synthesize the drug?" "That would be the right way to approach him. But it would have to be someone he respected and wanted to impress."

"A colleague, perhaps?"

"Yes."

"Can you think of anyone in particular?"

"Let's go back a step, Inspector. It has to be someone with a motive to ask him to assume this risk. I suspect there are fewer people who meet this criterion than friends or acquaintances he would want to impress."

"Quite right. Can you think of someone with a motive?"

"I don't have a clue. Isn't that your job? If you give me a list of people with a strong motive, I can tell you if my ex knows them and how he might respond to them. Mind you, my responses will be three years out of date."

Inspector Khan took another sip of his coffee. He was not doing well here, he thought.

"If only we had such a list, I would show it to you. Frankly, we don't have a clue about the identity of the murderer unless it is your ex-husband."

"Ian a murderer? That's a bizarre thought, Inspector. He may be many things but not a cold-blooded killer."

"You really don't think he would be capable of such an act?"

"I sincerely doubt it. I can see him synthesizing this drug as he is pathetically insecure. But murder, no."

"We do have a few people in our sights, but they have alibis or other reasons why we have discounted them. Three are students, who we have more or less ruled out. Then there's Professors Lundgren and Coates, both of whom were deeply aggrieved by Professor Mason's treatment of them or their students."

"I know Professor Lundgren, but not Coates. I can't imagine her as a murderer either, and Ian did not care for her in any case. He derided her as a poster child feminist and would not have been responsive to any appeal for help from her."

"Is there anything else you can tell me about your ex-husband that might help with the investigation?"

"Just that he's a creep. He's manipulative and dishonest. I'm not surprised he lied to you about the drug, as he lied to me about many things through our marriage. He gets a perverse pleasure out of misleading people and watching the consequences."

The conversation continued for another twenty minutes but provided no additional insight into the professor, with one important exception. Mrs Sousa noted *en passant* that she and her husband used to spend time at his parent's' home on the Dorset coast. It passed to him and his brother when his mother died. As far as she knew, they still owned it. She did not remember the address but gave him the location.

XXX: Thursday Morning

For the second time, Peter had gone to speak with Professor Bricknell's postdoc and two of his most advanced postgraduate students. They had been cautious and somewhat hostile on the first occasion. He did not expect it to be any different this time. He managed to schedule separate and consecutive appointments with them. The venue was a departmental office of a professor on leave that the chair had made available to him.

His first appointment was with the postdoc, who was even more defensive than on the prior occasion. He could not be pushed into saying anything negative about his professor and refused to speculate about the possibility of his synthesizing the anaesthesia whilst the lab technician in charge of the centrifuges was out for lunch. He pointed out that using the centrifuge would only be one stage of the process, and somebody would have observed him during the others.

"They might observe him," Peter suggested, "but would they necessarily know what he was doing?"

"We would because we know what he is working on. If he was involved in some procedure that did not seem connected to it, one of us would have asked out of curiosity."

"What if he did it when you weren't in the lab?"

"It's possible but unlikely."

"His colleagues would be less familiar with his research and might not notice. Would you agree?"

"Again, possible, but unlikely."

Peter finished the interview convinced that he was dealing with a dedicated student who did not want to believe that his mentor and the man on whose support he needed for his first academic appointment could be a criminal.

The other two interviews were basically a repeat of the first. He did, however, get one of the postgraduate students to admit that the professor was insecure and intolerant of disagreement. But he scoffed at the idea of the professor assisting someone in the double murders.

**

Inspector Khan rushed back to the police station to tell his colleagues what he had learnt from Mrs Sousa. Peter was still out, but Charlie Davidson had just returned from a court appearance. He had spent two hours in court but was never asked to testify because the defendant cut a last-minute deal with the prosecutor.

"I'm generally happy when this occurs," he told Inspector Khan. "I only wish they had done it before the court convened."

"I suppose it takes a looming trial to knock sense into many perpetrators."

"Anything interesting come up in your interview with the professor's ex?"

Inspector Khan summarized his conversation with Mrs Sousa and her belief that her husband could have synthesized the drug and lied to the police.

"I learnt that he inherited a family home on the Dorset coast. I've given the coordinates to one of the constables to get the address, and I'll ask the deputy commissioner to ask for a warrant to search it. Maybe this is where he made the drug after using the centrifuge in the lab. I'm going to call the head of the department and ask him if this would be possible."

"How do you think the deputy commissioner will respond?"

"I don't know. He's under pressure from his bosses to solve the case, and some of the media have described our searches of Professor Bricknell's home, office, and lab as police harassment. They will have a field day if we search his country home and find nothing."

**

Rhianna arrived at Professor Bricknell's office precisely on time. His personality and profession — perhaps the two were related — seemed to demand precision. He seemed eager to see her and invited her to take a seat. He closed the office door so they could speak without being overheard.

"It's good of you to meet with me, professor," she said.

"My pleasure. You seem to understand that I have been victimized by the police. I confess I hoped to see more about it in the *Cambridge News*."

"I did write it up. Surely you read the article? I reported how unhappy you were with the police searching your home, office, and lab."

"Yes, I read the piece. But your reporting was rather matter-of-fact and expressed no sympathy with my plight."

"Ah yes, I do owe you an apology here. My draft was very sympathetic, but the editor made me rewrite it. My guess is that the police put pressure on him. I'm a victim too."

"You have my sympathies. These people have no restraint. They get away with murder."

"I don't know that I would put it that way. But they are out of control. They have you in the frame for making the drug."

"Let me reiterate. I had nothing to do with it or the killings."

"They think otherwise."

"Still, after all their searches?"

"Because of them."

"What do you mean?" the professor said in a lowered and more measured tone of voice.

"My police sources tell me that they have an eyewitness who saw you making what they think was the anaesthetic."

"Do you know who this is?"

"No, I don't. They also have the tests back from your lab and believe they have confirming evidence."

"Why haven't they arrested me?"

"I don't know, frankly. Perhaps they are hoping to gather more evidence to make a tight enough case to be confident of a conviction."

Rhianna's observation was greeted by silence. Professor Bricknell was processing what she had said. She had evidently broken through his defences and decided to push her advantage.

"There is a way out or at least a way to improve your situation."

"And what would that be?"

"Go to the police and cooperate with them."

"Assuming, for the sake of argument, I was responsible for the drug, why would I want to do that?"

"Right now, you are in the frame not only for having produced the drug but for committing murder."

"I'm not a murderer," the professor said with emphasis.

"I believe you, and it's all the more reason to contact Inspector Khan."

"He's behind all this!"

"He's leading the investigation if that's what you mean. Mind you, just producing the drug for the killer is enough for them to convict you of accessory to murder. This carries a long jail term. If you were to turn yourself in and agree to name the person you supplied with the drug, I'm sure they would go much more leniently with you. In fact, you — or better yet, your solicitor — could propose a deal. You agree to confess your crime and name the killer in return for a greatly reduced sentence. You could also insist on a minimal security prison, where you are not likely to be beaten up or sexually abused by the other inmates."

The professor was silent again, and Rhianna sensed that he was mulling over what she had said.

"You should really call your solicitor after I leave and have him speak to the police. Once they have their ducks in a row, they will be less keen about a deal."

"I see your point," Professor Bricknell finally said. "If I had done this and knew who the murderer was, it would be the sensible thing to do."

Rhianna played along with this pretence and asked him some questions about his work that had nothing to do with the case. He became animated again as he described his research and some of its possible practical applications. They parted on friendly terms.

***

Professor Bricknell was deeply unhappy. He had done something very foolish, more than that, criminal. He had not seriously considered the consequences of his actions, something he would never have done with a scientific project. But this was a scientific project, and a challenging one, which is one reason why he did it. He had devoted a lot of attention to the intellectual problems posed by the synthesis of the drug and the secrecy by which it had to be carried out. He was overconfident and had failed to consider the ethical implications of his actions. He now recognized just how appalling they were.

He had wanted to help a friend and impress him with his scientific prowess. Entering into a conspiracy made it more exciting, something his life was sorely lacking. He had been fed a cock-and-bull story about why the drug was needed, and that made him angry. He didn't understand in retrospect how he had been so naïve as to believe it and not even try to check it out. He had been exploited and played for a mug. His "friend" must be laughing behind his back at how easily he had been manipulated. And look where it had led. He had been hounded by the police, embarrassed in front of his colleagues, likely to lose his job, and sent to prison if they made the charges stick. Prison was a frightening prospect; he shuddered at the thought of his loss of freedom, terrible food, and even worse if Rhianna was to be believed.

Professor Bricknell called his solicitor, who was unavailable. He left a message, stressing that it was a matter of great urgency. He then did the inevitable. He called Inspector Khan. Better to pre-empt, he told himself, than to be taken into custody when they had more evidence.

Inspector Khan returned his call within five minutes, and the professor told him he was interested in reaching some kind of deal.

"What do you have in mind?" the inspector asked.

"Assuming, for the sake of argument, that I did produce the drug and handed it over to someone who used it for criminal purposes. If I turn myself in, and give you the name of the person I suspect of being the murderer, could I bargain for a lighter sentence? Bearing in mind, I had no idea the drug was going to be used to murder someone, let alone two people."

"What did you think it would be used for?"

"I was told by a friend that his mother needed it to treat her painful arthritis and that the NHS wouldn't pay for it because it was too expensive. I really thought I was helping her out."

"I see. And you are prepared to give me the name of the person to whom you handed the drug?"

"When we work out our deal."

"I think we can do something to satisfy you. Do you want to come down to the station?"

"I've called my solicitor and want him present. He should negotiate the terms."

"This is very wise of you. Do you think we could meet sometime later today?"

"It depends entirely on my solicitor. What if I call you back as soon as I hear from him?"

"No worries. Let me give you my mobile number."

Inspector Khan was delighted by the conversation. Rhianna had worked magic. The previously arrogant professor was now begging cup-in-hand. He was certainly willing to do a deal with him, but he would have to clear it with the deputy commissioner and he with the prosecutor.

He called the deputy commissioner's office, telling his secretary that it was urgent and that he had good news to report. He also called Rhianna, whose phone was engaged. He left a short message that said he would call back. Before heading off to the deputy inspector's office, he stuck his head around the door of Peter's office to share the good news. He asked Peter to detail a constable to keep an eye on the professor.

"He's done a runner once, and I don't want this to happen a second time."

***

Professor Bricknell was also busy with his telephone. He phoned his solicitor's office a second time and stressed to his secretary just how urgently he needed to speak to him. He then called his "friend" for whom he had synthesized the drug. Here he was luckier, or so he thought, because his call was answered on the third ring.

"It's me, Ian. Can we talk?"

"Good to hear from you. This is not the best moment as I have someone in my office."

"I see. Could we meet somewhere later today? It's really quite urgent."

"Of course, my friend. What if I come around to your place early this evening? Say sixish? Would that be all right?"

"Yes, that would be fine. I'll be waiting for you."

As soon as he ended the call, Professor Bricknell began to have second thoughts about having made it. What did he expect to gain from this encounter? Personal satisfaction, he supposed. He felt an overpowering need to confront the man who had lied to him, manipulated him, and for whom he would now serve a prison sentence. At the very least, he wanted an apology and an explanation for why these two men had been killed. He would not be put off by another lie, which is what he now expected. He could imagine being told that his friend was merely the middleman and knew nothing about the murders, having passed the drug along to someone else.

Maybe he could reverse the power balance and get the upper hand. He would threaten to go to the police unless he received a full confession and explanation of why Professor Mason and the young lad were murdered. He would then, of course, go to Inspector Khan and spill the beans in return for a shorter sentence at a nicer, safer facility. With the details he extracted from his upcoming encounter, his story would be more convincing and helpful to the police and secure him a better deal. Maybe he could avoid prison altogether?

He was beginning to feel a little better and decided to go for a walk. In prison, this would not be possible.

XXXI: Thursday Afternoon

Peter was delighted that they were finally making progress. He agreed to post someone in front of the professor's home. He gave the assignment to the constable who had unwittingly let Rhianna follow him. It was a chance for him to redeem himself. Inspector Davidson and his team would keep the professor under more general surveillance. Everyone assumed that these were short-term precautions because they expected the professor to come to the police station as soon as his solicitor was free.

"I'm still troubled," Peter said to the two senior detectives. "We can agree that the professor made the drug, but I don't think he's the murderer."

"Not so fast," said Inspector Davidson. "He could have killed them both and now be trying to pin the deed on someone else."

"True," Peter said. "But this only works if we believe him, and we won't unless it is someone without an alibi, with a clear motive for the murders, and against whom we can find other confirming evidence."

"And it will go much worse for him if he tries a trick like this," said Inspector Khan. "I think he's in over his head. He had no idea the drug would be used to murder two people and is now very keen to cut a deal. I'm sure the deputy commissioner can convince the prosecutor to go along with it. I just hope the professor's expectations are realistic."

Inspector Davidson nodded his head. "Perpetrators have unreasonably high expectations of what they can negotiate, but their solicitors generally talk sense into them. Let's hope it happens this time."

"I know his solicitor," said Inspector Khan. "He's a no-nonsense kind of guy but will push us to get the best deal, that he can. All the more reason to see what the deputy commissioner can get the prosecutor to commit to."

***

Constable Krauss saw Professor Bricknell leave his house, cast a glance at him, and walk down the street towards where it ended, and the path began that ran between the river and college playing fields in the direction of Grantchester. He could not follow him with his car and called the station for instructions. He was told to follow him on foot and that someone else would be sent to Grantchester to track him from the other end of the path. When this happened, he was to return to his vehicle and wait for the professor to return.

Constable Krauss was pleased to escape from the monotony of sitting in front of the professor's house. It had been two hours, and he was desperate to relieve himself. He followed the professor at a polite distance but not far enough back to be unnoticed. The professor twigged him and periodically turned around to see if he was still being followed. He stayed on the path, moving rapidly through the several turnstiles en route. Constable Krauss decided he was unlikely to lose him and, at an opportune moment, ducked into the bushes on his right to respond to nature's call. He finished, zipped up his trousers and rushed back to the path, relieved in a double sense when he saw the professor, although now further ahead. The constable was still embarrassed at being followed by that journalist without having clocked it. He was not going to mess up an assignment a second time.

Just before the turnoff to the Green Man pub, the constable's phone rang. He was told he could return to his position in front of the professor's house, as another constable had him in sight from the Grantchester terminus. He reversed course and walked slowly back to Newnham. No rush, he thought, and certainly not to the boredom of a stakeout. He had a book and a newspaper in the car, and he could relax until the professor reappeared.

About thirty minutes later, Constable Krauss received a second call from headquarters telling him the professor would shortly emerge from the Newnham-Grantchester footpath. He reluctantly put down his book and waited for him to come into sight, which he did almost on signal, walking in his direction, up the path to his door, and then into his house. The constable looked at his watch and noted that he had almost two more hours left to his shift. He called the duty sergeant to report that the professor had returned home.

***

Our murderer was distraught by the professor's phone call. His accomplice was running scared. The police were almost certainly on to him, and he would be likely to make a deal. He would expose him to protect himself, and he really couldn't blame him. He would do the same if the circumstances were reversed. He would have to take care of his friend. No drugs this time. And Bricknell would be on his guard for some trick like this.

He returned home quickly, changed out of his professional clothes into jeans and a black T-shirt and put on a pair of dark coloured trainers. He went into his home office, took an Escher lithograph off the wall, and removed the key in the enveloped taped to the back of its frame. He went to his desk and reached down to unlock the bottom right-hand drawer. Inside, wrapped in a cloth, was the Luger his father had brought home from the war. Many soldiers had done this, and Lugers became a collector's item. The gun remained in service in Switzerland until the 1970s. Its 9mm Parabellum cartridges were easy to come by because they are used by many other military handguns. He kept the weapon oiled and cleaned and had fired off a few rounds in the woods the year before to make sure gun and ammunition still functioned. He relocked the drawer, returned the key to its hiding place, and went downstairs.

***

Professor Bricknell was refreshed by his walk but depressed. He wondered what kind of exercise he would have in prison. There would be a yard, for sure, but walking the same route for the duration of his sentence would be tedious in the extreme. He would also miss the changing of the seasons. He hoped there would be trees and plants in the yard; he could at least watch them go through their annual cycles. How many cycles he would have to do this was another source of depression.

His solicitor would likely have some idea, but he had to assume it would be at least five.

His mobile rang. He immediately answered it and was relieved to hear the voice of his solicitor.

"I'm sorry I could not call you earlier," he said. "I was with another client, someone serving time. They won't let you take a phone into the prison. I couldn't check my messages until I got out. How can I help you?"

Professor Bricknell filled him in on the most recent developments, and the solicitor listened without interrupting him.

"What do you think?" the professor finally asked him. "Can you cut me a good deal?"

"I think I can, provided you are willing to plead guilty, name the murderer, and testify against him. The prosecutor won't have to bring your case to trial, and your testimony will help convict the killer."

"So, what are we talking about?"

"Let me explain the law to you. If you aid and abet someone who commits a murder, the sentence can be the same as if you committed the murder. As the sentence for murder is life, you could, in theory, never emerge from prison. On the whole, life tariffs are only ever given to the most serious offenders. The sentencing guidelines suggest twenty-five years for murder if there was intent to kill beforehand. That would be the likely tariff for the killer in this instance. As you did not know a murder would be committed or that you were, in fact, assisting with it, you might expect five to ten years. Because you are turning yourself in, naming the murderer, and giving testimony against him, we may be able to bargain the prosecutor down to five or less."

"Five or less?"

"Yes, that's right. You're a first offender, correct? You don't have a record of any kind?"

"Me, a police record? I'm a law-abiding citizen."

"This may be hard for you, but you are going to have to act contrite with the police and the prosecutor. You must be humble and apologetic and avoid all sarcasm, and above all, suppress your sense of superiority. You must stress that you never would have synthesized the drug if you had known it would be used for any criminal purpose, let alone a murder. Is that clear?"

"Yes."

"Good. Now get dressed in a suit but bring along more comfortable clothes to wear in the holding cell if they deny your bail. Bring your toiletries with you. Oh, and bring your passport too."

"Would they deny me bail?"

"It's a possibility. Your willingness to surrender your passport will help your case. I'll arrange for a bond. Do you own your house?"

"Yes, outright."

"We will secure the bond against the house. I'll meet you in thirty minutes at Parkside Police Station."

"Do I just walk in?"

"The duty sergeant will be expecting you."

"One more question, if I may. Is there a chance I can be sent to some kind of low-security prison where… I am less likely to be treated badly by other offenders?"

"I think I can guarantee that. See you in a half-hour."

Professor Bricknell went upstairs to change and pack a bag as requested. He put on a pale blue shirt and took his best suit; he only had two. It was a grey-charcoal one and made for him in Portugal when he had been there the year before. He thought about wearing his college tie but decided against it and took a plain silk maroon one off the rack. He knotted it and looked at himself in the mirror. How very strange, he thought. Who was he trying to impress at the police station? Would anybody care what tie he wore?

He collected the few toiletries he would need and put them into a holdall along with another set of casual clothes.

He heard the doorbell ring as he was zipping up the bag. Maybe it's the cop out front, he thought, offering to drive him to the station. He came downstairs and, as he did, realized that it was the back doorbell. *That's odd. Who would be coming to see me at this hour and why the back door?*

"Who is it?" he said as he opened the back door. Standing on the porch on the other side of the screen door was his "friend."

"I wasn't expecting you until six."

"I finished early, and I thought I would come by. *Carpe diem* has always been my motto."

"That's fine. I'd rather have it out with you sooner rather than later, you bastard. Why are you wearing gloves in this weather?"

"Sooner rather than later is fine with me too."

His visitor reached into the little bag he was carrying and pulled out his Luger, dropped the bag, undid the safety catch and pointed it at the professor."

"What are you doing?" the professor asked.

The answer he received was a bullet through his heart. He fell back onto the floor. The screen door absorbed much of the first spurt of blood and more splattered against the wall as he fell. The visitor watched as the spurts ebbed away and were replaced by blood seeping from the wound over his victim's blue shirt and suit. If the spurts had stopped, so had the heart, and the professor was dead. He contemplated stepping inside and putting a bullet in his head to make sure but decided it was too risky. He was bound to get some blood on him, and it was possible that the cop at the front had heard the shot. He picked up his bag, put away his gun, and left via the back lawn the professor shared with a neighbour, coming out onto another street, where he had parked a short walk away.

Constable Krauss heard a pop but attributed no importance to it. He was engrossed in his murder mystery — the police were on the trail of a strangler — but did look up. He saw nothing and returned to his book. Thirty minutes later, his replacement arrived, and he drove off.

***

Michael Dubois arrived at Parkside Police Station five minutes early to be on hand when his client arrived. The duty sergeant called Inspector Khan to announce him; Inspector Khan notified Peter and then bounded the stairs two at a time to meet the solicitor. They shook hands, and the solicitor did the same with Peter when he appeared. Inspector Khan noted that, as usual, the solicitor was well dressed and that his shoes had a high polish. There wasn't a hair out of place on his head, and it was fine hair too, which made the feat more impressive. He had long ago concluded that there were two types of men in the world: those who had just stepped

289

off a page in *Gentlemen's Quarterly* and those who looked rumpled no matter what efforts they made. He unquestionably belonged to the latter category and had long ago learnt to accept it.

The three men made polite conversation whilst waiting for Professor Bricknell. After fifteen minutes, they began to wonder what had happened. Had he got cold feet?

"I think not," said the solicitor. "When we last spoke, he was reconciled to his fate and very keen to work out a plea deal. I'd say he was highly motivated to get here and on time."

Inspector Khan called Inspector Davidson and asked to check with the constable on watch if and when the professor had left his house. A minute later, Inspector Davidson appeared.

"He's still at home as far as we know. The constable said he hasn't left his house, and I've instructed him to go ring his bell and see what is going on. I told him to give him a lift to the station."

Inspector Khan introduced Inspector Davidson to Mr Dubois. Inspector Davidson's mobile rang, and he swiped it and put it to his ear.

"Yes?" There was a pause, and then his interlocutors heard him say, "Stay put. We'll send a team right over."

He put down the phone and addressed his colleagues. "He's not answering the bell. He could have snuck out the back entrance."

Inspector Davidson went over to the duty sergeant and asked him to get a couple of uniforms to the professor's house as quickly as possible. If he didn't answer the door, they should break in.

"Let's wait in my office," Inspector Khan said. "It's more comfortable."

The three policemen and solicitor trudged upstairs and dragged a third chair into an office that sat two comfortably at most.

Inspector Davidson's phone rang again.

"What's the story?"

The three men stood quietly listening to Davidson's end of the conversation.

"Shit. No, you did the right thing. Just stand guard, don't trample anything, especially any possible footprints in the backyard. I'll call the SOCOs, and we will be there as soon as possible."

There was another pause as the constable on the scene spoke.

"How many of you are there, did you say? Good. Two of you stand guard, one in the front and one in the back, whilst the others knock on doors to see if neighbours saw anything. Start with the houses in the back, as that's probably the route the murderer used to come and go. Put Constable Krauss on the phone, would you."

There was a brief pause in the conversation. Inspector Davidson looked across at his colleagues and the solicitor and grimaced.

"He's dead. Gunned down at his back door."

Inspector Davidson bit his lip.

"Constable Krauss? You're sure that nobody went to his door or approached the house from the street? I see. Yes, thank you. Wait where you are, and we will be around shortly."

Inspector Davidson ended the call but continued to hold the phone in his hand. "We'd better get out there. Just let me call the SOCOs."

Inspector Khan turned to the solicitor and said they would have to excuse themselves. He promised to call him later and provide more details about what had happened to his client.

"It's awkward for all of us," Mr Dubois said.

"Why all of us?" asked Peter.

"If I had been free this afternoon, Professor Bricknell would have met me here earlier and would still be alive."

"But you weren't," Peter replied. "And you could not have known this would happen."

"At least I would have known who killed him."

The three men looked at the solicitor.

"He was going to name the person for whom he synthesized the drug. Presumably, this person used it to immobilize the two men he killed and has now killed my client. I should have asked him who it was in our last telephone call."

"Why didn't you?" Peter wanted to know.

"He was under such stress; I didn't want to push him further. I deliberately avoided a long discussion about plea bargaining, telling him we could talk more about it at the station. I focused on getting him here as quickly as possible. It never occurred to me that something could happen in the thirty minutes between our telephone conversation and meeting here."

"It is more likely my fault," said Inspector Khan. "I sent a journalist to tell him that we had enough evidence to convict him. That's why he called you. She also helped persuade him — and she assured me it did not take much — that his so-called friend had played him like a chump. Whatever anger he might have had toward the police was directed, and properly so, at the person for whom he had synthesized the drug. I wouldn't be surprised to learn that he called him to give him a piece of his mind right after Rhianna left and shortly before or after he spoke to you. Peter, can you get an immediate trace on the number and other numbers he called?"

Peter turned to Mr Dubois and asked him what time he had called the professor. He had done this from his mobile after leaving the prison and checked the time and length of the call and read them out to Peter.

"It had to have been sometime after Rhianna left him and before Mr Dubois returned his call. If Professor Bricknell called after that, the murderer would not have had enough time to come by and kill him."

"Unless, of course, he was an immediate neighbour," said Peter.

"Correct. Let's check up on them as well. Ask a constable to get their names and run them through the computer to see if we have anything on them. Let's get some background information too."

"Yes, sir."

Three sombre men descended the staircase for the third time, filled in the duty sergeant on what had happened, and gave him the address to pass on to the SOCOs. They exited the back door and squeezed themselves into Inspector Davidson's small Ford.

XXXII: Thursday Afternoon II

They drove to Newnham, and there was little conversation en route. Inspector Khan looked behind them as the car turned from Lensfield Road onto Barton Road.

"I think she's following us," he said.

"Rhianna?" exclaimed Peter.

"Gotcha," said Inspector Khan.

"At a time like this?" said Peter.

"It relieves the tension."

"For you, maybe."

The police tape was already up when they arrived, and it formed a complete perimeter around the house. The tape was attached to trees and also to metal stakes that had been driven into the grass. Like every other crime scene on a sunny day, a crowd had gathered and was gawping and gossiping. Among them were presumably one or more of the neighbours the constables had interviewed. Everyone knew by now that something nasty had happened at Professor Bricknell's house. Inspector Khan was pleased to see that two of the constables, notebooks in hand, were interviewing people in the crowd.

The detectives went around to the back of the house and waited for the SOCOs, who arrived within minutes. They donned their suits, unpacked their equipment, and began by searching the backyard for footprints. They found indentations in the grass, photographed them, and then took impressions. The detectives watched as the SOCOs went silently about their business. They focused next on the staircase to the back porch. They took impressions from the shoes of the policeman who had walked up to the porch and discovered Professor Bricknell's body. They methodically photographed, dusted, photographed again, and made impressions on transparent plastic sheets. They neatly labelled all the impressions. The SOCOs kept well clear of the body and took photographs of it from a distance.

The coroner arrived, and Inspector Davidson filled him in on what had happened and gave him his estimate of when the professor was shot. One of the constables had started a crime scene log on his own initiative, which he now handed over to the inspector.

"I can't remember the last time I looked at the body of someone I knew when they were alive," the coroner said.

"Will it make a difference?" the inspector asked.

"I don't think so. I treat all corpses with respect but, like a surgeon, to do my job well, I must regard them as slabs of meat, bone, organs, and gristle. It's harder to do when you know the person."

The SOCOs called over to the coroner, who joined them to have a look at the body. The detectives followed up the steps onto the porch but stood at a distance on the porch to let the coroner could do his work.

The screen door had been opened by the SOCOs, and one of them had lodged a brick against it to hold it in place. The coroner, also in a protective suit, went inside and gingerly stepped into the pool of blood surrounding the body and bent down to have a closer look. He turned the body on its side, and a large exit wound came into view. He reached out with his right hand to feel the torso and neck.

"Shot through the heart. Death would have come very quickly. There were spurts of blood, two I think, as he fell to the ground. You can see the pattern they made on the screen and the wall. He angled left as he reeled from the impact of the bullet. The body still shows primary flaccidity, so dead less than two hours. As there is an exit wound, there must be a bullet somewhere in the kitchen."

"We've got it," one of the SOCOs shouted from inside. Malcolm's just pried it loose from the far wall. Judging from the location of the slug, the gun was held in a position parallel to the porch floor and, I would guess, at heart level. We'll know more when we enter all the measurements into our computer. The bullet looks like it came from a 9 mm cartridge, probably a Parabellum."

"That's military ammunition," Peter said.

"Yes, but widely available to civilians," one of the SOCOs said.

The head SOCO promised to send over reports on the bullet and the crime scene as soon as they were ready. The coroner did the same.

The three detectives walked over to the constables to find out what they had learnt from neighbours and other people in the crowd. The woman who lived immediately behind the professor had seen a middle-aged man crossing her lawn holding some kind of holdall. He was coming from the direction of the professor's house. She thought him cheeky for trespassing but did nothing about it, and he quickly passed out of her sight. And no, she had not seen him coming the other way and did not remember hearing any sound like a shot. None of the neighbours along the street parallel to the front of the Bricknell house saw anything other than a police car that now seemed like a permanent presence to some of them. Peter went to do a second interview with the back neighbour, who said nothing she had not told the constable. She was clear that the man was wearing a hat and sunglasses and held his head down as he walked. She did not get a clear look at his face.

***

Our murderer was at sixes and sevens. Normally he would have taken pride in his knowledge of the origins of that expression. In 1484, the Merchant Taylors and Skinners livery companies each claimed the sixth place of precedence. The Lord Mayor resolved the dispute by insisting that they alternate, so one year one of them would rank sixth and the next year seventh, and the following year the reverse. His erudition counted for little at the moment, he told himself. He was on the run, and it seemed possible that the police would track him down.

He had acted on the spur of the moment. He had no choice. His pathetic accomplice had somehow attracted police attention and was running scared. He doubted they had any real evidence against him, or they would have arrested him. He wondered if the journalist had not been sent by the police to frighten him in the hope of flushing him out. If so, their tactic worked. Professor Bricknell was in the midst of a panic attack when he had called, and no amount of sweet talk was going to convince him to keep quiet. He was shocked to discover that the drug he produced was used to enable two murders and that he was now an accessory to murder. Even if he could be persuaded to hold off on going to the police, he was going to do it sooner or later. Or perhaps, they would break him in a long interrogation session. He had to be shut up before that happened, and there was only one way to do that.

Given the constraints he faced, he did well. He had acted decisively. It was smart of him to keep a gun around and ammunition for it. He killed the traitor with one shot through the heart and did not have to enter the house to do it. He had quickly disposed of the gun and cartridges, his old trainers and some of the other clothes he wore. He had driven to a turnoff by one of the college playing fields, changed in the car, and when he saw nobody was around, removed the holdall with the gun, remaining ammunition, and gloves inside and the items of clothing he had taken off. He saw no bloodstains when he examined them, but better to play it safe. He took a shovel from the boot of his car and walked through an opening in the hedge at the end of the football pitch onto a farmer's field. It had recently been ploughed, and earth was still soft and upturned. He dug a hole and put the gun and ammunition in, and filled it in, trying as best he could to make it look the way it did before.

He returned to the car with the holdall and set off in the direction of Grantchester and the car park in front of Waitrose. He knew there was a skip on the street, discreetly blocked from view by hedges. He put the holdall in a black rubbish bag before leaving his car and dropped it into the skip when nobody was in his line of sight. Once having disposed of the evidence, he returned home.

He contemplated what to do next. He considered the possibility that Bricknell had already given his name to the police. If that traitor had dobbed him in, there was little he could do. But then the police would have wasted no time in coming for him. No, his secret had died with him. Bricknell had telephoned him in his office after speaking to his solicitor. The police would trace his calls, and this would put him in the frame. Being on their list of interested persons would be uncomfortable, but it was not the same as being arrested. They had no evidence against him to the best of his knowledge. He would come up with an innocent explanation for their telephone conversation. They were friends, after all, and Bricknell had sought his advice. He urged him to go to the police and tell them everything he knew and even offered to accompany him.

***

Rhianna was sitting at her desk trimming her nails when Inspector Khan called. She had just returned to her office from an interview with a woman whose husband had been falsely convicted — or so she claimed — of computer identity theft. She thought it might make a good story but was not convinced after spending time with her informant. She had heard nothing as yet of the events at Professor Bricknell's house.

"I have a scoop for you," said Inspector Khan.

"Super," said Rhianna, excitement evident in her voice.

"Let me ask you first when you need to go to press?"

"Not for another few hours."

"Good. We need to talk first."

"What's happened?"

"Professor Bricknell's been shot."

Rhianna paused to process what she had just heard.

"Shot, you say?"

"Yes, at the back door to his home."

"The BBC and other media will inevitably break the story first as we don't publish until tomorrow morning."

"They may know that he was shot but nothing more. You will have the details. We need to talk because we may have been the catalysts for his death."

"He's dead, is he?"

"Unfortunately. He was shot through the heart and died instantly."

"Poor bastard. Do you think my visit had anything to do with it?"

"Everything to do with it, I'm afraid. But I'm at fault. I put you up to it."

"Where would you like to meet?"

"What about King's College? Meet me in front of the gate where those pesky porters turn tourists away. We can get coffee inside and have a quiet tête-à-tête."

"I can meet you there in ten minutes."

"Good, see you then."

***

297

The SOCOs had been efficient and the lab even more so. The first report began coming out of the inspector's printer moments after he returned to his office after meeting Rhianna for coffee in the senior common room of King's College. The last time he had been to King's, he remembered, was with Peter during the early days of the investigation. This meeting was more intense, as he and Rhianna reconsidered and evaluated their motives for acting as they had with respect to Professor Bricknell.

Rhianna was less troubled than the inspector. She thought, and he had to agree, that they really had tried to do the professor a favour. By giving him the opportunity to turn himself in, they made it possible for him to negotiate a deal with the prosecutor and significantly reduce his jail time. They could not have known — and here, again, the inspector agreed — that he would call his accomplice and that he would be murdered as a result. They were both convinced that the killer had to be the person for whom the professor had produced the drug.

Inspector Khan had gone to see Rhianna with two ends in mind. He owed her a scoop, and he gave her what details they had. The media did not know that the bodies pulled out of the basin had been drugged, and they certainly knew nothing about the drug and how the murderer had obtained it. Rhianna could reveal these details in tomorrow's paper and the police suspicion that the dead professor had synthesized the drug in his Cambridge lab.

The killer had acted quickly and must have known about the police stakeout at the front of the professor's house. He went to the back of the house, where Bricknell opened the door for him. He undoubtedly considered him a friend. The SOCOs had found no recent fingerprints on the back door, other than the professor's, and thought it was rarely used. It had the stiffness of a door that had not been opened for some time. From the lawn, they had taken impressions of a male trainer, Size 11.5. It was a common brand and would not help them find their man. If they traced him by other means, and he had not disposed of his trainers — a big if — they could offer evidence of his presence at the house.

More interesting was the second message from the gun lab. The SOCO who pulled out the bullet from the kitchen wall was right; it was a 9 mm Parabellum. The name was an acronym for the Latin phrase: *Si vis pacem, para bellum* — if you want peace, prepare for war. This slogan provided justification for defence spending around the world. The lab thought it had been fired by a Luger of World War II vintage. It was a trophy weapon. They could be purchased, but most owners had inherited them from fathers, or even grandfathers, who brought them home as souvenirs. Many murderers disposed of their weapons, but if this one had sentimental value, its owner might keep it. It was difficult for Inspector Khan to conjure up a sentimental killer, especially one who had murdered three people in a premeditated way. The coroner sent over his report, and it contained nothing surprising. The professor had been killed by a single bullet through the heart, fired from a distance of only a few feet, and by a right-handed man of medium height. The victim was otherwise in good health; the autopsy revealed no health problems.

Peter rapped on the inspector's door and walked in even before being invited to do so. Inspector Khan handed him the report. "Not much there," he said, as Peter directed his attention to the reports.

Peter eventually handed them back. "You're right, as usual."

"We're almost back to square one," the inspector said whilst staring out his window overlooking Parker's Piece.

"Not entirely. I have some good news."

Inspector Khan turned to face him.

"BT got back to me with the phone logs. Faster than I thought they would, but I had the deputy commissioner make the request."

"Good thinking. What do we have?"

"A telephone call to his solicitor's office about three minutes after Rhianna left his house. Clever woman that she is, she noted her time of arrival and departure and passed them on to me. The call lasted less than a minute. Mr Dubois was visiting the prison, and Bricknell left a message for him to call as soon as possible. Mr Dubois confirms this, and so does his office. Two minutes later, Professor Bricknell called — do you want to guess whom?"

"Just tell me, if you would."

"Professor George Chester, head of POLIS."

"You interviewed him, I remember."

"He's the Latin-quoting, compulsive, son-of-a-bitch. Like the master, he assured me that Cambridge professors would never dream of murder. He nevertheless pointed me towards colleagues and students who might have a motive. I never thought about checking up on him."

"How long were they on the phone?"

"Thirty-two seconds."

"That doesn't tell us much."

"I think it does. Bricknell called him very soon after calling his lawyer. We can assume, and Dubois confirms, that he had decided to surrender himself in the hope of a plea deal. This was why he was calling his solicitor's office. Why would he call Professor Chester about some trivial matter right afterwards? It makes no sense. The call had to be connected with his decision to confess."

"I grant you that. But what if, for example, he had borrowed, say, the professor's robe for some college event or owed him money. He might want to clear this up before going to jail." "

"Certainly possible," said Peter. "But I think he made the drug for Chester and called to give him a piece of his mind."

"Then why was it such a short call?"

"I don't know. Maybe Chester was busy and asked him to call back later? Or maybe he volunteered to come right by so they could talk in person? It would explain the timing of his murder."

"Yes, it would," said the inspector. "I think we'd better have a talk with this professor. Best not to tip him off in advance. Take a constable and get over to his office, pick him up and bring him in. Let's interview him on our turf with a recorder going."

"Any chance we can get a warrant to search his home?"

"I'll ask the deputy commissioner, although I'm not sure how he'll respond."

***

The deputy commissioner's office had double windows overlooking Parker's Piece. The commissioner had been looking out on the park when the inspector entered the room. Without turning to face him, the deputy commissioner said, "It's a nice day out there. Am I in for a storm here?"

"Yes and no, sir," replied the inspector.

"Just like a weather forecaster, hedging your bets. Do I need an umbrella or sunscreen? Just tell it to me straight."

"You may need both, sir."

"Didn't I know it? There will be a storm, then sunshine? Or sunshine followed by a storm. The latter is more likely with you. You ask for multiple warrants, and all it does is give us a black eye and the media a field day. Then your fears prove justified when your person of interest is murdered — and with a police guard in front of his house. The BBC raked us over the coals on the news last night. And this morning, I read a story in the *Cambridge News* spilling the beans. This reporter has information that we have kept from the media until now. She makes us look justified in our interest in Professor Bricknell, but how did she get these details? First comes a murder, and then another bloody leak. I'd call those dark storm clouds."

"Let's start with the sunshine. We were right about Bricknell. He synthesized the drug used in the double murders, and we think we know whom he did it for."

"Who is that?"

"Professor George Chester, head of POLIS, the politics department. Peter has gone to bring him in for questioning."

"Did Bricknell point the finger at him?"

"In a manner of speaking, sir."

"Just drop the 'sir', will you please."

"Sorry. Bricknell was running scared and called his solicitor to arrange a deal. He was about to turn himself in. He called Professor Chester immediately after leaving a message for his solicitor and was killed half an hour after that. Chester had plenty of time to get from his office or home to shoot him."

"I see his motive if he was responsible for the double killings. But do we have anything to put him in the frame beyond the telephone call? It might have been made for any number of reasons."

"At the moment, no."

"I feel the barometric pressure dropping and the storm approaching. What do you plan to do next?"

"We will question him, check his alibis for the original murders and for this one. We will speak to Mrs Mason again and also Sid's colleagues to see what motive Chester might have had to kill him. I suppose we should also search for some relationship between him and Jaime."

"Jaime?"

"The young man killed with the professor."

"Of course, sorry for my lapse."

"And I would like another warrant."

"Another warrant?"

"Yes. We have a pretty good idea about the murder weapon and have identified the trainers the murderer wore."

"You don't really expect to find them in his house, do you? He's been one step ahead of us until now and has surely disposed of any incriminating evidence. What do you expect to find that might justify a search?"

"Probably nothing — unless we get lucky. But it will upset him and perhaps put him off his game. The same with the interview."

"Let's wait. Interrogate him and then report back to me."

Inspector Khan turned and headed for the door.

"Not so fast. There's still the question of the leak. How did the journalist get all this information?"

"Perhaps we should interrogate her too?"

"I think not. We treat the press with kid gloves unless we really have something on them. Leave her alone until you know where she got her information, and then go after her source. So help me, if I ever find the person responsible for this leak, I will wring his or her neck. You'll have a fourth murder on your hands."

***

Professor Chester was not in his office. His secretary said he was at a meeting and would return shortly. The constable agreed to wait outside, and Peter accepted the seat he was offered, took out his personal phone, and sent a text to Elaine in response to the one he had received from her. They were to meet this evening, and Elaine's message suggested in an elliptical way what was foremost in her mind. Peter became aroused and was struck by the surreal nature of thinking about sex whilst waiting to apprehend a murder suspect.

302

Fortunately, a few minutes elapsed between finishing his text and the professor's arrival. He came into the office and asked his secretary why there was a constable outside his door. At the same moment, Peter rose and flashed his warrant card before him. Professor Chester noted it and glowered at him.

"What do you want?"

"I want you to come with me to the station."

"You want me to come to the station?"

"That's right, sir."

"I have no intention of doing so. I'm a busy man. If you want to ask me some questions, do it here. I'm always happy to help the police. I can spare five minutes."

"That's not how it works, sir. You're coming to the station where Inspector Khan will question you for as long as he sees fit."

"It's a bloody police state. And if I refuse?"

"I wouldn't do that, sir. The big constable outside your door will cuff you and put you in the back of his patrol car. And who knows, somehow the press might get wind of your impending arrival at the station."

"I don't really have a choice, do I?"

"No, sir. Now, if you would be kind enough to accompany us."

The professor turned to his secretary, who was watching the encounter with her mouth open. He asked her to call his solicitor and tell him what had happened and ask him to meet him at the police station.

***

Mrs Mason was reading recent cases on-line about auto dealerships that refused to take any responsibility for the cars they sold. Her client's auto was an imported luxury sedan whose company had an excellent reputation. Maybe it had rolled off the assembly line the day Germany was playing Brazil in the World Cup. Something out of the ordinary had happened because there were numerous things wrong with it. At a certain point, despite the warranty, the dealer had begun to stonewall the owner. It was the kind of case she enjoyed. She would use her skills to help her client redress the power balance with the greedy lot that ran the dealership.

She had instructed the receptionist to take messages and not allow any calls to come through to her. She was surprised when her phone rang. She picked it up in a hostile mood but softened when she heard the voice of Inspector Khan.

"Sorry to bother you when you asked not to be disturbed, but it's an urgent matter. We are about to interview a suspect in your husband's murder and want to speak to you first."

Inspector Khan offered a succinct reprise of the events of the twenty-four hours since Professor Bricknell called his solicitor. "What can you tell me about Professor Chester, and how well did your husband know him?"

"He knew him well, of course. They were colleagues for years. They are very different personalities and would never have sought out each other's company if the university had not brought them together. Sid had — what shall I say — a tolerable working relationship with him. He thought him pompous, devious, controlling, very self-centred but skilful at portraying what he wanted as being in the common interest and building coalitions in support."

"And how did he regard your husband, if I may ask?"

"To be honest, I think he held a mirror image of Sid. It may explain why they got on well professionally. They understood each other and supported one another in their respective power bids. The biggest difference was that Sid could not restrain himself from lording it over others and exposing their pretensions or weaknesses with his acerbic barbs. Chester never did this. He is every bit as judgmental but more self-controlled."

"Can you think of any reason why Professor Chester would want to murder your husband?"

"No, I cannot. They were unindicted co-conspirators, so to speak, in departmental and university politics. You go after enemies, not allies, Inspector."

"I see. What about your relationship with him?"

"My relationship?"

"Yes. Did you interact with him much?"

"If I may be frank, I had my hands full with my husband. Why would I want to double my burden in this respect?"

304

"Perhaps I haven't made myself clear. I assume you met him socially from time to time. Did he ever seek you out and say anything about your husband, or anyone else, that struck you as odd?"

"He was very careful about what he said. He was entertaining but unengaged. I had the sense of interacting with a well-constructed façade rather than a real person."

"Was he in any way jealous of your husband?"

"He gave no evidence of this, but then I don't know what he really thought about anything. My guess is not, as they were both successful men and in different subfields, so not in direct competition."

Inspector Khan asked a few more questions but learnt nothing useful. Mrs Mason was doing her best to help. He was struck by her negative remark about her husband. From what he had heard others say about him, he could readily imagine that he had been a difficult spouse. None of this helped him fathom any motive Professor Chester had for killing Sid, let alone Jaime. And if he did not kill them, then he had no motive for doing away with Professor Bricknell.

***

Elaine was on a stakeout. The drug squad had yet another tip-off, this time from an informant who reported a drug shipment would be going out to Birmingham. The drug in question was relatively new and trendy, presumably now produced in Cambridge by somebody with appropriate expertise. Elaine thought about Professor Bricknell and his moonlighting and wondered if one of his colleagues or chemistry graduate students was doing the same. It was a phenomenally profitable, if risky, activity, although to the best of her knowledge, none of the producers, as opposed to dealers, had been murdered.

This tip-off was unique in her experience because there were allegedly two mules involved, and descriptions of both had been provided. They were on the lookout for a young man in his twenties with short blond hair, glasses, and likely to be wearing jeans and trainers. His companion, a woman of the same age, had dark hair and notably large breasts. Her male colleagues had a good time with that part of the description, several volunteering to tackle her rather than her companion

305

if the need arose. Elaine did not respond because she had now been working long enough with these men to understand them. They treated her with respect, and that was all she asked for. They could make all the sexist comments they liked as long as they behaved appropriately.

She was posted outside the station in civilian dress. She had been watching people come and go for over an hour and pretended to be waiting for a lift. An hour's wait was not credible, but the station was not a place where people hung around. She hoped that nobody had become suspicious. Out of the corner of her eye, she saw a car pull up and someone who looked like one of the suspects get out. She memorized the car registration and took her police phone out of her handbag to inform control that one of the mules had possibly arrived. She watched as the woman walked past her into the station. Other undercover police would presumably pick her up inside. Elaine remained at her post, hoping to spot the second mule. He appeared about five minutes later on the bus. She saw him get off and telephoned control again. She was told to wait in position in the unlikely chance either suspect exited or made a run for it. She kept her eyes on the exit in the hope that she would not have to confront either of them. If so, she knew whom she would tackle, and it would not be the one with the big breasts. It was a warm day, and both suspects were in T-shirts, and she had to admit that the account of the woman had been accurate.

Two minutes later, she was called and told to stand down. They had arrested both suspected mules and were bringing them into the police station, where they would presumably search them and their belongings. As she was the only female on duty, she was asked to return to the station to do the body search on the woman they had picked up. At the station, she was told that they had taken vials of capsules, which they assumed to be drugs, from the man's backpack and something similar from his companion. They would now search their clothing and bodies, and she would conduct the body search on the woman.

"This is not a task I look forward to," she said to two of her colleagues. "For the right sum, we could do a swap. Anybody want to make me an offer?"

Both men grinned. "No need to," one replied. "We've cut a peephole through the door. The latest in high-tech surveillance, you know."

It was Elaine's turn to smile, and she headed down the corridor to the room where the woman was being held.

***

Not far away, Professor Chester sat in an interrogation room waiting for his solicitor to arrive. He faced the same problem Professor Bricknell had. His solicitor was an authority on estates and property, not criminal law, and had to find someone from another firm to act for his client. He initially called Michael DuBois, whom he knew by reputation. DuBois explained why he could not take the case and recommended two other names. The first one was out of town on holiday, and the second agreed to come. All of this took time, and the solicitor did not get to the station until almost five p.m. Professor Chester had lost patience with the police long before then and was struggling to retain his sangfroid.

At seventeen thirty, Inspector Khan turned on the recorder, announced the time and the presence in the room of himself, Detective Sergeant Peter Leslie, solicitor Aaron Bornefeld, and Professor Charles Chester. It was the same interrogation room in which they had interviewed Professor Bricknell. The two detectives sat on metal office chairs across a rectangular table from Professor Chester and his solicitor. A constable in uniform stood inside in front of the door.

Inspector Khan had dealt with Mr Bornefeld on previous occasions. He was a good lawyer who looked after the interests of his clients and had a sharp eye for spotting any police irregularities. Inspector Khan was quite annoyed the first time his investigation came under such inspection but grudgingly acknowledged that the solicitor was doing his job. The two men had exchanged polite greetings when the solicitor arrived, and Inspector Khan told him to take as much time as he needed with his client and to ask the constable to summon him when they were ready for the interview. Twenty minutes had sufficed.

"For the record," Inspector Khan announced, "we are interviewing Professor George Chester in conjunction with the murders of Professors Bricknell and Mason and Jaime Peeker. *Ab initio*" — there's one in the eye to Professor Chester, he thought. "We are going to focus on the most recent murder, that of Professor Bricknell."

The questioning that followed was relatively routine. Professor Chester was asked if he knew Professor Bricknell, and how well, when he had last seen him, and if he could give an account of himself the afternoon of Professor Bricknell's murder. The professor looked across at his solicitor, who nodded his approval and proceeded to offer the minimal amount of information he thought the detectives would accept as answers. Inspector Khan was not prepared to let him off so easily.

"You say you went directly home from your office and that your secretary can vouch for the time you left?"

"That's right."

"You did not leave your home until you went to work the next morning?"

"Yes."

"And nobody else can testify to this?"

"As I've told you, I live alone. If I thought you were going to drag me here, I would have arranged for somebody to have come over to provide me with an alibi."

"Just to be absolutely certain, and for the record, you did not drive your car at all that day?"

"As I said, it was in my lockup. I walked to work and walked home."

"You didn't lend it to anyone?"

"No, I did not."

"You would be very surprised if it turned up on CCTV that afternoon in the vicinity of Professor Bricknell's house whilst you were at home?"

Aaron Bornefeld raised his hand in the direction of his client to forestall any response and asked Inspector Khan if he had CCTV images of the car and, if so, to give them copies.

"I don't as yet, but we're working on it. I assure you."

"This is a red herring intended to intimidate my client. I suggest you drop this line of questioning."

"Let me ask you then if you own a gun?"

"A gun? Certainly not. I abhor weapons of all kinds."

"You do not own a gun, a Luger pistol, to be precise?"

"I said no. Do I have to repeat myself each time?"

"What kind of relationship did you have with Professor Bricknell?"

"He was my friend, and I'm very upset that he's been murdered."

"Was he enough of a friend that he would synthesize a drug for you?"

"You don't have to answer that question," Mr Bornefeld said to his client.

"Let me be explicit," Inspector Khan said. "We know that Professor Bricknell synthesized the drug used to immobilize Professor Mason and Jaime Peeker. He did it for a friend who he thought would be using it for a benign end. He was planning to come to the station to plea bargain with his lawyer and promised that he would give us the name of the person for whom he made the drug."

"How interesting. Any idea of who that was?"

"Yes, we do."

"Why don't you arrest him then?"

"We've brought him in for questioning first."

"If I may intervene?" Mr Bornefeld said to the inspector.

"Of course."

"Do you have any evidence that would allow you to hold my client for even twenty-four hours?"

Inspector Khan looked across at Peter and then back at Mr Bornefeld as Peter rose and left the room in a hurry.

"In two minutes, I'll give you a definitive answer."

"They waited silently until Peter returned and shook his head before sitting down.

"We do not," the inspector said to Mr Bornefeld.

"Then may I suggest that you release my client unless you have additional and pertinent questions for him."

"He's free to go," said the inspector. "But remember, Professor Chester, you are now a suspect, and you cannot leave town for the time being. We will also be keeping an eye on you."

"*Satis verborum* — enough of words — especially yours," said the professor.

"Interview ended at eighteen fifteen," the inspector told his recording machine.

XXXIII: Thursday Evening

Inspector Khan and Peter walked to a nearby café to escape the confinement of the interview room. Peter ordered a cappuccino and the inspector a macchiato.

"I need something stronger to overcome the taste that bastard has left in my mouth."

"He is a piece of work, all right," Peter said.

"He's a psychopath. Having murdered Bricknell, he sits there and calmly laments the death of his 'friend'.'"

"And the uniforms have found no evidence of his car on CCTV?"

"I have three of them working on it. They are monitoring five cameras over a period of several hours. It will take a while."

"Too bad we can't use that clever constable who wrote the computer program."

"I thought of that. This is different as it involves visual identification of numbers, which is more complicated than searching a database where everything is already digitized. They will call as soon as we find anything. What worries me is that he has a second, unregistered vehicle stashed somewhere that he used for both his murderous outings."

"It's certainly a possibility. He's a clever enough bugger to have thought of this."

"What should we do?" asked Inspector Khan.

"Send Rhianna to smoke him out."

"You've got to be kidding!"

"I got you that time, sir."

"You did. I'll pay for the next round of coffee."

"What about talking to the Cambridge mafia again to see if any of them can shed any light on the professor's motive for the initial murders?"

"Let's do it. We should also revisit the question of Jaime and see if we can connect him in any way with Professor Chester. That would be a real feat."

***

Our murderer was at home sitting in a comfortable upholstered chair in his parlour. He was nursing a single malt whisky in a heavy-cut crystal glass and was deep in thought. He had removed the immediate threat, and the police could not connect him to the crime. But it was far from a perfect crime. He had disposed of the gun, ammunition, and relevant items of clothing, but there were still ways of tracing him. There was his car, for a start. He had taken the precaution a couple of weeks back of preparing a decal with a phoney registration that could be overlaid on his. It could only be used once but had the virtue of leaving no evidence behind, unlike paint. His car was a common make and model and had no visible features to distinguish it from others.

He had recognized from the beginning that his murder of Sid was not the perfect crime. There were two people who could link him to it. The first was Yobbo, whom he needed to kidnap and immobilize Sid, and whom he had neatly removed from the scene. The second was Bricknell, who had prepared the drug and whose car he had borrowed. His cooperation was essential, and he played successfully on his insecurity to gain it. He was convinced that Bricknell would never do him in, because he had no idea of why he really wanted the drug. He had bought his story that it would save money for a friend's mother who desperately needed it to treat her arthritis. A problem had arisen when those damn bodies were discovered, and the clever coroner had figured out they had been drugged before being killed. Then everything began to unravel.

In retrospect, he should have done him in right after the bodies were dug out of the basin, but he had no idea that they could identify the drug or that someone would consider the possibility of it being synthesized in a Cambridge lab. He had to admit that the police had done good work here and that he had underestimated them yet again. Should he sit tight in the expectation that they could not pin the crime on him? He would probably get away with it but would be on the defensive and forever in their gaze. This was a very uncomfortable reversal. Until now, he had been entirely in the background, like a wind that blows in from nowhere, does its damage and leaves as invisible as it arrived. This he enjoyed as much as the damage he wrought. It gave him a feeling of omnipotence, which he no longer felt. Now, he was more like some cell, stained and mounted between sheets of glass and put under a microscope to be minutely examined. His secret was still out of sight, but he was not.

Interesting too, he recognized, were the emotional effects of this transformation. His erotic charge had been replaced by an uncomfortable sense of insecurity and relative powerlessness. It made him squirm and feel ill at ease with his body. He had worried that the former pleasure would not last, now he worried that the current, most unpleasant state of arousal would endure a long time. It made it difficult, but not impossible, to play a waiting game. Even if victorious in the end, it was not a contest he would enjoy.

The other problem was Cynthia. He went to his bookshelf and removed his latest photo album. It was filled with shots he had taken of her without her knowledge. She was a good-looking woman and just right for him. Thoughts of what he would like to do with her brought immediate arousal, but they too were problematic. He had lusted after her for a long time and removing her husband had not brought his fantasies any closer to realization. He had expected otherwise, which made further postponement of them more difficult to take. Here too, he realized, he had created another problem. The sensible thing to do was to push Mrs Mason out of his mind for the time being. But he rebelled at the thought. She was at the centre of it all, and any victory over the police could end up being self-defeating in a more fundamental sense.

There was another course of action. He could be bold, regain the initiative, and perhaps win his love object. He immediately warmed to the prospect and the challenge of overcoming all the obstacles in his path. However, there were many obstacles, he well knew, and his planning to date had not found ways around them all. The biggest question mark was Cynthia herself. Success would ultimately require her cooperation. It was a *va banque* strategy. Was he up to it?

312

***

Rhianna had invited Rudi, as she now called him, for coffee at the same café where they had met previously. She dressed more conservatively on this occasion. Her previous outfit had made at least some of her charms more visible and, she was convinced, had its effect on Rudi, as it had on the constable whom she had aroused. Now it was time to be more proper and appeal to a different side of this intriguing inspector. The circumstances were also different. The professor was dead, his murderer still free, making the occasion sombre. She was still in jeans but wore a loose-fitting dark top that came up to her neck. Her subtly applied makeup lent her a touch of elegance.

Rhianna very much enjoyed being part of the action in contrast to her usual role of observer. She wanted to stay involved and help in some way to bring the murderer to justice. She had no idea how she might do this and further realized that there was no way Rudi would use her as an intermediary again, given what had happened to Professor Bricknell. She would keep alert for any new developments that might provide an opening for her.

She brought their coffees to the table and waited for Rudi to speak. He asked her about work and whether her interview with Professor Bricknell had got her into trouble at the paper.

"None whatsoever. But then my editor has no idea what I said to the professor. He assumed it was the normal interview, where I asked questions and someone else provided answers. What about you?"

"The deputy commissioner is furious, but not at me. He knows that you passed on information about our investigation to the professor and would like to strangle your source and you as well. I wouldn't be surprised if he didn't have you hauled in for questioning."

"Does he use thumbscrews?"

"Does the idea turn you on?"

"No, what about you?"

"No, although Peter and I think it would be more fun than waterboarding."

"I won't break under either form of torture, so your secret is safe with me."

313

"If Bricknell had said that to our murderer, he might still be alive," said the inspector.

"I'll bet the murderer has a real set of thumbscrews and no compunction about using them."

"That wouldn't surprise me."

"What is new with the case?" Rhianna asked.

"Nothing really, although don't put that in your column."

"This is all off the record. Chatham House Rules, I assure you."

"There's really nothing new. We're still checking CCTV recordings looking for Professor Chester's car and trying to figure out any reason he might have for wanting either Professor Mason or Jaime Peeker out of the way."

"Do you mind if I interview him?"

"Are you sure you want to?"

"You never know. He might tell me something interesting."

"It could be risky, and frankly, I don't think you will learn anything from him. If we couldn't do this at the station, you're unlikely to in an interview."

"I don't know about that. I have ways of making men want to speak to me that you don't. And I don't need thumbscrews to do it."

"Well, I'm glad to hear that. But please be careful. Promise me you won't interview him at his home, but in your office or on neutral public ground where there are plenty of other people around. I'm worried about you."

"I'm touched. Any questions you want me to put to him?"

"You could ask him his motive for killing Professor Mason."

"Even my charms are unlikely to coax that out of him."

***

Rhianna wasted no time in calling Professor Chester, whom she reached at home. His number was not in the directory, but she had no difficulty in procuring it. The professor picked it up on the third ring and asked who was calling.

"It's Rhianna Johnson from the *Cambridge News*."

"Yes."

"I was hoping to interview you."

"If wishes were horses, beggars would ride."

There was silence on the line as Rhianna waited for her interlocutor to continue, but he said nothing.

"I really would like to speak to you."

"I don't want to speak to you. The last suspect you interviewed was murdered not long afterwards."

"Surely that's not going to happen to you!"

"I certainly hope not, but I'm not prepared to speak to you. Leave your mobile number, and if I change my mind, I'll call you."

Rhianna gave the professor her mobile number. He repeated it back to her and hung up.

XXXIV: Friday Morning

Inspector Khan and Peter were back at the station. The inspector reported the gist of his conversation with Rhianna and how he tried, unsuccessfully, he thought, to discourage her from trying to interview Professor Chester.

"At least I made her promise not to go to his house, but why should she listen to me?"

"She likes you. Haven't you noticed?"

"You're trying to get two free cups of coffee, and I'm not falling for it."

"I'm serious. She has the hots for you."

"Come on!"

"It's how she looks at you and her body movements when she's in your presence."

"Since when have you become an expert on women?"

Peter's refusal to be drawn prompted the inspector to break the vow he had made to himself to say nothing about what was, he clearly discerned, his partner's budding, but as yet unannounced, relationship. "Have you picked up these new detective skills from your new partner?"

"You know about her?"

"Of course, I do."

"We've been trying to keep it secret for obvious reasons."

"Obvious reasons?"

"Workplace romances raise eyebrows, if not worse."

A workplace romance, the inspector thought, quickly racing through the list of eligible women at Parkside Police Station. Only a couple came to mind, and none of them seemed Peter's type. One was very attractive but had sent clear signals from the outset that she intended to keep her professional and social lives quite distinct. Peter would indeed get ribbed by his colleagues if she was his paramour, but more from envy than disapproval.

"May I ask who she is?" the inspector said. "I'm happy to keep her name under my hat."

"I wasn't going to say anything, but if I don't, those little grey cells of yours will undoubtedly double their firing rate, and we will get drawn into a game with you trying to find out and me trying to keep it secret."

"Her name is Elaine, and she works at the railway police station."

"I'm very happy for you, Peter, and delighted to hear that it's someone outside the building. I don't think it matters that she's a cop. She doesn't work with us, so no problem really."

"It may be more difficult for her if her colleagues find out she has paired off with a detective sergeant. She's a newbie at the station and on the lowest rung of the ladder."

"I won't tell a soul, although at a certain point, it's bound to become public knowledge."

"We'll cross that bridge when we come to it. And I won't say a word about you and Rhianna."

"Me and Rhianna? I've told you there's nothing to say."

The conversation paused a second time until the inspector asked Peter if the constables had found anything.

"Yes and no. The CCTV coverage in Newnham is relatively light, and our friend obviously knows where these cameras are. It's no surprise that his registration did not turn up. I suspect he took a roundabout route, but there are only so many ways to get near Bricknell's home. Our original and expanded search turned up a number of vehicles of the same year and make, but none with his registration. Constable Gilliam used his computer programme to run them quickly through the database, and we found one with an unlisted registration."

"Two in one investigation?"

"Unlikely to be a coincidence, isn't it? Let's suppose he played the same trick as before and altered his registration. Can our computer genius reason backwards again from it to the original registration?"

"He's working on it now. It raises a different question that we've never discussed. Why is it that the car with the altered registration on the day of the murder led us to Professor Bricknell, not to Professor Chester?"

"I've also wondered about that. I think we can rule out Professor Bricknell as the murderer. The only question would be if he somehow had assisted, and I just can't see him doing that. I think he was honestly shocked to learn that the drug he had synthesized was used for homicidal ends."

"I concur. I also think it's unlikely that our computer boffin made a mistake about his identification of Bricknell's car as one of, what was it, six possibilities."

Inspector Khan nodded his head. "Yes, there must be some connection here. Perhaps Chester used Bricknell's car? He might have borrowed it, changed the numbers, and returned it after the murder."

"That would really have been clever and yet another reason for Bricknell's fury when he put two and two together."

"He was really played for a chump."

"And paid for it with his life."

"What about your interviews with colleagues?"

"Davidson and I went separately to speak to four of them. To cut to the chase, people are surprised that he is in our sights, and none of them can think of why he might want to kill Professor Mason. Perhaps the most insightful comments were by Professor Lundgren, who described him as a kind of cipher. After years of interaction, she still has no idea of who he really is. He's very careful, she said, to be polite and reveal little of himself. So much so it borders on pathology. She doesn't trust him and would not be surprised to see him implicated in something unpleasant but added that she knows of nothing to suggest such behaviour."

"Anything from the others?"

"Not really. The master knew him only incidentally. He had been to dinner at the college sporadically over the years, most often as a guest of Sid. He detected no tensions between them. Another colleague described him as a good head of department and personally aloof. He too was surprised that we were asking questions about him."

"Not much to go on, is it? No known hostility to Sid, no hint of a motive for his murder, and certainly no connection to Jaime. It makes it sound like we are barking up the wrong tree again. But my instinct says not."

"Mine too if it's any consolation. He's been fooling his colleagues for years and running rings around us. I'm at a loss to know what to do to get evidence against him."

***

Our murderer listened to the most recent telephone calls made by Mrs Mason. It was less than a week before her departure for Central Asia and the Silk Road. Once she made another life for herself, he reasoned, it would be more difficult to make her his woman. He had better act before this happened, and her trip could be his catalyst.

He had worked hard to prepare for this eventuality. He had stocked his redoubt with everything he thought he would need, and then some. He would get there in his car with an altered registration, but with a different set of numbers than he used the day he eliminated Bricknell. He worked out and rehearsed his plan for Mrs Mason. He had made his last dry run a couple of days back, in disguise, and a good one. He was pleased again by his ingenuity but upset by not being able to dictate the timing of his plan. Mrs Mason's departure spurred him to action, but so did the call from that Nosy Parker at the local rag. Why would he want to talk to her? Her call left no doubt that neither the police nor media would leave him alone, and he would soon be fielding impertinent questions from colleagues and neighbours. It was time to act.

***

Mrs Mason was feeling good about herself for the first time since her husband's death. Serving papers on the car dealership was enough to bring them to their senses. She and their solicitor had settled the matter in a friendly and fair way in the course of a ten-minute telephone chat. He would send papers for her client to sign along with a cheque. The pest wanted to come in, but she had dealt with her on the telephone as well. Her colleagues in chambers more or less treated her as they had before the murder, and this too was good. Most uplifting was the contemplation of her forthcoming Silk Road trip. She had always dreamt of an adventure of this kind but could never convince Sid. His idea of travel was to visit great cities of Europe and other locations there, especially in Italy, known for its art and food. She had enjoyed this kind of travel but was keen to do something different outside of her comfort zone.

She left her office early to do some last-minute shopping for her forthcoming trip. She was planning on going home after that and working there but had received a call from a local journalist keen to speak with her. She had no interest in publicity, but this journalist, whose by-line she had often seen in the *Cambridge News*, said that she had some information to share with her about her husband's disappearance and murder. She was surprised and put off at first. Inspector Khan had periodically briefed her about their investigation, and if he was withholding anything from her, she thought, it was probably for a good reason. But she had some free time, and why not let this journalist have her say.

They met in a café not far from Mrs Mason's office and on her way home. The two women exchanged the usual pleasantries and agreed to address each other by their first names. Rhianna volunteered that the interview would be entirely off the record. Whatever story she ran in the paper, Cynthia's name would not be mentioned, nor any information she learnt solely from their conversation. Rhianna then asked her if the police had told her about their suspicions about Professor Chester.

"They did ask a few questions about him," she confided, "but never said he was a suspect."

"Oh, he definitely is, for Professor Bricknell's murder and for your husband's."

"But how could that be?"

"You're surprised?"

"Very. Ever since the police asked me about him, I can come up with no motive he might have had for either murder."

"I can provide one for Professor Bricknell." Rhianna explained how he had synthesized the drug used to immobilize her husband and Jaime and was apoplectic when he found out how it had been used. He was about to meet his solicitor at the police station to grass on the killer and plea bargain. But the killer got to him first, as Bricknell had telephoned him to express his anger.

"He must live nearby. Did Bricknell make the drug in return for money?"

"The police don't think so."

"Then he must have been a friend. That would explain his response. But how did he know about the connection between his drug and the murder? I've seen no mention of any drug in the press."

"I told him."

"You told him?"

"May I take you into my confidence here?"

"I'm a solicitor. My practice depends on my discretion as much as it does my professional skills."

Without incriminating Inspector Khan, Rhianna explained what had happened, how her interview had backfired, and how terrible she felt about it. Cynthia sympathized with her and wondered if she was about to let the genie out of the bottle again.

Rhianna told her at length about suspicions the police had about Professor Chester and how they had dragged him down to the station for a long interrogation.

"But why Professor Chester?"

"That's whom Professor Bricknell called immediately after my interview. A reliable source tells me he made only one other call — to his solicitor. The police reason that he is their man."

"You are well informed."

"It's my job."

"So, what is it you want to tell me?"

"About the police interest in Chester and the link between him and Bricknell. All that's missing is a motive for Chester wanting your husband dead. I thought perhaps you might have some ideas."

"None whatsoever. As I told the police, my husband had a perfectly satisfactory relationship with him over the years. I've met him on numerous occasions. I never detected any hostility or emotions of any kind, for that matter. I can think of no reason whatsoever why he would want him out of the way. In fact, I rather think they enjoyed each other in a funny kind of way."

"Would you care to elaborate?"

"They were allies in department and university matters and respected each other's political skills."

"I see. You are as stymied as the police?"

"More so, as I know Professor Chester."

With their coffee and conversation finished, the two women got up to leave. Cynthia was walking home, and Rhianna asked if she could accompany her as she was in need of fresh air and exercise. They headed off in the direction of Newnham.

***

Our murderer was parked not far from Mrs Mason's house. He mulled over one more time his plans for her abduction. It was now or never, and he was ready. She should be coming down the street any minute in the direction of the town centre, and he would nab her in this spot where there were no CCTVs. He had carefully checked and had planned an escape route that got them almost out of town, away from the eyes of these prying lenses. What an infringement on civil liberties they were! He was amazed that the citizenry had not objected more vocally and restrained their now nearly universal use.

Mrs Mason came into view and, to his chagrin, was not alone. As the two women drew closer, he struggled to identify her companion. He was sure he had seen her face somewhere, but try as he could, he could not place it. What was he to do? He couldn't kidnap two women, and he couldn't make off with Mrs Mason whilst her companion was there. And this was his last opportunity before she left for the Silk Road. He started his car and drove off in a fury.

Back home, he accessed the recording of his tap on Mrs Mason's telephone. He had previously listened to her conversation with Inspector Khan and was pleased that she threw cold water on his suggestion that he might have killed her husband. She was incredulous, which was a very good sign. Maybe she really liked him.

Judging from the time, she called her daughter within minutes of arriving home. She wanted to say goodbye before leaving on her trip. The conversation was not particularly interesting, although he always felt a certain arousal in listening to her voice. He had played several of the recordings over again for this reason before erasing them. He couldn't afford to leave any evidence in his house in case the police searched it. For the same reason, he had disposed of his photo album of pictures he had taken of Mrs Mason. He listened to the conversation with one ear as he reflected on his situation. His attention was riveted on the call again when he heard Mrs Mason describe a meeting she'd just had with a journalist from a local paper. She passed along new information about the police investigation, including the name of one of Sid's colleagues, who was now their prime suspect. She described the reporter as politely aggressive, an attitude that was probably necessary in her job, and all the more so as a woman.

"I was careful what I said to her," she told her daughter. "I quite liked her, and we walked back here together."

The murderer reached into his jacket pocket and took out the piece of paper on which he had written the reporter's name and number. Rhianna Johnson from the *Cambridge News*. So that's who it was. The nosy bitch had thrown a spanner in the works. He shut off the recording and went to pour himself a stiff drink. He sat in his usual chair, fuming about the recent turn of events.

A solution gradually presented itself. He was a fool, he told himself, to have focused so intently on Cynthia. She was a means to an end, not an end in herself. He did not seek her but rather domination. She was appealing because she would be a challenge to dominate, and success would bring more satisfaction as a result. This insight was a source of liberation. It created a new world of possibilities. It was also psychologically uplifting as it freed him of his uncomfortable dependence on Cynthia and made him feel more dominant.

A new plan quickly formed in his mind. It involved a clever substitution and required a couple of important psychological twists. His mood improved as he worked out the details.

XXXV: Monday Morning

Inspectors Khan and Davidson and DS Leslie were sitting in the police station canteen, giving vent to their frustrations. They had been so close to nabbing the perpetrator, but Professor Bricknell had been killed before he could give them his name. They knew who it was from his telephone call but had no evidence against him. Professor Chester had an alibi for neither the double nor follow-on murder. He insisted he had been at home and claimed that his telephone logs could prove it. They did indeed show calls, but they were short ones. Peter speculated that he could have rigged some timer to his phone to make the calls whilst he was out. Inspector Davidson thought that a bit over the top but agreed that they were dealing with a killer smart enough to have resorted to such a ruse.

"I remain perplexed about his motive for killing Professor Mason and Jaime," Inspector Khan said. "I agree he's our man, but why is it that neither we nor any of his colleagues can think of any reason why he would murder Sid and Jaime? I'm scheduled to see the deputy commissioner at ten, and he's going to probe me hard on this one."

"There's not even any speculation," said Peter. "Colleagues all report the two men got on well. Perhaps something came up between them that the others don't know about."

Inspector Khan reviewed his telephone conversation with Mrs Mason. "She characterized him as a man so much in control of himself that he never shows much, if any, emotion. She's had no access to the real Professor Chester."

"I heard something similar from his colleagues," Peter said. "He's a pleasant cipher, in their opinion. The only trait he reveals, and in abundance, is arrogance. I certainly encountered it in my interview with him at the outset of our investigation. I thought I would need a Latin dictionary for the other day's interrogation and was surprised that he uttered only one Latin phrase. You did too, for that matter."

"Did you understand it?" asked Inspector Davidson.

"Yours yes, his no. I looked it up afterwards. It means 'enough of words'. I assume he was signalling his disinclination to say anything else to us."

"It could also mean that it's time for action," said Inspector Davidson.

The three men pondered this more ominous interpretation.

***

Deputy Commissioner Braham welcomed Inspector Khan into his office and was facing him this time as he did.

"Please take a seat."

Inspector Khan sat down in the chair opposite his desk and waited for the deputy commissioner to speak.

"Any progress, Inspector?"

"We know who did it but can't prove it." Inspector Khan described their frustrating interrogation of Professor Chester. He pre-empted any question about motive by confessing that they had none, nor could Mrs Mason or any of his colleagues think of one."

"And you still think he's your man?"

"None of us doubt it." Inspector Khan once again restrained himself from saying "sir".

"And you've come to ask for another search warrant."

"No." Inspector Khan shook his head. "This killer has been very successful in covering his tracks, and I can't imagine he has anything in his house that could be used against him."

"I see. What do you intend to do?"

"Nothing for the moment."

"That's unlike you. You have a reputation for leaving no stone unturned."

"I appreciate that, but in this instance, being too meddlesome could be counterproductive."

"As it was with Professor Bricknell. Have you any lead on who briefed him on our investigation?"

"I do, but I think it best to keep it under my hat for the time being. I hope you will trust my judgment here."

"Do I have a choice?"

"There's always waterboarding or thumbscrews."

"Ah, the good old days. All right, I'll give you the latitude you request — especially as you didn't ask me for a warrant. I was really going to come down on you hard if you did."

"The murderer has been ahead of us until now and knows we have nothing on him. But, for the first time, he knows that we know who he is. This has to be uncomfortable and may lead him to do something that will make our task easier."

"I see your logic. I hope you are right."

***

Before leaving his office, our murderer googled Rhianna Johnson, looked at her personal webpage and the one posted by the *Cambridge News*. He studied her picture carefully, read several of her articles, including exposés posted on her website and the newspaper's. The more he read, the less he liked her. She was an aggressive bitch who stuck her nose in other peoples' faces, as she had in his. Her obvious intelligence aside, she was the opposite of Cynthia in every important respect. Cynthia was attractive, minimalist in figure, dress, and manner. Rhianna was voluptuous and flaunted it in low-cut and tight outfits. Cynthia was soft-spoken and subtle, whilst Rhianna was loud and direct. Cynthia liked to work quietly behind the scenes, and Rhianna craved publicity. In bed, he imagined, Cynthia would be pliant and melting, responsive but following his lead. Rhianna would be all over him like a rash and possibly more demanding than he wanted. If Cynthia was alluring, Rhianna was a succubus.

He had fantasized endlessly about abducting Cynthia and winning her love through a clever combination of physical restraint and psychological pressure. He had devoured with interest everything he could get his hands on about the Symbionese Liberation Army and their 1974 kidnapping of nineteen-year-old newspaper heiress Patty Hearst. She developed political and personal loyalties to her Black radical abductors and joined them in a bank robbery. This phenomenon was later dubbed Stockholm syndrome — in reference to a similar event. It has been characterized as a form of bonding arising from trauma that leads kidnap victims or hostages to develop positive feelings towards their captors to the point of identifying with and defending them. Psychological dependence is achieved through bondage, abuse, harassment, and humiliation.

On his leisurely walk home, he calculated that some three weeks in captivity, but certainly no longer than a month, would be enough time to affect this transformation. Patty Hearst and some other captives were younger, and accordingly, less mature, worldly, and self-assured than Cynthia. He convinced himself that for other reasons, Cynthia would be more receptive to his grooming, and it would take no longer to bring her around.

How would this work for Rhianna Johnson? She was younger but more experienced and tougher, he judged, than Patty Hearst. He might need more time. But then there were mitigating factors. He considered aggressive women the flip side of passive women, and there was no doubt that Rhianna was somewhere towards the end of the aggressive side of the continuum. He guessed that it would be easier and faster to have her flip from one end of the continuum to the other than to coax her from the centre to either extreme. The more he thought about it, the more challenging and enticing the prospect became. Despite his distaste for her personally, he was sufficiently aroused that walking was becoming an unpleasant activity. He sat down on a bench along the river, looked up, and tried to focus on clouds and their shapes. A couple of them looked uncomfortably like parts of Rhianna's anatomy.

As this diversion was not working, he returned to his fantasy about how he would dominate Rhianna. His goal with Cynthia had been to make her beg for sex with him and in a manner that would demonstrate and establish her submissiveness. Rhianna was a whore who probably put out for anyone. A smile came across his face. He would make her passive but abstemious. She could beg for it, but he wouldn't rise to the bait until she was reduced to desperation and tears.

His strategy brought to mind a joke one of his American colleagues had once told him about former Vice President Hubert Humphrey. The left-leaning politician was famous for his non-stop oratory. At the outset of World War II, he had been Mayor of Minneapolis but enlisted in the

Army Air Force. In the story, he is a bombardier on an American B-17 that is shot down over Germany. He is captured and interrogated around the clock. After two days of this treatment, the Gestapo major descends from his office to Humphrey's cell, slides back the metal shutter to peer inside, and observes the interrogator slap him in the face and shout, "Vee haf our vays to make you stop talking!" He would do the same, and then some, with Rhianna Johnson. He got up and continued his walk home.

***

Peter and Inspector Davidson decided to revisit the bombing of Leinster College. They reread the file hoping that time away from the event and evidence might suggest new connections or leads. They also had some additional reports from experts they had consulted about bomb preparation.

They agreed that the unique feature of the event was the effort to which the perpetrator had gone to make certain the bomb would not explode. It was an attempt to scare, not to destroy, and possibly a diversion somehow connected to the murder of Professor Mason. The diversion angle was attractive because of the possibility the bombing and the double murders were carried out by the same person. They now had a suspect for those murders and wondered if there was some way of connecting him to the bombing. They tried to reason in reverse: from their suspect to the bombing rather than from the event to a possible perpetrator.

They checked with the master to see how often Professor Chester had visited or dined in the college. He was not a frequent visitor and certainly did not have access to any private rooms, let alone the set of Professor Nejami. The college was going over to a card key system, but it had not yet been installed in Professor Nejami's entryway. An old-fashioned key was still necessary. Neither the professor nor his predecessor had lost one, and the master considered the maids and porters beyond suspicion. There was no evidence that Chester knew any of them and no suggestion that anything else irregular in the college could be traced to the staff. Key and motive remained a mystery.

It is gospel among police that legwork reaps dividends. Everyone could think of cases where it led to proverbial needles being found in haystacks or to important clues that weren't recognized as such until paired with other ones that were the product of tedious background research and endless interviews. Useful evidence also comes from people who remembered something the third or fourth time they were interviewed. Efforts of this kind were not only tedious but also demanding on personnel and money. Detectives and their bosses, usually deputy commissioners, make strategic decisions about when to ramp up an investigation and when to call a halt. In the case of a double murder that had garnered national publicity, and with the University of Cambridge and national police authorities pushing for a resolution, personnel and money were available. This was also true for the bombing once Detectives Khan and Davidson had convinced the deputy commissioner that the two events were probably related and that their investigations should be combined.

Inspector Davidson accordingly felt no compunction about a third round of interviews with Leinster College staff, faculty, and students. He coordinated these efforts with Peter, who dispatched a sergeant and several constables to conduct the interviews. This time they carried photographs of Professor Chester with them. One of the constables hit the jackpot when interviewing a student. On the afternoon of the bombing, she had not only seen Professor Chester in college but was certain she had eyed him coming out of the "N" entryway, where Professor Nejami had his set. Another student had seen him on the main court and knew the precise time because he was on his way to his three-p.m. tutorial. A porter thought he saw him leave around that time. The police already had a list of other occupants of the "N" corridor: the IT office on the ground floor, Professor Nejami and an engineering postdoc on the first floor, and two student rooms on the third. They checked with everyone, and nobody in the corridor knew Professor Chester nor had been visited by him on the day of the bombing.

This was circumstantial evidence of his involvement. The detectives were convinced of it, but they knew it was not enough for the prosecutor to take a case to court. They pushed for something more substantial and finally hoped they had found it. Later in the morning, they received a report from one of the London labs they had consulted on the bomb and its manufacture. Professor Chester had slipped up. He left a partial fingerprint on the cellophane wrapper of the clock he used as a timer. It made perfect sense. He presumably had removed the cellophane and disposed of it, then put on rubber gloves for handling the clock and other parts of the bomb. Static electricity is created whenever two surfaces come into contact and will separate if one of them is an insulator, that is, with a high resistance to electricity. Given its opposite polarity, the odd bit of cellophane had remained stuck to the clock and had not been destroyed because the bomb had not gone off. Professor Chester's fingerprints were on file because of a security clearance he had in conjunction with work he had done for the government. There was a good partial match with his index finger.

Fingerprints are no longer considered infallible, and prints of one finger, less so. But it was hard evidence and certainly enough to bring him in for another interrogation. The two detectives called Inspector Khan and the deputy commissioner and reported the good news.

"We are finally getting somewhere," Peter exclaimed.

"Imagine getting that fingerprint from the wrapper!" said Inspector Davidson. "How clever of the lab to find it."

"We owe them a big vote of thanks."

Peter was instructed to grab a uniform and go bring in Professor Chester. Inspector Khan said he and two or three constables would sit in the room with the door closed in the meantime to raise its temperature. He also promised to leave a set of thumbscrews in plain sight on the table.

"Now I know you are kidding," said Peter.

"No free coffee for me on this one."

"You already owe me two!"

***

Professor Chester's secretary told them that her boss had left for the day as he had no appointments on his calendar. She thought he had almost certainly headed home. Peter summoned assistance in the form of a patrol car with two uniforms inside. Once at the house, the constables who met them ran around to cover the back exit. Peter and Constable Krauss —

why was it always Constable Krauss, Peter asked himself — walked up to the front door and pressed the buzzer. There was no response. They waited a minute and buzzed a second time. There was still no reply, and no sound came from within. Peter's heart sank as he wondered if history was repeating itself. Would they find a second professor lying dead on his kitchen floor? He left Constable Krauss at the front door and ran around the back where the two constables had quietly positioned themselves to prevent any escape via the back door. They went up to the house, peered in through a large window, and saw nothing beyond a well-ordered kitchen.

Peter telephoned Inspector Khan to report that Professor Chester was evidently not at home. He was instructed to wait for a bit and return to the station if the professor didn't show but to leave a couple of uniforms behind. Constable Krauss pleaded with him to be allowed to stay, and Peter did not have the heart to turn him down. He thought with two of them there, what could go wrong?

Inspector Khan called Professor Chester's office again and caught his secretary on her way out. No, she informed him, the professor had not come back to his office and was almost certainly at home, unless, of course, he had stopped to do some shopping en route. The inspector called the deputy commissioner, informed him of the new evidence and the possible disappearance of the professor. The deputy commissioner agreed to request a search warrant and hoped they might get one within the hour.

***

Our murderer entered his street on foot and saw a police car in front of his home, some hundred metres away. He turned around and walked back the way he had come. The last thing he wanted was another encounter with the police. Professor Bricknell's house was not far away, about a ten-minute walk. He had a key and had taken the precaution of copying his car key when he had borrowed the car. He walked down Marlowe Road and turned right on Eltisley Avenue, keeping an eye out for the police. The coast was clear, and he walked towards the house. Once inside, he searched for and found a small bag and packed it with a few

331

items of clothing. The two men were about the same size, and he had most of what he needed in any case at his redoubt. He rummaged around and found a pair of gloves, which he put on. He exited through the kitchen, which now showed no sign of the murder, and headed across a concrete path to the lockup. He opened it up, backed out in the professor's car, closed the garage door, and drove off.

***

The deputy commissioner worked his magic, and Inspectors Khan and Davidson had their warrant thirty minutes after requesting it. Inspector Khan arrived with his lock pick, and the detectives were inside without having to break down the door. The constables followed and began a careful search of the premises. They were looking for anything that might connect the professor with the three murders. An hour's perusal of the premises turned up no smoking gun and nothing at all when they used a crowbar to open the desk drawer that was locked. There were a number of photographic albums, which Peter flipped through. They documented foreign travel and included many pictures of the professor standing or dining with people, who were presumably colleagues, at conferences at diverse venues. There were several photographs in beach cafés, one on a balcony with what looked like the Alps in the background. A nice life, Peter thought.

The house was as fastidious as Peter had described the professor's office. Everything in the kitchen was in place, and the pots and pans that hung from a ceiling rack were arranged in order of descending height. The same order characterized the closets where the professor kept his clothing. Inspector Khan noticed a gap in the row of shoes and wondered if it might have been filled by the running shoes that left marks in the grass behind Professor Bricknell's house and, for this reason, might have been subsequently disposed of. There had also been a gap in the photo albums, and perhaps that too might have been filled by an album with some photographs he didn't want to fall into the hands of the police.

They returned to the station empty-handed. The SOCOs had removed the professor's computer and various other electronic items.

Inspector Khan doubted they would find anything of interest. One IT person remained behind to trace a wire that ran from the computer into the basement.

XXXV: Tuesday Morning

The following morning, Inspector Khan and Peter met in the former's office for their usual coffee. Peter noted that his boss hardly drank tea any more. He wondered if this reflected a change in taste or a response to the pressures of this seemingly endless murder investigation. There was a knock on the always partially open door, and the face of Danny Miller, their chief IT investigator, came into view. Inspector Khan waved him forward, and the lanky, jeans-clad young man sauntered in but remained standing as there were only two chairs in the room.

"I've found something extraordinary," he announced.

The two detectives waited for him to continue.

"I traced the wires and electrical cords attached to Professor Chester's computer, and there was nothing unusual there. But there was a cord on the floor, with a FireWire connector, that disappeared through a hole drilled through the floor into the basement. I traced it to a receiver, which further aroused my curiosity. Yesterday afternoon, after bypassing the computer's password protection, I went back to the house and plugged the wire into the appropriate port. Professor Chester has been tapping somebody's phone and recording conversations on his computer. He's deleted any stored files and turned the downstairs receiver off. I was nevertheless able to retrieve fragments of the files he deleted, and the phone belongs to a woman named Cynthia."

"Cynthia!" Peter exclaimed and looked across to his boss.

"How interesting," said Inspector Khan.

"You know her?" Danny asked.

"If it's the Cynthia we know, she is Professor Mason's widow."

"The guy they pulled out of the catchment basin?" Danny asked.

"One and the same," said Inspector Khan.

"Wow!" said Danny. "This could really be something important?"

"At the very least," said Inspector Khan, "it gives us grounds to arrest someone we suspect of murder but have no evidence connecting him to the crime."

"I have a request, Danny," said Peter. "Could you extend your search and see if the name Jaime Peeker pops up anywhere?"

"Happy to oblige," said Danny. "Anything else I can do for you?"

"For the moment, that will do," said Inspector Khan. "And by the way, I will tell the deputy commissioner how helpful you have been."

"That's great," said Danny, who promptly took off for his lab.

"We'd better get a security team over to Mrs Mason's house," Peter said, "and see if we can find any evidence of her phone being bugged."

"Yes, but we need to inform her, and best yet, get her consent. But she left this morning for Central Asia. I had her give me her schedule."

"I bet she has her mobile or her computer so that her office can contact her, if necessary."

"Maybe," said Inspector Khan. "Why don't you call them and see if they can reach her. Somebody there may have a key to her house. Whilst you do this, I'll brief the deputy commissioner and this time ask for an arrest warrant."

***

Our murderer was all set to go. He was pleased with himself. He was now driving Professor Bricknell's Toyota because his own car was in his lockup and inaccessible as his house was being watched, if not occupied, by the police. He congratulated himself on his foresight in making a copy of Professor Bricknell's car key. It offered a sharp contrast with the police, who had failed to keep an eye on his car and house.

He would use another EpiPen to subdue Rhianna. He had a difficult calculation to make. With the bastard and Yobbo, the dosage and its purity did not matter. He wanted them both dead, and it mattered not a whit if they died from an overdose or drowning. This time he wanted his victim immobilized for the journey but conscious and unaffected by the drug afterwards. He had found medical manuals that gave dosages for the drug when used in operations. They varied by the weight of the patient and how long they would be anaesthetized. He guessed at

335

Rhianna's weight and aimed for two hours of sedation. He knew his drug was not of the same purity but hoped it would still have roughly the same effects. Better, he reasoned, to give a lighter dosage than too strong a one. If Rhianna began to regain consciousness, he could give her more of the drug. If he gave her too much, she might never recover.

Now that everything was ready, he took the piece of paper out with Rhianna's mobile on it and punched the numbers into the throwaway phone he had bought for the occasion. She answered almost immediately.

"Rhianna here."

"This is Professor Chester. I don't know if you remember me."

"Of course, I do. How can I help you?"

"I very much hope you can. As you know, the police think I murdered Professor Bricknell."

"You didn't?"

"No, I didn't. I say that *ab imo pectore* — from the bottom of my heart. Although I can understand why they think I did because he called me the afternoon he was killed. Inspector Khan believes it was to complain about how I had exploited him."

"It wasn't?"

"No. I'm his friend, and he needed to talk through his situation with someone he trusted. It was unfolding rapidly, and he was about to leave for the police station to meet up with his solicitor and make an arrangement with the police. He felt awkward, even guilty, about naming the murderer because he had been a friend of many years standing, but it was the only way he could protect himself. I told him he should feel no guilt whatsoever. He had no responsibility to protect the murderer, only himself and others by giving up his name to the police."

"How did he respond?"

"With relief. I think it's what he wanted to hear. He was engaging in what psychologists call post-decisional rationalization. When people make decisions involving the prospect of loss, they must reduce anxiety before they can confidently move forward. This is what he was doing."

"And why are you telling me this now?"

"I would like my side of the story told. Initially I did not think that was necessary. I hoped the police would find the murderer and I could return to my life as a professor. But this hasn't happened."

"This may sound like an impolite question, but why should I believe you?"

"No, it's not impertinent. I have evidence concerning my innocence and also some idea of who killed my friend."

"Might I ask why you haven't given this information to the police?"

"That's another good question."

"I am a reporter, after all."

"And a very good one."

"How would you know?"

"I've read stories of yours, including your exposés."

"Did you like them?"

"Very impressive indeed."

"I'm happy to hear that. But let's come back to you and the evidence you have. Why haven't you spoken to the police?"

"Oh, I have spoken to the police. More accurately, they spoke to me. They made me wait in an overheated and windowless room for hours and then grilled me mercilessly. They just assumed I was guilty and had no interest in anything I said to the contrary. By the end of the session, I had no inclination to help them. But I've thought about it since, and the advice I gave to my friend Bricknell. It's advice that I should act on myself."

"Then call up Inspector Khan and arrange to meet him with your solicitor."

"I will do that but not before I speak to you."

"I don't understand, not that I'm unhappy, mind you, to get your story."

"I need to protect myself. I'm going down the same path as Bricknell, and he was killed not long after speaking to me on the telephone. Somebody knew he was about to be dobbed in and shot him to prevent it. This could happen to me too."

"How does speaking to me protect you?"

"Unlike Bricknell, I've written down the murderer's name. In fact, I've posted you a letter with the man's name but also arranged to have it communicated to you and the police by other means. There's no way the murderer, even if tipped off, could keep you and Inspector Khan from getting his name."

"What is it you want me to do?"

"I want to meet with you tomorrow morning and lay out my suspicions to you. You have a better track record than the police in getting at the truth, and I am going to give you a head start. You're free to publish anything I tell you whenever you think it appropriate. There is protection in this for me and a scoop for you."

"Can I come back to the murder of Professor Bricknell for a moment? Do you really believe his killer was tipped off beforehand?"

"I don't doubt it for a moment. It is too much of a coincidence that he was murdered in the short period that elapsed between his telephone call to me and his impending departure for the police station."

"But who knew about it?"

"Certainly, the police and people in his solicitor's chambers."

"You don't really think one of them is the murderer or tipped him off."

"Indeed, I do. And here's what I suggest we do. I am keen to avoid publicity. Let's not meet at my place or your office or a café where we are likely to be observed."

"All right, what do you have in mind?"

"What if we meet at eight thirty tomorrow morning outside and somewhere to the right of Parkside Police Station. It will depend on where I can park or pull over. I'll be in a metallic grey Toyota Auris. We can sit in the car and talk."

"OK. I'll see you then."

"Wonderful. Enjoy the rest of your day, Rhianna. May I call you Rhianna?"

"Yes, that's fine. See you tomorrow."

***

After ending the call, Rhianna reflected on what Professor Chester had said and what she had agreed to do. It was conceivable that he was telling the truth, but she considered it unlikely. Rudi did not try to pin murders on people or harass them. But it was possible that Chester was not a murderer. He didn't sound like one over the phone, but she knew that pathological people could often be terribly convincing. She was keen to see him on the off chance that he had some information about the murder. It would make a fine story, but she would check it out with Rudi and publish only if he had no objection. She was happy to follow his lead on this because she would still be the first with the story.

If Professor Chester was interested in protecting himself, she was too. She went to her editor's office to tell him about the forthcoming interview, its location, and her intention to return to the office right afterwards. She should be back by nine thirty, ten at the very latest. She would also check in with him by phone as soon as the interview ended. She wondered if Professor Chester had chosen the road in front of the police station to reassure her. If so, he had succeeded. It was good to know that help would be nearby. She would not tell Rudi about her impending interview, convinced that he would do his best to persuade her from it or have police waiting to arrest the professor when he parked his car.

She considered what to wear and decided to dress conservatively. It seemed appropriate in the circumstances. She would have her mobile in her bag in recorder mode and turn it on before getting into his car. With any luck, she would return with a good story and maybe even some important new evidence to pass along to Rudi. She would rather be getting into Rudi's car. She had always encountered him on foot. She wondered if he ever thought about her.

***

Deputy Inspector Braham called Inspector Khan to tell him that he had his arrest warrant for the professor. The inspector was delighted and dispatched Peter and a constable to the professor's office. He did not expect to find him there, as he had not returned home the previous night. However, word of the police appearing with an arrest warrant would spread rapidly around the department, if not the university. Somebody might come forward and tip them off as to his whereabouts. The police would make very clear to his secretary and anyone else in earshot that harbouring a fugitive was a criminal offence. Inspectors Khan and Davidson worked out a schedule of interviews with the professor's colleagues, hoping that one or more of them might have some idea where he might be found.

The previous afternoon they had alerted the railway police and sent over a picture of the professor. Elaine and her colleagues were given copies and instructed to be on the lookout for him. Elaine reasoned that if he left Cambridge by train, he had probably already done so, as a good hour had elapsed, between the time he was reported to have left his office, and their receipt of his photograph. Inspector Khan had Deputy Inspector Braham contact the police at Stansted, Birmingham and Heathrow airports, and the Met. They passed around photographs, but nobody sighted the suspect at these airports or London train stations.

Elaine thought it unlikely they would do so this evening. Professor Chester would hardly come to the station and expose himself to police he knew must be on the lookout for him. She nevertheless patrolled the perimeter of the station with one eye scanning for the suspect and the other watching for anything else out of the ordinary.

Inspector Khan went to interview the master. This was the fourth time he had been to see him and expected to do so again in his office. Instead, the porter on duty escorted him to the master's lodge, where he buzzed him in and instructed him to ascend the main stairs. The master met him at the top and directed him towards a large sitting room with nice views over one of the courts. He offered the inspector a drink, and as the sun was almost over the yardarm, he accepted. A steward appeared in short order with two snifters with single malts. Inspector Khan brought the master up to date on the investigation and their belief that they had found their man. The master did not conceal his delight that Professor Chester was from outside the college and called his friend at the professor's college to pass on the news and ask him if he could come by to talk to Inspector Khan. He agreed to go over immediately.

The three men chatted amiably, and the inspector declined a refill. The first drink had been stiff enough. With glass in hand, the sociologist from Professor Chester's college listened to an abbreviated version of what the inspector had told the master about the current state of their investigation.

"Do you have any idea of where he might be?" the inspector asked the rather rotund and tow-haired professor.

"None whatsoever, I'm afraid. I last saw him some four days back at a departmental meeting. We exchanged a few words and afterwards went our separate ways."

"How did he strike you?"

"Same as always. He was calm, polite, and responsive to colleagues, and very clearly in control of the meeting. There was nothing out of the ordinary."

"Was he in college often?"

"Several times a month, for lunches mostly. I did persuade him to attend one of our feasts last year, which I think he and his wife both enjoyed."

"What about Professor Nejami? Does Professor Chester know him?"

"Almost certainly because they are in the same department. To the best of my knowledge, they are not friends."

"Whom was he closest to?"

"George is a pleasant companion but could hardly be considered warm. He treats social encounters like poker games and never shows his cards until he has been called. My guess is that he had more acquaintances than friends. A possible exception is Professor Carducci in the history department."

Inspector Khan thanked the master and professor and took his leave.

XXXVI: Wednesday Morning

At 8.29 the following morning, Rhianna walked past Parkside Police Station and wondered if Rudi was in his office. She continued along the street on the lookout for a grey Toyota Auris. She saw one on the opposite side of the street adjacent to Parker's Piece. The driver's window was down, and Professor Chester stuck his head out, smiled, and waved to her. She had to wait for a break in the traffic to cross the road. The professor leaned across to open the door on the passenger side. Rhianna slipped gracefully into the car and sat back against the seat. She suddenly felt something like a bee sting when the EpiPen went into her carotid artery. She lost consciousness before she could yelp.

The EpiPen worked like a charm. He saw Rhianna stiffen, her mouth opened to say something, but then went slack along with the rest of her body. He reached across to steady her and, with some effort, fastened her seatbelt. Wonderful things, these seatbelts, he thought. He eased her down in the seat so that her head was resting on it. If anyone looked in, they would assume she was napping. He reached across again, this time for her bag, and rummaged through it for her mobile. He pulled it out, opened it and removed the battery.

He headed out of town in the direction of Ely. He passed the turnoff he had taken the last time he had drugged passengers in his car. He smiled, thinking about how well that had come off but also how many unforeseen consequences had followed. He was a great fan of Thucydides and thought about his account of the Peloponnesian War. Athens' great leader Pericles convinced the otherwise reluctant assembly to take Corcyra into an alliance. This led to war with Sparta, which Pericles had hoped to avoid, but if not, he intended to wage a defensive war and ultimately negotiate a peace that would leave his city in a stronger position. He lost control of events. The expected Spartan occupation of Athens' countryside led people to seek refuge in the city, protected by its walls and the long walls down to Piraeus and the sea.

Crowded together, the population was more susceptible to the plague that arrived from Egypt. A third died, including Pericles, who was replaced by the demagogue Cleon. He pursued a different strategy, and the war escalated and dragged on.

He had done something similar to Pericles. He had devised an excellent plan, but unforeseen events had interfered. He fell to neither plague nor police, and was able to respond appropriately, unlike Cleon. But there was something to learn from Cleon. Carried away by daring and hope, Cleon devised a crazy scheme that brought Athens surprising initial success. His abduction of Rhianna was a parallel — he looked across to make sure she had not stirred — and unlike Cleon, Alcibiades, and Athens, he would stop when he was ahead. A classical education was turning out to be more useful than he had ever imagined.

The drive to his redoubt in the North Broads took almost an hour. About ten miles north of the city, near Wroxham, he turned right and headed towards the Bure Marshes Nature Reserve. Once in the vicinity, he turned on to a dirt road — one that went past two farms. After the second, he turned right onto a smaller dirt road that ran past a field on the left with woodland on the right. Several hundred yards down this now increasingly bumpy road, there was a largely grass-covered track that led through the woods to a simple, frame house. He stopped in front of the house, got out, opened the passenger door and, with some effort, dragged Rhianna out of the car and into the house. He knew carrying a dead weight would be difficult. He was in good physical shape but still had to stop once to catch his breath.

Inside, everything was prepared. The house contained a sitting room, bedroom, kitchen, and bathroom. Behind it was a cabin that he had set up as a workshop. In the sitting room he laid soft, black plastic mats on the floor, the kind people work out on in gyms. He had screwed a number of eye sockets into beams and had various cords running through them. He dragged Rhianna into the sitting room, laid her down gently on top of one of the mats and put a pillow under her head. She remained motionless, but he was pleased to see she was breathing regularly. He stretched out her legs and arms and attached restraints to each that were connected to cords, which in turn were clipped on to eyelets in the wall.

The restraints were padded, also loose, but tight enough that she could not wiggle her hands or feet free.

He smelled urine and realized that the drug, also a muscle relaxer, had loosened the sphincter at the base of her urethra and that she had emptied her bladder. He freed her legs from restraints, removed her jeans and wet knickers and went to the kitchen to get a cloth to wipe her off. He had bought an assortment of women's clothes and put new underwear on her after cleaning her up. For this he had to raise her buttocks and do so again to slide on and pull the replacement jeans. He couldn't help but notice what a nice bottom she had and what a pleasure it was to squeeze. Rhianna was about the same size as Cynthia, and the clothes he bought with her in mind fit without difficulty.

He replaced the restraints and went off to the kitchen to brew a cup of tea. He took fresh milk from the refrigerator and reached into the cupboard for a biscuit tin. There was nothing to do but relax until Rhianna came round. She was likely to feel seriously hungover, and he had aspirin and water at the ready. One more task awaited him, he suddenly realized. He left the house, locked the door, and drove off the way he had come in. After a few hundred yards, he turned on to another, even less distinct track that ran down to an embankment along a small river. There was a crossing here, a concrete path that was useable when the water level was relatively low, as it was at this time of year. He drove the Toyota across, accelerating a little when he came to the dirt path that ran along the other bank of the river. In a couple of minutes, he turned off onto a grassy sward and came to a stop in the woods further downriver. He locked the car after grabbing the wellies he had on the back seat and used them to wade across the river. His house was a two-minute walk on the other side. He re-entered and had a quick look at Rhianna to discover that she was still fully sedated.

***

The editor of the *Cambridge News* was busy in a meeting with his layout team, and it slipped his mind that Rhianna had not called. At about 9.15 a.m., as the meeting came to an end, he looked at his watch and only then did he think of her. Oh well, he thought, she'll be along soon, and he headed down the hall to his office. At 9.45 a.m., she had not returned, and he called her mobile. He was immediately shunted to her voicemail.

What was she up to? She had been concerned for her security and had told him to call the police if she wasn't back by ten a.m. Rhianna was the dramatic sort and was now probably sitting in a café, having forgotten all about her backup request. But just possibly, she had run into trouble. Better to overreact, he thought, than to sit on his butt only to find out later that something had happened to her. He reached for his phone.

***

Inspector Khan was in Pembroke College talking to Professor Carducci, whose set was two flights up with a pleasant view of a small court and garden. It was cluttered with mementoes presumably collected on his travels. Framed lithographs of three bearded men hung on the little wall space not devoted to bookcases. He recognized Marx, and when asked, the professor explained that the other two men were Max Weber and Emilie Durkheim. They were the three fathers of sociology.

Professor Carducci acknowledged a certain friendship with Professor Chester but was quick to caveat it.

"He really does not open himself to anyone. Maybe he does more so to me, but he's still very guarded. I know little about his past, his aspirations, or why he never married."

"I'm sorry if this sounds impertinent, but this is a murder investigation. Can you tell me anything about his sexual preferences?"

"I understand. I think he's straight, but I have no confirming evidence. I remember him looking at Mrs Mason once at a college dinner in what I thought was a lustful manner. It made a strong impression on me as it seemed so out of character."

Inspector Khan pursued this further, but his interlocutor had nothing further to add.

"Perhaps you can help us in a different way," the inspector finally said.

"Professor Chester has left town, knowing that we would sooner or later come for him. Do you have any idea where he has gone?"

345

"No. I don't. Perhaps he's visiting a colleague at another institution?"

"Do you know whom that might be?"

Professor Carducci named several people in his field, including a sometime co-author at University College London. Inspector Khan thought it would take some effort to contact them, but Professor Carducci came to his rescue. He had a list of the heads of UK sociology departments and promised to email it to the inspector. He could check to see if any of them knew of Professor Chester's whereabouts.

"Is there anywhere else he might have gone?"

"I really don't know. Oh, wait a minute. A couple of years back, he told me that he had a cabin or a house. Somewhere in the North Broads, I think."

"You don't remember where?"

"No, I'm sorry. I don't think he ever told me. He likes to watch birds, and I surmise it's somewhere close to a lake or river."

"No other thoughts about its location?"

"I'm afraid not."

"No problem, you've been very helpful. One last question, if I may. Would he have told anyone else where his house was or perhaps have taken someone to visit?"

"It's possible, of course. But nobody comes to mind."

The inspector thanked him and was getting up to leave when his phone rang. It was the editor of the *Cambridge News*.

***

Inspector Khan rushed back to the station after calling Peter to relay the news about Rhianna having gone missing. By the time the inspector returned, Peter had ordered a copy of the CCTV coverage on the street in front of the station and had a constable checking car rental agencies to see if the professor had by any chance rented one. He did this after calling the constable on duty in front of the professor's home and having him check that his car was still in its garage. It did not occur to him, or to anyone else, to check Professor Bricknell's garage.

346

Inspectors Khan, Davidson and DS Leslie were on edge when they met in Inspector Khan's office. They did not know where Professor Chester had found a car or where he had driven Rhianna. The best bet, Inspector Khan insisted, was the North Broads, where he appeared to own a property. Inspector Davidson suggested the quickest way to find its location might be to contact his insurance company. He might have insured this house and his Cambridge one with the same agent. Peter pointed out that he would have to pay council tax on any properties he owned and would have a couple of constables start checking with local authorities in the region. This would take time but was sure to show something if Professor Carducci's information was correct.

***

It was taking longer than Professor Chester hoped for Rhianna to shake off the anaesthetic. He had drunk two cups of tea, taken a short walk, and relieved himself against a tree in the woods. He was careful not to let any urine drip on his trousers and thought about the effect of the drug on Rhianna. He could have left her in her wet knickers. It would have been a double shock when she awoke. He decided against it as her initial readjustment would be difficult enough. She would have no idea where she was and would immediately discover that she was restrained. She could stand up but not move off the mat. He had calculated just how much tension on her restraints would be necessary to keep her in place. Only later would she realize that she was not in her own jeans or knickers. This would constitute another shock, and she would immediately wonder if she had been violated. This would make her more vulnerable still. He would reap the benefits of raping her without having done so.

Around midday, Rhianna began to stir. He heard her cough and wheeze and rushed into the room to make sure she was all right. Her breathing became normal again, and he noticed movement in her fingers. Her left leg twitched, she yawned, and her right eye opened. It looked like all would be well, so he crept from the room. She needed time to wake up and go into shock and worry about what might happen to her. Aristotle was a clever old bugger. He distinguished fright from fear. The former he described as a physical and emotional reaction to immediate

347

danger, as when one encounters a ferocious wild animal. Fear was reflexive. It was about horrible things that might happen in the future and required imagination. Fear was induced by the thought that one might meet a ferocious predator whilst on a hike. He wanted Rhianna to overcome any fright she might have and to think about her situation and its apparent hopelessness and become increasingly fearful. Only then would he make an appearance.

***

Rhianna felt awful. She had a terrible headache, felt sore in all of her limbs, and at first, was unable to move. She wondered if she was dreaming and struggled to open her eyes. They felt glued shut, a feeling she sometimes had when awakening from a deep sleep in the middle of the night. She persevered and succeeded in opening one eye, only to shut it immediately because of the blinding light. She gradually felt in touch with her extremities. She was able to wiggle her fingers and toes and then move her hands. She tried opening her eyes again, but the light was still blinding. She raised her right hand to block out some of it but discovered that she could only move her hand part way towards her face. She couldn't imagine why this was so.

Rhianna stopped moving and took a few deep breaths in the hope of gaining more strength. She opened both eyes, but only partially, and once again tried to raise her right hand. It was restrained by something. She could feel a pull on her wrist that kept her from moving her arm more than a few inches upwards. She moved it sideways but to no more effect. She tried with her left hand and discovered it was also restrained. She moved her legs, one after the other, and they too were in some kind of restraints. Her head was now clearer, and she opened her eyes a little wider. She could make out a room of some kind and realized that she was awake, not dreaming. Where could she be, and what the hell was limiting her movements?

It came back to her that she had gone to speak to Professor Chester and entered his car. The last thing she remembered was leaning back in the passenger seat and feeling something like a bee or wasp sting in her neck. Then everything went black. What could have happened? Then it dawned on her. She had been drugged. That son-of-a-bitch Chester had done this to her. He must have used the same drug which he had used to anaesthetize the men he murdered. So much for his protestations, and so much for her naiveté in agreeing to meet him.

Unlike his other victims, she was alive. He had kidnapped her and taken her someplace. But where? And what was she going to do about it? More to the point, what could she do, given her restraints? Maybe she didn't have to do anything, at least immediately. Her editor would know something had happened and would call Rudi. He would find her. She realized she had an irrational trust in him, but in the circumstances, maybe that was a good thing. She sat up and tried to stand. She was still weak and giddy from the drug, but the second time she made an effort, she succeeded. She examined her restraints and realized there was little she could do about them. They were professional looking and, whilst she had some movement, she certainly couldn't bring her hands together or bring either to her face where she might use her teeth to loosen or bite through the restraining cords.

She directed her attention to the room. It was a parlour but a rustic one. She heard bird song outside but no traffic, which also convinced her that she was somewhere in the countryside. She must have been out for some time. She looked at her watch, but it wasn't on her left wrist. The bastard must have removed it. There were two windows in the room, and the sunlight was streaming in. She knew it was theoretically possible to calculate the time from the angle of the sun, but she couldn't see it and couldn't do the calculation in any case. She guessed it was midday. How long was she going to have to stay like this? What if she had to relieve herself? She looked down and discovered she was not in her own jeans. She was sure about that. How had that happened? Had he raped her whilst she was unconscious? She bridled at the thought and focused on her body. She knew how it felt after sex, and it did not feel that way now. But why would he put her in different jeans? This was another mystery.

Within thirty minutes, her interest in her condition and surroundings had diminished somewhat. She was bored, angry, and increasingly frightened. She tried not to think about what could happen to her but found it very difficult to keep unpleasant — and worse — thoughts — from her mind. She hoped Rudi would get here soon.

XXXVII: Wednesday Afternoon

Inspector Khan was trying to fathom Professor Chester's motive for kidnapping Rhianna. Did he plan on killing her as he did his three other victims, or had he taken her hostage? To reassure himself, he got the deputy commissioner's permission to send a couple of SOCOs to the catchment basin where the last bodies had been found, and if there was any evidence of recent activity, to dispatch a team of divers to the scene. He realized this was somewhat irrational because he reasoned Chester had dropped the bodies there in the hope they would decompose and not be discovered. Why would he dump Rhianna's body in the same place unless, of course, it was to humiliate the police?

He called Peter to check up on how the search of the tax records in Chester's name with local authorities was going. Inspector Davidson had put a call through to Chester's civilian solicitor to get information about his insurance company and had met with resistance. The solicitor told him the information was confidential, and Davidson replied that he was investigating a murder. He was told to get a warrant, and the firm would be happy to provide the information. Davidson explained the urgency of the matter; they were trying to free a kidnapped reporter before something dreadful happened to her. That softened up the solicitor, and another three minutes of pleas and promises on his part succeeded in extracting the information. He put down the phone at about the time a constable came by with a cup of tea.

"I need a drink, not tea," he thought. He took the tea nevertheless and thanked the constable. The call to the insurance company was a replay of that to the solicitor. The information was confidential, he should get a warrant, and how did they know he was the police. He told them the same story and asked them to call him back at Parkside Police Station to verify his identity. In the end, the insurance agent also caved and went to check Chester's file. Davidson was disappointed to learn that he had only one property insured, and that was his Cambridge home.

Peter kept his eye on the constables and made some calls himself to hasten the search process. It was tedious work and very disappointing, as there was no central national register that held tax information of this kind. By noon, they had eliminated a number of locales, but there were others to check out. Their breakthrough came unexpectedly. Professor Carducci remembered that Professor Chester had a sister and called Inspector Khan to tell him about her. He did not know her name or where she lived but thought if anyone knew about his second home, she was likely to. The inspector called Professor Chester's solicitor back, but he was filing papers at court and did not call back for a frustrating hour. And then he was not forthcoming when asked if the professor had made a will and whom he had named as beneficiaries of his estate. Inspector Khan finally convinced him that client privilege was overridden by the need to free a hostage whose life was in danger. It was the same argument he had made previously, and he had to do it again.

The solicitor called him back ten minutes later with the name and address of the sister. She was indeed his principal beneficiary. She lived in London, and he had her telephone number. Inspector Khan called, but nobody answered. He googled her only to find out that her details were only available on two social network sites, to neither of which he belonged. Quick calls around the office found that Constable Krauss belonged to both, and he was asked to log on and find out everything he could about her. He retrieved the information quickly and passed it on to Peter, who thought it about time the constable did something useful.

Mrs Lewis was a younger sister who worked in arts management for a company that represented performers and musicians. Her webpages indicated an interest in the arts, which was understandable, but also in travel, cooking, and gardening. Inspector Khan called her again with no luck and then sent an email. He called her company to see if she was at work but was told she was on holiday and not due back for another ten days. They would not provide any contact information, and the woman on the other end of the line scoffed at his explanation of why he needed it urgently.

From his experience of helping to bust a London drug ring, Inspector Khan had some useful contacts at the Met. To go through official channels would take too long, and he called one of them up, explained the circumstances, and was promised immediate assistance. He gave the name and address of the woman to whom he spoke at the agency. Thirty minutes later, his Met contact called him back with the information he needed.

"How did you pull that off?" he asked.

"I sent a detective over with two constables in full riot gear and automatic weapons. When the detective flashed his warrant card, backed up by two Darth Vader lookalikes, your truculent woman suddenly became extremely compliant. She telephoned me immediately with the information and has promised to remain at her desk in case you need additional information."

Inspector Khan smiled when he conjured up an image of the office with its staff cowering in fear. He dialled the overseas number he had been given. It was a resort in the Seychelles. The receptionist was a fluent English speaker and confirmed that Mrs Lewis was a guest. She didn't know where she was at the moment but would take a message. He persuaded her to send someone to look for her at the beach and elsewhere in the grounds. He would wait on the line. Ten minutes went by whilst he listened to maddening rock music, but at least it had the virtue of confirming that he was still connected. The receptionist finally came back on the line to report that Mrs Lewis was nowhere to be found. She must have gone out for dinner, and she would pass on the message when she returned. Inspector Khan told her it was about her brother and extremely urgent. He realized that she would think something terrible had happened to him. He didn't care. There was nothing to do but wait, which is the most trying task in the detective business, as it is in many others.

***

Rhianna's courage was fading fast. She had been awake now for several hours by her calculation. The sunlight was fading, although she thought it would still be light for several more hours. She had given up trying to loosen her bonds and was unable to find any comfortable position to sit or stand. The best she could do was to sit on the mat with her partially stretched arms at her side. She was thirsty, hungry, and would not have minded a visit to the loo. She really did not want to see her abductor but recognized that she needed him. Otherwise… she tried hard not to think of what would happen otherwise. She heard a noise, coming, she thought, from the other room behind the closed door. Chester was probably there and no doubt taking pleasure in her predicament.

Another hour went by. Rhianna's mouth was parched, her stomach was growling, her arms were sore, and she itched in several places she could not reach to scratch. Her bladder was sending signals, not yet of the urgent kind, but intense enough that made them difficult to ignore. She tried pulling as hard as she could on one of her arm restraints in the hope that it would loosen it from the wall, or she could somehow slip her hand through it. It didn't work, and the effort left her feeling even more uncomfortable than before. She started to hyperventilate but brought this under control by closing her eyes and concentrating on a pleasant memory. She began yoga-style exercises of short cycles of inhalation and exhalation. She felt a little better, but only in the sense of not losing it completely.

More time passed, and she was significantly more uncomfortable in every respect. Her headache had not gone away, her thirst and hunger were more acute, and she was having more difficulty in controlling her bladder. She didn't know if she could hold out much longer without wetting her pants. She was feeling sorry for herself but also angry at having fallen for the professor's pitch. If she had listened to Rudi, she would not be in this predicament. She began to hyperventilate again but brought her breathing back to normal more quickly this time. She achieved this state at a price. Yoga breathing required getting her muscles to relax, and as they did so, she lost temporary control of her bladder. She struggled to limit the damage and knew it was only a matter of time before nature would take its course. She tried without much success for the next twenty minutes to concentrate on other things, but it was a losing battle. Her sphincter finally relaxed in spite of her best efforts, and she wet her pants. She felt great relief but also humiliation. And soon, she recognized, she would feel a different kind of discomfort from her wet knickers and jeans. Her socks began to feel damp.

***

Professor Chester forced himself to finish the novel he was reading to pass the time. It was now ten past five in the afternoon, and he thought the timing right. Rhianna must be softened up and ready for him to begin his programming. This would be a challenge, but one to which he looked forward.

He opened the door and walked into the room. Rhianna saw the movement and immediately looked in his direction whilst rising to her feet. *She still wants to treat me as an equal*, he thought. *That won't last.*

"Why have you done this to me?" she shouted.

"You must learn to remain silent unless asked to speak," he said in a soft and barely audible voice.

"Fuck you."

"Outbursts like this won't get you anywhere."

"You're a total nutter."

Professor Chester had placed the mat toward the centre of the room so he could easily walk around her, which he did. Rhianna could crane her neck, but she couldn't turn around and had only partial vision behind her. Once more or less out of her sight, he undid the belt around his trousers, pulled it out, held it behind him and brought it down hard, but not too hard, on her lovely, round but tight bottom. She gave out a yelp, and he laughed.

Still standing behind her, he walked as close as he could get without touching her and whispered into her right ear, "Silence is the key to freedom."

She craned her head again, hoping she might spit at him, but he had backed off. He moved around to face her and looked at her and smiled.

"Thirsty, are we?"

"You know damn well I am!"

"Now, now. Let's control our foul mouth."

"Go fuck yourself."

"Have it your way, then." Professor Chester left the room and closed the door behind him.

***

354

Rhianna was enraged. The bastard kidnapped her, tied her up, starved her, hit her, and had the gall to complain about her language. Just wait until she got her hands on him. Her rage quickly subsided, unlike her headache, thirst, hunger, and wet and itchy crotch and thighs. She sat down on the now wet mat and thought about her situation. For the moment she was completely in his powers. It wasn't at all obvious what he wanted from her. She was fairly certain that he had not raped her, although he had certainly changed her jeans. He was violent but had only hit her once and not very hard. There were no torture devices in sight. His primary interest during their brief encounter seemed to be to get her to follow his instructions, only speak when invited to, and not to curse at him. She was willing to do this if it got her drink and sustenance.

On one level, their encounter had been a relief. She knew she had not been left alone to starve to death in an isolated house. He intended to keep her alive, for whatever reason, and would sooner or later look after her needs. It was probably best to humour him to get what she needed, and as quickly as possible. She would play his game and stall for time. Rudi would ultimately liberate her.

***

Rudi was sitting by the phone nursing a now cold cup of coffee. Sensing his mood, and sharing it, Peter had gone out to buy them coffee and pastries from the nearby café even though it was the inspector who owed him. Whilst in the queue, he called Elaine to see how she was doing and to report that it was likely to be a late night at the office. He knew better than to say anything more on an insecure mobile line but did not hesitate to say no when Elaine asked him if they were making any progress.

Peter returned to Inspector Khan's office and, a moment later, Deputy Commissioner Braham knocked on the half-open door. He was immediately invited in. Peter rose to give him his chair, but the commissioner held up his hand to restrain him.

"Any progress?" he asked.

"We're still trying to locate his hideout," Inspector Khan replied. He described their efforts and their wait for Professor Chester's sister to return his call.

"I've spoken to my counterpart in the Norfolk Constabulary. He's a nice bloke. Met him at one of those ghastly refresher courses, a couple of years back. He's willing to help in any way possible."

"We will need him once we find out where Chester has holed up. I'm wondering if it wouldn't make sense for me to go up to Norfolk to be on hand if and when we locate his whereabouts."

"Go ahead if you like. Have a uniform drive you up. Charlie and Peter can manage the search at this end."

"Are you sure?"

"Yes, go. Maybe pack a bag if you need to overnight."

Inspector Khan made his exit, and the deputy commissioner took his chair and joined the vigil by the telephone.

***

Professor Chester poured a glass of wine and took out of the fridge one of the prepared meals he had purchased at Waitrose. He put it in the oven to heat up and wondered if the aroma of his *bœuf bourguignon* would waft into the other room and make Rhianna hungrier still. He thought about opening the door and walking in with wine glass in hand but realized that would only further arouse her ire. Best to let her stew whilst he savoured his stew. He would go back to her later with a glass of water in hand. To drink, she would have to display compliance. He poured himself a second glass of Burgundy.

***

Inspector Khan had Constable Bates drive him to his flat, where he hurried to pack a small suitcase with what he might need over the next couple of days. He returned to the car, and they took off at a good clip for Norwich.

"Shall I put on the siren, sir?" the constable asked.

"No need. I'm going there on the off chance our killer turns up. Just take your time, and we can both relax and enjoy the ride."

The constable looked dejected.

356

"I'll tell you what. If I get a call telling us that they have found Professor Chester, you can put on the siren and drive like a bat out of hell."

"Yes, sir," the constable said in a snappy voice.

Inspector Khan was beginning to relax. There was nothing to do but sit back and watch the scenery as they headed east on the A11 towards Newmarket. The last time he drove this way, it was in expectation of a long bike ride in Thetford Forest. He had been summoned back to watch Professor Mason and Jaime being pulled out of the water.

That's when it all began, he thought. *Wouldn't it be nice if I got another phone call as we approach the forest, informing me that they have found Chester, and are preparing to move in on him?*

There would be a nice symmetry to it all, but he recognized that this rarely ever happens.

***

Professor Chester judged the time right and returned to the parlour with a glass of water in hand. Rhianna stood up and glared at him but said nothing.

"You're learning," he said. "Would you like a drink of water?"

Rhianna nodded her head.

"Good girl," he said. He put the water down just out of her reach and walked over to the wall, where the restraining cords attached to her right arm and leg were connected to eyelets in the wall. He reached out and released the clip and then pulled on the cord until her arm was almost perpendicular to her body. He refastened the clip and did the same with the leg restraint. He walked to the other side of the room and repeated the process until Rhianna looked like Leonardo da Vinci's famous drawing of Vitruvian Man with his arms and legs outstretched. He knew he was not a genius like Leonardo but thought he still ranked high in creativity and cleverness. He looked at Rhianna. Cleaned up and naked, she could be a work of art. He was pleased he had remembered to bring his camera.

Rhianna continued to restrain herself from speaking.

"You may wonder why I've done this," he said.

She remained still.

"I can give you water without you pulling any tricks." He approached her and held the glass to her lips. He tilted it a little so she could drink.

When she saw him approach with the glass, Rhianna thought about spitting the first mouthful in his face but did not. The momentary satisfaction this provided would be more than offset by the longer-term unpleasant consequences. Instead, she leaned forward, opened her mouth, and slowly began to drink. The water felt unbelievably refreshing, and she finished most of the glass, compelling him to raise it higher so the remainder ran into her mouth. He took a handkerchief out of his pocket and wiped her moist lips.

"I'll be back," he said.

In less than a minute, he re-entered the room carrying a washcloth, towel, and what she recognized as her own knickers and jeans.

"I've washed them," he said. "You wet them earlier."

So that's what happened, she thought to herself. He changed my clothes whilst I was still anaesthetized.

He approached her, knelt down, and undid the metal button on her jeans. Rhianna moved away from him as well as she could. He inched a bit closer on his knees, undid her zipper, and pulled down her trousers. This was difficult because her legs were spread apart and wet. He had to adjust her restraints so her legs could move closer together. With some effort, he got the jeans over her knees and on down her legs. He unclipped one restraint, held out her leg, pulled it out of her trouser leg, and refastened the clip on the restraint. He did the same with her other leg, and the remaining trouser leg came off easily as he had long ago removed off her trainers. He then reached for her knickers. Rhianna twisted away from him but to no effect. He peeled them off and repeated the process with the restraints to remove them.

He stepped back to admire his work.

Rhianna was red with rage but forced herself to remain silent. It could be worse, she reasoned, and pushed away the thought. She watched as he approached again and kneeled with his washcloth in hand. He carefully wiped her down, starting with her ankles and calves and working his way up. She was disgusted by this intimacy but greatly relieved that all he did was clean her up. He didn't touch her directly with his fingers or do anything overtly sexual.

He stepped back and picked up her clean knickers and jeans and put them at her feet.

"Would you like to be dressed again?" he asked.

"Yes," she replied.

He used the procedure with the restraints, but in reverse, to get her into her knickers and jeans. He buttoned them and gave them a little hike with his hands, so they rested on the right place on her hips.

"Are you hungry?" he asked.

"Yes," she replied.

"I'll be back."

He exited the room, leaving her to reflect on what had just transpired. Rhianna was at a loss. Chester was not a rapist and was looking after her physical needs. He was evidently some kind of control freak. She would humour him to buy time.

Her captor returned with a plate of food and a glass of wine. It looked like some kind of stew, and she had to admit it had a wonderful aroma. If she was a good girl, he told her, he would loosen her hand restraints enough that she could feed herself. She instantly agreed, thinking that she might be able to free herself and overpower him. He was a big man but did not look particularly strong or fast, and she was both. She positively relished the idea of a fight with him. It was not to happen. Before loosening the arm restraints, he took two small locks out of his pocket and attached them to metal rings embedded in the wrist restraints. She was able to sit down and eat but could not free herself from the restraints. He left the room only to return with another glass of wine for himself and a bottle of water to refill her glass. He pulled up a chair and sat across from her.

"You thought you would get a scoop, did you?"

Rhianna was chewing a mouthful of meat and did not answer.

"I won't disappoint. You'll find I never do. As you've figured out, I did away with Professor Bricknell and those other two useless men."

"What did you have against them?"

"Bricknell was about to turn me in. I thought that would be obvious to a woman of your intelligence."

"I was interested in the other two."

"What I had against Sid must remain my secret for the time being. If we become closer, I might tell you. When you plead with me to embrace you, I'll know the time has come."

Rhianna could think of few things she would rather do less. She would be happy to pass up the scoop if this was the price.

"What about Jaime in that case?"

"On first-name terms, are we?"

"Why did you kill him?"

"He was a useless yobbo, and the world is better off without him."

"You knew him well?"

"Ah, that was the beauty of the scheme. He was a lowlife who dealt drugs. I picked him up on the street and made him an offer he couldn't refuse. He thought he was going to get rich, but he ended up in a ditch. It served him right."

"Then you hardly knew him?"

"That's right. The police spent fruitless hours trying to establish a connection between him and Sid, and both of them and anyone else. But there was no connection. I imagine they're still looking for one."

"And what about me?"

"That depends. We have lots of time to work out our relationship because you're not going anywhere in the near future. You are an independent woman who lives alone. One of these modern types who do what they want, and I can imagine what you do on off-time. Nobody at work is going to miss you for a while, and when they do, they will have no idea of where you have gone."

Rhianna again bit her lip and remained silent.

"Would you like some more wine, my dear?"

"No, thank you. But another glass of water would be nice."

Professor Chester passed the water bottle over to her, and she helped herself to a glass.

"How about some music?"

"I would appreciate it," she said, convinced it could do no harm and maybe put him in a better mood.

He turned on the radio, and the sound of organ music filled the room. She thought of the scene in one of those *Pink Panther* movies where

Inspector Dreyfus has kidnapped the professor's daughter and entertains her by playing the organ. If life imitated art, the mad professor should now develop a severe toothache.

XXXVIII: Wednesday Evening

Mrs Lewis enjoyed a lovely dinner with a couple she had met at the hotel. They were Glaswegian and also on a package deal but had arrived two days earlier. The man was a travel agent who owned a franchise of a nationwide firm, and his partner worked there as well. They had a good sense of humour and regaled her with stories about the customers and the naiveté and boorishness of some of them. Mrs Lewis had the impression that the man was married to someone else, and the couple had come to the Seychelles to conduct their affair in privacy. Her speculations about their relationship lent an additional frisson of excitement to the evening. They had Mai Tais before dinner and a bottle of white wine with it, and she was feeling no pain.

They walked back from the restaurant; it was only a few hundred metres down the coast road from the hotel. They had brought torches, knowing that near to the equator, the sun sets early regardless of the time of year. Their passes were checked at the entrance, and Mrs Lewis was told she had a telephone message.

It's the last thing I need at this hour, she thought.

She nevertheless dutifully went to the desk and was handed an envelope. Inside was a handwritten message, neatly written on a folded piece of stationary. It asked her to call Inspector Khan of the Cambridgeshire Constabulary on an urgent matter relating to her brother. Her new friends stood by as she opened and read the letter.

"Nothing serious, I hope," said the woman, her arm linked in that of her partner.

"I'm not so sure. It's the police. They want me to call them about my brother."

"Oh dear, that doesn't sound good. Might have been in an accident or something."

"Possibly. Not much I can do about it from here. It's too late to make any travel arrangements, even if it's an emergency. Maybe I should just sleep on it and call them in the morning when I'm alert and more up to coping."

"If you need to, you can still change your flight. Remember, back home it's four hours earlier."

"I suppose you're right."

"We're happy to wait here whilst you call in case you need support or travel advice."

"That's really very kind of you. I'll bite the bullet then. It's the responsible thing to do."

Mrs Lewis had her mobile in her purse and carefully punched in Inspector Khan's number. Peter was returning from the loo when he heard the phone ring and rushed back to grab the phone on the fourth ring.

"Inspector Khan's office, DS Leslie speaking. May I help you?"

Mrs Lewis identified herself and said she was returning Inspector Khan's message. Peter told her how pleased they were she called and hoped he had not inconvenienced her terribly."

"Is my brother all right, Inspector?"

"Yes, I believe so. It's the person he's with that we're worried about."

"I don't understand."

"I didn't think you would." Peter explained the situation to her as delicately as he could. How do you tell someone that their brother has murdered three people and taken a fourth hostage? There was silence on the line when he finished his account, and he wondered if he had lost her.

"Are you still there, Mrs Lewis?"

"Yes, I'm here. I'm trying to make sense of what you said. You really suspect my brother of having done something terrible."

"I'm afraid so, Mrs Lewis. But we're mostly concerned with the wellbeing of his hostage and want to get to her as quickly as possible. I assure you we intend no violence against your brother."

"What if he doesn't give her up?"

"This rarely happens. Our hostage negotiator is very skilled. We want them both unharmed."

Peter judged the moment right to ask her about her brother's house in Norfolk. She knew it, although she had visited it only once, a couple of years ago, to give her brother advice about a vegetable garden he was contemplating.

"Can you tell me where it is?"

"Oh dear, I was afraid you were going to ask me that."

"Is there a problem?"

"I don't remember. It's north of Norwich, outside of some lovely village. I just can't recall the name."

"Take your time, please."

"It's no good, Inspector. I'm not going to recall it. All I can tell you is that the village is strung out along a road, has two lovely churches, one of them Norman. There's a large and very popular pub at the end of the village, on the right, along the river."

This could describe a hundred villages, Peter said to himself. "Is there anything else distinctive about it?"

"Distinctive? It's like so many of these Norfolk villages. Hold on. I remember now that it's not far from a prison, a women's prison, I think my brother told me."

"And what about your brother's house? Is it near the village?"

Mrs Lewis did her best to describe it as somewhere near the river but on the other side from the village and almost in sight of another town along the river that had a beautiful old Norman church perched on a hill above it.

Peter didn't think he was going to get anything else useful from her and thanked her profusely. He assured her there was no need to return home and that they would do her the courtesy of calling her back when they had more news about her brother.

Mrs Lewis ended the connection and looked at her new friends. They appeared very concerned, and she realized that they had heard her end of the conversation.

"Are you all right?" the woman asked.

"Yes, I think so."

"Would you like to talk about it?"

"Yes, I would. It's all very strange. But first I need another Mai Tai."

***

Peter picked up the phone this time to call the Norfolk police. It was more urgent to get them involved than to update his boss. He passed along the information to Detective Sergeant Cross, who was their designated point of contact. Peter had recorded the call with Mrs Lewis and had made handwritten notes but remembered clearly what Mrs Lewis had said. He looked at his notes only to confirm that his memory was accurate. Detective Cross listened closely and did not interrupt until Peter mentioned the women's prison.

"Yes, that would be right," he said. "I think I know the village. It's strung out along the road and has two nice churches and a pub along the river. There's a walking trail past the park by the pub, and you can go as far as the other town she describes with the Norman church. For the life of me, I can't think of its name either. Let me call up a Norfolk map on my computer."

Peter waited whilst he did this, and in less than a minute, Sergeant Cross was back on the line.

"It's Wroxham," he said. "The women's prison was the giveaway. Tell me again where she said the house was."

Looking at his notes this time, Peter repeated what Mrs Lewis had told him.

"That's not much to go on, but it sounds like it's not far at all from the town, at least as the crow flies. I'll get on to the tax authorities immediately and the local police and, with any luck, get an address, and we can move in."

"I'll call Inspector Khan; he's on his way to Norfolk now. He would very much appreciate being part of your operation."

"He'll be an asset as he knows the principals. And it will take a little while to get the address and set the operation up."

Peter now called his boss, who was having a catnap. He had stayed alert until Thetford Forest when his eyelids began to feel heavy. His body had always reacted to stress this way. He functioned well as long as necessary and collapsed once the danger passed or task was completed. Driving to Norwich was a temporary respite, and his body was trying to make the most of it. His dream dissipated before his conscious mind could make contact with it. He struggled to open his eyes as he fumbled for his phone. He answered on the fourth ring, which, he thought passable in the circumstances.

"Mrs Lewis called us, and we're zeroing in on her brother. The Norfolk police agreed to include you in the operation if you get there in time."

After ending his call, the inspector turned to Constable Bates. "I'm going to make your day. Turn on your siren and put the pedal to the metal."

The constable smiled, and did as instructed. Inspector Khan had second thoughts when the constable pulled out into the other lane to pass a lorry, compelling drivers coming the other way to take refuge on the verge.

***

Professor Chester enjoyed his time with Rhianna. She was getting used to her constraints, physical and verbal. Tomorrow morning, she would need to bathe, and he would assist. In the course of time, she would not only become accustomed to being touched by him but welcome it. He thought how nice it would be to soap up her body and rinse it off, watching her clean skin glisten. He would clean out her mind too, although that would take considerably more effort.

His reverie was disturbed by the sound of a car passing slowly on the dirt road that ran some hundred metres from his house. He listened as it went by without pausing or stopping. It reminded him to double-check that his alarm was turned on, as it had not sounded. He excused himself and went into the kitchen to look at the screen. It was indeed on, but the volume was low. He turned it up so he would hear it sound in the sitting room. It was a good system. He had certainly paid enough for it. There were three cameras, two of them placed a hundred and fifty metres apart and facing the road running past his house in opposite directions. The third was by the turnoff where he had initially parked. Any passing person or a car triggered the alarm. This gave him early warning of unwelcome visitors. He wasn't expecting any, but better to be prepared.

***

It was remarkable how quickly a bureaucrat could do something in response to a request from the deputy commissioner of the Norfolk Constabulary. Within five minutes, she had located Professor Chester's tax record and address and read out what little information they had in the relevant file. The most important details of all taxpayers were now filed electronically, but more was available in the older paper files.

Detective Sergeant Cross alerted his boss, Inspector Keene, that they had the address of the house, and that Inspector Khan would shortly be joining them. Inspector Keene, in turn, alerted the two constables who routinely patrolled Wroxham and the surrounding area, asking them to meet them in the car park of the pub of an outlying village. He had previously asked his emergency action team to prepare for a hostage rescue mission and now told their chief where they would be going. He would accompany them, and they would leave as soon as Inspector Khan arrived.

The emergency team gathered infrequently, and its members had other duties that consumed most of their time. One of them was on holiday, and a second was home with a bug of some kind. That left five skilled officers, enough, their leader thought, for an operation of this kind. They would be augmented by Inspectors Keene and Khan and DS Cross. DS Leslie had told them that Professor Chester owned a Luger, which he had used to kill a Cambridge colleague, so he might be armed.

A Luger, the chief thought, *how quaint*.

But he knew a 9 mm Parabellum fired from it was nothing to laugh at. They would take no chances and use stun grenades before entering the house. They would station a sharpshooter outside and cover any other exits. Their last operation, against a drug gang, had come off like an exercise, and he wanted to chalk up another success.

Inspector Khan was overjoyed when they arrived. He judged the drive more threatening to his life than any police operation he could contemplate. He was unsteady on his feet at first but felt himself after a few steps. DS Cross was waiting for him outside the door to the police station. They entered, and he made the usual rounds of introduction, starting with the deputy commissioner.

Interesting, Inspector Khan thought, *that protocol must still be adhered to in an emergency situation*.

They finally prepared to move off, and a constable arrived with coffee and a sandwich for him. This aspect of protocol he greatly appreciated.

He went in Inspector Keene's car and listened to him describe their operational plan. He asked Inspector Khan if he had any suggestions, and he said he was content to trust in their expertise. Inspector Keene was relieved, and all the more so by his colleague's willingness to wait outside with him whilst the assault team did their job.

They discovered the pub car park filled with cars and locals staring at the cavalcade of police that suddenly arrived. The assault team exited their vehicle to stretch their legs, which caused more of a stir among the crowd when they caught sight of their automatic weapons and grenade launchers. One of the barmaids emerged, her apron fastened at her waist, and she asked Inspector Khan what was happening. He looked across at Inspector Keene for guidance.

"Just preparing to nab some underage smokers when they come out of the bar."

"You're joking surely?"

"Indeed." Inspector Keene said nothing more, and the barmaid got the idea.

"Well, I hope you get your man," she said as she pulled a pack of cigarettes out of her apron pocket.

"Would you like to see proof of my age, Inspector?"

Inspector Keene smiled. "I would indeed, but on another occasion."

She smiled at him.

The deputy commissioner arrived in an unmarked black sedan and went to chat with the head of the assault team. They then walked over to where the two inspectors were standing.

Two members of the assault team climbed into the back of the deputy commissioner's car. He knew the area well and would drive them to within five hundred yards of the house. He would then return to headquarters whilst they positioned themselves and waited for the rest of the team to arrive. The deputy commissioner was holding a helicopter in reserve but was loath to use it unless absolutely necessary because the sound it made would tip off anyone within a couple of miles that something was up.

The inspectors waited for the rest of the assault team to depart in their special vehicle and then followed at a respectable distance. They did not speak for most of the fifteen-minute ride. Inspector Khan hoped that Rhianna was unharmed and struggled again to fathom what possible motive Professor Chester had for abducting her.

The vehicle transporting the assault team slowed to a crawl as it turned off the metalled road onto a deeply furrowed dirt one. They followed but continued to maintain their distance. After perhaps half a mile, they turned on to a smaller dirt road that ran past a field on one side and woods on the other. Not long after, the vehicle ahead of them stopped. They did the same. They watched the assault team get out and creep forward on opposite sides of the road. They exited their car and walked behind them, stopping well short of the spot where the assault team had assembled. They could see its members fanning out and disappearing into the wood on their left. The two inspectors took up a position well behind where the team had assembled.

It was high summer, and the sun would not set for another hour and visibility was good. The evening was generally a quiet time of day in the Norfolk Broads. The wind had died down, farmers had called it a day, and there was no sound of machinery. Even the birds seemed to have repaired to their roosts.

How different from Cambridge, Inspector Khan thought.

***

Professor Chester was in the midst of a rather elaborate procedure necessary to make Rhianna more comfortable for the night. He had brought out a mattress, a couple of pillows and a duvet and told her that he would loosen her restraints so she could lie down. He insisted on removing her jeans and knickers as this way she could relieve herself if necessary. After completing this laborious procedure and relocking her constraints, he put a bedpan next to the mattress. Rhianna was naked from the waist down and wondering how she would ever get to sleep. Then the alarm sounded. Rhianna had no idea what was happening but saw the professor run from the room towards what she assumed was his kitchen.

Professor Chester looked at his monitor and saw helmeted men carrying assault weapons slowly advancing up the road.

How the hell, he said to himself.

But that was for later. He had to get out of there. His car keys were still in his trouser pocket, and he had a suitcase with wheels all packed just in case. He left the cabin quickly and made his way down to the river, his wellies in hand. He put them on and carried his shoes and suitcase across the river and stayed in his boots until he reached his car. He put the suitcase in the boot, changed back into his shoes, and tossed the wellies into the rear footwell. He started the motor and slowly drove off. Somehow, they had smoked him out, but he still had a few tricks up his sleeve.

***

The assault team was in place. They were hiding behind trees, with the front door in their sights, as one team member crept around behind the house. Sergeant Wilson had positioned himself deeper in the woods but with a clear eye on the shed. The two inspectors stayed where they were, waiting for the operation to begin. When the team member behind the house was in place, the team leader looked at the other members and gave the thumbs-up sign. They emerged from their hiding places and crept up to the house. One of them peered through the kitchen window and signalled to his colleagues that the room was empty. A second looked into the other room, where he could see a semi-naked woman sitting on some bedding in the middle of the floor. There was no sign of Professor Chester. The two policemen crawled around to the front and waited by the door. The head of the assault team tapped his colleague on his shoulder, and he immediately rose, and they used a ram to break through the door. Three members of the team ran inside weapons at the ready, and safety catches off. They fanned out into the kitchen and bedroom, found nobody in either room or joined their colleague in the sitting room. The head of the team then came into the house. They all stood looking at Rhianna, who was now standing and staring at them.

"Don't just stand there," she said. "Get me out of these restraints."

One of the assault team approached after handing his weapon to a colleague and took a knife from a sheath on his belt. He cut the first rope before he discovered that the wrist collar to which it was connected was locked.

"I'm afraid I'll hurt you, ma'am, if I slip the knife underneath." One of his colleagues went into the kitchen and returned with a pair of scissors that he used to cut his way through the collars on her arms and legs. It was slow going as the nylon was tough, and the scissors were not very sharp.

The head of the team went back outside once they had determined that the professor was nowhere in the house. He took the colleague who carried the ram and went to the constable guarding the shed.

"No need to break down the door, sir," said the officer with the ram. "I can cut through the lock." He put down the ram and unhooked heavy shears from his belt. He caught the metal loop of the Yale lock between its jaws and pulled tightly on the handles. The lock snapped, the constable unhooked it and opened the door. There was a light switch inside to the right of the door that the constable turned to the on position. The room was a combination workshop and storage area. They backed out, leaving it uncontaminated for the SOCOs. The assault leader called the deputy commissioner to report that they had liberated the hostage. She was unharmed and freed from the restraints locking her in place. Their job now was to find the professor. There was no sign of his car, and he certainly had not driven past them. He would report back after questioning the hostage.

The deputy commissioner volunteered to alert the police nationally about the professor and send out his photograph and other details. They had no idea where he had gone but assumed he had a car somewhere. The deputy commissioner ordered the helicopter aloft to identify traffic in the vicinity and sent uniforms out to set up roadblocks at convenient choke points. Everyone thought the professor had probably flown the coop by then, but it was still worth the effort in case he had not.

The head of the assault team walked back to the dirt road and summoned the two inspectors to join him. He briefed them on what had happened and invited them to join him in questioning Ms Johnson. They walked in the direction of the house at a rapid pace.

Rhianna was now freed from her constraints, had slipped into her knickers, and was putting on her jeans when the head of the assault team and two inspectors came into the room.

"Rudi," she exclaimed, "I knew you would rescue me!"

"I'm very relieved to see you, Rhianna. Are you OK? And were you undressed?"

"I'm just fine," she said as she zipped up her jeans. "The bastard tied me up and had me naked from the waist down."

"Did he… "

"No, he didn't molest me, at least not sexually."

She began to explain what had happened but was interrupted by Inspector Keene.

"When did he leave?" he asked.

"No more than five minutes ago. Some kind of alarm sounded in another room, and he rushed out. I heard a door open, and bang shut. Not long after, your team broke in."

"Does he have a car?"

"Yes." Rhianna described how she had been drugged once she had sat down in the passenger seat. She was unconscious from the moment she felt the needle until she had come to in this room and knew nothing else. "Please, can you tell me where I am?"

"Outside of Norwich," Inspector Keene explained. "And I think we should get you to a doctor."

"I don't need one. But I do need to call my editor and tell him that I'm OK. I assume he called you when I did not show up at work?"

"Yes," Inspector Khan replied. "It was smart of you to use him as a backup alarm." He thought but did not say how stupid it was of her to agree to an interview with Professor Chester and to get into his car.

"What do we do from here?" she asked.

"We get you back to Cambridge, and Inspector Keene and his team try to find our professor."

Inspector Khan stepped outside to call Peter and tell him what had happened. He volunteered to call Mrs Lewis back and ask if she knew of any other place her brother might seek refuge.

XXXIX: Wednesday Night

Professor Chester felt increasingly secure as he put more distance between himself and Wroxham. He worried that he would encounter a police blockade or checkpoint, but there was nothing of the kind. They were slow in responding and had not twigged that he was driving Bricknell's car. This meant his new identity was probably safe as well.

He thought about how nice it was to rub the washcloth over Rhianna's shapely legs and soft skin. If only he had more time, he could have won her over. He allowed himself a reverie of Rhianna begging him for sex and of a somewhat rough kind. He would have to figure out a way of seeing her again. Wouldn't it be wonderful if he could kidnap her again and take her to some place where the police would not disturb them. He wondered how they had traced him. If they knew about Bricknell's car, they might have tracked him on CCTV, but that would have taken them a long time, so he discounted it. He would know for sure in another couple of hours.

Somebody must have tipped the police off. Who knew about his redoubt? He couldn't remember telling any of his colleagues about it, but perhaps he inadvertently had. His sister knew about it and had helped him plan his garden. Maybe they had called her and asked? Good police work on their part, either way. It was satisfying to outwit the police, and all the more so when they were worthy opponents. There was no honour gained in running rings around oafs. He thought the score was tied at the moment. He had kidnapped Rhianna, they had found her, he had escaped, and they had not found him, at least so far. He would regain the upper hand if he continued to elude them. His best way of doing this, he had concluded, was to leave the country. For this reason, he was en route to Harwich and the ferry to the Hook of Holland. It left at eleven p.m., giving him just enough time for a relaxed drive. Once assured he was past any imminent danger of interception, he pulled off the road, took out his phone, and booked tickets for himself and his car.

Peter knew it was too late to call Mrs Lewis in the Seychelles. He would ring her tomorrow morning. He thought it worthwhile speaking to a couple more of Professor Chester's colleagues to see if they had any thoughts about where he might be heading. His appointment earlier in the day with the professor's secretary had been unsatisfactory. She was attached to her boss and could not believe that he was wanted for murder or would kidnap a journalist. She would not volunteer any information that might lead to his capture, and Peter came away with the feeling that she would have liked to have been his kidnap victim.

Let's go in the opposite direction, Peter told himself. *Who likes Professor Chester the least and is thus more likely to be forthcoming with helpful information?*

The answer was clearly Professor Lundgren. She definitely had it in for Professor Mason, and he could not imagine that she had any warm feelings for Professor Chester. He may have been supportive of her career but probably made sure that she knew what battles he had fought on her behalf and expected payment in kind. He gave her a ring, and she seemed pleased to hear from him. He invited her for coffee and suggested they meet at the same café as last time. She countered with the suggestion of a drink and mentioned a wine bar within walking distance of both of them. He immediately agreed.

As interesting as Professor Lundgren was, it was not the woman Peter had been hoping to connect with this evening. He telephoned Elaine, brought her up to date on the investigation, and they both agreed how dumb and lucky Rhianna had been. He promised to call back after his meeting, and she, in turn, promised to hold dinner for them. He wanted to know what she was cooking and was pleased to learn that it would be a seafood risotto. With multiple appetites aroused, he headed off for his drink with Professor Lundgren.

He remembered his informative conversation with her the last time they had met and how she had told him about the Japanese distinction between the week above and the week below.

They arrived at the wine bar at almost the same moment and agreed to sit at the bar because all the tables were occupied. She ordered a New Zealand sauvignon blanc, and he was happy to follow her lead.

"They make good wines, these Kiwis. Their sauvignon blancs are distinctive, very different from their French counterparts. They produce good pinot noirs now too, but they are oddly priced."

"How so?"

"With sauvignon blanc and Riesling, quality and price are directly correlated, which makes shopping for them easy. With the pinot noir, there is no necessary relationship."

"How odd."

"I think so. You're a detective. Maybe you could look into it once you catch whoever committed these murders."

"We know who it is."

"You do?"

"We're absolutely certain it was your colleague Professor Chester."

"George! You've got to be kidding!"

"I'm afraid not."

Peter filled her in on Professor Bricknell's synthesis of the anaesthesia at Professor Chester's request, how it had been used to immobilize Professor Mason and Jaime, Bricknell's subsequent murder, and Rhianna's kidnapping and rescue that afternoon. She was stunned. Peter told her how he had escaped and how they had no idea where he was headed, or for that matter, where he had found another car.

"If it were me," she said, "I'd hightail it out of the country. I remember now; I once had a conversation about this with George."

"You did?" said Peter, whose turn it was now to show surprise.

"Yes, even in the context of a murder."

Peter looked at her in astonishment.

"It's not quite what you think, Inspector. And may I call you by your first name? You may call me Rose."

Peter nodded, and Rose commenced her tale.

"We ran into each other at Covent Garden at the first interval of a performance of *Don Giovanni*. Do you know anything about the opera?"

"Not really. Just that he seduces women and is ultimately taken to hell by a statue."

"Not hell, but the underworld. But yes, that's the gist of it. The statue is a monument of the Commendatore, whom Don Giovanni ran through with his sword when he tried to rescue his daughter from his clutches. The Don later rapes a woman, and the men of Seville organize a posse to hunt him down. He uses several ruses to avoid capture but stays in town rather than fleeing and has the temerity to invite the speaking statue he encounters to dinner. This final act of hubris leads to his demise."

"What does this have to do with Professor Chester?"

"I'm coming to that. With drinks in hand, we discussed the Don's behaviour. I suggested that it was stupid of him to stay in town with a posse and a statue after him. He was a rover by nature. His sidekick Leporello sings a famous aria early in the opera about the 1003 women Don Giovanni has seduced all over Europe, Turkey included. It made sense for the two of them to go somewhere far away, where he could try for new sexual triumphs. George told me I did not understand. Sex for the Don was an exercise of power, and so too was his commitment to remain in Seville and outwit the posse. Running away would be a sign of weakness."

"You think he will stay in Britain and possibly even return to Cambridge?"

"I wouldn't be surprised. But like the Don, he will need a new identity to pull this off."

"A new identity?"

"Yes, Don Giovanni compels Leporello to change clothes with him, and his poor assistant gets caught and is almost run through with a pitchfork by one of the posse. The Don, dressed as Leporello, fools, and then roughs up one of their men, the young man engaged to the woman he raped or tried to rape. There's some ambiguity here that gives those staging the opera freedom to decide."

"A clever stratagem, but it's an opera."

"Opera mimics life, and the reverse is true as well. And our professor appears to have had his Leporello."

"You mean Professor Bricknell."

"The one and the same."

"It seems a bit far-fetched to me. Suppose he followed your line of argument and left for greener pastures. Where do you think he would go?"

"That's a good question and might require a refill. What do you think of the wine?"

"It's excellent. Tell me the name again."

Peter took out his omnipresent pad and wrote it down. "I'll top us up."

"I could do this," said Rose.

"No need. The deputy commissioner is in a good mood since we found and freed Ms Johnson, and I'm going to hit him with the bill."

Professor Lundgren smiled as Peter signalled to the barman.

Peter ordered their drinks and returned his attention to Rose.

***

Inspector Keene had one of his men drive Inspector Khan and Rhianna Johnson back to Cambridge. He walked them to the waiting car, and they thanked him for carrying out such a successful operation.

"Partially successful, I'd say. We freed you, but that Chester bloke eluded us."

"I'm sure we'll find him," Inspector Khan said.

"We will interview people in nearby towns and petrol stations to see if anyone saw him, but identification is more problematic without some idea of what kind of car he was driving."

"He has an advantage there," Inspector Khan agreed. "But unless he has another hideout, which I doubt, he is on his own, with few possessions, and he can't return to Cambridge to gather more. We've stationed uniforms round-the-clock at his home and office."

They shook hands and parted, and Rhianna gave him a peck on the cheek as she again expressed her joy in being liberated.

"I'm sorry that we caught you with your pants down," the inspector said.

"I'm thrilled that you did," she replied with a smile.

Neither party said much on the ride back. Inspector Khan wondered what she had looked like when they broke into the building, but was pleased he had not been there. His relationship with Rhianna was a professional one, but she, it seemed, wanted to make it personal. Eyeballing her naked from the waist down would have complicated matters and made it more difficult for him to keep his distance.

Rhianna was exhausted but relieved and quickly fell asleep, the motion of the car acting as an effective catalyst to this end. Her head rested on the inspector's shoulder, and he did not have the heart to change position. He had to admit that he was enjoying it.

***

Professor Chester reached Harwich in good time and eased into the queue to board the overnight ferry. He was peckish and thought he would get himself something to eat once aboard the ship. He also needed the loo, but that could wait.

The boarding process was handled professionally. He had to present his ticket and passport to an official. In the background, he could see a heavily armed policeman. He guessed that they were mostly interested in people coming the other away: illegal immigrants and drug smugglers. They gave a quick glance at his passport and ticket and ran the appropriate page of the former through the standard reader. His documents were handed back, and he was instructed to return to his car and drive on to the ferry. He was waved aboard and then motioned into a lane by a woman in a high-vis jacket and finally told where to park by another one. He exited his car, found the lift to the decks above, and got out on the one advertising the restaurant. He stopped first at the loo, meticulously washed his hands, and headed off for the restaurant for a sandwich and a drink. The wine looked like cheap plonk, and he settled for a beer. He had booked a cabin for the overnight passage and was looking forward to a good night's sleep. He always slept well at sea.

XXXX: Thursday Morning

Peter and Inspector Khan met for their early morning coffee in a local café rather than at the police station. Everyone there would be abuzz with gossip about yesterday's operation, and the inspector would be mobbed with well-wishers. The deputy commissioner had asked to see him first thing, and that would take time too. Best to talk to Peter before going anywhere near the station. Two of their colleagues came in for coffee and saw them ensconced in leather chairs talking in low voices. They were sensitive enough to leave them alone and merely nodded in recognition as they walked by.

The inspector filled Peter in on yesterday's events, and Peter asked only the occasional question. Like Inspector Khan, he was baffled by Professor Chester's motive. Why had he abducted Rhianna, and what did he want from her? It seemed evident that he was acting out some kind of sexual fantasy. Why else would he have tied her up and undressed her? But this, too, was baffling because he had not molested her. The search of his house revealed a tap on Mrs Mason's phone, and she seemed to be the object of his affections — if that's what they could be called. Why had he redirected his attention to Rhianna?

"She's a younger and sexier woman," said Peter.

"But if that's what he's after, then why the interest in Mrs Mason in the first place? One could surmise that he killed her husband to make it possible for him to make a move on his wife. After all that planning and effort, why switch objects of affection?"

"Maybe Mrs Mason was not accessible? She's out of the country."

"True enough," said the inspector. "If we get evidence that he's gone abroad, I suppose we should get her itinerary and get someone abroad to offer her protection."

Peter briefed the inspector about his conversation with Professor Lundgren and her belief, based on his argument about Don Giovanni, that the professor might well return to Cambridge.

"We have uniforms at his house and home. I suppose we could alert them. But he must know we have his home and office under surveillance. Is there anywhere else in town he could go? What about his college?"

"I've made inquiries there already. I'll call the master of his college now, and alert him about our suspicions. He can ask the porters to keep their eyes open."

"Good. What would you do if you had to go underground in Cambridge?"

"Oh, I have a place to hide. I'd be happy to give it a try if you like."

The inspector smiled. "Yes, I know exactly where I could find you."

"I do have a thought," said Peter. "Chester's secretary is very protective of him and was unwilling to tell me anything that might help us find him. I wouldn't be at all surprised if he didn't call her for assistance. She could get whatever he needs without attracting attention and then meet him somewhere out of town. He could even be staying at her place."

"Worth a look. I'll ask Braham for a tap on her office, home, and mobile telephones and a search warrant. We would look very foolish if it ever came out that he was hiding under our noses."

The two men finished their coffee and walked back to the station. Peter disappeared into his office to call Mrs Lewis, report on their successful operation, and see if she could provide any more useful information.

***

Deputy Commissioner Braham was in a sour mood, which Inspector Khan interpreted to mean all would be well. He was offered the usual seat and was pleased to see the commissioner take the seat opposite him.

"Would you like some coffee?" the deputy commissioner asked.

"No thanks. I'm just back from the café."

"They do have better coffee, don't they?"

Inspector Khan nodded his agreement. The commissioner asked for an account of yesterday's events, and Inspector Khan repeated what he had told Peter. They agreed that the professor's motives were not self-evident and that he had to be found soon. At Peter's request, he had alerted airports and ports. But he discovered the Norfolk Constabulary had already done this.

"Helpful, were they?"

"First-rate, sir."

"Then why did the professor escape?"

"He must have had some kind of warning. Ms Johnson reported that he left in a hurry some minutes before the police arrived."

"Do you think he was tipped off?"

"Unlikely."

Inspector Khan's telephone rang, and he looked across at the commissioner who signalled him to take the call. The commissioner sat silently and waited for him to finish.

"That was Inspector Keene. We have our answer. The professor installed a sophisticated surveillance system on both sides of the road leading to the house.

"He had a monitor in his kitchen and an alarm rigged to go off if the cameras detected vehicles or people. The assault team parked some distance away but were picked up by one of the cameras as they crept up along the road."

"I see. And how did he make his getaway?"

"He planned well for that, too. He parked his car on the other side of a river that runs near his house and waded across at a point where it is passable. The SOCOs found his tracks, and they led to where he parked his car, some hundred and fifty metres upstream and with easy access to a road. Given the lay of the land and the roads, it's several miles at least by car from where the police had parked."

"A clever bugger. What's he going to do next, and how are you going to prevent it?"

Inspector Khan shared Professor Lundgren's speculations, and the deputy commissioner agreed immediately to ask a judge for the taps and search warrant.

"Let's go through the secretary's office and desk as well, why don't we."

"Fine by me, sir."

"Do I remember correctly that we confiscated his passport when we searched his house?"

"We did indeed."

"He doesn't have a second one, does he?"

"Not to my knowledge, but I'll check on that."

"If not, he can't leave the country very easily, and he's still likely to be around somewhere."

"That's our conclusion too. You didn't hear anything from the ports or airports?"

"Nada."

"Maybe that's because you asked them to check for a George Chester."

Inspector Khan described Peter's conversation with Professor Lundgren in detail and suggested it would do no harm to see if they had any record of a Leporello or a Donald Giovanni leaving the country last night. And the name Bricknell, too."

"Bricknell? Why him?"

"He played Leporello to Chester's Don Giovanni. Maybe Chester got hold of his passport. Have we maintained a watch on his house since his murder?"

"I don't know. Did you order one?"

"Only until the SOCOs had finished."

"It's possible that he went to Bricknell's home once he knew we were on to him and took whatever he needed from it, including his passport."

"And his car. He had a car when he abducted Rhianna, and we can't figure out where he got it from because his is in his lockup."

"All right. I'll add Bricknell's name to the others, and you get someone over to Bricknell's house to see if his car is still there."

There was silence for a moment until the commissioner spoke again.

"The news of Ms Johnson's abduction and rescue has gone viral. The phone has been ringing off the hook, and I've scheduled a press conference for ten a.m. You'll appear with me, of course, and we will distribute photographs and information about Professor Chester and ask for the public's help in finding him. We will both praise the Norfolk Constabulary for their excellent work. How nice it will be, for a change, to have good news to report."

"Absolutely, sir." Inspector Khan wondered if Rhianna would be at the press conference. He doubted it. She would probably be holding one of her own.

***

Her colleagues greeted Rhianna as a returning hero. They wanted to know all the details, and she gave them an edited version, leaving out the part about being stripped by her abductor. Her tale evoked a lot of sympathy and a slew of questions about how she felt to be restrained for that length of time. She answered in a calm way. It was far and away the most exciting thing that had happened to any reporter at the *Cambridge News* in anyone's memory.

"You're the story now, not the reporter," said one of her colleagues.

She smiled and thought how strange this felt. Rather than ferreting information out of people, she was now trying to hold it back and be very careful about what she said to her colleagues and the media more generally. She had an earlier conversation with Rudi in the car once she had awakened, and they agreed to keep a lid on certain details to make it easier for the police with their investigation.

Her editor told her that everyone from the BBC on down wanted an interview but that he wanted an exclusive. This was her big break, she thought, and she wasn't going to let some provincial editor stand in her way. He was a nice fellow who had always done right by her, and she would give him something. They went into his office to negotiate an arrangement. That afternoon's paper would carry her story and photo on the front page. She could do radio and TV interviews after that, and he had already booked her with the local BBC. He thought it likely that the interview would be broadcast on the national news.

Rudi had allowed her to tell the public about how she had been sedated and that it was the same method and drug used in the earlier murders. He was relieved because she did not want anyone to think she was some hopeless skirt who passively allowed herself to be kidnapped and restrained. Neither he nor the Norfolk Constabulary would say anything about her state of undress, for which she was grateful. She was fascinated by how he and Peter had tracked her down and made a mental note to write a thank you note to Mrs Lewis when this was all over. In her account and interviews, she would emphasize her resistance and refusal to cooperate with her captor even though she was restrained and starved. She would make no mention of the dinner she had been offered.

She went down the hall to her office to collect her thoughts and write her story. *Who knows*, she thought, *perhaps a fat book contract could come my way.*

***

Professor Chester had a long and tranquil night's sleep. He awoke refreshed and treated himself to a full English breakfast in the restaurant, excepting those awful baked beans. He could understand how people ate them during the war when almost everything else was rationed and unavailable. But today was another matter. It showed how much people were creatures of habit, and this was good, he thought, because it made them easier to predict, exploit, and evade.

The ship docked on schedule, and Professor Chester waited in his car for the signal to drive ashore. He could hear clanging noises as the ferry docked, and its ramp was wound down and made a loud grating sound when it made contact with the concrete surface of the dock. Car engines started, and traffic began to move off the boat. He drove out into a surprisingly blue morning. Dutch officials had checked his passport and car registration earlier aboard the ship. He imagined that they had some kind of scanner to read car registrations and would pull over anyone not on their list of cleared vehicles. They must have some way too of checking on passengers.

He drove through the town and headed for Germany, planning a nice lunch when on the other side of the border. The Netherlands and Germany are both in Schengen, and the border was wide open, and he could pass through without showing any identification. Once across, he would dispose of his car and complete his journey by train. The weather was good, and even though it was not a weekend, traffic was light. There were, however, numerous lorries and articulated lorries on the road. He amused himself by checking their number plates and found some from as far away as Poland and Slovenia.

***

The press conference went well, and the deputy commissioner complimented Inspector Khan on the job he had done. Inspector Khan felt more relieved than pleased. He hated these events and always expected the media to distort his remarks and those of his colleagues to portray them in a bad light. He didn't think that would happen today. There were no barbed questions and no sign of hostility from any of the news people. Their questions were good ones and politely put. They did not push as they usually did when he or the deputy commissioner declined to answer something on the grounds that it might hinder their investigation. At the end of the conference, they received a surprising round of applause. On their way out, news representatives were given flash drives with a photograph and information about Professor Chester. This was an innovation, and the IT people thought it would expedite the dissemination of the professor's picture. Inspector Khan excused himself as politely as he could and returned to his office.

***

Peter and Inspector Davidson had organized teams to search the office and home of Professor Chester's secretary once the warrants were in hand. He told the team that would monitor the telephones what they should be listening for. His phone rang, and he picked it up, expecting yet another request for an interview. It was Professor Lundgren — Rose — as they were now on a first-name basis.

"Since our talk, Peter," she said, "I've thought more about where George might go if he did not return here to Cambridge. I don't know of any bolthole that he has overseas, but he likes spending time in Germany, especially in Berlin. He has colleagues there, friends by now, I assume, who invite him frequently to give talks. He told me they pay him in concert tickets. Last summer, I know he went with one of them to the Handel Festival in Halle."

"Where is that?"

"In the old East Germany."

"You think he might be on his way to Berlin?"

"I really don't know but think it a possibility worth looking into. I would in your shoes."

"And just how do I find him in a city the size of Berlin?"

"I would start by getting the names of his contacts there from his secretary."

"She's not forthcoming. Is there anybody else who would know?"

"I would think she's the best source. She's fiercely loyal to him for reasons I can't understand, and you might have to put some pressure on her."

"Any thoughts of what buttons to push?"

Peter heard a rap on his door and looked up to see Inspector Khan in the doorway. He motioned him in but put his finger over his lips to signal he wanted to continue his call. The inspector sat down and let him get on with it.

"Not really. Perhaps you could ask someone higher up, even the vice-chancellor, to have a word with her."

"That's not a bad idea. Any suggestions about where we might look in Berlin?"

"As I said, he loves music. The Philharmonie would be the venue to watch. He loves books too, so maybe some of the better-known bookstores. If he's run off on the spur of the moment, as you suggest, he'll be desperate for something to read, and it won't be the kind of book you find at airport shops."

"That's very helpful, thanks. If you think of anything else, please do call back."

Peter ended the call and turned his attention to Inspector Khan. He listened to his account of the press conference and his early meeting with the deputy commissioner. He agreed that they both should have thought of continuing surveillance of the Bricknell house. His solicitor was the executor of his estate and had been given access to the house after the SOCOs departed. He promised to keep it under lock and key.

It was Inspector Khan's mobile that sounded this time, and he took it out to answer.

"Khan here."

There was a pause as he listened to his caller.

"I see. Thank you." After another pause, he said, "No reason to close the barn door after the animal has left."

He put the phone down and looked across to Peter. "As the deputy commissioner expected, Chester has keys to Bricknell's home and lockup and made off in his car. He may have taken his passport too, and we've added Bricknell's name to the watch list."

"That was a big slip up on our part. Was Braham angry?"

"Surprisingly, no. He was delighted that we smoked Chester out from his hiding place and brought Rhianna back unharmed. Now we can put out a nationwide alert on Bricknell's car."

Inspector Khan's phone sounded again, and he took it out of his pocket a second time.

"Khan here." He listened to his caller's voice. "That's interesting. We owe Professor Lundgren and Don Giovanni votes of thanks."

Another silence.

"Yes, sir. She thinks he might be on his way to Germany. We'll need to enlist some help there, and I don't know how we do that. It's not like calling a contact in the Met or Norfolk Constabulary." There was a short silence followed by, "Thank you, sir."

Inspector Khan put his phone back in his pocket and looked back at Peter. "Maybe I should just leave it on your desk given the frequency it rings? The bastard is still a step ahead of us. He left the country on last night's ferry from Harwich to the Hook of Holland."

"Let me guess, in Bricknell's car and using his passport?"

"Go to the top of the class."

"How did he get away with it? He doesn't look like Bricknell."

"Remember, passport photos are only headshots, and the two men have similar hair and eye colour."

"I'm really impressed that you clocked those details."

"Don't be. If I were clever, I would have left a uniform at the house."

"What do we do now?"

"The deputy commissioner is alerting Interpol and giving them information about Chester and Bricknell's car. The Foreign Office will send along Bricknell's passport details. Braham is also finding someone to make contact with the Berlin police and wants us in his office in thirty minutes."

"It's now in somebody else's hands."

"It looks that way. Frustrating, isn't it?"

"Very."

XXXXI: Thursday Afternoon

Deputy Commissioner Braham called an acquaintance at the Met who handled foreign liaison. He passed him along to the official who did this for other police forces throughout the country. She was stationed in Slough and was forthcoming and business-like. She took all the relevant information and promised to call back as soon as she had made contact with her counterpart in Germany.

In the interim, Inspector Khan and DS Leslie made their way to the deputy commissioner's office. He invited them to take the seats behind his desk, a position from which they were most often the targets of his criticism. But today, he was positively avuncular. Collectively, they speculated about the nature and extent of the media coverage they could expect. The deputy commissioner said he had already heard a report on BBC radio.

"It was reasonably straightforward and actually got the facts right. Must have been written by a newcomer who hasn't yet had proper training."

The three men chuckled.

"I'm curious to see what Rhianna has to say," said Inspector Khan.

"No worries there," said Peter. "It will be effusive in its praise for the constabulary and single out its gallant Inspector Khan."

"How do you know?" asked the deputy commissioner.

"He rode to her rescue, and in her fantasies, does more riding than that."

"Peter, please," said Inspector Khan.

"I'm simply stating an obvious truth. You've been nothing but correct with her, but as I've said before, it's obvious she has the hots for you."

Inspector Khan was relieved to hear the ring of the deputy commissioner's telephone. Commissioner Braham picked up the handset and pressed the speakerphone function so his colleagues could listen in.

The official in Slough had made contact with the *Bundeskriminalamt*, or Federal Criminal Police Office, located in Wiesbaden. They, in turn, spoke to the Berlin police, who agreed to help. The British liaison officer gave them a name and number in Berlin to call. She assured them that Senior Inspector Fabian Wundt spoke excellent English. Earlier in his career, he had done a tour of duty at the German embassy in London.

Inspector Khan and Peter returned to the inspector's office, where he dialled the Berlin number. It wouldn't go through. The inspector tried again without success.

"Maybe your phone is blocked for international calls?" Peter suggested.

"Bloody hell. You're probably right."

"Perhaps they heard about your interest in Las Vegas?"

The inspector laughed. "That would do it."

He called the deputy commissioner's office and explained the problem to his secretary. She agreed that Peter was probably right and would submit a request to unblock his telephone.

"Pennywise and pound foolish," she said. "It's the motto of modern policing. It will undoubtedly take some time for my request to work its way through the system, so come up here and use the deputy commissioner's phone."

"He's comfortable with that?"

"He will be."

Peter and the inspector trudged back up to the deputy commissioner's office, where, to the inspector's great surprise, he was invited to sit at the deputy commissioner's desk and make his call. The deputy commissioner put the console back on speakerphone mode and took a seat behind the desk alongside Peter. The call went through without a hitch, and Inspector Khan reached someone he assumed to be Inspector Wundt's secretary or assistant.

Drawing on his best university German, he said, "Darf ich mit Inspektor Wundt sprechen, bitte."

"This is he speaking. Would that be Inspector Khan?"

"Yes. Delighted to make your acquaintance."

"The feeling is mutual. Tell me how I can help you."

Inspector Khan summarized developments in Cambridge from the abduction and murder of Professor Mason and Jaime Peeker to the liberation of Rhianna in Norfolk. He gave their reasons for believing that Professor Chester might be heading for Berlin.

"Your murderer is a Cambridge chemistry professor?"

"No, that was one of his victims. He's a political scientist," Inspector Khan said.

"Remarkable. Here in Germany, we think all murders in Britain occur in Oxford or Midsomer."

"They do," Inspector Khan said. "This is most unusual for us."

The deputy commissioner and Peter smiled, and Inspector Khan wondered just what kind of detective he was dealing with.

"If you give me a number," he told his German interlocutor, "I'll send you the list of names and addresses of the professor's colleagues and friends in Berlin."

"That would be helpful. We could contact all of them, but that might tip the professor off that we're on to him. What do you advise?"

"That's an interesting question. None of them, I assume, would want to harbour a murderer, but all of them would be willing to host a friend."

"Where do they work?"

Peter handed Inspector Khan the list, and he read out the names and institutional affiliations.

"Most are affiliated with the Free University, located in Dahlem. We can put the political science building under surveillance, but if your professor is in town, he may want to lie low at one of their homes. I think it best to speak to the lot of them and make sure they understand that it is a serious offence to take in someone wanted by the police."

Inspector Khan passed along the observation of Professor Lundgren that her colleague loved classical music and attended concerts when in Berlin. She remembered him saying that colleagues in Berlin had bribed him to give a talk there by offering him concert tickets.

"That's useful to know. Does he like symphonic or chamber music?"

"She didn't say."

"No matter, we'll monitor the main auditorium and the chamber music hall at Philharmonie and show the ushers and sales staff his photograph. It might give me the opportunity to attend a concert on police time and money. Any other tips?" Detective Wundt asked.

"Our professor is a cultured man, and our informant says he's almost certain to browse bookstores. You must have a lot of them, and I'm not sure how helpful this is."

"Very useful. A man of his tastes is likely to head to Dussmann in the *Kulturkaufhaus*. He could browse books and then listen to classical recordings in the basement. Then there's "Marga Schoellers Bücherstube" near the Kurfürstendamm. There's another possibility if he has a perverse sense of humour?"

"A perverse sense of humour. Why do you ask?"

"He's an English murderer, and there's a bookstore, well known to locals, that specialises in English *Krimis*. It's called "Krimibuchhandlung Miss Marple," and is in Weimarer Straße. This is also near the Ku'damm."

"Now you're kidding."

"We Germans are famous for our sense of humour."

"You're serious then?"

"Oh yes. We'll stake out these bookstores and distribute pictures of the professor to the sales staff. Is there anything else I ought to know? Is he armed?"

"We're not sure. We haven't recovered the gun he used to kill Professor Bricknell. He could have taken it with him."

"You'll send the specs?"

"Of course. It's a vintage Luger."

There was a short silence at the other end. "A Luger?"

"I'm afraid so."

"OK. We will be on the lookout for it. I'll get back to you the moment anything turns up."

Before hanging up, the two inspectors exchanged mobile numbers.

"I think you are in good hands," the deputy commissioner said. "And I see that Chester's secretary was finally forthcoming. I hope my intervention with the vice-chancellor's office did the trick."

"It was the thumbscrews, sir."

"The thumbscrews?"

Peter and the inspector looked at each other and smiled.

***

Professor Chester improvised the next part of his journey. He drove to Bremen in expectation of taking the train north to Hamburg and then changing for his onward journey to Berlin. The north German plain is thick with industrial sites and dual carriageways and generally free of fog in the summer. He made good time and checked into a hotel in Bremen, using Professor Bricknell's passport for identification. The drive had left him stiff. He had a good walk around the town before lunch and then took in the art museum. He was drawn to the Blaue Reiter artists and their Weimar successors, and the Kunsthalle had a good collection of Lovis Corinth, Max Liebermann, Max Beckmann, and Paula Moderson-Becker. The latter died of an embolism at the age of thirty-one in 1907 and was a pioneer modernist, known especially for her nude portraits of women. He walked along the river past allotments, carefully tended by residents. He left Professor Bricknell's car in a siding by some kind of warehouse, thinking it was likely to sit there unnoticed for quite some time.

The following morning, he took the train to Hamburg. Its principal art museum is close to the train station, as is the *Miniatur Wunderland*, the world's largest model railway. Professor Chester was in no hurry, and his connection left him with time for one of these attractions. He opted for the model railway and marvelled at the detail and diversity of the multi-floor layout in an old warehouse by the river. Most impressive of all, he thought, was the miniature airport, where planes came through openings in the walls to land and take off.

He returned in plenty of time for his train, found his way to his reserved seat, and had a nice nap en route to Berlin. He wished British trains were as clean, comfortable, and on time. Germany appealed to him in its precision and respect for authority. This had declined considerably ever since the 1960s, and many Germans regarded the loosening up of their society positively and evidence of successful distancing from their authoritarian past. He lamented this change. The Berlin Hauptbahnhof was an impressive post-modern structure, and his friend, Hans-Jakob, was waiting for him at their agreed meeting place. They went by S-Bahn to Charlottenburg and walked to Hans-Jakob's Victorian-era house.

It was conceivable, Professor Chester reasoned, that the police would contact his foreign friends in Germany and elsewhere if they believed he had fled the country. He thought this unlikely because they had undoubtedly searched his house again and found his passport. It would probably not occur to them that he was travelling on Bricknell's passport, but that too was possible. He had developed a grudging respect for Inspector Khan. He was a credit to the constabulary and more evidence, if that was needed, about how Britain benefitted from immigration. He would be careful and avoid any professional friends whose names and addresses might be extracted from his secretary or computer. One of the many benefits of his host Hans-Jakob was his refusal to communicate by email. He wrote letters — the old-fashioned way — with an ink pen and expected the same in return. It was frankly a nuisance, but in the circumstances, a blessing. There would be no electronic trail for the police to follow, and he never kept any of his letters, and no paper trail either.

He had met Hans-Jakob some years back at the chamber music hall of the Philharmonie. Hans-Jakob had two tickets to the concert, but his friend was ill-disposed, and he returned his ticket to the box office. Professor Chester had just arrived in Berlin and went to the concert hall in the hope that a ticket might be available, and voilà. Hans-Jakob had struck up a conversation with him as soon as he was seated, telling him how happy he was that somebody was able to make use of the ticket he had returned. He bought Hans-Jakob a drink during the interval, and the two men chatted away in German, in which Professor Chester was reasonably fluent. They quickly became friends and had met subsequently in Berlin, London, and Rome.

Hans-Jakob told him about his early retirement plans from his insurance company and how he intended to do a graduate degree in art history. He envied his English friend's university life and was always keen to hear about his activities. Professor Chester told him that his career was prospering and that he had received several invitations to lecture in the U.S. He would go to Cornell and Chicago in the autumn when he was on leave. Of course, he said nothing about his criminal activities and doubted Hans-Jakob would believe him if he did.

XXXXI: Friday Morning

The following morning Professor Chester had a leisurely breakfast with his friend. Hans-Jakob ate yoghurt and fruit for breakfast but knew how much Professor Chester liked pumpernickel and had gone to the bakery early to buy fresh bread to supplement the sausage and cheese he had in his fridge. They both drank strong coffee that Hans-Jakob made on his Italian machine.

He did not want to overstay his welcome; he had always lived by the rule that fish and guests begin to smell after three days. He thought he might nevertheless extend his stay on this occasion because he had nowhere else to go. He had not yet figured out what to do after what he hoped would be a pleasant Berlin interlude. Money was not a problem, at least in the short term as, over the decades, he had banked and invested in Germany whatever money he earned on the continent. Berlin would be his preferred place to settle down, but that was easier said than done.

He had always lived alone as an adult but thoroughly enjoyed his time with Hans-Jakob. They shared many common interests and somehow lived under the same roof without any stress, albeit for short periods of time. He and Hans-Jakob had never talked about relationships, but he was fairly certain that his friend was gay. He suspected that Hans-Jakob would not be averse to a more intimate relationship. He, however, was unremittingly straight. Too bad Hans-Jakob was not a woman, he thought.

Hans-Jakob left for work, and Professor Chester lingered over a second cup of coffee and then cleaned up after them both. He had planned his day carefully. He would start with a walk through the garden and woods of Schloss Charlottenburg. Best to do it now, he decided, because rain was predicted for the afternoon and evening. He would return, shower and change, and take a bus to Mitte. His first stop would be Philharmonie, where he hoped to pick up a ticket for that evening's chamber music concert of Shostakovich quartets. If he couldn't get one, he would try next door, where the Berlin Philharmonic would be performing. Then he might take in a museum, have lunch, and visit a bookstore. He would like to, but did not dare, check his email. The life of a fugitive was liberating but also constraining.

***

Senior Inspector Wundt was promised whatever resources he wanted within reason because the *Bundeskriminalamt* was keen to display its efficiency to the British and even more to the *Bundestag* on whom it depended for funding. The inspector did not think he would need much in the way of help. He had forces on hand to check out bookstores and concert halls and leave the professor's photograph and a number to call if he showed up. Managers at these several institutions promised to brief their respective staff. He stationed an undercover policeman at the KaDeWe department store, whose famed oyster bar was an attraction for sophisticated foreign visitors. He did the same at several of the major city museums. He also had a squad on short notice to descend on any venue where the professor was spotted. There was nothing more to do but sit tight and wait.

***

Waiting was also the name of the game in Cambridge, and they had been at it for longer. Since their telephone call to Berlin, there was nothing more for them to do. The deputy commissioner had passed along Professor Bricknell's name and car registration and Professor Chester's photograph to his contact, who forwarded it to the Dutch and German authorities. British cars are not all that common on the continent, and much less so in Holland and Germany than in France. Highway police in both countries would now be instructed to look out for a Toyota Auris with Bricknell's registration. As Chester had changed the number plate in the past, instructions went out to stop any British Toyota that had any two of the numbers or letters of the actual registration.

There was no evidence that Chester was going to Berlin. For all they knew, he could be heading south to Paris or elsewhere in France. Half of the Cambridge professoriate seemed to have second homes on the continent, most of them in France. For lack of anything better to do, they called around his colleagues to see if he had any friends in France. The consensus was that his interests and friends were more Italian than French. He was a frequent visitor to the European University Institute in Fiesole, just outside of Florence. Once again, they had the deputy commissioner call his contact to get the Italians involved. If he was headed for Italy, it seemed unlikely that he would drive there, and they asked Interpol to do a check for a passenger named Bricknell on European flights, but especially ones to Berlin or anywhere in Italy.

At four p.m., they received their first call from the continent. The Bremen police had found Professor Bricknell's car just on the city outskirts. They thought it had been abandoned and towed it to a police garage. Their experts were ready to pore over it if there was anything the British police wanted them to look for. Neither Inspector Khan nor Peter thought it worth the effort. The question for them was whether the professor was still in Bremen or had moved on. The Bremen police would do a sweep of hotel registers, looking for an Ian Bricknell and give his photograph to the appropriate people at the local airport and train station.

***

Professor Chester had a lovely walk around the Schloss and had showered, put on a different outfit, and taken the bus to Tiergarten. He changed at the Zoologischer Garten for the Number 200 bus that would drop him off right in front of Philharmonie. He stood in a short queue at the Kammermusik Hall only to find out that the concert was *ausverkauft* (sold out). He was disappointed but not yet distraught and walked out and a little further along the street to the entrance to the main auditorium. There was no queue here and, to his delight, a ticket was available. He paid for it in cash and thought about the old German proverb: *"In der Not, frisst der Teufel Fliegen"* — in a famine, even the devil eats flies. This was a very nice fly, he thought, pocketing his ticket.

He left the concert hall in the direction of Potsdamer Platz. It was new and ugly, utterly soulless, and typical of urban planning. He would find a place to eat and then headed off to the Museum Quarter in the old East Berlin.

***

The police had spoken to the right people at the Philharmonie, and everyone working the box office had been briefed about Professor Chester and given a photograph to keep in view but out of sight of customers. No sooner had the professor walked out the door of the chamber music hall, the clerk behind the counter reached for the telephone and called the number the police had written on the photograph. An apprentice answered the phone, noted the time, took the information, and called Inspector Wundt. A couple of minutes later, the phone rang again. This time it was from a female clerk at the main concert hall. She was fairly certain that the man the police were looking for had purchased a ticket. She had written down the seat number. For the second time, the apprentice called Inspector Wundt. The inspector was delighted with the news and returned to the station to get everything organized for an evening arrest.

He instructed the leader of his special team to go over to Philharmonie to see just where the seat was but to plan on arresting Professor Chester before the concert. When he returned from the Philharmonie, they would meet again and go over the deployment plan. The team leader thought a smaller team was less likely to attract attention. His men and one woman would be in mufti and carry handcuffs. They would have a van outside with more heavily armed police ready to swing into action if needed. Inspector Wundt endorsed the plan. He wanted to capture Chester, but discreetly, so as not to cause an incident at one of the city's premier cultural venues.

Two hours later, the intern received another call, this time from one of the policemen posted by the Bode Museum. He thought he had seen Chester approach but not enter the museum. He was walking in the direction of the Pergamon and Islamic Art Museum. The officer was instructed to follow but at a good distance. It was critical that Chester did not know the police were on to him. The team was instantly assembled and dispatched to Museum Island, where they were to wait out of sight until summoned.

Professor Chester ambled along, giving the Bode Museum a miss as he had been there on his last visit to Berlin. He continued down Am Kupfergraben and then turned right over the bridge to Museum Island into the Bodestrasse. He noted how fast the river was flowing. He crossed the road to avoid some repairs, walked between the Neues Museum and the Altes Museum and then turned right on into the Lustgarten. The policeman followed, but at a good distance, as instructed. The professor turned the corner and walked diagonally through the crowd in the Lustgarten towards the river. The policeman turned the corner and didn't see him, but finally saw him climbing the stone steps and then disappearing into the Altes Museum. He called headquarters to report that he had entered the Museum. The quick response team was ordered into action.

Five of them went up the steps into the museum whilst a sixth remained on the top of the steps with the officer who had called in the sighting. Anyone coming out the main door would have to walk right past them. A sixth team member went behind the museum to a service entrance, showed his ID to the guard and was told that nobody had come through the exit recently. He waited there just in case. Once inside, the five men approached the ticket desk. The deputy director also appeared. He had received a call from police headquarters telling him what was about to happen. The team leader showed the photograph of Professor Chester to the young woman behind the ticket counter. She thought he might recently have come in. She had just admitted a sizeable group of American tourists and was very busy and didn't really look at the people to whom she sold tickets. They questioned one of the guards who inspected tickets upon entry. He thought the face looked familiar but was by no means certain. The director of the team stayed behind to keep a lookout on the two-winged grand staircase leading to the first floor. The remaining four members went up the staircase and fanned out on opposite sides of the rotunda to walk through the various rooms of the collection in search of Professor Chester.

The director led the team chief into the rotunda, where they admired the statues. Professor Chester was nowhere to be seen. The team members upstairs fared no better. He was not visible among the Etruscan, Greek, and Roman statues, or other art on display. The two groups of two policemen met, briefly consulted, and continued to circumnavigate the rooms just in case their colleagues had missed him. They met again where they had begun and saw that the staircase to the second floor was blocked with a rope. One of them climbed the stairs and noted with satisfaction that the door at the top was locked. They went downstairs, searched it thoroughly, including the toilets and gift shop. Professor Chester had eluded them.

The team director informed headquarters that Professor Chester was nowhere to be seen. Headquarters confirmed that the officers at the two entrances had not seen anybody emerge who resembled the professor. The team was stymied and had a second look around but with the same result. Inspector Wundt wondered if they had missed him or if the officer on the street had mistakenly identified him. He recalled the team. They would have a second chance that evening at Philharmonie.

XXXXII: Friday Afternoon

Professor Chester had no idea of the commotion he had just caused and was calmly walking down Unter den Linden reacquainting himself with this elegant avenue. He walked by the State Library and Humboldt University before reaching the Brandenburg Gate. He doubled back and found an Italian restaurant in a side street, where he had a quiet and pleasant lunch. He ordered *burrata*, followed by *vitello tonnato*, and washed it down with a bottle of sparkling mineral water. He would now head to a bookstore and then home for a nap. He wanted to be alert for this evening's concert.

He remembered there was a good bookstore near Kurfürstendamm that specialized in murder mysteries in multiple languages. He could read German easily but before going to sleep found English easier going. He paid his bill and headed off for the U-Bahn.

***

The police had been to Marga Schoellers Bücherstube and left several photographs of the professor. The manager of the bookshop promised to brief his staff and alert the police if he showed his face. The manager was amused by the prospect that a real murderer might want to read "Krimis" and wondered if he was drawn to highly stylized mysteries like those written by Agatha Christie or to the grittier, more realistic, and violent style associated with Scandinavian noir. If he were a killer, he thought, he would like the more escapist kind of novel, but then maybe he could pick up some useful tradecraft from Kurt Wallender, Harry Hole, or Inspector Rebus. His staff was divided in their opinion but unanimous in their belief if the professor showed his face, it would be to browse something other than *Krimis*. They were famous for the literature in many languages and at one point had been a *Treffpunkt*, or meeting place, for members of West Berlin's literary scene. In the Nazi period, they had remained open and sold banned books under the counter that they kept hidden in the basement.

Professor Chester walked into the shop and up to the large wooden counter in the centre, displaying recent works of literature, and flanked by polished wood bookcases on both sides. He felt at home, as he did in almost any bookstore or library. He worried, as a friend of his had put it, that literacy was a passing fad. His students read, although their writing skills had declined over the years. But they read mostly academic journals and seemed oblivious to the world of literature. Outside of Oxbridge, he knew, it was worse. The media did not help as so many of the newsreaders on the BBC could not themselves speak the Queen's English. Their newsreaders and reporters made numerous grammatical errors.

He thumbed through several novels in English and German and looked up at one point to see a very pretty young woman, carrying a pile of books, staring at him, or so he thought. She was obviously an employee as she placed the books on the shelves and then disappeared downstairs. He picked up an English language novel, paid at the counter, and walked out onto Ku'damm.

***

Brigitte was convinced that she had just spotted the man for whom the police were searching. She had been told that he was dangerous and that she should give no sign of recognition but rather call the number she had been given immediately. She went downstairs to do this, thinking she would not be observed and could talk in a normal voice. The police line was engaged, and she waited a minute and dialled again. This time she got through, and the intern asked her to speak calmly and slowly as she took down the information. She told her to go back upstairs and to call again if the target left the shop. She should note the direction he went but not follow him. Police would arrive momentarily.

The intern phoned Inspector Wundt, who realized that his team, which had just returned to base, would take some time to reach the store. Professor Chester would be long since gone. He accordingly asked his superior to divert the nearest available uniforms to the store. The two policemen who were summoned did not arrive until after the professor had paid for his book and left the shop. Brigitte and the manager were waiting for them and breathlessly described what had transpired. The police had no idea what Professor Chester looked like, but the manager had a photo in hand and gave it to one of the policemen. They raced out of the shop and took off down Ku'damm in the direction indicated by Brigitte.

A hundred metres ahead, they spotted their quarry looking into a shop window. They approached him stealthily, to the extent that this can be done on one of Berlin's busiest streets and grabbed him from behind. They handcuffed him before he knew what had happened. One of the policemen held the suspect, now screaming at them, whilst the other telephoned in their good luck. He was instructed to check their man for weapons and hold him, whilst a high-security van, and additional police, were sent to collect him. The police dispatcher arranged for the pickup then called his superior, who called Inspector Wundt to report their success.

Wundt left his desk in a hurry to make his way to the police station near Ku'damm, where Professor Chester was to be taken. Once a positive identification was made, he could dismiss his team and notify his British colleagues of their success. Someone at their end would then presumably prepare the necessary extradition papers, and the professor would be sent home to stand trial.

A crowd of curious onlookers surrounded the two policemen and their suspect. People would have been attracted by the sight of two policemen flanking a handcuffed man, but what really drew a crowd was the screaming. In seemingly native German, the handcuffed man was cursing the police and demanding to be freed. The policemen stood there in silence, waiting for the van to arrive, which only made their suspect more enraged. It pulled up, and four heavily armed policemen emerged. The crowd parted as they moved forward towards the suspect. Two of them lifted him off his feet and carried him back to the van and placed him inside. They then climbed over him. One of the others locked the van from the outside, climbed in the front, and it drove off with its blue lights flashing and sirens wailing. The crowd dispersed, and the two policemen, relieved of their burden and suddenly redundant, phoned their station and were told to return to base.

The van pulled up at the back entrance to the police station, and the handcuffed man was removed from the van and frogmarched into the station and down the hall to an interview room. Here he started screaming again, but his police guard, used to this kind of behaviour, stood by quietly. People on drugs not infrequently acted this way.

The suspect thoroughly exhausted himself from his bouts of screaming. When he quieted down, one of his guards gave him a cup of water, but only after a thorough frisking and removal of his wallet and mobile phone. To his repeated question of why he had been forcibly abducted, they told him to await the arrival of the detectives and a legal representative. They knew nothing other than there was a warrant for his arrest, and they had been instructed to pick him up.

"The way I am being treated," he told them, "you'd think, I was a terrorist or FIFA vice president."

One of the policemen broke into a smile, whilst the other stood there expressionless.

Five minutes later, Inspector Wundt and a local detective entered the investigation room.

"Maybe I'll finally get an explanation," the handcuffed man said.

Inspector Wundt knew something was wrong. His associate instructed one of the police guards to remove the handcuffs.

"Professor Chester," he said, "I'm Inspector Wundt. Please have a seat."

"Professor Chester? I'm not Professor Chester. My name is Ludwig Neumann. Why have you arrested me?"

"I'm told that until now you passed yourself off as Ian Bricknell. You're a resourceful fellow."

Inspector Wundt reached out and put his hand on his colleague's arm to restrain him. "*Lassen Sie es mal gut sein.*"

"Is this your wallet, Herr Neumann?

"Yes, it is."

"May I have a look?"

"Please."

Inside he found the usual EC-Karten — debit cards — a German driver's licence, a gym membership card, and a photo ID issued by the Stiftung Preußischer Kulturbesitz — the Prussian Cultural Heritage Foundation. The photos on the licence and the ID were those of the man sitting before him. Inspector Wundt took Professor Chester's photo out of his shirt pocket and held it out in front of him to look at it and the professor. It was additional confirmation that they had picked up the wrong man.

"Herr Neumann, I believe a great mistake has been made. Is there somebody at work who would recognize your voice on the telephone?"

"*Naturlich.*"

Inspector Wundt dialled the number after checking that it was indeed the prefix for the Stiftung Preußischer Kulturbesitz and asked to be put through to the colleague Herr Neumann had named. He handed over the phone, the two chatted for a minute or so, and Herr Neumann returned the phone to the inspector. The colleague confirmed that he had just spoken to Ludwig Neumann.

Inspector Wundt offered a profuse apology to Herr Neumann and explained to him why the error had been made and how keen the police were to pick up this English murderer walking the streets of Berlin. He offered to have someone drive Herr Neumann to anywhere he would like to go.

"Thank you for freeing me, Inspector, and for your offer. But I think I've had enough of the police for one day. May I just walk out of the station and take the bus to my office?"

"You may indeed."

Herr Neumann shook hands with the two inspectors and was escorted from the interview room by his police guards, who suddenly transformed their demeanour from gruff to as close to charming as they could pull off.

A dejected and embarrassed Inspector Wundt sat down to compose himself. This was Berlin, not Munich or Vienna, Inspector Wundt told himself. Such *Schlamperei* was simply unacceptable.

***

Like Inspector Clouseau at the Oktoberfest, Professor Chester was utterly oblivious to the several unsuccessful attempts to stop him in his tracks. He walked down Ku'damm to the bus stop to take him back to Charlottenburg. He arrived without incident and let himself in with the key his host had kindly given him. He undressed, got into bed, and quickly fell asleep.

***

Inspector Wundt returned to his office and met up with the head of his special team. They had done nothing wrong at the Bode Museum; a policeman had given them a false identification. That made two today. It was not at all evident that Professor Chester had visited the Marga Schoellers Bücherstube, although Brigitte insisted that he had when one of his assistants interviewed her. Other police had called or spoken in person to the professor's colleagues at the Free University, and all of them denied having any contact with him since the police had last been around. Without certain identification that the professor was in Berlin, he was not going to call his Cambridge colleague. For all he knew, the people at the Philharmonie box office could also have been mistaken. They would find out this evening.

Inspector Wundt briefed his colleagues on the day's events. Nobody needed to be told that they did not exactly reflect credit on the force. They all wanted to get it right tonight, assuming it was the professor who had bought the concert ticket. They would only know if and when he appeared at Philharmonie. Inspector Wundt looked up the programme on his computer and discovered it was an all-Mozart evening featuring his twenty-first piano concerto played by Maria João Pires. He hoped they captured the professor as he sauntered into the concert hall, but one part of him would not mind hearing the concert and arresting him during the curtain calls. He imagined that Professor Chester might not be averse to such an arrangement and may agree to turn himself in if he were allowed to listen first. Assuming he showed up, it might be the last concert he would ever attend.

The team, which had now increased to some dozen officers, conferred for over an hour about how they would position themselves that evening. They finally agreed that two of them, clad in mufti, would wait by the bus stop, and two more, similarly dressed, would stand just inside. There was also an entrance in the back for people arriving from the direction of the Potsdamer Platz. Two more officers would be stationed inside those doors and two more by the staircases leading up to the section where the professor would be sitting. Inspector Wundt had arranged for the box office to telephone the subscribers who held the seats adjacent to the professor and tell them a cock-and-bull story about why they had to be moved tonight. They were offered better seats and free drinks at the bar and readily agreed. The inspector and one of his officers would sit in their seats just in case somehow the professor eluded the police cordon — or, the inspector thought more likely, did not appear because he was not in Berlin. There would be more police outside in uniform and with assault weapons, but out of sight, and a van to transport the professor, if apprehended, to their police station. It seemed a fool-proof plan — unless it was not Professor Chester who had bought the tickets or somehow twigged that the police were on to him.

The only real worry Inspector Wundt had was the rain shower forecast for this evening. It would not deter concertgoers, but it would make it more difficult to identify the professor in a sea of umbrellas. And all the more so if they were angled forwards into the wind. The professor would have to fold up his umbrella before entering the concert hall and would then be clearly visible to those awaiting him. If he got by them somehow, the inspector and his colleague would grab him. If he arrived at his seat just before the concert began, they would wait until the interval to arrest him. He wondered if Madame Pires would perform the piano concerto in the first or second half of the evening; he would have to buy a programme to find out.

***

Hans-Jakob came home early from work and told George he had a pleasant surprise for him. A friend at work had to bow out of tonight's concert at Philharmonie because family was unexpectedly visiting. Knowing how much Hans-Jakob liked classical music, he gave him his two tickets and categorically refused to accept any money in return.

Hans-Jakob would prepare a light meal, and they could drive to the concert. Sometime back, another friend had given him a *Geheimtipp* — a secret tip — about where to park, and it never failed. George had to confess to his friend that he had already purchased a ticket.

"No worries," he said. "My sister's partner is out of town at the moment, and I would have taken her if you were not visiting. Let me call and see if she's free to join us."

Emilie was delighted to accept the invitation to the concert and a light supper beforehand. George followed Hans-Jakob into his kitchen to keep him company whilst he prepared a starter of melon and prosciutto to be followed by a simple pasta dish: freshly made tagliatelle with aubergine, garlic, pepper, and olive oil he had brought home from Umbria.

"Taste this oil," Hans-Jakob said to George as he poured some on his finger to taste."

He licked his finger and swirled the oil on his tongue. "It's not anything like what Waitrose has on offer."

"You can get some good oils here, but you pay through the nose. I bought tins of the stuff, along with wine, and this prosciutto, when I was in Todi last month. The prosciutto is from further north."

Hans-Jakob took a cloth off of the stand that held his ham and a long sharp knife from a magnetic rack.

"It has to be cut very fine, and it took me a while to learn the trick." He slowly cut two slices and offered one to his friend.

"It's delicious, and that's quite a knife."

"I have a set. They're made in Solingen and need regular sharpening. But they cut much better than other knives."

XXXXIII: Friday Evening

The buzzer rang, and Hans-Jakob went to greet his sister. She was three years younger and a plastic surgeon. She also lived in Charlottenburg, in what used to be their parents' home. Like his house, it had escaped damage in the war, although it was a near thing. In the mid-fifties, in the course of renovations, an unexploded bomb had been found buried in the ground next door. The entire neighbourhood was evacuated until the bomb squad safely defused and removed the device.

Emilie was full-figured but graceful and had a nice smile. She gave her brother a hug and then a bouquet of mixed summer flowers. He admired them and reached up to a high shelf for a vase he thought appropriate, but not before introducing his sister to his visitor.

Hans-Jakob did his best to arrange the flowers with Emilie looking on but not offering any suggestions. "This will do, I think," Hans-Jakob said. He went into the dining room and put the vase on a blue patterned Dutch tile that sat atop an old walnut table.

He returned to the kitchen. "Let me open some wine, and we can eat."

He turned to George, holding up a bottle of Nebbiolo. It's Piemontese, not Umbrian, but not too high in alcohol and just right for a summer evening. What do you think?"

"I agree. It won't put me to sleep in the concert if I have a glass or two, and I think I will. This evening is already on its way to becoming something very special."

George and Emilie set the table and then helped Hans-Jakob bring in the supper. They sat down, and he poured the wine and brought out a bottle of sparkling water.

***

It was an hour earlier in London, and Inspector Khan was still at work. The Bremen police had phoned to report that there was no sign of Professor Chester, although they would continue to keep their eyes open for him. He had met earlier in the day with the deputy commissioner, who was pleased by Rhianna's story in the *Cambridge News*.

"Listen to this," he said to the inspector. "The Cambridge police left no stone unturned to discover where the maniac Chester had taken me. They tracked down his sister on holiday in the Seychelles, who knew vaguely where his Norfolk retreat was located. The Norfolk police diligently checked local tax records to find it whilst Inspector Khan hightailed it up to Norwich.'

"And there's more: '"The police rescued me at just the right moment. The mad professor had my arms and legs in restraints attached to opposite walls. He was trying to get me giddy with wine, but I wanted nothing to do with him. He had an alarm system that gave him advance warning about the police and took off as soon as they came up the dirt road leading to the house. I never felt so happy to see three helmeted and heavily armed men in my life. After searching the house for him, they cut me loose and gave me some water to drink. Inspector Khan, always a gentleman, escorted me back to Cambridge'."

"You're a great policeman and a gentleman. I can't think of a higher compliment."

"I'm glad to see you're smiling," the inspector said.

"Oh, I am."

The deputy commissioner reached into his desk and took out a bottle of malt whisky. "Do you think it's too early in the day for a little nip?"

"Not in the circumstances," Inspector Khan said, a smile on his face.

"I suppose we shouldn't become too celebratory until our fugitive is arrested and extradited. Any word from Berlin yet?"

"No, sir. I'm sure they will call as soon as they have anything to report. It's a big place, and it may take them some time to find him — if he's there."

***

The rain came as predicted, and the shower was intense. Inspector Wundt and his assistant looked outside and saw people scurrying for cover. Soon the rain became heavy enough that it was difficult to see out the window.

"*Es schüttet wie aus Eimern* — it's raining cats and dogs"— Inspector Wundt exclaimed.

He worried that the rain would make it more difficult to identify the professor. His assistant had made sure that everyone on the team had studied his photo, and they agreed, given the false identifications earlier in the day, that they would not move until they had two independent reports of his appearance. If the professor was spotted outside, the police watching for him should not move in but alert control. They would follow him inside, and if colleagues inside the concert hall agreed that this was their man, the four of them would close in and make the arrest.

Part of the team and control arrived quite early, as the concert hall had a bar that served pre-concert snacks and was frequented by many people. Control was in an unmarked van parked near Philharmonie along the road used by buses, taxis, and cars to drop people off. The inspector's assistant was inside, along with a communications officer and the intern who had begged to be included in the operation. She began to have second thoughts after sitting for an hour in the confined space of the van. Team members in position checked in every ten minutes with control, and nobody had anything to report.

The concert was scheduled to begin at eight p.m., and the crowd began to build up thirty minutes before. There was a queue of people waiting to collect pre-purchased tickets and another one hoping for returns. It was periodically scanned by one of the team, but nobody expected to see the professor in the queue as he already had a ticket. By seven thirty p.m., everyone was in place, and communications had been tested and found working. Best of all, the rain had stopped. Only the odd umbrella was still open, and those by people not yet convinced that they wouldn't get wet. Two of the team were smokers and had been given outside duty by the team leader. People often went outside to light up, and they blended in nicely.

***

The *Geheimtipp* was indeed just that, and Hans-Jakob was able to park a five-minute walk from Philharmonie. The space was narrow, and it took a bit of manoeuvring to get his BMW sedan nicely aligned with the kerb and not touching the cars in front or behind. Emilie and George congratulated him on his parking skills. He thanked them but credited his skill to the camera at the back of the car that projected his position on the dashboard screen.

It had stopped raining, but they decided to take umbrellas as a precaution. Emilie had arrived with one, and Hans-Jakob kept two in the boot of the car. They were quite large and advertised an Italian aperitivo. Hans-Jakob promised to tell George later how he had come by them.

They had to cross Potsdamer Strasse to get to Philharmonie and did so at the traffic lights. Professor Chester was impressed by the willingness of Germans to wait for the green pedestrian signal before crossing even empty roadways. He saw it as a commendable sign of order, not a hangover from the authoritarian past. In discussions with friends who regarded it as authoritarian— and many Brits and Americans did — he pointed out how this practice had long prevailed in democratic, peaceful Scandinavia.

The moment the green crossing light came on, the rain began again. Professor Chester and his friends unfurled their umbrellas and held them forward as the wind was blowing rain towards them. They were not alone in doing this, and the plaza was filled with open umbrellas and a big crowd by the door as people tried to wait until the last minute to take down and close their umbrellas. It was all but impossible for the two officers monitoring the crowd to see anybody's face let alone spot the professor.

Hans-Jakob, George, and Emilie made it to the door and passed through into the large anteroom of the concert hall. Inspector Wundt had positioned himself by the coat check counter, thinking that most people would queue to check in their umbrellas and raincoats and that he would have a good view of them. Indeed, Hans-Jakob collected the three umbrellas and stood in the queue to check them in. Emilie and George went to their respective washrooms, Emilie to check her hair, and George to relieve himself. They met Hans-Jakob outside and headed off to two different staircases. Emilie had George's single ticket, which was behind the orchestra, and was accessible by staircases on either side. Hans-Jakob and George had seats in row "G" in front of the orchestra, one of them an aisle. They chattered away as they joined the mass of people heading up the stairs toward their entryway.

They entered the auditorium, and Hans-Jakob led George to their seats. He insisted that his friend take the more comfortable aisle seat. They sat down but had to get up twice to let people move by them to seats beyond them in their row. Hans-Jakob observed, and George agreed, that people in the absolute centre of a row always arrive last and inconvenience everyone.

***

The team was on the lookout but missed Professor Chester when he came through the back door in a crowd of people who opened and shook out their umbrellas as soon as they were inside. Inspector Wundt missed him at the check-in counter because he was not there. Nobody was posted in the *Herrentoilette*, and the man who worked there, who had been shown the professor's picture, was only interested in tips. When Hans-Jakob, George, and Emilie met in the lobby, one of the policemen thought he spotted their target but was not certain because he looked somewhat different from the photo. In the passport photograph, the professor had a scowl and longer hair. Inspector Khan and another officer had taken up their positions by the two staircases the professor would have to use to reach his seat, but nobody close to him in looks walked past them. The orchestra was on stage, and they heard people applauding the concertmaster as he came out from the wings. They could wait no longer and went in and inconvenienced six people in their row to get to their seats. There was an attractive middle-aged woman in the professor's seat. It was not the professor unless he was an absolute master of disguise. He was not at the concert, or the staff had made an error with his seat. There was nothing Inspector Wundt could do now but sit back and enjoy the music. And to his great pleasure, the programme indicated that Madame Pires would perform the opening piece.

One of the policemen in the foyer thought he saw the professor walk up a different staircase than expected. He reported his sighting to control, who duly noted it and informed other members of the team in the area. Nobody else reported seeing him, but control then made sure everyone knew of a provisional sighting.

Inspector Wundt received this message just before shutting down his communication system for fear of making a noise during the performance. There was nothing he could do, sandwiched in between people in the middle of a row with the concert to begin momentarily. He sat back and cast one more sideways glance at the woman in what was alleged to be the professor's seat. He had the foresight to bring a small pair of binoculars with him, and in the forty-five seconds or so before the lights dimmed, he took them out and scanned the audience seated behind the orchestra. He did not see the professor, but then he did not have time to do more than scan one row.

***

The conductor and soloist came on stage to a round of applause and shook hands with the concertmaster. Madame Pires sat down at the piano stool, made a small adjustment to it, positioned herself carefully and nodded to the conductor. He raised his baton and held it momentarily before moving it down sharply in a signal for the orchestra to begin. The piece opened with a march and then shifted quickly to a lyrical melody that alternated with a wind fanfare. The music grew louder, and the march returned, this time played by the violin section. It was followed by a quieter interlude featuring the horns. Madame Pires, who had remained motionless, now joined in with a short cadenza that resolved itself in a trill. The piano introduced a new theme in C major, which then migrated through G major to G minor. The audience was impressively silent.

Inspector Wundt tried to concentrate on the music but, to do so, he first had to convince himself yet again that there was nothing he could do but sit there and enjoy the concert. He was *hors de combat* and had to hope that his colleagues in the lobby of the concert hall were conferring on how best to position themselves to nab the professor at the interval — if he was in the concert hall. He sat back in his seat again, stopped fingering his binoculars, and let Mozart's music transport him into that ordered and beautiful world that only great art is capable of creating. Professor Chester would not go away, however, and he periodically had to concentrate to push him from his conscious mind.

Outside the auditorium, members of the team were conferring with their chief. One insisted that he had seen the professor go up a staircase. If so, he could be anywhere on the second level of the auditorium that wrapped around much of the concert hall. They agreed to arrange themselves to get the best view of people coming down the various stairways at the interval. Two team members would eyeball the exits from outside. The team chief would resume his role of control in the van, and the intern would accompany him.

The Mozart piano concerto consisted of three movements. The final rondo began with the full orchestra playing. There was a short cadenza in which the piano elaborated the opening theme and then a short "call and response" section where piano and orchestra exchanged themes and figurations. The main theme then returned, and the concerto ended on a triumphant note.

There was a burst of applause, and Inspector Wundt took out his binoculars, intending to scan the rows behind the orchestra. The applause continued, and members of the audience stood to offer another sign of their enjoyment of the performance. Once a few people stood, others joined them, and soon almost everyone was standing. This made it impossible for the inspector to use his field glasses. He was desperate to get out, but his row was not going anywhere. He looked at his assistant, who asked him what they could do. The inspector took out his warrant card, as did his assistant. He tapped the person to his right on his shoulder, flashed his warrant card and asked to pass. The man looked at him as if he was rudeness personified but finally backed up against his seat when Inspector Wundt told him that he was responding to an emergency call. The two policemen slowly edged their way to freedom. His assistant stepped on the foot of a woman, and she glowered at him even though he apologized. Once at the end of the row, they were caught again, as the audience was now filing out from other rows. Their section funnelled out through two narrow passageways, and it took a good four minutes for them to get to the mezzanine and then another minute plus to reach the ground level. The crowd moved as fast as the slowest person, and two of the concertgoers in front of them were supported by sticks. A third was in a foot cast. The inspector wondered how the fire department could ever have approved this bizarre and dangerous architectural design.

***

Professor Chester and his host had an easier time of it because they were in an aisle and adjacent seat, and there were fewer people in the section behind the orchestra. Neither man relished hanging around. They left after two rounds of applause and had no difficulty finding their way to the exit doors and the mezzanine. They had agreed to meet Emilie by the booth that sold programmes, but outside the concert hall, if it had stopped raining, which it had. They walked quickly through the mezzanine around to the staircase that led them down into an open grassy area and walkway around it, to the left of Philharmonie.

The team members inside Philharmonie were all on the ground floor and did not see the professor depart from the mezzanine level. Two of them decided to check out the men's loo. It was crowded, but there was no Professor Chester unless he was in a stall, and neither of them was keen to have a peek. Two others went out on the mezzanine floor promenade where smokers gather. They went up the stairs and inched their way through the crowd to get there. They had a good view over the concrete and grassy area below. At almost the same moment, they shouted to one another, "*Dort ist er!*" and pointed in the same direction. They pulled out their phones and called control. One of them shouted into his phone, "He's at the back of the grassy area to the left of the Philharmonie. He's in a grey suit with a blue shirt and maroon tie. "*Wir schnappen ihn uns* — we're going after him."

***

The movement of two arms pointing in his direction caught the professor's eye, and he looked up to see two men with telephones in their other hands. He stared long enough to see them put away their phones and begin to push their way through the crowd towards the staircase that led down to his level. They had to be police.

"See you later," he said to his host and began running towards the exit to the Bendlerblock. He made it outside to the street but had to wait for a bus to pass before crossing it. He ran up the wide-angled ramp, called the "Piazzetta," which led to the Gemäldegalerie. It houses a world-renowned collection of art from the thirteenth through eighteenth centuries, but culture was far from his mind at that moment. He intended to run behind the museum and then find some way to double back and meet Hans-Jakob by his car at the end of the concert. He would miss the second half of the concert, which would give him time to plan his next move.

He never made it to the top of the Piazzetta. It was wet because of the earlier rainfall and was notoriously slippery. The Berlin government had received numerous complaints about the Piazzetta since it was built. The professor felt one foot slew out to the right. He turned to stabilize himself, but there was nothing to grab, and his body was in an awkward position as he fell. He heard a crunch and felt a sharp pain in his foot after hitting the pavement. The pain grew in intensity until it was excruciating.

The intern was restless and asked if she might get some air and perhaps keep an eye out for the professor. The team leader told her to go do it but to be back in ten minutes. No sooner had she climbed outside with the intent of mingling with the crowd than she saw a man run by and heard shouts of "stop him" from one of her out-of-sight colleagues. She gave chase, hoping that it was Professor Chester, and closed the gap between them because of the bus that caused him to wait. She followed him onto the Piazzetta and was almost close enough to tackle him when he fell. He was facing her when he hit the ground, and she knew in an instant that he was the man they were after. She unclipped her handcuffs from her belt and met no resistance when she put them on him. In less than a minute, colleagues surrounded her. They cordoned off the Piazzetta and carried the screaming professor to the waiting van.

***

Inspector Wundt missed all the action. He and his assistant arrived on the scene when the wounded professor was being hoisted into the van. The head of the team was standing by silently. Before calling Inspector Wundt, he contacted headquarters to request the services of an orthopaedist and a patrol car to collect him as soon as possible. The inspector and his assistant returned to the police station. They were relieved that the professor was in custody but curious about why and how he had eluded them inside the Philharmonie. Inspector Khan had warned them that they faced a clever adversary, and indeed they had.

"How did he do it?" the assistant asked.

"Wenn ick det wüsste — I don't have a clue—" said Inspector Wundt, using some local slang. "We'll have to interrogate the team leader, but only after he has debriefed his officers. I wonder if the box office made a mistake about his seat or if he somehow managed to swap tickets with someone."

"The officer who spotted him going up the stairs said he was with another man. The two officers who eyed from the promenade confirmed this. We need to find out who he is."

"Indeed, we do. If the professor has his ticket stub, we could have the box office check to see who sat on either side."

"Maybe they will get it right this time."

***

At the police station, the police had a stretcher waiting and gently lowered the professor onto it, and six armed officers then escorted him inside. He was booked and taken to an interview room in lieu of a cell as there was more room in the former and no chance in his condition that he would make a break for it. Not long after, the orthopaedist arrived. Sirens blaring, he had been sped through the city by a police cruiser. Inspector Wundt thought it odd that with police assistance, a murderer was about to jump to the head of the queue for medical treatment. He wondered how many more deserving patients would receive delayed care as a result.

Professor Chester had been sedated because of his pain and was at the edge of consciousness when the orthopaedist arrived. The doctor cautiously removed his right shoe and sock, the latter effort causing the professor to twitch involuntarily. He then rolled up the professor's trouser leg and asked the policeman to hold it out of the way so he could have a clear look at his leg and foot. Another policeman moved a lamp as close as its cord would allow. The doctor examined the professor's foot, heel, and lower leg carefully and then directed his attention to his heel. At one point, he poked it gently with his finger, and the professor almost jumped in response.

The orthopaedist addressed Inspector Wundt. "I believe he's fractured his calcaneus, or heel bone. It's the biggest of the tarsal bones and the largest bone in the foot. It is the insertion point for three muscles, and he may have torn one or more of them as well. I'll know more when we do an X-ray. He's got to be moved to a hospital."

"We can arrange that," said Inspector Wundt. He looked across at the team head."

"Yes, it has to be done. I'll have the duty sergeant call an ambulance. I'll put two team members inside, and we will follow in a car."

Inspector Wundt reached down, put his hand into the outer breast pocket of the professor's jacket and pulled out his ticket stub. It was indeed for a seat in the section behind the orchestra. He conferred briefly with the team leader before going upstairs to his office. They made an appointment to talk the following morning. The team leader already knew about the companion, and members of his team were looking into it. He also had the mobile number of the concert hall manager and would call him first thing in the morning to see if he knew why the professor had not been in the seat for which he had purchased a ticket.

The inspector walked upstairs to his office and slumped down into his desk chair. He suddenly realized how exhausted he was; presumably, he thought, from the tension of the chase. It was over now. The professor would be treated in the hospital and extradited to Britain to stand trial for multiple murders. The British government would, of course, have to present evidence to a German court to secure his extradition.

The inspector remembered he had one more task to perform before he could go home, shower, change, and have a welcome drink. He picked up his office phone and asked the police operator to call Inspector Khan in Cambridge. He made sure the operator had his mobile number. It was one hour earlier in Britain, so not too late to call, and if he were in Inspector Khan's shoes, he would want to know as soon as possible that his killer and kidnapper had been apprehended.

Inspector Khan was watching a football match on the sports channel. His mobile sounded during the replay of a near goal, and he reached across to the coffee table to pick it up. He swiped the screen and put the phone to his ear.

"Khan here."

"Fabian Wundt calling. How are you this evening?"

"Very well, thank you. And you?"

"Splendid, absolutely splendid."

Inspector Khan anticipated good news after a statement like that and was not disappointed.

"We've got your man."

"That's marvellous. Congratulations!"

"Your informant was spot on about his cultural tastes. We staked out — I think that's the term — museums, bookstores, and concert halls, and nabbed him at an orchestral concert at Philharmonie." Inspector Wundt neglected to tell his colleague about the false sighting at the Bode Museum, the embarrassing arrest of the wrong man at the bookstore, and how Professor Chester had eluded an entire team of police at the concert hall and would have escaped if he had not slipped and then been cuffed by a female intern.

"Was he going under the name of Professor Bricknell?"

"Probably. He had credit cards in that name in his wallet. But we haven't recovered his passport yet or determined where he was staying. I'll pass this information along as soon as we have it."

"I'll inform the deputy commissioner. He'll want to alert our solicitors and the Foreign Office so they can get the documents ready for an extradition hearing."

"There's no rush," Inspector Wundt said. He explained how the professor had fallen whilst being chased and broken his heel.

"His heel, you say?"

"Yes, that's right, his right heel. He's just been taken to the hospital for X-rays and will presumably need an operation or some kind of treatment. I really don't know yet. But I doubt he will be able to travel for some days."

"I can wait. As long as you have him in custody, it really doesn't matter when he returns."

"He's in safe hands, I assure you. Members of our assault team are taking turns guarding him in the hospital."

"I'm reassured. He's really a nasty piece of work. He comes across as a sophisticated but smarmy Latin-quoting professor. But he's a cold-blooded killer, and he didn't even really know one of his victims."

"He's still quoting Latin. It's not my forte. I never studied it in school. But our intern did, and she said that he kept repeating the phrase '*alea jacta est*' after being sedated."

"Then he was really in pain?"

"Oh, absolutely."

"It almost gives me pleasure to hear it, but don't tell anyone I said so."

"I understand completely."

"Too bad we don't have an appropriate Latin saying to mock him when he becomes — shall we say — 'compos mentis' — again."

"Bravo, Inspector Khan. As I said, I never did classics, but I am an authority on movie classics and a line from Marx springs to mind."

"Karl Marx? Did you grow up in the East?"

"No." Inspector Wundt chuckled. "I'm from the West. I grew up in Konstanz. And I wasn't thinking of Karl Marx, but of Groucho."

Inspector Khan waited to hear the bon mot his German colleague obviously had up his sleeve.

"In the movie *Go West*, Groucho exclaims, 'Time wounds all heels'."

Both men laughed and agreed to speak again in a day or two.

EPILOGUE

X-rays revealed a hairline fracture in the professor's heel and a torn muscle. Rest was the indicated treatment and total absence of any pressure on the foot. They wrapped the heel appropriately, and the police removed him to a secure facility where he could be held until the German foreign ministry approved a British extradition request. This took less than a week, and Inspector Khan and DS Leslie were given the honour of travelling to Berlin to escort the professor home. They were greeted at the airport by Inspector Wundt and his assistant and lavishly treated. When Inspector Wundt discovered that his British counterpart loved classical music, he arranged for them to go to a concert together at Philharmonie. He showed him beforehand how they had stationed their team and how the professor had made a run for it. He warned Inspector Khan to be very careful when walking on the "Piazzetta."

The trio flew to Heathrow in business class with Professor Chester handcuffed to Inspector Khan. They were dressed in suits but attracted a lot of attention, as the inspector knew they would. Peter suggested that most passengers would assume that he was the prisoner, as he was dark-skinned and younger, and the professor, a high-ranking police officer, as he was white and distinguished-looking. Inspector Khan agreed and wondered if he should make a break for it. Peter read his mind and warned that he would have to shoot him but that this would be less painful than thumbscrews. The two men had a good laugh, and the morose professor stared silently at them.

The evidence against the professor was overwhelming, and he was quickly convicted of three counts of murder and one of kidnapping. He was given a life sentence. The case was widely covered in the media. Inspector Khan and DS Leslie did their best to shun interviews but were pushed into them by the deputy commissioner. The favourable publicity they generated for the Cambridge constabulary was too good to pass up. Inspector Wundt was repeatedly interviewed by the British media and

Inspector Khan by their German colleagues. The *Bundeskriminalamt* was delighted by the outcome and the publicity.

After his call from Berlin, Inspector Khan telephoned Peter, Inspector Davidson, and the deputy commissioner in quick order to report the good news. Then he called Rhianna. He still owed her a scoop and gave her the details of the arrest of Professor Chester in Berlin. She was pleased and relieved and rung off to write up the story. She promised to email him a copy and begged him to have a look to make sure she got it right.

The day after the arrest, Inspector Khan paid off his debt to Peter by buying him a large cappuccino in their local café. But the barista would not let him pay, insisting that it was on the house. The inspector was not only a celebrity, he explained, but had rescued a local woman from the clutches of a murderer. Inspector Khan tried to explain that it was really the Norfolk police who had done this, but the barista would brook no objections.

Back in the police station, he and Peter were invited to the deputy inspector's office. It was too early for a dram of single malt — they all agreed. Deputy Inspector Braham told them he had something almost as good and asked the inspector to approach him. He took a medal out from his pocket — authorized by the grand poo-bahs in London, he explained — and pinned it on his lapel. Inspector Khan thought how ridiculous it was to hand out medals in the twenty-first century and decided to pass it on to his niece.

His family was thrilled by the publicity, and nobody more so than his niece. With his permission, she took the medal to school and showed it to her teacher and friends. For the first time, his parents conceded — albeit grudgingly — that maybe policing was not such a bad profession.

Inspector Khan was invited to appear on a TV dance show. He was greatly amused and wondered how they had found out about his dancing skills. If he had a partner, fine, the producer's assistant said, but if not, they would provide one. He remembered that Peter had told him what a fine dancer Rhianna was. He called her up to ask if she might be interested in joining him. She instantly agreed.

"This could be the beginning of a beautiful friendship."

"Please, I've heard enough old movie lines for the week."

Mrs Mason returned from her journey down the Silk Road. She had a wonderful trip, hit it off well with her roommate, and met a number of interesting people. She took a lot of photographs and made sure she did not inflict any of them on her friends or legal colleagues. She was delighted to learn from Inspector Khan that her husband's murderer had been apprehended. He had called her after telephoning Rhianna and apologized for the lateness of the hour. She told him he could call at any hour with news of this kind. She wanted to know why George had killed her husband and Jaime Peeker. Inspector Khan promised to come to her chambers the following morning to explain. It was creepy and not the kind of thing, he thought, to tell someone before they went to bed. He called Mrs Peeker next, who also expressed relief at her son's murderer being caught. Inspector Khan promised to send Peter around the next day to provide a full account of what had transpired.

The inspector sat in the café sipping a cappuccino and Peter, an Americano with milk foam on top. The detectives were besieged by well-wishers. They nevertheless managed to conduct the first of what would be several post-mortems of the case. The inspector asked Peter if he remembered his earlier invocation of Mozart's opera *Don Giovanni*. Peter did and observed that Professor Lundgren had been wrong. Unlike the Don, Professor Chester had fled the scene of his crime, and not just to the next city. The inspector explained that Don Giovanni was relevant in another way. The opera ends dramatically and musically when the Commendatore grabs Don Giovanni's hand and drags him down to the underworld. It is the counterpoint to the opening scene in which the Don runs the Commendatore through with his sword. The opera's overture ends with a sustained D-minor chord, as does the Don's descent to the underworld. But the opera doesn't end there, the inspector explained. There is a final sextet in which the remaining characters come together to moralize over Don Giovanni's fate but also to lament their lives. The music is lacklustre, and the scene is anticlimactic. Some authorities speculate that it was tacked on to appease the censor, and the occasional conductor, beginning with Gustav Mahler, banished it from their performances.

"We're like the characters in the sextet," the inspector said. "Mrs Mason has returned home to an empty house after an exciting trip and must continue her efforts to make a new life for herself. Mrs Peeker has lost a son, and knowledge that the murderer is behind bars is small compensation for her loss. I have to find a new crime to keep me from getting bored as the high of solving this one is quickly wearing off. Rhianna has had her fifteen minutes of fame and needs to resume her life as a provincial reporter covering disputes about unleashed dogs and planning permission applications. The only upbeat members of Mozart's sextet are Zerlina and Masetto. They have each other and look forward to supper and a roll in the hay. That's you and Elaine — and I very much expect to be introduced to her. And I promise... I will not behave like the Don."

"And what did he do?" Peter wanted to know.

"Don't ask."